Where He Left Me

ALSO BY NICOLE BAART

The Long Way Back

Everything We Didn't Say

You Were Always Mine

Little Broken Things

The Beautiful Daughters

Sleeping in Eden

Far from Here

Beneath the Night Tree

The Moment Between

Summer Snow

After the Leaves Fall

Where He Left Me

A Novel

NICOLE BAART

ATRIA PAPERBACK

New York • Amsterdam/Antwerp • London
Toronto • Sydney/Melbourne • New Delhi

ATRIA
PAPERBACK

An Imprint of Simon & Schuster, LLC
1230 Avenue of the Americas
New York, NY 10020

For more than 100 years, Simon & Schuster has championed authors and the stories they create. By respecting the copyright of an author's intellectual property, you enable Simon & Schuster and the author to continue publishing exceptional books for years to come. We thank you for supporting the author's copyright by purchasing an authorized edition of this book.

No amount of this book may be reproduced or stored in any format, nor may it be uploaded to any website, database, language-learning model, or other repository, retrieval, or artificial intelligence system without express permission. All rights reserved. Inquiries may be directed to Simon & Schuster, 1230 Avenue of the Americas, New York, NY 10020 or permissions@simonandschuster.com.

This book is a work of fiction. Any references to historical events, real people, or real places are used fictitiously. Other names, characters, places, and events are products of the author's imagination, and any resemblance to actual events or places or persons, living or dead, is entirely coincidental.

Copyright © 2025 by Nicole Baart

All rights reserved, including the right to reproduce this book or portions thereof in any form whatsoever. For information, address Atria Books Subsidiary Rights Department, 1230 Avenue of the Americas, New York, NY 10020.

First Atria Paperback edition November 2025

ATRIA PAPERBACK and colophon are trademarks of Simon & Schuster, LLC

For information about special discounts for bulk purchases, please contact Simon & Schuster Special Sales at 1-866-506-1949 or business@simonandschuster.com.

The Simon & Schuster Speakers Bureau can bring authors to your live event. For more information or to book an event, contact the Simon & Schuster Speakers Bureau at 1-866-248-3049 or visit our website at www.simonspeakers.com.

Interior design by Yvonne Taylor

Manufactured in the United States of America

1 3 5 7 9 10 8 6 4 2

Library of Congress Cataloging-in-Publication Data is available.

ISBN 978-1-6680-6617-1
ISBN 978-1-6680-6618-8 (ebook)

For Aaron
In every world.

PROLOGUE

The night was black and thick with ghosts.

Shadows peeled from the branches, fingers of fog poking through the dark forest just steps from where Sadie stood trembling. She was barefoot, wearing nothing but Felix's old sweatshirt, and a damn fool.

A scream had dragged her from bed, sent her racing through the unfamiliar house and down the front porch steps. Her whole world was reduced to cold grass, a throb of tangled trees, the jut of a craggy peak, shiny as a dragon's scales in the light of a quarter moon.

It was an animal. It had to be. Something small and injured. Maybe a coyote. A wolf? But it didn't sound like any of those things. It sounded human.

"Sadie!"

In a moment she was in his arms, caught from behind with her back pressed tight to his naked chest. "What are you doing?" Felix whispered.

"I heard . . ." Sadie trailed off as a shattering, keening wail made her clutch at her husband's arms where they wrapped around her chest. "What is that?"

"A fox," he soothed, lips against her hair. "It's just a fox. Their pups are being born right about now and they're very territorial."

"It's awful," her voice broke, and the last remnants of the

nightmare that snatched her from sleep began to dissipate. Sadie was home. Not *home* home—that designation was reserved for their small bungalow in equally small Newcastle, Iowa—but in the house where Felix grew up. A ramshackle two-story craftsman with dormer windows and mossy eaves planted deep in the heart of the North Cascades, a place so different from their quiet, Midwestern town they might as well have moved across the world. A winding, hard-packed dirt road, an isolated homestead on a mountain that felt like it exhaled long and slow beneath her bare feet. Waiting. What she really wanted to say was: *I hate it here.*

"I know." Felix rubbed his hands on her upper arms to warm her. "But we're safe."

"Safe," she huffed, her heart still drumming high in her throat.

"I've got you." There was something fierce in Felix's voice, base and radiant. Never mind the screaming fox, the chilly late-spring night, the fear that still clutched at Sadie even though she was folded into her husband's chest. Felix said, "Look up."

And although she just wanted him to take her inside, away from the awful noise and the impenetrable gloom, Sadie did as he asked.

Above them, stars spilled across the cathedral of the night, so numerous they looked like spindrift, a vapor of mist and sparkling foam. Despite herself, Sadie gasped. And that made Felix laugh. His smoky chuckle drowned out the fox's screams until they finally, blessedly, faded away entirely.

"I've never . . ." Sadie started but couldn't finish.

"I know," Felix said. "'Earth is crammed with heaven' or something like that."

It was beautiful to him, Sadie knew, vast and mysterious. But for the first time since she'd met Felix Graham, when Sadie looked up at the night sky, it felt glacial and aloof. So distant as to be cruel. A tidal wave of galaxies and universes and worlds that cared not one bit about her or Felix or anyone.

Sadie must have stiffened, because Felix tightened his grip and kissed the top of her head. "It's okay," he said, as if reading her mind. "I'm here. I'm not going anywhere, promise."

But even though her heart was beginning to keep time with his, Sadie couldn't shake the feeling that the mountain had cracked open something between them. A rift of dark space, cold and impassive as the stars.

CHAPTER 1

SUNDAY

They say Hemlock House is haunted, and when the lights flicker and then snuff out completely, I believe it—if only for a moment. It all comes back in a whoosh: the Bluetooth speaker pouring soft jazz into the room, the chandelier over the dining room table; the exhaust fan whirring above the stove, the rusty wall heater *tick-tick*ing under the bay window as it tries in vain to warm the drafty rooms. The world is instantly whole again.

Safe.

I barely have time to register the way my fist has tightened around the butane lighter. I force myself to take a deep breath. Flicking the strike wheel, I touch the flame to the tapered candle in my other hand. The wick catches and glows so merrily, I can almost pretend that nothing happened at all.

The two-story house is old and creepy at the best of times, but with Felix gone it feels almost menacing. Small rooms, creaky floors, a staircase that is so steep and narrow I walk up and down the dark tunnel with my palms pressed flat to the plaster walls for support. There are shadowy corners and inexplicable sounds—a high-pitched whistle from the attic on days when the wind blows just right, a low moan that seems to emanate from the root cellar beneath the mudroom, disembodied sighs and whispers and groans. It's a quiet cacophony that I should be able to ignore.

I can't.

I set the candle in the middle of the table, and Felix's mother's bone china glimmers in the dancing light. The patterned dishes sat untouched in the hutch for decades after she died, all twelve place settings whole and accounted for, with a matching gravy boat, soup tureen, and several serving platters collecting a thick layer of dust. When Felix and I first arrived at Hemlock House over five months ago, it took me the better part of a morning to wash each piece, scour the hutch, and then methodically put everything back just the way I found it. Tonight is the first time we'll use the fancy dishes, a tribute to the occasion—and the woman I never met.

Satisfied that everything looks perfect, I slip my phone from the pocket of the apron I'm wearing to protect my velvet dress. It's ridiculous, probably—the mid-length, terra-cotta gown with the plunging neckline—but Felix loves it, and I want to take his breath away when he walks through the door.

Getting close? I type with my thumbs. And then quickly add: *Don't read this. Keep your eyes on the road. See you soon. Love you!*

I try not to focus on all the unanswered texts. My husband is an accidental Luddite—casually disinterested in his phone—and he regularly misplaces it or forgets to respond to calls and messages. Still, he was supposed to land in Seattle just before three o'clock this afternoon, and I thought he'd at least touch base. But my *Welcome (almost) home!* message is the first of five to glow blue and lonely on the screen of my phone.

He didn't want to waste any time getting on the road, I tell myself. I-5 during rush hour is a nightmare, and Felix always stashes his phone in his backpack when he's driving. A glance at the microwave clock—7:09—confirms I don't need to be too concerned.

Yet.

I bend to check the beef bourguignon in the antique gas oven. It's a wonder the cast-iron monstrosity works at all, but when I lever open the door, it's hot as a blast furnace inside and fragrant with the aroma of the wine-soaked stew. I'm not much of a cook, but this I've mastered, and with the white cheddar popovers and the rest of the bottle of burgundy that I've been saving, it'll be a feast. I didn't bother with dessert; I wore the dress. Felix loves to run his hands all over it, fingers brushing the creamy fabric until he begins to pluck loose the satin bow.

Pouring myself a glass from the decanting bottle of wine, I grab my laptop from the kitchen table. I have more edits to do, and the final scene of my as-of-yet-untitled debut novel isn't quite perfect, but these long days alone have been nothing if not productive.

"It'll be great," I promised Felix when he brought up the conference a few weeks ago. "My manuscript is due November first, and I can use the alone time to finish it up."

"You won't mind being out here by yourself?"

"Hemlock House and I are old friends," I assured him, patting the balustrade of the oak archway between the small dining room and the equally tiny living room. There was just enough space for a brocade couch, a coffee table, and one spindly chair. Felix perched in the chair, laptop open on his knees and the table before him strewn with papers, journals, and notes.

He glanced up at me, arching one heavy brow. "Are you, now?"

"I love it here," I lied.

"Oh, you do?" His mouth pulled to the side so that his one dimple poked a divot in his cheek. This expression was skepticism and sincerity and delight and so much more. It was Felix himself, his half smile calling my bluff.

"I'll be fine," I said, holding his gaze, wanting him to believe me, because even though I hadn't warmed up to life on a mountain, the last thing I ever want to do is hold Felix back. He couldn't turn down an invitation to speak at the Planetary Sciences Symposium.

I should love it here, I know that, and as I settle into Felix's favorite chair with my computer, I try to quiet my unease. The mountain—*our* mountain—is undeniably gorgeous. But while it is lovely and serene, it's equally as dangerous and savage.

"Carry a bear whistle, be aware of your surroundings, never stray too far from the path," Felix has told me a hundred times at least, but his exhortations aren't necessary. I tend to stay within easy sight of the little clearing where the buildings of Hemlock House mark the four points of a compass at all times. I feel—if not *safe* exactly—*familiar* with the clipped grass of the square and the run-down buildings that Felix assures me were once practical. It's hard to believe him when the greenhouse glass is clouded with lichen and lime, the small stable is leaning, and the tool shed bristles with rusted tools and wicked-looking scythes.

7:55

The face of my watch glows like a full moon—impossible to ignore. Felix should be here by now. Even accounting for traffic, over five hours is more than enough time to make the drive from Seattle. *Maybe he stopped for gas. Or for something to eat.* I whip my laptop closed without hitting send on the work-in-progress update email I was crafting to my agent. I didn't exactly slave over supper, and my hair was in desperate need of a good wash, whether or not Felix would be home to appreciate it, but the sting of disappointment pinches deep in my chest anyway.

I don't know how to be a wife.

The thought saddens and humiliates me. When I fell for

Felix, my mom—widowed at thirty-five—offered me the best advice she could: "Whatever you do, don't love him too much." She didn't know it was already too late. Everything about me and Felix was an extravagance, lush and decadent, far too much. But the particularities of life together, of weaving our two into one, is a far more complicated endeavor than tripping headlong into love.

I push myself out of Felix's chair and go to turn off the oven. There is no "keep warm" setting, so I crack the door a bit and let the hot air out into the already stuffy kitchen. The stew is just this side of burnt, and I can smell the charred onions and bits of carrot that are surely sticking to the bottom of the pan. The eggs, cheese, and milk that I had set out for the popovers are now lukewarm and sweating, good only for the trash, which is where I dump them. I blow out the guttering candle with a sigh.

Sweeping open my phone, I tap the call icon and try Felix again. Straight to voicemail.

He's nearly two hours late.

Climbing to our bedroom on the second floor, I try to recalibrate. He doesn't know I planned an elaborate dinner. Or that after three days alone in Hemlock House I'm basically salivating at the thought of some human contact. Yes, I drove the Ranger—a multipurpose utility task vehicle with bucket seats and a dump bed—down the mountain to Requiem, the tiny village that sits at the end of the logging road, for coffee every morning. Sure, I hopped on an hour-long Zoom call with my editor about the final, revelatory scene in my coming-of-age, not-so-great American novel. But I'm not too proud to admit that I miss my husband terribly. His husky baritone singing everything from the Chainsmokers to Elvis Presley as he grinds coffee beans in the morning. How he winds my hair up in one fist and lifts it to kiss the back of my neck. All the ways he touches me throughout the day: his calloused fingers on my jaw, a playful tug on my ponytail, a brisk smack on my ass followed by a wink that says a thousand words. If I'm a house cat, moody and private, Felix is a Labrador retriever, all wanderlust and vigor and joy. I miss him so much it aches.

As I pull off the dress and slip into a pair of faded leggings and a sweatshirt, I feel the teeter-totter of my emotions tip from annoyance to worry. It's not like Felix to ignore me. Yes, we're independent, maybe even a little unconventional. But we're in love. Our tiny, campus greenhouse wedding was matter-of-fact but heartfelt. I don't wear a wedding ring because I don't like the feel of it on my hand. And we both decided that it would be best if we didn't tamper with our names. I'll be Sadie Sheridan until the day I die, even if my heart belongs to Felix Graham.

And we don't feel the need to tell each other *everything*, which suddenly seems irresponsible—maybe even wrong—when I thumb through our texts and realize that I haven't had so much as a "hello" from my husband since the day he left.

How is that possible?

Thursday morning, Felix brought me coffee in bed before he was scheduled to leave at seven. He kissed me on the forehead, deposited my favorite mug on the bedside table, and then winked and turned to go.

I caught his hand. "No goodbye?"

"I thought that was implied," he said, his voice low and a little flat.

"I thought you were going to wake me up." I was drowsy, but I remembered how he had clasped my wandering hand in his and given me a chaste kiss the night before. "I'm so tired, Sadie," he'd said. "Tomorrow morning?" But standing beside the bed just after sunrise, it was clear he was ready to go. Felix was freshly shaved and wearing a light jacket over his favorite burnt-red sweater, his backpack slung on one shoulder. There would be no lingering goodbye.

"It's just a few days," he said, rubbing my cheek with his thumb. I'll see you Sunday night. You'll be fine, right?"

"Of course." I pushed myself up on the pillows. "What's the worst that could happen in three days? Spontaneous combustion? Death by bear? A solo Sasquatch sighting with no evidence and no witnesses to corroborate my story?"

"Hey, don't even joke about that."

I grinned in spite of myself, but Felix's smile was fleeting. "I'm going to miss you," I told him seriously. It was hard to believe, but it would be our first time apart for more than a night since our wedding day over a year ago.

He paused at this, then bent and pressed his lips to mine, delicately, as if the kiss was a breakable thing. When he pulled away, he whispered, "In every world I'd find you."

"And in every world I'd love you, Felix Graham."

Then he was gone.

◆

Back downstairs, I gather the day journal I keep on a desk in the kitchen breakfast nook we jokingly call my office and push open the double wooden doors that lead to the main floor study. I'm not forbidden from entering Felix's office, but it feels strange to be here all the same. His work requires reams of data, special hi-res monitors, and a pair of supercomputers that can download and print images from the James Webb Space Telescope. Felix learned less than six months ago that his proposal had been selected by the Space Science Telescope Institute, and his research would include observing time with the world-famous instrument. He had been ecstatic. To study brown dwarfs for NASA was a dream come true. And Hemlock House was the perfect place to unplug, focus, and realize that dream.

The room hums even in his absence, the computers with their tall towers merely sleeping, while an oscillating fan whirs to keep everything cool. It's his laboratory and his playground, the place where his lucid dreams and most fervent hopes unfurl against the backdrop of science, cold and fragile as spun glass. Lifting a long curl of paper still tethered to the oversized design printer, I study the fantasy that is deep space. A jagged swirl of gas cloud the color of Spanish saffron. A starburst of white light. An unknowable sorcery. I drop the printout as if the paper burns.

"Maybe I have the date wrong," I say to the wilting philodendron on the windowsill. It's the only other living thing in this house, and suddenly I need to hear a voice, even if it's just mine. "Maybe he's supposed to come back on Monday." But both my digital and handwritten planners confirm Felix's Sunday return, and I realize I'm in his office because I already knew they would.

I begin to rifle through Felix's things. I'm careful at first, afraid of disturbing anything important or disordering his meticulous research. But then the mantel clock perched on the wide window ledge chimes ten o'clock, and my heart turns to ice in my chest.

Felix is too late. Too late for there to be any safe, logical explanation for his absence. His flight landed on time—I double-checked hours ago—and the only thing that could've prevented him from pulling down our sinewy, dirt drive by now is tragedy.

But my mind skitters away from the particulars of that thought as my vision becomes a star-spangled mess. I'm hyperventilating now, so I slide out Felix's chair and crash into it, trying to hang on to a shred of reason so I can make a plan.

I'll call again. And then reach out to the local police. Maybe I should try the hospitals, but between Sea-Tac and Requiem there must be dozens. I should call the hotel where he stayed, or the conference director. I'll call his boss—his department chair, I think—or the team that funded his research.

My breath returns, but my heart is beating too hard and fast for comfort. Before I can wrestle the situation back under my control, there's a mechanical *ding*, the universal sound for an alert. The computer monitor in front of me glows to sudden, unexpected life, the password-protected home screen temporarily overridden.

It takes me a while to realize what I'm looking at. Before we moved to Hemlock House, Felix told me about his father's obsession with the unknown. Wraiths and will-o'-the-wisps, unidentified aerial phenomena, and even the elusive Sasquatch. His father had installed trail cams around the property and cataloged everything, from unusual scat to video malfunctions that (if generously misinterpreted) could appear to be messages from the great beyond—whatever that was. The word LOOK spelled out in gnarled tree branches, IF in a twist of grass. And once, a barely there HELP when the video feed blurred to snow for no apparent reason at all.

"That's insane," I told Felix when he warned me about the elaborate recording system his father had created years ago. "Tell me we're not moving to a Pacific Northwest version of Skinwalker Ranch."

He laughed, kissed my forehead. "No trail cams or conspiracy theories, I promise. We have real work to do."

Now, staring at Felix's oversized computer screen, I understand that my husband lied. I'm looking at an infrared feed, the far corner of the greenhouse on the northernmost point of the maintained property, if I can believe my own assessment.

There's just a slice of white building on the lefthand side of the screen, and then the snarl of forest beyond. I squint at the web of trees, the impenetrable blackberry brambles.

Something triggered the camera. When a gray shape parts the branches, my mind tries to make sense of it. An animal, but far too big to be a rabbit, bobcat, or fisher. But then the figure unfolds, stands, and it's not one of the big cats or a moose that wandered south, or even Bigfoot himself. It is a man. He wears a dark hoodie pulled low over his forehead and a knit hat that grazes his brow.

Felix? Something unspools in my chest, yearning toward him, but then the figure lifts his face to the camera.

Not Felix. His eyes blaze hot and hollow, and I would swear he's looking straight at me.

Terror is a slow-moving train, black and hulking and incomprehensible, until it finally hits head-on.

There's a man standing at the edge of the forest, and I'm trapped in Hemlock House.

Alone.

BEFORE

MONDAY, NOVEMBER 16
NEW MOON / TAURIDS METEOR SHOWER / URANUS AT OPPOSITION

Later, after the feel of his fingertips against the line of her jaw was nothing but a fading memory, Sadie told herself that she'd imagined it all.

The whole thing was reckless, a last-minute lapse in judgment that made her pocket her car keys and turn away from the parking lot of the humanities building toward the dark north entrance and the quad. It was November in Iowa, a night so cold and dark, the first prick of brittle late-autumn air was keen as a freshly honed blade. She almost turned around. But Sadie had been in Newcastle for over two months, and still working past ten on an ordinary Monday night. She was lonely, just gathering the courage to admit it, and the flyer tacked crooked on the bulletin board in the English Department pod felt like an invitation.

The heels of her sensible flats tapped a rhythm on the flagstones of the courtyard as she hurried, then jogged, between the science building and the campus commons toward the football field. Of all places. But there was a certain exhilaration in having somewhere to be that wasn't her office, a classroom, or the condo she rented on the outskirts of town. Sadie wound the scarf tighter around her neck and bunched her fists beneath the long cuffs of her wool coat. She told herself the spontaneity of it was thrilling.

The poster had promised "Stargazing on Steroids," with a couple of the science department's portable telescopes set up for viewing both a meteor shower (Sadie had already forgotten the name) and something to do with Uranus—which would've sent the middle schoolers she used to teach into hysterics. The poster had crackled with energy, a guileless enthusiasm that made the crisp night air feel clean and fresh as newly fallen snow. Full of possibilities.

The Brantford Memorial Stadium (*Go Newcastle Knights!*) was cloaked in darkness, the streetlights extinguished for what she could only imagine was an attempt to cut down light pollution for the stargazers. But Sadie wasn't afraid as she hustled beneath the brick arch to the knot of people gathered at the fifty-yard line. Her eyes had adjusted to the ink-black world, and Newcastle was safe. Like, *leave your keys in the ignition, don't lock your front door* safe. Though she still did both, and carried a personal alarm clipped onto the strap of her purse—a relic from her days teaching eighth-grade English in downtown Milwaukee. The only thing Sadie had to fear tonight was putting herself out there, a directive her mother had barked at her only a few hours before: *Don't be such a mouse. Put yourself out there!* Wouldn't she be surprised when Sadie told her she'd done exactly that. If she remembered the conversation at all.

Twenty or so people were clustered in a semicircle around a man who stood between a pair of telescopes mounted on silver tripods. No one glanced up when Sadie folded herself in at the edge of the crowd, grateful for the cloak of the deep, moonless night. She was also—she *hoped*—indistinguishable in the small crowd of students, perhaps a faculty member or two. Her light hair was pulled back in a low ponytail, navy peacoat belted tight. Maybe no one had to know that the newest member of the English Department had made her first social appearance since arriving on campus in late August.

But anonymity wasn't the point of this outing at all. Maybe there had already been introductions and she had missed her chance to share that she was Dr. Sadie Sheridan, assistant professor of creative writing (though her degree was in English lit, but beggars couldn't be choosers), recent transplant from Wisconsin, French cuisine aficionado, so pleased to meet you. She began to back away.

"I want you to take your shoes off," the man between the telescopes instructed, cutting straight through Sadie's distraction. She was so surprised by the strange direction, she froze mid-getaway. "Grounding has some incredible health benefits," he continued. "Research suggests that the negative charge of the earth's surface can neutralize free radicals, regulate our nervous system, and synchronize our circadian rhythms."

"It's cold, Dr. Graham!" someone complained, but it was good-natured, and more than a few of the students laughed.

"Well, we could talk about the benefits of cold therapy, Landon, or you could trust me on this. Stargazing isn't just a fun hobby, it's an art. A way to ground yourself in time and space as you contemplate the infinitude of the cosmos. To connect with both the world around you and the baffling beyond. I find it helps to feel the earth beneath me before I turn my attention to the stars."

"Dude's a wannabe poet," a student muttered, but everyone bent to remove their shoes.

Sadie couldn't see Dr. Graham, not well, yet something

about the way he spoke made her toe off one camel flat and lower her bare foot gingerly onto the clipped grass of the football field. It was definitely cold, and a bit damp, but it also felt like green growing things and summertime and childhood. It made Sadie smile because she couldn't remember the last time she'd stood barefoot on grass, so she quickly slid off the other shoe, wiggling her toes in the carefully maintained turf.

"I'm going to pass out binoculars and star charts," Dr. Graham said. "I want you to spread out on the field and find a place to lie down. There are blankets if you want them. Once your eyes have adjusted to the dark, you can watch for the so-called falling stars of the Taurids meteor shower, or see if you can find Cepheus, Cassiopeia, or Pisces."

"I'm here for the Starlink satellite train!" This brought a gale of laughter, and as the crowd filed forward to accept a pair of binoculars and a star chart, Sadie could just make out the flash of white teeth as Dr. Graham smiled.

"I'd keep my eyes on Taurus if I were you," he said. "The meteors will radiate from the center of the constellation."

A girl passed Sadie a pair of binoculars and a laminated star chart over her shoulder. Sadie wanted a blanket, too, but Dr. Graham was already talking about the telescopes and Uranus at opposition, so she just stepped back into her shoes and wandered off to find a spot that wasn't already claimed by prone bodies curled close together.

Looking around, she had no doubt there were more than a few couples in the crowd. Young love and all that. Was stargazing the perfect first date, or hopelessly cheesy? And was it pathetic that she was here, among them?

When Sadie finally lay down, the vast expanse of sky made her dizzy, like she was falling and flying at once. She dug her fingers into the grass and tried to concentrate on Dr. Graham's calm directions, his nearly whispered guidance for locating the Andromeda galaxy by star-hopping from the W-shaped valleys of Cassiopeia to the great spiral solar system itself—the most distant object visible with the naked eye, he claimed.

Sadie had no idea what she was doing, but his voice became the quiet soundtrack to her exploration, and as the sky became darker still and the stars and planets and far-flung galaxies poured across the velvet scroll of forever, she lost herself. There were whole universes contained in each pinprick of golden light, and she was so very, very small. A single heartbeat. A whisper.

"Did you want to look through the telescope before I pack it up?" Suddenly, Dr. Graham was standing over her, his face in shadows, hand outstretched.

Sadie propped herself up on her elbows and glanced around, confused. She felt lightheaded, almost drunk, and she realized that the field was emptying, the stargazers wandering back to dorm rooms, the all-night diner, or perhaps Joe's, the one seedy but welcoming bar in Newcastle.

Embarrassment coursed through her, and she fumbled for the discarded star chart, the binoculars that she had abandoned long ago. The wonder of it all spilled out of her, a tipped cup. She regretted coming.

But if Dr. Graham thought her a fool, he didn't let on. "It's magical, isn't it?" He loved it, Sadie realized. The sky, the stars, the limitless possibilities of the great beyond.

"Yes," she said belatedly. It *was* magical, and she had been utterly transported, but now she felt stiff and cold. Ashamed that she had let herself get so lost in space. Literally. Sadie curled her feet beneath her and tried to stand, but her thigh-length coat was making it tricky, and she ended up dipping sideways.

"Here," Dr. Graham said. He leaned down, slipped an arm around her, and helped Sadie to her feet in one swift movement. "Did you know that some physicists believe there are more universes than the human mind can comprehend? It makes me believe in, well, everything."

"Everything?" Sadie parroted as his hand fell away. She was freezing, her body trembling, protesting the time she had spent in the grass. She wrapped her arms around herself to both ward off the cold and hide the fact that she was shaking.

"Maybe *anything* is a better word." Dr. Graham ran one hand through his black hair. It was thick, wavy, and just a little too long to be respectable. "It's hard not to believe in anything and everything when our understanding is so rudimentary."

Her eyes had grown so used to the dark she could see that he had a dimple when his mouth pulled into a half smile. Closed lips, but his expression was warm and sincere. She couldn't help but smile back.

"'There are more things in heaven and earth, Horatio, than are dreamt of in your philosophy.'" Sadie was mortified the second the line popped out of her mouth.

"Sadly, the name's not Horatio." Again, the crooked smile. The dimple. "It's Felix Graham. Science Department. But I'm guessing you already knew that. You must be the new assistant professor. I'm sorry we haven't crossed paths."

Sadie's chest burned when he stretched out his hand, and she was grateful that he couldn't see her pinked cheeks. "Dr. Sadie Sheridan," she managed. "English Department."

"Thus the *Hamlet* quote."

"I'm just a walking cliché." She didn't realize her fingers had turned to ice until Felix wrapped both of his warm ones around them.

"Shakespeare is always applicable. But I'm truly sorry for the hypothermia I've clearly caused tonight." He gave her hand a light squeeze, and when he let go, she tingled all over.

"It's fine. I'm fine. I saw your flyer as I was leaving tonight and decided to stop by. Kind of a last-minute thing." Tucking her aching hands deep into her pockets, Sadie surprised herself again by continuing, "You know your Shakespeare."

"I took an English lit class as an undergrad and the prof was obsessed with *Hamlet*. If you had quoted *Macbeth*, I would've been clueless."

He had a very slight accent, or maybe a lisp. A softening of his consonants, vowels rounded as if he savored each word like something sweet on his tongue. Sadie found herself squinting at him, grateful for the cover of night as she tried to discern more than just dark hair, dark eyes. Felix was taller than her by a few inches, wearing nothing but a thick sweater, though the night was becoming almost unbearably cold. "Can I—" she began at the exact moment he blurted: "Would you like to see Uranus at opposition?"

Sadie almost giggled at that, the punch line of a bad junior high joke, and Felix must have caught the glint in her eye because he grinned. "My astronomy students have a new one every day. Uranus jokes will always be funny."

"Will they?" Sadie raised one eyebrow.

"You're right," Felix conceded, shaking his head. "Only funny to twelve-year-olds and lovers of planetary science."

"Yes." Sadie dismissed the bite of the November night, along with her self-consciousness. "I'd love to."

There was something easygoing and authentic about Dr. Graham. Sadie had finished her doctorate just a year ago, a few weeks after her forty-first birthday, and breaking into higher ed at her age was a lesson in humility. It was why she'd accepted a position at a relatively unknown small college over five hundred miles from home. From the quaint assisted living facility where her septuagenarian mother—her only family—lived. Sadie had left everything behind for Newcastle, and so far she wasn't convinced it had been worth it. Her course load was intense, her lectures packed. She didn't have time to make friends.

But Felix acted as if this moonlight meeting was as normal as bumping into each other after faculty assembly. "Once a year, Uranus comes into opposition," he said, leading Sadie to the single telescope left standing.

Everything else had been packed away into cardboard boxes. How had she missed that?

"The Earth and Uranus pair up on this side of the sun—only two point eight billion kilometers apart."

"Practically touching," she said, and felt like an idiot. But she was rewarded with a light chuckle.

"Next-door neighbors," Felix agreed. "It's a piece of cake to spot it with binoculars, but you can see the planet's distinct blue-green marbling with this telescope. Did you spot it earlier?"

She could've lied, but Sadie shook her head and admitted, "I got distracted."

"Totally understandable. Here, let's start with these and work our way up." He handed over the binoculars he'd rescued from one of the boxes, and pointed at the night sky, telling her where to find Uranus in relation to the Great Square of Pegasus. Sadie had no idea what he was talking about, but gave it her best shot, squinting into the smudged lenses until Felix stepped behind her. "May I?" he asked, and before she could answer, he touched her.

It was nothing really, just a fingertip or two on her jaw, lifting her chin a few degrees. "You have to look up a bit more, Sadie."

Her name on his lips was an unlocking. In a single moment, Sadie's whole heart fell loose and open.

"It looks just like a star," Felix said, oblivious, "but it's not. The diameter of Uranus is four times that of Earth, and it possesses the coldest atmosphere in the solar system."

But Sadie wasn't listening anymore. Her skin flamed where he had touched her. She felt naked and exposed. "Thank you," she choked out, shoving the binoculars in his direction. Could he tell? Did he know how he affected her? Sadie knew she had made an absolute spectacle of herself. Coming to this stargazing event, whispering under a moonless sky with a colleague like she was a flirty teenager instead of an academic—a professor!—in her forties.

"In the telescope you can—"

"Thank you," she said again, interrupting. "I'm afraid I have to go. Maybe I can see it another time."

Of course, there wouldn't be another time. Once a year, he had said. A special event. Something unique and disruptive and extraordinary. As uncommon as Sadie Sheridan doing something impetuous.

"This was . . . informative," she said, gathering herself and trying to force the wayward pieces back into place. Midnight stargazing with strangers was the most un-Sadie-like thing she could have possibly done, and the impulsivity of it felt rash and uncomfortable. "It was nice to meet you, Dr. Graham."

"Felix," he said, but she had already turned away. "You can call me Felix."

Sadie wanted to tell him that he was the most interesting person she had ever met. That she believed she could spend the entire night looking at the sky with him and never once get bored. But the lightness in her chest, that uninhibited exhale that made her tingle all over, was ridiculous.

Sadie knew herself. She liked her life safe and predictable, her two feet firmly planted on the ground. A thoughtful plan outlined. Don't forget the cost/risk analysis and a foolproof exit strategy.

She simply wasn't built to be untethered.

CHAPTER 2

MONDAY

The closet stinks of mothballs. I can smell them before I open my eyes.

I know exactly where I am.

I know why.

I'm surprised that I slept, even if it was just for an hour or two with my cheek pressed to the cold, back wall of the cramped hideaway.

8:24

The face of my watch frowns in the dim light. Felix is fifteen hours gone, lost or hurt or God knows what. The thought makes me shudder, and every inch of my stiff body protests.

I'm alive. Last night that didn't feel like a given, but as I part the heavy curtain of coats and fumble for the door handle, I feel a quick beat of humiliation. I spent the night in a closet. The closet of Felix's study, to be specific, where I had to shove aside boxes and tunnel beneath old garments like a field mouse in winter. If he could see me now, the line between Felix's eyes would deepen in concern. He'd lift me into his arms, rub my hair between his fingers. Whisper *cielito* against my neck. *Little Sky*.

A white-hot pulse of want throbs through me. I want my husband here, with me, his voice sanding away the lethal corners of last night, his hand wrapped tight around mine. He would've known just what to do, his height and breadth a commanding deterrent, even if he had no weapon to wield.

I emerge into the sun-bright room, squinting at the cheerful new day, and question everything.

Last night, after seeing the strange man on Felix's monitor—too lanky and furtive to be my dependable, confident husband—I slid to the floor, my brain downshifting toward survival without any conscious decision to do so. I crawled through the study toward the living room, avoiding windows so that the twinkling snow globe of the house wouldn't project my every move. At the front door, I double-checked the lock and then wedged Felix's favorite chair under the handle, a tricky endeavor as I crouched on the floor, trying to keep my head below the windowsill.

I had to kill the lights.

I army crawled then, arm over arm, heart pulsing in my throat, until I could snake one hand up and flick off every switch on the main floor. When it was done, the darkness was thick and absolute. Even the motion-sensing light over the porch had been lulled to sleep. The man was lurking behind the house where shadows stalked at the forest's edge. But I knew my way in the dark, and now he couldn't see me creeping around like a caged animal on display.

I hurried to the mudroom, the hairs on the back of my neck tingling as if the stranger was already in the house, a mere step or two behind me, reaching. There were two locks on the back door: one on the hard little knob of the handle, and a dead bolt that slid closed with a satisfying *thunk*. But that was it. I had done everything I could do to defend myself and protect Hemlock House from whoever was prowling outside.

My phone had been abandoned on Felix's desk, and I rushed back to the study, ready to call for backup. But as I slouched to the floor, I drew a blank. Who could I dial—911? The nearest police station was over an hour away. And what would I say? I saw a man on a trail cam? He hadn't approached the door or threatened me. Yes, Hemlock House was situated on an impressive stretch of private property halfway up a dead-end logging road. But people liked to explore the relatively untouched wild of the Cascades. Sometimes they wandered onto our land. They hunted and fished, went berry-picking and foraging for mushrooms. They got lost.

At nearly eleven o'clock on a cold, autumn night?

I warred with myself, knowing that a stranger in the blackberry bramble was not okay. Not something that could be ignored or explained away. His presence there was ominous. Yes, I had a lifelong tendency to catastrophize, to take what might be an ordinary situation and twist it into a worst-case scenario. I had earned that right, but admittedly my bent toward pessimism often created problems.

"It's fine," I whispered, comforting the plant hanging in the darkened window, the starry printouts, myself. "He'll realize he made a mistake and turn back."

Turn back where? Our mountain unfurled into another and then another, all the way into British Columbia. Requiem was four miles down the logging road and then another three past the turnoff along the highway. The nearest campground was more than thirty miles away.

What was he doing here?

Maybe he's a ghost. The thought skittered through my mind like an insect, and I shook my head to dislodge it. Spinning to my knees, I peered over the edge of the desk at Felix's monitor. It had gone dark during my covert operation around Hemlock House, and I wondered for a moment if I had imagined it all. But the trail cam was recording again, the same spot highlighted in ashy whites and grays. The man was still there. Still standing, though facing away from the camera, his back a black smudge against the twisting vines. He parted them carefully, heading deeper into the forest.

I exhaled slowly, watching him go with a sort of fearful, rabid fascination. Maybe I would never know. Maybe these frantic moments of pure, uncut panic would be nothing but a hazy *what if* against the backdrop of a new day. But then he shifted, sweeping the branches aside with his outstretched arms, and a second figure appeared.

There were two of them.

That sent me scrambling for the closet, gripped by a terror so raw it was feral. I wasn't myself—college English professor, soon-to-be published novelist, head-over-heels newlywed—I was a single exposed nerve, diminished to nothing but the electric spark of my fright. I hid and listened, my entire body taut as a rubber band as I waited for the sound of boots on the porch, breaking glass, my entire world imploding.

It never came.

Now it all seems so stupid.

I try to turn on my phone, but it's dead, the battery used up during the hours-long and nonexistent siege of Hemlock House. As the silence stretched on in the closet, I dared to risk the glow of my device to surf the internet, making a list of all the hospitals I could find along Felix's route home. Then, when an hour had passed with no sign of forced entry, I called. Whispering at first, then later asking in an almost-normal voice if a man named Felix Graham had been admitted overnight. "No," came the answer again and again. "We are not treating anyone by that name."

More internet searching turned up a western Washington incident site, but it looked like someone had dumped birthday sprinkles on a map of the coastal counties. Still, I clicked on each dot, noting the category and nature of each case and reminding myself that if the police were involved in whatever happened to Felix, it was likely too soon for it to be documented online.

I was typing emails to friends with my thumbs when I fell asleep.

Now, plugging my phone into the charging cord that snakes across Felix's desk, I hope I didn't type anything too desperate. Too mortifying. What if my panic is unwarranted and Felix isn't missing at all? What if he just doesn't want to come home? I didn't think my heart could sink any further, but it does. The thought of my husband leaving me is too awful to consider.

The sun is high and pouring warm light through the windows, smooth as melted butter. Outside I can tell there's a gentle breeze, it weaves fingers through the aspens beside the old stable and dislodges spent leaves so that the air shimmers with gold like confetti. It's perfect. Postcard-worthy and contemptuous of my midnight ravings and proclivity for hyperbole. For experiencing the world with the sensitivity of someone who has lost much and learned to live carved out, a hollow husk that—until Felix—could never be filled.

A quick glance out the window assures me that my husband didn't return in the middle of the night. The drive is empty, the spot where we usually park the Jeep nothing more than tire tracks that are already being overtaken by wild ginger. There's also no sign of the intruders. For just a moment, it all feels like a dream. Even Felix.

God, I miss him. It's a bone-deep ache, sharp and bitter, and it overrides any residual fear that makes Hemlock House seem alien and strange. I can deal with whoever trespassed and cursed me with a sleepless night later. But right now, I need to find my husband.

The UTV is an old Polaris Ranger outfitted with a six-inch lift for off-roading and a dump bed for disposing of whatever debris Felix collects around the homestead. He was especially excited about these two features when we first arrived at Hemlock House, although I didn't pay much attention to the particulars. It had surprised me, this rugged side of him. It was hard to square my bookish, empirical husband with the outdoorsy nature lover that emerged when we spotted the mountains on the horizon. For a man who spent nearly the whole of his time studying the heavens, he clearly had a deep love for the terrestrial. At least, when the ground beneath his feet was the Cascades.

My hand trembles when I fit the circle key into the ignition of the UTV. I've somehow managed to brush my teeth, pull my hair into a topknot, and throw on a pair of jeans and a sweater, but I know Cleo will take one look at me and know something's wrong. That's fine. I need her resolve.

No police department will take my missing person report too seriously after less than twenty-four hours, and my support system in Requiem is threadbare. There's Cleo. That's it.

The trek into Requiem is beautiful under any circumstances, but I barely notice the crisp snap of the autumn air, the crystalline sunshine, the susurrus of the wind in the trees. The logging road is a squiggle of hairpin curves and loose gravel, and it requires all my focus to keep the oversized tires of the side-by-side from slipping off the edge. I'm driving too fast for comfort, a speed that just yesterday would have felt impossible to me, nearly out of control. I live for predictability, constancy, order. This isn't me, but what choice do I have? I press down on the gas a bit more.

Requiem is more of a village than a town, a hodgepodge

collection of buildings lined up on both sides of the highway that caters to tourists. There's a hardware store that sells hiking essentials, a gas station, a small family restaurant. Felix once told me he remembers shopping at Timber Co. with his dad, and his mom used to send him to Gus's for gallons of milk and loaves of bread when he was a teenager. But there are newer additions, too. A tiny distillery with a landscaped yard lures visitors to lounge at the painted picnic tables for hours. On weekend nights during peak season, a taco truck pulls up to the curb and does brisk business feeding the buzzed revelers queso and hot, salty chips to balance out the rich sips of Remy's famous smoked maple pecan bourbon. I once asked Remy how he could possibly make a living off the flights of small-batch whiskey he sells for twelve bucks a pop, and he laughed and pointed to the rows of boxes printed with *Requiem Rye* lining the back wall. "You, too, can take home two bottles of house-made, organic rye for the low-low price of ninety-nine dollars, Sadie." I laughed and did exactly that.

Next to Requiem Rye, is my destination: Trilogy. Like the distillery, it's a trendy new build with whitewashed floors and exposed brick. It's light and airy, with stunning views of the river through floor-to-ceiling windows across the back. Trilogy is part coffee shop and part workspace, with a dash of diner. Cleo built it with the sizable life insurance policy her husband left behind after he died. She jokes that her investment is just as demanding and high-maintenance as her late husband, but the La Marzocco makes better coffee.

I park the UTV at the curb by Requiem Rye, surprised to see that all the spots in front of Trilogy are taken. I've been writing here every day, tucked into an oversized leather chair near the impressive windows, and practically had the place to myself. The avid hikers and family road-trippers are mostly gone for the season, back to school and life as normal instead of posing at scenic overlooks for their social media feeds. The just-over-two-hundred permanent residents of Requiem need the vacationers to survive, yet after only a summer here, even I feel the tension between wanting to preserve this perfect slice of creation for those of us who call it home and needing tourist dollars to do so. The bustle of people in Trilogy on a Monday in mid-October is unexpected.

An old-fashioned bell above the door announces my arrival, but Cleo doesn't even look up from the counter. Her head is bowed over the cash register as she rings up what seems like a sizable order for a pair of park rangers in their gray button-downs and green pants. Two of the tables are occupied, and my favorite chair is holding a hiking pack for a couple enjoying the view with coffees in hand. This wasn't what I had in mind when I decided to enlist my friend's help.

Just then, Cleo finishes the transaction and looks up. "Sadie!" she calls, a grin blooming. "Happy Thanksgiving!" My confusion must be evident, because she clarifies: "Canadian."

That explains it. We're not far from the border, and an autumn day like today is a siren call.

"Hazelnut cappuccino?" she asks, though her smile slips a bit when she gets a good look at me. Her hair is braided loosely over one shoulder, the color of hot apple cider with strands of silver steam, and she flicks it back as I come near. "What's wrong?"

"Felix." I almost choke on his name. "He didn't come home last night."

"What do you mean? Was his flight canceled?"

I shake my head. "On time. I've called and called. I texted a dozen times at least. He's not answering."

Cleo's eyes flick to her waiting customers, and she waves me behind the counter so she can continue to work on orders. I sag against the bakery display case while she pulls an espresso shot. "Maybe he extended the trip," she says, not meeting my eyes.

"What for? Why wouldn't he tell me?"

"Maybe he got busy. I'm sure he'll call today."

Something about her response feels off. Dismissive and cool instead of the compassionate understanding I was expecting. "Something's wrong," I tell her, a quiver in my voice. "Felix wouldn't do that. He wouldn't forget to call. We're not like that."

Cleo pours frothed milk over the espresso and pops a lid on it. Setting it beneath the PICK UP HERE sign, she calls, "Large vanilla latte, double shot!"

"I called all the hospitals between here and Sea-Tac," I tell her, pushing off the display case so I can shadow her steps. "I've written emails to our colleagues and friends. I don't know what else to do. I was hoping you would."

Cleo sighs. "Sadie, hon, I've known Fee since he was a baby. I think you're overreacting. Forgetting to call is exactly something he'd do. I'm sure there's a logical explanation."

I can't help but bristle at both her casual dismissal of me and her use of a nickname Felix hates. I want to say, "You don't know him the way I do." But that's not true. Cleo has known Felix his whole life. He's been in mine for less than two years.

When we moved to Hemlock House, I expected Felix's homecoming to be happy. And it was, sort of. Felix came alive on the mountain in a way that I had never seen before. The Cascades and Hemlock House were home in a way our sensible one-story brick house in Newcastle, Iowa, never could be. But memories lingered in the musty rooms, and it was obvious they weren't all good.

I can admit that Felix has been quiet, maybe even cagey about his past. The people he introduced me to in Requiem have all been kind but guarded. Careful. His family clearly has a reputation, and though I can't put my finger on why we're treated with wary deference, I inherently understand we're set apart somehow. Given a wide berth. It never really bothered me until now. Until the closest thing I have to a friend out here—never mind that she's almost twenty years my senior—is giving me the cold shoulder.

"Felix is missing," I say with more heat than I intend. "My husband is missing, Cleo, and you're acting like you don't care at all."

She presses her lips together, finishes up a second coffee, and hands it to the park ranger who's waiting on the other side of the counter. "I care," she tells me, laying one freckled hand on my arm. Her colorful bracelets jangle. "But I can't say this is terribly surprising."

"What's that supposed to mean?"

Turning from me, Cleo suddenly snags a towel, wrenches open the oven door, and pulls out a bundt pan. The scent of caramelized sugar floods the shop. She sets the coffee cake on the butcher-block counter to cool, and says over her shoulder, "I can't get into this with you right now, but that family is flighty, you know?"

I don't know. Cleo must catch the glint of tears in my eyes because she drops what she's doing and wraps me in one of her signature hugs. It's tight and intense, and my arms are pinned to my sides, but I'm grateful for it anyway. For just a moment it feels like her arms are the only thing holding me together.

"Hey," she says, her chin tucked over my shoulder. "Give it a day or two."

"He's not flighty," I say. "Felix isn't like that."

Cleo pulls back, grasps my shoulders in her strong hands and gives me a half smile. "Maybe not. But just give it some time. He'll be back. You'll see."

I leave without a cappuccino and without saying goodbye, but Cleo is too busy to notice. It's like she didn't even see me. Like I was hazy and indistinct, the mere impression of a person instead of flesh and blood—someone she didn't have to acknowledge. To take seriously. It's so reminiscent of my half-life before Felix found me, that an unexpected fury takes hold. I want to scream on the sidewalk in the middle of Requiem. To make someone really look at me. *Listen.*

What does Cleo know that I don't? The question rips through me, and I realize I feel worse after my trip to Trilogy, not better. What now? I can't stop myself from glancing at my watch. *11:01.* Over seventeen hours gone.

"Excuse me?"

I whip around to find one of the rangers standing a few feet away, his hands up as if to assure me he means no harm. My nerves are on a hair trigger, and as my heart steadies, it dawns on me that I didn't even have a chance to tell Cleo about the strangers at Hemlock House.

"Didn't mean to startle you," the ranger says, ducking his head a bit. He's an older man with a full head of silver hair and a national park uniform that fits like it was tailored to his body. He doesn't extend his hand or offer his name, but there is something genuine in his sepia-colored eyes. "I couldn't help but overhear your conversation with the barista."

"Cleo owns Trilogy."

He shrugs. "I just wanted you to know that we take missing persons very seriously out here. Was your husband in the park? Hiking or fishing or something?"

"No," I say, but then think better of it. "I don't know. He

was supposed to be coming home from Sea-Tac last night. I expected him around dinnertime."

His face stiffens a little. "Contact the state patrol. And it wouldn't hurt to file a report with the park. We handle all sorts of calls and can keep an eye out for his car. If he doesn't reach out to you or turn up today, we'll want to take every precaution to make sure he's not stranded somewhere in the Cascades. There's a storm brewing."

I glance at the azure sky, as deep and clear as a polished stone, and can't square his words with the warmth of the sun on my face.

"It's nice now," the ranger admits, "but mark my words, snow will fly before the end of the week."

A single bead of dread bubbles to the surface. I'm not ready for this. Felix warned me about winter in northern Washington, icy roads and deep snow with the power to make us involuntary hermits. We bought boots and snowshoes and heavy, down parkas because in his words: "There's no such thing as bad weather, only bad clothes." Still, I don't feel prepared for the darkness and isolation, the long nights. Especially with Felix missing. And unknown men lurking around Hemlock House.

"There were strangers on my property last night," I blurt. It feels crucial that somebody knows about the intruders.

"Say what?"

It's a lot, I know, a missing husband and a trespassing accusation. An impending storm to complete the trifecta of personal disaster. I wonder if he even believes me. "I don't think they did anything," I say. "There were two men lurking at the edge of the property. I saw them on one of our trail cams."

The ranger takes a step toward me, his eyes flinty. "You need to be very careful, ma'am. It could've been an innocent mistake—a navigational error—but poachers are armed."

"Poachers?"

"They'll shoot anything that moves—cougar, wolf, elk, bear . . ."

I can feel the blood drain from my face.

"Be sure to tell the state patrol about them, too," he says. "My jurisdiction only covers the park, but we work with local law enforcement when the situation warrants."

"Thank you," I tell the ranger. "I'll call." But my voice hitches, and he catches it. He gives me a sympathetic smile and doesn't patronize me by saying that everything will be okay. Instead, he nods goodbye, and I swear he'd tip his hat if he was wearing one.

"Hey," I call when he's nearly reached the door of Trilogy. "How long until the snow flies?"

The ranger swivels and studies the washed-clean slate of sky as if he can read the forecast in the crooked cross of contrails at the farthest edge. "It's going to turn fast," he says eventually. "Two days, three at most. Get ready, okay? It can be dangerous up here."

CHAPTER 3

MONDAY

The turnoff for Hemlock House is a blink-and-you-miss-it, two-track lane through a tangle of almost impenetrable underbrush. When we first arrived nearly six months ago, we had to turn back to Requiem so that Felix could buy a brush-clearing sickle from Timber Co. to cut down the blackberry canes that had grown over the path. I eyed the wicked carbon steel blade and short, blunt handle, unconvinced that such a compact tool could make a dent in the fairy-tale thicket that made our new home seem like Sleeping Beauty's castle.

Felix read my mind. "There's a gas-powered brush cutter in the shed," he said, a glint in his eye. "All I have to do is get to it."

I'd believed, foolishly, that the property was overgrown because Felix had been gone for so long. Sure, he'd contracted with a local realtor to make sure the place didn't completely fall apart, but Hemlock House sat empty for years, the forest slowly reclaiming the patch of land his family had worked so hard to cultivate for over a century. But beating back the wild was an almost daily chore, something that required time and attention so that the house and grounds weren't swallowed up by nature.

At first I'd found the riotous vegetation lovely. The five-petaled white stars of innumerable blackberry blossoms, the bright pink cups of creeping bindweed, the tufts of old man's beard that scaled the cedars and draped the branches like long, lacy Christmas garlands. But Felix pointed out the way they choked the trees and smothered the bleeding hearts that his mother had planted in the shade along the north side of the house. On a trip into Requiem for groceries, he showed me a rusted-out truck in a shallow ditch that had been strangled by ivy and wild blackberry. I could barely make out the shape of the abandoned vehicle beneath the shroud of virulent green.

Now, steering the UTV onto the narrow path home, I feel like the mountain is closing in around me. The forest has eyes and arms in the form of creeping vines that could stealthily overtake me. Nothing about Hemlock House feels safe or civilized. The heavy metal gate is open—just the way I left it—and the homestead is quiet and undisturbed. It feels abandoned. Almost ominous.

Felix is nowhere to be seen as I park in a strip of gravel near the front porch.

"It's okay," I tell myself, trying to stifle the panic building in my chest. "Everything is going to be just fine."

My words ring painfully hollow, and hysterical laughter bubbles up in my throat. I try to suppress it, but it escapes as a sob, a cry that is instantly absorbed by the lush landscape around me. There's nothing for me to do but bury my face in the crook of my arm where it rests on the steering wheel and weep.

When I'm done, I feel fragile and empty, but also cleansed somehow, like I've rinsed the toxic thoughts away and the only thing left is the truth of what I'm facing. My husband is gone, and—as far as I can see it—there are three possible reasons why.

He's dead. I force myself to hold that thought in my hands, a burning coal that hurts so badly I gasp. But pretending won't do me any good, so I don't. Felix, my beautiful husband, could have had a terrible accident and is yet to be found.

He's missing. Maybe his Jeep went off the road and he's injured or unconscious or confused. He could have taken a wrong turn on an isolated stretch of highway, lost somewhere remote without reception.

He left me. It's unthinkable—and something I would have never even considered a mere eighteen hours ago. But I know firsthand that life, and people, are unpredictable, capable of blindsiding you in the most shocking, untenable ways.

Not my Felix.

Everything inside me rebels against this grim practicality, this careful assessment of the impossible situation I find myself in. And yet, what choice do I have but to move forward, clearheaded and sure? I'll do what I always do: make a plan and follow it. By myself, apparently, which is how I have always worked best.

I open the half door of the UTV and step onto the quilted lawn of Hemlock House. The ground is spongy here, thick with the scrubby grass that grows in rocky soil and patches of almost whimsical clover that fill in all the gaps. As I brush the tears from my cheeks, a pair of whisky jacks soar down from the canopy of trees that hem the yard, chasing each other around the stubby fingers of our leaning electrical poles. Their whirling pattern is a game, a dance, and I would be charmed if I didn't know that they're scavengers. Felix told me months ago, when I first admired their soft gray feathers and white bellies, that they don't migrate but winter in the mountains, eating carrion that predators leave behind. I shiver, thinking of impending snow and carnivorous birds that look as if they might alight on your finger, but would do whatever they must to survive.

I look up the number for the Washington State Patrol like the park ranger suggested, so I can report my husband missing. I pace the homestead yard as I do so, walking tight circles as I click different links on my phone until I finally find the contact info for the office in Whatcom County, the closest jurisdiction.

It's a frustrating conversation, stilted and inconclusive because my instincts were right, and the officer doesn't seem overly concerned about Felix's whereabouts.

"I've taken everything down, Mrs. Graham. We'll keep an eye out for him and let you know if we find anything," he says when I've shared every relevant detail I can think of.

I switch my phone to speaker and tap open Notes. "I'm afraid I didn't catch your name," I tell him, though I remember full well that he introduced himself as Chief Colin Brandt. I type out his name as he repeats it, the time of our call, and then record the number that he tells me to use in case Felix shows up.

When I hang up, I don't feel like I've done anything at all. But short of taking off in the Ranger and driving the route to Sea-Tac myself—both ridiculous and illegal—there's nothing else I can do.

I'm buzzing, strung tight as steel wire, and vibrating with a directionless energy. My heart is broken, of course, but I'm also angry and confused and helpless and God knows what else. A therapist would have a heyday pulling me apart, but I've spent my whole life holding all my shattered pieces together with grit and good old-fashioned Midwestern pigheadedness. I'm not about to crumble now.

Closing my eyes, I turn my face to the pale, October sun. It's not warm, but cool and impassive. A warning. The air smells of pine, but beneath that there's rot: fallen leaves, decaying trees, moss and fungi hidden in the dark and secret places of the wilderness all around me. *Snow*. The scent is faint, but bright and threatening, and I know the park ranger was right to warn me. Today may be the perfect fall day, but it will not last.

This mountain is new to me, but winter is not. I know all about storm doors and double-hung windows, winterizing yards and homes and cars.

There are a pair of worn, leather gloves in the tool shed, lying flaccid and cool on the rough-hewn work bench. I slide my hands into them, and for just a second I can feel Felix over my shoulder.

They're too big for you. A perfect fit.

It's what he always says when I wear his clothes, which is often. His flannels are thick and sturdy, lined with pockets for my little notebooks and pens. Felix's sweatshirts are well-worn, threadbare in places, but oh so soft and forever smelling faintly of his warm skin, no matter how many times we wash them.

The first time I threw on one of Felix's sweatshirts—cold from a late-night lunar eclipse viewing—he caught me in the act. "There's no question," he said, coming up behind me and wrapping his arms around my middle. "It looks better on you."

I felt a flush of shame then, frustration with myself for being vulnerable, for pretending that Felix and I were connected in a way that rendered territory meaningless. My mother had been a cold woman, her boundaries sharply drawn, and I had learned as a child that it was better for everyone if I held myself apart. Self-possessed, carefully contained, and separate. I hadn't even realized I was beginning to love Felix without borders.

"I'm sorry," I said. "I should have asked."

"Never. It's yours, Sadie. All of it."

What he meant was: *all of me*.

Clapping the gloves together sends a cloud of dust into the air, and it's enough to dispel the memory. Felix is coming home, I tell myself, and when he does, he won't have to worry about burst pipes or ice dams on the roof.

It takes me several hours to prepare for the impending storm. I drain the outdoor faucets and wrap them in burlap, then prop the old ladder against the house so I can dig the debris from the gutters. When I bring the first bucket of muck to the burn barrel, I scream at what I find curled on top of the festering pile of grass clippings: a snake. Even as I jump away, I know that my imagination has played a trick on me—it can't be a snake, not this time of year—and I creep back to peer over the edge. It's not alive, just a perfect snakeskin, desiccated but whole, and coiled as if ready to strike. The ghostly silhouette is as thick as my wrist and several feet long.

A shudder rolls down my spine, and I quickly upend the bucket over the lifelike husk. It feels like an evil omen, but I refuse to fixate on it, instead squirting lighter fluid on the contents of the burn barrel. When I toss a match inside, a whump of flame bellows black smoke into the air.

The last thing I do is prepare the UTV. The Ranger is open to the elements, but I find cab enclosures in the shed and meticulously attach the sealing strips until the marine-grade polyester is stretched taut across the sturdy vehicle.

I'm sweating by the time I'm done, sleeves rucked up past my elbows and tendrils of hair that have escaped the topknot cling to my damp cheeks. I've been so busy I've forgotten to obsessively check my phone, and I sink to the porch steps, peeling off Felix's work gloves so I can do just that.

Nothing.

No calls or texts from anyone with news, just a few emails from Iowa friends telling me they haven't heard from Felix but: *How can I help?* I have absolutely no idea.

Twenty-two hours gone, I realize, staring at my phone screen. At this time yesterday, I was just putting the beef bourguignon in the oven and heading upstairs for a shower. At this time yesterday, I had no idea my life was about to change.

The sound of an engine snaps my head up and sends a flock of crows screeching into the sky. Because the forest is so thick, sound doesn't carry here, so Felix and I are only aware of visitors once they're already upon us. My heart leaps into my throat, choking me with hope, but it's not our Jeep pulling onto the homestead yard, it's Cleo's silver hatchback.

She waves when she sees me standing on the porch steps, and I can tell from the slant of her mouth that she's come to apologize. She emerges from the car with a wrapped bundle in one hand and a to-go cup in the other.

"No news?" Cleo calls.

I shake my head.

"A peace offering," she says, crossing the space between us, and thrusts the cup at me. When I take it, she wraps me in a one-armed hug.

"I didn't realize we were at war."

Cleo flaps her hand dismissively. "Tomato potato."

"I don't think that's how it goes."

"I know, but I like my way better."

She sits down on the porch with her feet on the top step and pats the boards beside her as if this is her home and she's inviting me to stay for a while. I sink down beside her and take a sip of the coffee. It's a perfectly creamy hazelnut cappuccino, still warm in spite of the long drive over.

"I brought coffee cake, too," she says, holding out the paper-wrapped bundle. "I had to bake a second because I sold out of the first in an hour."

"Busy day." I take the package and peel back a corner to expose a thick hunk of cake. I want to be bitter, but I'm suddenly ravenous. Besides, I don't have enough friends in Requiem to nurse a grudge.

"Tell me everything," Cleo says after I've taken a few bites.

The afternoon air starts to cool as the sun dips below the tree line. I suppress a tremble and roll down my sleeves, taking another sip of the coffee to warm myself a bit. It doesn't help, but Cleo doesn't suggest we move inside. Like Felix, she's so fully acclimated to life here it's like she's part of the flora and fauna. I'm convinced she'd be comfortable in any weather at all in her rotating wardrobe of different-colored North Face half-zips and sturdy jeans.

There's nothing for me to do but tell Cleo everything, bolstering myself with nibbles of her sugary coffee cake and nips of cappuccino until both are gone. She seems satisfied when they are and takes the empty cup and greasy paper from me so she can recycle them later. It strikes me that this is exactly what she wanted to do when she came: feed me. It's so characteristically *Cleo*, I can't help but be touched that even though she ignored me earlier, she cared enough to trek all the way to Hemlock House to make it right. Felix has softened me in dozens of ways, but I often still bristle at being taken care of. Yet in this moment, I'm grateful. I lean into Cleo until our shoulders bump. It's a thank-you and she knows it.

After a few hours of trying to forget, I realize I'm exhausted. I want someone else to take charge, to tell me what to do or how to find Felix, but instead of outlining a game plan, Cleo heaves a massive sigh. Goose bumps rise along my skin.

"What?" I ask, my voice flat.

"Well, he's not dead, is he?" Cleo squints through the growing shadows at the spot where our winding driveway disappears into the trees. "If Felix was in an accident or something else terrible happened, someone would have called you by now. He has his ID on him."

I nod. Of course he does. He drove. He flew. He needed his license for both. "What if it was a single-vehicle accident and no one was around?"

"The route to and from Sea-Tac is well-traveled, Sadie. I guarantee you: someone saw something if Felix was in a wreck. And if anything happened at the convention, you would've already received a call."

I know she's right, and it both comforts and scares me. "So where is he?"

Cleo fixes me with a sober look until understanding dawns behind my eyes. She smiles gently and lays her hand on top of mine. It's warm and dry on my clammy skin. "He'll come back when he's ready."

I feel as if she's slapped me, but I know that it won't do any good to try and convince her that Felix isn't like that. That he wouldn't just abandon me at Hemlock House. I swallow. "You said the Grahams are flighty. What did you mean?"

Cleo looks away, then pulls her braid over her shoulder, slides the elastic off the end, and begins to unravel it with her fingers. "They were always just *different*."

"I'm going to need more than that. I never met them, remember?"

It's true, I never met Felix's parents or his sister. But there's more to it than bad timing. Felix and I rarely talk about our families of origin. That's strange, I know it is, and yet, in the beginning it felt right for us to keep our sad stories far away from the new life we were creating together. My childhood was unhappy, his unsettling, and we avoided discussing them. It was enough to know that we had suffered and emerged more or less intact. Now we talk about our people carefully, tending old wounds that split open far too easily. It's irresponsible, maybe, a willful ignorance that feeds the naive belief that we can simply forget everything that came before we fell in love. But I am made of loss. Felix of perfection that grows from a deep need to keep his world ordered and safe and calm. My mother left her mark all over me. I know Felix's family did the same to him.

"I don't want to speak ill of the dead," Cleo says eventually, "but the Grahams were eccentric. Living way out here, keeping to themselves, you know. They never really made friends in Requiem."

"So? Being private is hardly suspicious."

"They were." Cleo shoots me a sidelong glance, then begins re-braiding the hair she just unwound. I can tell that she's decided to give me the unvarnished truth and I'm grateful. "David Graham was a bachelor—living out here alone—until one day he showed up with a wife half his age. She was small, pretty, could barely speak a word of English. The joke was that Lucia was a mail-order bride."

I bristle. "That's cruel."

"Do you want me to tell you or not?" Cleo doesn't wait for an answer. "Felix was born right away, Gabriella less than two years later. We only knew about them because Lucia showed up in town with one baby in a sling around her chest, and the other on her hip. It wasn't obvious they were David's kids, but she paid with his bank card, so."

Cleo's hair tie has slid off her knee and fallen to the porch step, and I bend down to grab it for her. "Still not strange."

"I'm getting to it." She takes the tie, secures the braid, and then leans back with her elbows on the porch floor. "So, Lucia and the kids would disappear for long stretches of time—"

"Back to Mexico," I interject, because I know this part. "To see her family."

"I guess. But it's almost like David and Lucia and the kids weren't really a family at all, because whenever she came back, *he* disappeared."

"Where?"

Cleo bobs one shoulder. "Who knows? David was really into the supernatural—like, lots of people around here talk about the Sasquatch, but it's not *real*, you know? We don't actually believe in it. He did."

I think of the hunting cameras, the phosphorescent glow of strange men in the darkness, and feel the hair rise on the back of my neck. "So, what? He was off tracking *Bigfoot*?"

"I guess. David Graham was always banging on about one crackpot theory or another. Rumor had it he was working with a film production crew on a documentary about paranormal activity in the Pacific Northwest, but I don't know if that's true or not. Have you heard of the Wendigo?"

I shake my head.

"Skinwalkers? The Ogopogo?" Cleo tries. When I don't bite, she goes on. "Doesn't matter. He was big into Indigenous mythology. Bit of an expert, from what I understand. He was always chasing the next sighting, the next story."

"Flighty," I say, using her word.

"Strange," she counters. "Disengaged, isolated, prone to taking off. By the time Felix and Gabi were teenagers, David Graham was gone more than he was home. It didn't seem to bother Lucia much. I think they all did better when he wasn't around."

"And you think Felix is the same way?" I can't keep the hurt out of my voice.

"Hey." Cleo sits up and drapes an arm around me, pulling me closer for just a moment. "That's not what I meant. I don't think Felix is crazy or indifferent to you and what you must be feeling. But he grew up with a revolving door at Hemlock House. If he wasn't leaving with his mom and sister, his dad was. Now Felix is home, back in the place where all his childhood heartaches occurred . . . Coming and going was simply a part of his life. There wasn't much stability, you know?"

"Stable" is exactly the word I would use to describe my husband. Steady, dependable, sure. But my mind skitters to his office—printouts of the ink-black heart of deep space, galaxies spread out like radiated bone, the gunmetal clouds of the Pillars of Creation and their war waged against the backdrop of a bloody sky—and I know that he inherited his father's curiosity, his dark wonder. And compulsion. Felix's monsters are well documented, but they are not entirely knowable. He chases them with the single-minded intensity of a hunter.

"I'm just saying, coming home a day late from a conference wouldn't be a big deal for Felix. It's Graham family modus operandi, you know? Give it a day or two, and if he doesn't turn up, *then* we'll start to worry."

Too late, I want to tell her, but instead I say, "I guess every family has their quirks."

"The Grahams were more than quirky!" Cleo laughs, seemingly relieved that I'm not crushed by her revelation of my husband's strange family dynamics—or possible proclivity to repeat them. "Felix even landed on our couch a few times. I was his sixth-grade teacher, you know, and we had quite a close relationship back then . . ."

"Thank you," I say, which is stupid, and Cleo brushes me off.

"Lucia had a beautiful heart, but that family was messed up. Living with David was nothing but misery for all involved."

Cleo slaps her hands on her thighs, a sure sign that the conversation is over, and pushes herself to stand.

I rise, too, and fix a pained half smile on my face. It isn't hard.

"Go grab some things," Cleo says. "The guest room is ready for you. I washed the sheets a few days ago."

"What?"

"Well, you're coming home with me, of course." Cleo zips her fleece up as far as it'll go and stuffs her hands into the kangaroo pocket against the growing chill. "I have some leftover potato soup, and we can watch a movie. We'll make it a fun girls' night."

"I can't," I tell her, my voice strangled. "I can't leave Hemlock House. What if Felix comes back? What if he needs me and I'm not here?"

The look on Cleo's face says it all: I'm crazy. Crazy to stay out here by myself, and crazy to cling to the notion that something's wrong when she's made such a compelling case for both the genetic factors and learned behaviors that would enable my husband to simply not come home as planned. Maybe she's right. Maybe I'm making way too much of this. But I don't care.

"He can call you, Sadie. If he comes home and you're not here, he'll call."

"It's okay," I tell her. "I'll be fine. I'm sure you're right—he'll turn up soon, and I want to be here when he does."

Cleo narrows her eyes, skeptical, but I hold her gaze and don't waver. I was planning to tell her about the trespassers, but I tuck that little tidbit away, knowing that she wouldn't take no for an answer if she realized I wasn't quite out here alone. But I have to believe the park ranger was right: the men were poachers who didn't find what they were looking for in my backyard. They won't be back. And I refuse to leave.

"I don't like this," Cleo tells me as she pulls me in for one last hug. Her left hand is balled around my used coffee cup and wrapper, but she rubs my back with her right. "Call me if you need anything—and I mean *anything*. Your faucet leaks, I'm your girl. Feeling lonely? I'll come get you in the middle of the night."

"I'll be fine," I tell her again, then try to appease her by saying, "I'm sure Felix is on his way as we speak." I'm shocked I don't choke on the words.

Cleo nods but turns away quickly to hide the doubt that suddenly clouds her eyes. She's not fast enough. I see it, and know that deep down, she's worried, too.

I watch her drive away, the dramatic smudge of a crimson sunset bleeding between the fingers of the trees that line the yard of Hemlock House. Something about the dark draw of approaching night, the red claw marks of a gory sky, and my own deep isolation conspires to disturb me. I cross my arms against the night, unsettled by Cleo's stories and the history of this beautiful, toxic place. There is a reason I both love and hate it here, the relentless, arcane beauty and the malicious, encroaching wild: it's haunted. By sadness and loneliness and the ghosts of David Graham's futile search for imaginary demons.

I shiver, and not from the cold. As if the lines have been conjured by an unspoken spell, I remember the witches of *Macbeth*. It's been years since I memorized the scene, but it floats back to me in bits as a gust of wind sweeps down from the mountain, scattering the carpet of brown leaves at my feet.

Round about the cauldron go.

I don't know why I never thought of it before. Haven't wondered why Hemlock House isn't River Run or Summit View or Cottonwood Estate—all of which would be perfectly apt names for this sprawling mountain homestead.

But hemlock is poison.

I turn to the house, the windows opaque and unknowable as if they are keeping secrets. Maybe they are. Maybe they always have been. And maybe, if I want to know what happened to my husband—where he is and why—I'm going to have to do some digging.

I can't help myself. I say the last bit out loud: "Root of hemlock, digged in the dark."

BEFORE

FRIDAY, DECEMBER 20

WAXING GIBBOUS MOON / URSIDS METEOR SHOWER / WINTER SOLSTICE

Sadie's office looked like it belonged on the set of *Dead Poets Society*. Newcastle University provided the bones—creaky hardwood floors, dark paneled bookshelves, mullioned windows—but she leaned into the aesthetic with overflowing stacks of old books, a leather-and-bourbon-scented candle, and a gilt frame that contained one willowy, hand-lettered word: *Ardently*. There was an antique map of Middle Earth and an African violet on the windowsill that had just unfurled three perfect lavender blooms like an early Christmas present. The office was small, but to Sadie, it was perfect. Rich and delicious as warm pumpkin cake.

The students were gone for semester break, and the English pod was silent but for the quiet hum of central heating and the rap of snow on the window. The flakes were hard little crystals, dry as cut diamonds because of a cold snap that had plunged temperatures into the single digits. It was late on a Friday night, and Sadie knew she should take the remaining Introduction to Creative Writing short stories home to grade, but her office was far cozier than her condo. Besides, she had told her mother weeks ago that reception was poor in the garden-level English

Department, and when Alice's aides knew Sadie was working, they rarely allowed her mother to call.

Sadie had a mug of peppermint tea, a space heater under her desk, and the muted glow from a strand of white Christmas lights that she had draped across one of her floor-to-ceiling bookshelves. What more could she possibly want?

When the door to the department pod creaked open, it sounded thunderous in the silent space. Sadie felt a stab of irritation, because the peaceful cluster of offices after hours was her own private kingdom. She nursed an irrational, proprietary claim on the anteroom—with its mismatched sofas and burbling water cooler—since her colleagues were all married with children at various ages and stages, who raced home at the first opportunity. They didn't seem to notice the knitted throw she had carefully positioned over the dark stain on one of the couch cushions, or the snake plant that now graced a low table near the glass-paneled door to the hallway. Sadie sighed, hoping whoever it was had simply forgotten something and would be in and out in minutes. Still, she turned down the volume on her speaker in case the velvety instrumental arrangement alerted the interloper to her presence.

A gust of cold air was accompanied by the light thump of a palm on Sadie's half-open office door, and it nearly sent her to the ceiling. She gasped like the heroine in a Regency romance and pressed one hand to her chest.

"Whoa," Felix Graham said, stepping into her office uninvited. He crossed the narrow space in two large strides. His dark eyes were sheepish, but the lift at one corner of his mouth betrayed amusement. "Didn't mean to startle you."

Sadie was struck dumb. Felix Graham was in her office. She hadn't spoken to him since the night on the football field, though she had hoped to. For a couple of weeks she idly wondered if there was a way she could orchestrate an accidental meeting, and had even gone so far as to walk through the science building en route to different locations on campus. Once, she caught sight of him after a guest lecturer had presented in Newcastle's stately chapel, but after hurrying to catch up, she stopped so quickly it was as if she was tethered, and someone had yanked the chain. *What was she thinking?* She was hopeless at relationships, and she knew it. A botched romance—no matter how attracted she was to Felix—would be her undoing. She simply couldn't risk it. Instead of catching up to him, Sadie took a shuddering breath, straightened her pencil skirt, and cast a furtive glance around to make sure no one was watching. Then she'd walked off in the opposite direction.

Now he was standing at her desk. Towering over her, actually, as she sat with a red pen in one hand and her mouth slightly agape. She snapped her teeth together. "You surprised me."

"Sorry, I've been meaning to stop by and keep getting sidetracked. It's been a busy semester." He raised one knowing eyebrow at the untidy stack of papers on her desk.

"It has," she said, putting down the red pen and pushing back her chair. "Very busy semester. Can I get you a cup of tea?" Sadie's manners were coming back to her slowly. Felix's shoulders were dusted with snow, as if he had been sprinkled with powdered sugar, and his hair sparkled white. "You must be freezing."

Felix shook his head, sending a fine spray of droplets across the room. "Not at all. I like the cold." Then he looked down. "Nice slippers."

Sadie had forgotten she was wearing them. She kept a pair of fluffy, faux fur–lined slippers beneath her desk. Often, her favorite part of the day was when she sunk into her ergonomic office chair and kicked off her shoes so she could slide her toes into the soft, warm slippers. Looking down, she realized they were ratty and worn. One discolored sole was peeling loose.

"Oh, these old things?" She laughed, her heart light for the first time in weeks. "Now that you've seen them, I can't let you leave this office. No witnesses."

"I solemnly swear your secret is safe with me." Felix crossed his heart with a finger and then settled into one of two chairs Sadie used for student meetings. He seemed perfectly at home in her space, as comfortable as if they'd known each other for ages.

"Peppermint?" Sadie asked, lifting the last remaining tea tin from the bookshelf that doubled as a drink station. "Or peppermint? It's getting a little lean around here. Christmas break and all."

"I'll go with peppermint." Felix looked around her office curiously, his gaze raking over the knickknacks and books arranged alphabetically by genre until they landed on a photograph of Sadie and Alice. They were obviously mother and daughter: blond and lean, with the same narrow nose, small mouth, and gray-green eyes. He didn't comment on it, but said, "Speaking of Christmas break, what are you still doing here?"

Sadie set the electric kettle to boil and pulled a pyramid-shaped teabag from the tin. "I leave tomorrow." She tried to keep the angst out of her voice. She was looking forward to seeing her mother, but holidays were especially hard. It's why she had chosen to linger in Newcastle as long as possible. "What about you?"

"Nowhere to go," Felix said with a candor that didn't veer into self-pity.

Sadie released a shallow breath she didn't realize she was holding. She hadn't known for sure if Felix was unattached until that very moment, and although she didn't want it to matter, it did. "Where's home?" she asked, grabbing a mug from her stash and checking to make sure it was clean.

"Newcastle now. But I was born in Washington state. I've also lived in Oregon, Arizona, and Nebraska. My mom's family is from Mexico City. I spent part of my summers there when I was a kid."

"A true nomad. I'm from Wisconsin," Sadie offered. "Lived there my whole life until I moved here a couple months ago."

"A Midwestern girl through and through." Felix accepted the mug of hot tea and motioned toward the framed photo on Sadie's desk. "You look just like your mom."

Sadie curled one hand into a fist as she took the chair beside Felix. She'd discovered long ago that it was best to get this part out of the way as soon as possible. Hiding the biggest defining event of her life only made things awkward later on. At best, people felt like she'd kept important information from them; at worst they felt lied to. "My dad and older brother were killed in a car wreck when I was four. It's just the two of us."

Felix had the grace not to look stricken. Instead, he studied her carefully, his eyes penetrating hers as if looking for the veiled grief of the left behind. She fought the urge to look away. Sadie didn't miss her father or brother, per se, but she felt their absence like a bomb-size crater in her world. It never grew over, and her mother had never healed. Sadie had known from a very young age that it was her job to be everything Alice had lost: her partner, her son, the life she was supposed to have. Sadie tried, but she was never, ever enough.

"It's okay," Sadie said when the silence between them stretched on. "It was a long time ago."

Now Felix seemed shocked. "*Is* it okay?"

No, Sadie thought, and felt a rush of something that was dangerously close to affection for the enigmatic professor.

Wasn't he supposed to be cold? Closed off? Weren't scientists aloof and passionless?

Before Felix could express his condolences or probe deeper into the mechanics of her sad little family of two, Sadie asked: "What about you?" Now that the hard part was over, she was eager to steer the conversation away from her life. She didn't want his pity or his scrutiny. And she definitely didn't want to talk about Alice. How her mother had never been satisfied, never okay. Always wanting—*demanding*—her daughter's time, attention, and focus. Alice Sheridan was quicksand, a gaping chasm of need with razor-sharp edges that ensured Sadie could never escape. Sadie was only here—nearly thirty-eight years later and a couple hundred miles away from the assisted care home—because of Alice's dementia.

Occasionally, Alice forgot the accident had happened at all, and then remembered in a rush that was as devastating as the first time she'd heard the news. But she frequently forgot Sadie. "Who are you?" she'd ask, a snide barb in her voice when Sadie visited. Or, "Not another new girl," though Sadie never wore the smart plum-colored scrubs that were the uniform at Valley Rest Senior Care Home. "It's me, mom," she'd say over and over. "Your daughter. Sadie Noelle." Then she'd lean forward, and against all odds, take her mother's dry, brittle hand in her own. Trace the veins like rivers on a map to a place she longed to visit but never could.

"My parents have been gone for a while," Felix said. "My sister, Gabrielle, still lives in Washington. We're estranged."

His voice didn't waver; he was stating a fact, nothing more. Sadie felt a prick of compassion for him, and then her cheeks warmed because she knew what he was doing. She shared something ugly, so he was doing the same. It was an offering of sorts.

Felix's hands on the mug had Sadie mesmerized—slender,

elegant fingers that she suddenly longed to touch—so she pulled herself roughly back to reality by blurting, "What are you doing here?" It was rude, to say the least, and she softened it by adding, "I mean, how did you know I was here?"

It was a few days before Christmas. It seemed like everyone else had taken time off.

Felix's cheek dimpled. "There's exactly one office on campus lit up tonight. I knew it was yours."

"How?"

"You have a reputation, Dr. Sheridan. Just a few months in and you're already known for being hardworking and a student favorite."

"But . . ." She rolled her hand, encouraging him to get to the less flattering bits.

He shrugged. "You're also known for lingering in your office until all hours of the night."

Sadie groaned theatrically to cover up the sting of his words. "I'm pathetic, aren't I?"

"Of course not." Felix seemed genuinely confused. "You take your work seriously. You should."

She wanted to tell him that she wasn't just writing lesson plans and grading student papers when she lingered in her office past midnight. Sadie was busy on her own project, too. Her book had sparked the interest of a literary agent she'd met at a writing conference in Austin over a year ago, and they'd been in touch throughout the rewriting process. Addison was young, a budding agent who was still building her client list, hoping to discover the next Marilynne Robinson in a sea of hopeful contemporary novelists. "You write with such a subtle beauty," she'd told Sadie over cups of weak hotel coffee on a sun-soaked terrace. "There's something real and aching in your words. But your story needs a lot of work."

Sadie had been working. Writing and rewriting, sitting through master classes on Zoom, hiring freelance editors to take a crack at ten pages here and there. Her book wasn't bad, but it wasn't good yet, either. The bottom line was, it wasn't publishable, and she knew it. But she wasn't about to tell Felix any of that—even if it was tempting. Sadie believed he'd be a good listener. She thought he'd understand.

Felix took a sip of his tea, then set the mug on her desk and reached into his coat pocket. "Anyway, I'm sorry to barge in on you, but I've been meaning to swing by for weeks. I wanted to give you this."

It was a small piece of paper about the size of a postcard. When Sadie took it, she saw that it was a picture of a sparkling blue orb surrounded by concentric rings.

"It's Uranus," Felix said. For just a moment they stared at the card together, and then he made a sound like he was choking, and they both erupted in laughter. Sadie laughed so hard she hiccupped, which only made the whole thing even *more* funny, and she howled until tears ran down her cheeks.

"I'm sorry," she finally managed, brushing the heels of both hands beneath her eyes. "I promise I'm not usually this immature."

"I told you; Uranus will never not be funny."

She quirked one eyebrow at him. "I can't decide if the double negative makes that sentence work, or if it ruins it."

"Don't think about it too hard. Just look at the photo." He tapped the blue marble with one finger. "That's the planet you were supposed to see that night on the football field. Of course, this is an image taken by the James Webb Space Telescope. It would have looked nothing like this through Newcastle's Celestron, but I felt bad you didn't get a chance to see it."

Sadie studied the photograph, the almost neon blue of the

planet and the dusty white glow of the rings. "It doesn't look real," she said.

"Uranus has been photographed before," Felix told her. "Once in 1986 by the Voyager 2, and later by the Keck Observatory in Hawaii using advanced adaptive optics. But the James Webb images are in another stratosphere. Pardon the pun."

She glanced at him out of the corner of her eye and gave a wry smile. "Funny guy," she said drily.

"Flip it over," Felix instructed her, and then reached for the paper as if to help. When his fingers brushed hers, Sadie felt his touch echo in her bones. For just a moment they stayed there, hands sparking in all the places they touched, like the tip of a struck match, and then slowly Felix shifted. Reluctantly? Sadie couldn't tell. He bent over the image and pointed out a couple pinpricks of glittering light.

"This wider view features all the moons. Uranus has twenty-seven of them, most of which are too small to be seen, but you'll recognize the names of these." He tapped three of the larger arctic blue coronas in succession and said: "Oberon, Titania, and Puck."

"*A Midsummer Night's Dream*," Sadie exhaled, unable to hide her delight.

"Most celestial bodies are named for Greek mythology, but it seems appropriate that these would be christened after magical spirits. They look like—"

"Fairies," Sadie finished.

"I thought you might appreciate it." Felix sat back in his chair, clearly pleased with himself. "Being a Shakespeare devotee and all."

"Thank you," she told him, strangely touched by this thoughtful, unusual man who had the mind of a scientist and the heart of a bard.

"You're welcome."

They sat there for a moment, Sadie running the tip of her finger along the edge of the cardstock that Felix had used to print the images. He opened his mouth as if to say something, seemed to think better of it, and reached for his tea instead. Taking a quick sip, he deposited it back on her desk and stood in one fluid movement.

"I'd better leave you to it," Felix said.

The glimmer in the room was gone. That brief, luminous heartbeat or two where the world seemed astonishing and intentional, as if everything was scripted and they were playing their parts flawlessly. Exactly as they were always meant to.

"Oh," Sadie rose, too, hoping her disappointment wasn't evident in that one syllable. What was she wishing for? Dinner, drinks, the promise of another impromptu drop-in? *More*, she realized as he shot the cuffs of his heavy coat and stepped around the chair. She simply wanted more time with him.

"Goodnight, Felix," Sadie said, but the words didn't seem like enough. She wanted to lay her hand on the navy wool of his coat, over the place where a neat, square pocket covered his heart. Tugging the sleeves of her cable-knit cardigan over her knuckles, she added, "Merry Christmas."

Felix paused at the open door. Turning toward her, he smiled slow and soft, like he was savoring the moment or keeping a secret. "Happy Midwinter Night, Sadie."

CHAPTER 4

TUESDAY

It's dark when I open my eyes, the starry glow of my laptop screensaver the only light in the quiet house. The air is thick and anxious as a pent-up breath, and I whip my head around, suddenly sure that I'll catch a glimpse of something—*someone?*—in the shadows. But there's nothing there. I'm utterly alone.

I've fallen asleep sitting up on the couch, my computer still in my lap and my phone pressed against my hip. Bleary-eyed and confused, I run the back of one hand over my mouth and tap the phone screen with the other. 12:04.

30 hours gone.

I didn't mean to fall asleep.

My neck is stiff, my lower back aching from an afternoon of manual labor and an hour-long catnap pretzeled on the sagging couch. Still, I'm shocked I dozed off when dread sits like a stone in my belly.

I've been busy trying to track down any information I can find on Felix's possible whereabouts. The Planetary Sciences Symposium was in San Diego, and a quick online search told me it was being held at the Marriott Marquis & Marina. But when I called to find out if Felix had checked out or if I could be patched through to his room, the front desk clerk refused to give me any information.

"I can pass your name and number along to my manager?"

she said, the end of her sentence lifting as if she was asking a question instead of stating a fact. I could tell she was new.

"I expect a call back first thing in the morning." I didn't even try to be cordial.

Thwarted on that front, I spent the rest of the night doing the one thing I had promised Felix I wouldn't do: I scoured Hemlock House.

After we moved in, Felix had shut the doors to several rooms and assured me we didn't need the space. The house had never been properly cleaned out, and we were temporary sojourners at the homestead. "This place is a crypt," he said, one side of his mouth tugging down in disgust. Then he hauled anything we didn't want or need into the attic and closed the doors to his and Gabi's childhood bedrooms. It was clear he wanted me to stay out, and it never occurred to me to be suspicious of why.

When David Graham passed away from a quick and brutal battle with pancreatic cancer, the homestead had been more or less abandoned. Lucia had died nearly seven years earlier. Felix was living in Arizona at the time, finishing a PhD in astrophysics at ASU, and working on his dissertation on quantum mechanics and black holes. He and Gabi were barely on speaking terms, and what Felix told me about their tragic homecoming and unhappy reunion was that neither had time to go through the house. Gabi was pregnant, hugely so, and preparing to give birth to her first baby, a feat that she seemed to think Felix should be more excited about. But Felix was neck-deep in research, crippled by imposter syndrome, and facing his own demons at the death of his not-so-beloved father.

It had been a stalemate. Felix and Gabi held a subdued, poorly attended service for David at the tiny Lutheran church in Requiem, said goodbye to their father, and left the house untouched. The siblings never spoke again.

"Never?" I gasped when he told me, shocked that this man I loved could be so cavalier about his own flesh and blood. It stung, actually, because even then I might have traded the love we had to undo what had happened to my family. The thought of seeing my father and brother—to talk to them, to hear them laugh, to know the kind of man that Matty would've become—was enough to steal my breath away. I couldn't imagine choosing estrangement over a living, breathing sibling.

But Felix had given one tight jerk of his chin, a rare show of contempt, and the conversation was over.

"I'll go through everything," he told me when he closed off parts of the house. "Just leave it, okay?" Felix phrased it as a request, but it was an order.

Five months into our sabbatical, the closets are still filled with musty clothes, the drawers crammed with faded towels, yellowed bricks of Ivory soap, old sheets. A junk drawer in the kitchen is a graveyard of dried-out pens and half-used tape dispensers, trail maps, and rubber bands. Hemlock House is a mausoleum, the resting place of a life interrupted. We've cleared out space for ourselves, but much of it remains untouched. Sometimes, I feel like if I move fast enough, I might catch the shadow of Felix's mother among all her old things. A silvery wisp of her slender hand, spectral and reaching.

Now, I'm surrounded by flotsam and jetsam in the form of whatever I could find that might offer me some insight into the Graham family. Who they were, what made them tick. I found nothing so providential as a journal or a diary, but I collected an old photo album, a banker's box filled with a messy tangle of crumpled receipts, bank statements, jotted notes, and two of David Graham's black composition notebooks. I'm pretty sure Felix shuttled most of his father's "research" to the cellar when we moved in, but I found these tucked into the cupboard above the sink. They had been slid upright between an old rum bottle with an inch of cloudy liquid in the bottom and the perpetually damp cabinet wall. I've already thumbed through one of the notebooks and found it filled cover-to-cover with scribbled commentary, awkward sketches, and oddly proper-looking formulas.

Carefully, I close my laptop and slide it onto the coffee table. Then I reach my hands overhead and interlace them, stretching first to the right and then to the left, trying to work the kinks out. After just a couple hours' sleep on the closet floor last night and an uncomfortable couch doze, I know I should brush my teeth and head to bed. Try to get some real rest. But my mind is once again whirring so fast, I know sleep would be impossible.

Instead, I decide to brew a pot of coffee and keep going. Maybe Felix thought it was too spendy to stay at the Marriott Marquis and opted instead for a cheaper option nearby. The grant money covers work-related travel, but Felix is frugal and unfussy. He'd be just as happy in an outdated roadside motel as a five-star resort. I'll make a list of hotels within walking distance of the Marriott and start calling.

But as I head toward the kitchen, I notice a soft glow emanating from Felix's office. Earlier in the night, I watched the monitors for any sign that the trespassers were back, but gave up after the only thing that triggered the sensors was an owl that swooped through the trees. Even now, still yawning and bleary from my unexpected nap, I expect another false alarm. The strange men from last night are surely long gone.

Except they're not.

My heart jolts and threatens to beat out of my chest when I step into the office and see the same, white-haloed figure from last night. Same dark hoodie, same knit hat, same round-shouldered posture as if he has something to hide. I frantically scan the periphery of the frame, searching for the second intruder, but it seems the tall figure is alone. As I watch, breathless, he jogs across an open expanse of yard to the greenhouse. Looking around furtively, he grabs the handle and gives it a pull. There's no lock on the door, but it sticks. I know that rotten wood has warped the metal around the strike plate; that you must give the door an almighty jerk, that it'll screech loudly when it eventually yanks loose. I can't hear what's happening, but it all plays out in front of me just as I know it will. The man tugs, tugs again, and when the high-pitched shriek of metal-on-metal finally pierces the night, he spins around as if caught red-handed. His eyes blaze hollow and phosphorescent on the hi-res computer screen.

I gasp, fingers tingling with fear, and throw myself toward the living room and my phone. The house is dark, so I don't think he—or anyone else—can see me moving behind the windows, but I stay crouched anyway as I fumble over the couch. The device has slid between the cushions, and when I eventually grasp it, a bolt of adrenaline slides through me. My hand trembles as I try to thumb it open, but the screen remains stubbornly black.

My phone is dead.

Kneeling on the hardwood floor, I curse myself. I've been throwing my phone on a charger repeatedly throughout the day, but just enough to stop it from slipping into low-battery mode. It's finally caught up with me.

The ranger's proclamation has me spooked. Poachers are terrifying—really, anyone with a gun is—and I'm desperate to call 911, Cleo, *anyone*. I won't make the same mistake I made last night. Whoever the man is, he shouldn't be here.

My charger is in Felix's office, and I hurry back there. A few seconds of juice should be enough, and while I make the call,

I'll be able to keep an eye on the stranger. The cord is hiding beneath some of the papers that I've already gone through, and I sweep them to the floor in my desperation to connect the phone.

On Felix's computer screen, the man has disappeared into the forest again, leaving the door to the greenhouse open. My pulse is thrumming in my ears, my breath quick and jagged, and when he reappears I physically recoil.

He's carrying someone in his arms.

It's a struggle for the stranger to clear the bramble with a body gripped to his chest, but he lowers his head and pushes through. One small, dangling leg catches on a blackberry cane, but the man doesn't stop. Instead, he surges forward, ripping a long branch of thorns straight out of the ground in his effort to keep going. It drags behind the stumbling pair like a broken shackle.

Is he carrying a woman? A child? Terror bubbles up in my throat. Try as I might, I can't square the scene before me with anything rational or understandable. Am I watching a rape in progress? An abduction? And why *here*? The answer is swift and almost painfully obvious. Because Hemlock House is huge and isolated. Because it's haunted.

I tear my eyes away from the scene unfolding before me to check my phone, but the screen remains stubbornly dark. Tapping it with my fingers, and then hitting it in frustration, I feel a cry wrench free from my throat. I can't just sit here. I can't let this man do whatever he plans to do without at least trying to stop him. Even if I could call the police right this second, they would never arrive in time to prevent whatever is happening in the greenhouse.

But *I'm* here.

I rattle the phone, wiggling the charger in the port to try to make it come to life, but the screen remains resolutely black. Calling for help is out of the question right now, and every second that ticks by is one more moment the stranger is alone in our greenhouse with someone who is vulnerable and at terrible risk.

I need a weapon.

My cheeks are damp with tears, my chest heaving, but the thought is crystal clear and somehow galvanizing. The man is weighed down with a body in his arms, with whatever evil he plans to carry out. But I am unrestrained. I can be quiet and strong. Formidable. I have the element of surprise on my side.

We don't have a gun, not even for hikes. Felix swears bear spray is safer and more effective if we were ever to encounter a grizzly out here, and I can only imagine how it would affect a man. But as I hurry through the house toward the mudroom where our hiking gear is always carefully organized and easily accessible in clear plastic totes, I worry about the spray discharge in the close confines of the greenhouse. "This stuff'll blind you," Felix warned when he showed me the canister and how to use it months ago. "Never spray into the wind." He hadn't said anything about enclosed spaces.

The cool cylinder of bear spray feels disproportionately heavy in my hand, consequential, but I decide saving someone's life is more important than worrying about collateral damage. Still, when I slip into my hiking boots, I also grab the crowbar propped against the mudroom wall. Before he left for San Diego, Felix had been peeling off the moldy baseboard in the constantly damp, chilly room.

I slip into the night without my coat, my eyes already adjusted to the dark and my body too keyed up to feel the bite of the cold air. Around the corner, the greenhouse glows faintly in the pale moonlight, a sickly iridescent green from the moss that's grown over the warped glass.

Creeping slowly across the lawn, I flick my gaze between the door of the greenhouse and the spot at the tree line where the man has created a sort of path. My heart sinks at the thought that there were *two* men last night, and the second has yet to appear. I almost lose my resolve, but the bear spray has a maximum range of thirty feet. If someone comes skulking through the bramble, I can fog them before they even realize I'm there. It occurs to me that a hunting rifle has a much longer range than a canister of bear spray, but I push that thought from my mind with a ferocity that surprises and emboldens me.

The moon is a sickle above my head, sharp and pale as a shard of broken seashell. It witnesses me trip over a mole hill, nearly fall, then catch myself with a whisper of a sob that I have the foresight to swallow. My feet don't make a sound on the springy carpet of untamed lawn, and I'm grateful that Felix didn't have time to cut it before he left. I'll take whatever small advantage I can get on this fool's errand, because with each step closer to the greenhouse and whatever—*whoever*—waits inside, I am more and more convinced I'm making a terrible mistake.

Too late. It's too late to worry about that as I near the small building. A few feet from the limed, crooked door I can hear shuffling, a quiet voice muttering in the dark, a muted thud. Then, a piercing cry of pain. Fear? It doesn't matter. The sound is a final, savage push, and I feel every ounce of hurt and terror and fury pool into one hot and holy purpose.

I kick the door of the greenhouse open with a scream. I want to shock the man inside, paralyze him with the sound of the crowbar singing against the iron doorframe, blind him with the double row of HPS lights. The clang of the crowbar echoes when I hit the switch with my forearm, bathing the long building in a sudden, artificial daylight that leaves my eyes watering and my vision blurred.

"Stop!" I shout, because that's all I want him to do right now. Stop whatever he's doing long enough so that he turns toward me, and I can get a clear shot at his face. My thumb twitches on the actuator tab of the bear spray. "Stop or I'll shoot!" I plan to shoot anyway.

It takes a few seconds to untangle what I'm seeing. The man is crouched on the floor at the far end of the greenhouse, a body curled in a fetal position on the ground before him. As I watch, the intruder whips around, shielding his eyes from the glare of the lights, affording me my first unobstructed, in-real-life look at him. Two things are immediately apparent: he's not a man at all, and he's terrified.

"Please!" he says, his voice cracking. "Don't shoot!"

I watch as he scrambles to his feet, legs gangly and graceless as a colt's. His hair is long, dishwater blond, and curling beneath his dirty beanie. Pimples dot his sharp chin, and he's sporting an impressive black eye that shines bright purple in the harsh light. Although the boy is tall, he's teenager-thin, and I marvel at how I could have possibly mistaken him for a grown man. Both his black sweatshirt and his jeans are baggy on his narrow frame and look as if they haven't been washed in ages. They're stained and fetid, the sweatshirt ripped with a sizeable hole over his right shoulder. Bare skin peeks out from underneath. I can smell him even from twenty feet away, the sharp tang of his body odor and a primal, animal fear choking the space between us.

"Please. We just need a place for the night," he continues, palms raised as if to hold me at bay. "We'll be gone before sunrise, I promise."

I'm stunned speechless. I don't move an inch. He may be just a kid, but his expression is wild, his gaze unhinged. He's folded in on himself, possibly afraid to move, but he balls his hands into fists and then shakes them out anxiously as if he would like to take a swing at me. I don't trust him, and I keep the canister of bear spray raised between us, the crowbar dangling beside my leg as extra leverage.

"We'll go," he says when the silence stretches too long. I realize all at once that I've forgotten to speak. I must cut an unnerving profile: wrathful, silent. With poison in one hand and a weapon in the other, my hair a nimbus of snarled waves, my cheeks streaked with dried tears. I probably look insane.

"Who are you?" I croak, my voice thick with disuse.

"Henry," he says. Did he pause? I can't read his expression.

"Henry who?"

"Just Henry."

"Where did you come from, Just Henry?"

He thrusts his head over his shoulder, back toward the forest and the path through the briar.

"The mountain?"

Henry nods.

"There's nothing out there," I tell him, frustrated that my words come out shaky. My hands are quivering, my core molten.

He shrugs, clearly starting to realize that I'm not quite as menacing as I seemed at first.

I want to yell at him, but I was a teacher long enough to know that yelling is the fastest way to make him shut down even more. If I want to get any reliable information out of him, I have to take a different approach. Sucking in a deep breath, I reach for the self-possession that used to get me through long days filled with teenage hormones and interminable adolescent drama.

"What are you doing here?" I ask, trying to project authority and calm.

"Just need a place to spend the night. It's getting cold out there and . . . " Henry trails off.

"Did you sleep in the greenhouse last night?" Understanding dawns as I remember the first time I saw him on the trail cam feed. His obviously well-worn track through the undergrowth.

Henry pauses, wrestling with himself. I can almost see him weighing his options. Finally, he nods, just once.

"How old are you?"

This answer comes immediately. "Eighteen."

I don't believe him for a second. He's fifteen, tops. His height would suggest a growth spurt, but the fullness in his cheeks betrays the fact that it happened recently. He has yet to lose the last of his little boy fat. But I don't press him on it. He's composed himself a bit, and by the way his eyes flick over my shoulder to the door behind me, I know that he's weighing his options. If he threw himself at me, how quickly would I go down? Could I hit him with the bear spray before he knocked the canister away?

"You can't spend the night in the greenhouse," I tell him, because of course he can't. That's absurd. Unthinkable. "You have to go home."

At this, his eyes cloud over. "No." It's one word, but he says it with such heat, such vehemence, I clutch the crowbar tighter. "We're not going home."

We. The surprise of finding myself face-to-face with a teenager instead of a fully grown man—a poacher or human trafficker or God-knows-what kind of monster with evil intent—nearly made me forget about the person on the ground. "Move," I tell Henry, taking a threatening step forward and using the crowbar to point him to the right.

He stares at me for a moment, and then, doggedly holding

my gaze, takes one step away from the body still prone on the floor.

It's a boy.

Like Henry, he's wearing dirty clothes and a knit hat that's seen better days. His jeans are mud-streaked, frayed at the hems, and the torn blackberry cane is still attached to one pant leg. I worry for a moment that the thorns have not just punctured the fabric, but his skin, too. The child is slight, curled on one side with his hands fisted at his chest. His eyes are closed, and his hair coiled in dark, greasy ringlets against one ghostly white cheek. He looks like he's dead.

"Who—"

My question is cut off when the boy moans, a sound so pathetic it rips at my heart.

Henry drops to his knees, ignoring me and the danger I pose him, and brings his fingers to stroke the boy's head. "Finn?" he says softly. "Finn, can you hear me?"

The most Finn can manage is another moan that subsides into a confused, delirious mumbling. I can't make out any intelligible words, but there's a cadence to his monologue. He's talking to someone in a fever dream.

"He's sick?" I ask.

Henry doesn't answer but pulls his filthy sweatshirt over his head and tucks it around Finn. Beneath the thin garment, he's wearing a paper-thin tank top that must've once been white. He's got to be freezing, but he doesn't show it. Instead, Henry murmurs to the boy, true tenderness in his tone.

"Who is he?" I ask, and when Henry doesn't answer, I say it again: "*Who is he?*"

"My brother."

I look at the bear spray in my hand, and then at the crowbar. At once it feels foolish, even cruel to still be clutching them. As if I would use a weapon against children. I shudder a little at the thought. "I'm going to set these down," I tell Henry. "I won't hurt you. I promise."

Henry glares over one shoulder, clearly as distrustful of me as I am of him. I drop the bear spray and crowbar just outside the greenhouse door and offer him my empty hands, a tight-lipped smile. "I might be able to help. Do you have any water? Ibuprofen? Blankets?"

It's clear he doesn't, and the shame that floods his face makes me regret asking. "I have all of those things," I tell him. "And a phone. We have a portable cell tower on the roof, and even though there's no signal out here, we get great coverage—"

"No!" Henry's outburst startles Finn and the boy trembles alarmingly, his little body jerking on the hardpack floor. Henry seems not to notice, but he grips Finn's shoulder protectively, angling his body between me and the sick boy. "I swear, if you call *anyone* and tell them that we're here, I'll take Finn and disappear. You will *never* find us. No one will. I know this mountain like the back of my hand."

I can tell it is not an idle threat. The thought of Henry slinging Finn over his shoulder and melting into the forest makes my blood run cold. There's a frost warning for tonight, a storm on its way, and something seriously wrong with Finn. "Okay," I tell him, patting the flat pockets of my jeans and turning a slow circle so he can see I'm not carrying anything. "I don't even have a phone with me. I won't call." *Now*, I think.

"May I see him?" I ask again, taking a tentative step forward.

I can tell that letting me anywhere near his brother is the last thing Henry wants to do, but he also understands that he doesn't have much of a choice. Finn clearly needs help, and only I can offer it.

Wordlessly, Henry shuffles to the side. He crouches knee to

knee with his brother, offering me the space by Finn's chest and head. I walk over slowly, making sure my movements are measured and smooth, nothing to worry about here. Then I kneel beside the boys.

Up close, the stench is almost overpowering. My middle school teaching years inured me to sweaty boys and rapidly maturing girls, but this is next level. I have so many questions. I want to ask them where they came from and how long they've been roaming around in the wilderness. There's nothing out here but Hemlock House, and I can't even begin to imagine how they found themselves on this patch of forsaken ground of all places. I want to ask where their parents are. Surely their mother is losing her mind, wherever she is. This kind of neglect doesn't happen overnight; these boys have been missing for a while. And up close, I can see that Henry's black eye is painfully swollen, a recent injury that has yet to fade even a little.

But as many questions as I have, nothing is so immediately pressing as the needs of the little boy before me. His skin is glossed with a sheen of sweat, but his lips are cracked and dry. High on his cheekbones there are two bright dots of color, the twin stains of a high fever. I put out a hand to touch him and then glance to Henry for permission. He gives me a barely perceptible nod.

Finn's skin radiates heat long before my fingers brush his forehead. It's been years since I pressed my palm to a child's skin to gauge temperature, but this is beyond anything I've ever experienced. It almost hurts to touch him.

"He's burning up," I tell Henry, alarmed. Moving my hand to Finn's narrow chest, I can feel the rattle behind his quick, shallow breaths. "I think his lungs are full. He could have pneumonia."

Henry and I stare at each other for a moment, and the fear

in the older boy's eyes gives me the courage to try again. "Look, he really needs a doctor."

"No." Henry whispers it this time, but there's steel in that one small word. He knuckles away a tear that escaped from the corner of his good eye and says it again. "*No*."

When he shifts to stand and slings one of Finn's limp hands over his shoulder, half hoisting the boy into his arms, I give in. "Okay, okay," I say quickly, against my will. "I won't call anyone. Just put him down."

Henry loosens his grip and Finn slumps back to the ground, seemingly unaware that anything has happened at all. It takes everything in me not to cradle his head, to brush aside the lank hair that's clinging to his temple.

In one way, I've never had children of my own, but in another, I've had hundreds. I think about Emily, who showed up to school with the raised, red welt of a burn peeking out from the collar of her shirt. Or Ivanna and Alexander, refugees who didn't speak a word of English. Of Hudson, whose mother died from breast cancer halfway through his seventh-grade year. He used to lean against me, lightly at first, and then, when I didn't give way, slumping the full weight of his body against mine, a tangible knowing that he was not alone. That someone would hold him up when he felt like he might fall. I loved them all in my way, and I feel that same sudden, irrevocable beat of connection with Finn. He needs me, and I'm here. Even if I have no idea what that means.

"What are we going to do?" Henry asks after a moment, determinedly avoiding my gaze.

But I don't respond. I'm stuck on that one word: *we*.

There is no we, I think. Until Felix, it had only ever been *me*. And now here I am, alone at Hemlock House with two strange boys—one of whom is sick. I'm at a loss. For the span of a heartbeat or two, I long for my husband with a yearning that nearly levels me. I want him here, beside me, making everything okay in the way that only he can. *What am I supposed to do?*

I was afraid of the unknown men who were lurking outside Hemlock House. But in some ways, the reality of this situation is even worse. With Finn shaking before me, I feel a new kind of fear slide through me like a knife. It's bottomless. Otherworldly.

It feels like a little boy's life is in my hands.

CHAPTER 5

TUESDAY

I can't bring Henry and Finn into the house. I just can't, and maybe that's wrong of me, but less than an hour ago I thought they were bent on destruction. And even though I now believe that's not the case, I have no idea who they are or why they've sought sanctuary at Hemlock House. I don't know them, and I don't trust them.

So, I leave the brothers in the greenhouse and hurry back across the lawn to gather supplies. Quilts from the hall cupboard, bottles of water. There's ibuprofen in the medicine cabinet above the bathroom sink, and cough syrup that hasn't yet expired. I don't know if I can give a child cough medicine intended for adults, and I have no idea how much Finn weighs, but the kid is in bad shape. Maybe a half dose would be better than none at all.

At the last minute I think of Henry in his old, ribbed tank top and climb the stairs to our bedroom. There's only one small closet with a pocket door, my clothes and Felix's mingled together in a knot of knits and soft cotton. It hurts to run my fingers over Felix's shirts, and I select an old blue sweatshirt he rarely wears. I want to bury my nose in it, but I resist the temptation.

Back downstairs, I deposit the provisions on the dining room table and jog to the office to grab my phone. I promised Henry

I wouldn't call anyone, but that doesn't mean I can't at the very least search home remedies for lung infections. Maybe if I can convince Henry that Finn needs medical intervention, he'll give in and let me call for help. But when I lift my phone from the desk, it remains dark.

"Damn it," I mutter, dropping to my knees to fumble along the wall for the outlet. As I suspected, the prongs are barely clinging to the slots. I must have yanked the cord out just enough to detach it in my haste to plug my phone in. After slamming the connector into the outlet all the way, I rise to check that my efforts paid off. This time, a white apple appears on the screen.

Relief floods through me, but it'll be a while before the phone is usable.

On my way back to the boys, I panic. I left the bear spray and crowbar against the outside wall. What if Henry's found them? What if this was all an elaborate ploy? But when I get close I peek behind the bricks and moonlight glints off my makeshift weapons. They're right where I left them. And when I slip back into the greenhouse, it seems as if Henry and Finn haven't moved, either.

"Here." I hand Henry the sweatshirt and carefully kneel to ease the rest of the supplies to the ground. He glowers at me for a moment, but I can see the goose bumps all along his arms, and in the end, he pulls the shirt over his head without a word of thanks.

"Try to get him to swallow these," I say, tapping two ibuprofen into my palm. I hand them over to Henry, along with one of the water bottles.

He just stares at the little orange pills in his hand. "What is it?"

My jaw actually drops. "*Ibuprofen*. An anti-inflammatory. A painkiller and fever reducer." When I realize that Henry's not buying it, I grasp his wrist and squeeze. "Trust me. It'll help."

He looks between me and Finn, contemplating. But it's clear to both of us that Finn is suffering, and it seems like Henry is at the end of his rope, willing to take the risk. As he lifts Finn's head and coaxes him to gulp one round tablet at a time, I use the quilts to create a sort of nest. I've forgotten a pillow, something to elevate Finn's head and chest so that he doesn't choke on any mucus.

"I'm running back to the house," I tell Henry. "Try to get him to drink as much of that water as you can."

Henry scoffs but doesn't bother to glare at me as he gently wipes away liquid that has spilled all over Finn's chin and neck. But it looks like the pills went down, and as I stand, I see Henry tip the water bottle to Finn's mouth again.

When I return, I have three couch pillows, a bucket of cold water, and a couple of washcloths. I get Henry to help me move Finn to the improvised bed, his upper body elevated on the pillows. We pull a double-thick blanket up over the boy's shoulders, and then I dip one of the rags into the bucket and squeeze it out. Henry watches as I wipe Finn's face, drawing the cloth across his eyes, cheeks, and mouth. Wiping away the grime that coats every inch of his exposed skin. As I do so, I realize he's adorable. Button nose, bow mouth, and thick, long lashes that any girl would envy. Finn moans, and when he does, a deep line appears between his eyes. I want to smooth it away but settle instead for dragging off his greasy hat and brushing his hair back. Henry doesn't say anything until I rinse the washcloth for the last time, wring it out, and lay the cool compress on the little boy's burning forehead.

"Where'd you learn how to do that?"

I'm not sure what he means. Use ibuprofen? Make a bed out of blankets? I decide it doesn't matter. "My mom," I say tightly. After Dad and Matty died, the only time she ever showed me tenderness was when I was sick. A slight fever and she nursed me like her life depended on it. Of course, when I got better and my need for her wasn't so immediate, Alice Sheridan went straight back to being distant and aloof. But I clung to those rare moments of connection like a lifeline, and I used to pray for strep throat, a flu bug, a case of good old rotavirus. They proved to me that somewhere, deep down, my mother loved me enough to want me to be well.

Henry must have mommy issues, too, because his jaw goes rigid, and he looks away. "What do we do now?"

"Wait."

"How long?"

"Depends. If the pills work, his fever will come down." I shoot Henry a sideways glance. "Have you never taken ibuprofen before?"

He pauses just a second too long before saying, "Yeah, ours just don't look like that. I didn't know if . . . "

I let him trail off and don't press the point. "Look," I tell him, "I know I came in here a little aggressive. You were trespassing on my property, and I didn't know who you were or what you were doing. You scared me."

Henry grunts, and I take it to mean the feeling is mutual.

"But I'm not going to hurt you. And I swear I won't hurt Finn."

It's an olive branch of sorts, but rather than accept the truce, Henry folds his arms across his chest and leans against the leg of one of the shelves that stretch the length of the greenhouse. He fixes me with a haughty look. "As soon as Finn feels better, we're gone."

I bite back an incredulous laugh. As if I'm keeping them here against their will. As if *they* aren't the ones trespassing on *my* property. "You do that," I say, settling against a shelf across from him. We're facing each other, the narrow center aisle of the old greenhouse between us. Finn's makeshift bed links me and the surly teen, with the sick boy's head at my hip and his feet at Henry's. If Henry wasn't watching me like a hawk, like he half expects me to strangle Finn even though I've just done everything in my power to make him comfortable, to ease his pain, I'd rake my fingers through Finn's hair. Maybe touch his cheek or curve just a bit closer to let him know that he's not alone. I remember being sick, how scary and isolating it was, and how much better it felt when I knew someone was keeping vigil with me. But rather than reach for Finn, I ball my hands together in my lap.

The adrenaline that kept me focused and sharp from the moment Henry appeared on Felix's computer screen is starting to drain away. In its absence, I become aware of just how cold it is in the greenhouse. How bright the overhead lights are. How weary I am.

"I'm going to get a few more things," I tell Henry, levering myself up from the ground. I realize too late how weak I must look clinging to the wooden shelving as I rise. I'm a forty-something English professor, and without the aid of the bear mace and crowbar, I'm no match for an angry eighteen-year-old, no matter how malnourished he seems or how doubtful I am about his real age. I'm pretty sure he's taller than me—pushing six feet—and his arms, exposed earlier in the saggy tank top, are ropey and strong. Henry is no soft-bellied gamer. That kind of lean muscle mass comes from hard work, and I have no doubt he could overpower me if he wanted to. Still, before I leave, I say, "Dip one of those washcloths in the cold water and hold it against your eye. You'll feel better."

When I return to the greenhouse for the last time, I'm carrying a battery-powered lantern and both of our sub-30 sleeping bags. I've slipped on my winter parka, and in the pockets, I have boxes of raisins and several of the protein bars that Felix likes. I'm also packing a small but wickedly sharp paring knife with a protective sleeve clicked over the blade, but I don't want Henry to know about that. Glancing at the boys huddled on the floor, I berate myself for grabbing it at all. And then Henry looks up with hate in his eyes and I'm glad I did. He didn't take my advice. The extra washcloth sits untouched beside the bucket.

"I'm going to shut off the main light," I say, indicating the lantern. It's already lit, glowing faintly, and will hopefully allow Finn to get some rest without leaving me alone in the dark with Henry. I don't wait for an answer but hit the switch. The world is instantly black, the soft light of the lantern barely enough to illuminate even the first step I have to take. But I grip the knife inside my coat pocket and make my way carefully over to the boys.

"Here." The tightly coiled sleeping bags are pinned under one arm, and I drop them into Henry's lap. "One is for you, and I want you to open the other one up in case Finn needs it."

"In case he needs it? It's freezing in here."

"We don't want him to overheat," I say, settling back onto the floor. "He's buried in blankets—if the temperature drops much more, we'll have it handy, but he's okay for now."

Placing the lantern on the floor between us, I lean over Finn and cup his face in my bare hands. Does he feel slightly cooler? I can't tell, but the moisture at his temples reminds me that he needs to keep hydrating, and I raise the water bottle to his mouth for a few small sips. He drinks obediently but chokes on the last swallow and begins to cough. It's a wracking, convulsive bark that is both wheezy and wet, and tears leak from the corners of Finn's eyes as he struggles to breathe.

"What did you do to him?" Henry is on us at once, shoving me aside, though there's nowhere for me to go. My shoulder slams into the rough wood of the shelf and I stay there, panting, while Henry attends to his brother. "Hey, buddy. You okay? I'm right here. It'll pass."

The coughing fit does pass a few moments later, but Henry stays where he is, half on top of me. He barely seems to register that I'm there at all. I want to throw him off—I feel panicked and trapped with his rank body over me—but I don't want to trigger him. So I ease myself out from the cramped space between his steely side and the rough-hewn wood, yanking the hem of my coat when it wrenches me back. Henry doesn't budge.

"It's good for him to cough," I say when I'm safely on the other side of the aisle. I'm breathless and fighting the urge to run back to the house and lock the door. Call 911, even though Henry swore he'd take Finn and disappear. The boy's small hand curled like a chrysalis in the gentle maw of his brother's much bigger fist is the only thing that stops me.

"How can that be good for him?" Henry asks after a few tense beats of silence.

"It clears his throat and airways, loosens up the mucus in his chest. Better out than in." It's what my mother used to say, rubbing my back as I bent over a pot of steaming water with a towel thrown over my head. "I have cough syrup, too, but I want to see how he reacts to the ibuprofen before we medicate him more."

Henry doesn't respond to this.

For a while we focus on the raspy breath raking in and out of Finn's lungs, then I ask: "How old is he?"

"Fourteen," Henry says.

It's another lie. Finn is ten, eleven tops. I don't understand why Henry feels the need to inflate their ages. Why not just tell the truth? But then Henry hands me the answer as if I voiced the question out loud.

"I'm his guardian. I make all the decisions about what happens to us. No one will take him away."

Bingo. For some reason, Henry is afraid that he and Finn might be separated. A drop of respect for Henry bleeds into the picture I've been painting of him. I would lie, too, if it meant I could keep my brother with me.

My thoughts splinter, fracturing into a dozen questions and then a dozen more. But now that we're finally settled, and Henry and I have more or less suspended the hostilities in our shared desire to help Finn, exhaustion sweeps over me like a flood. I'm warm enough, and the dim smolder of the lantern is almost homey. I know that I should fight sleep, keep vigil for both Finn's sake and my own—I don't dare turn my back on Henry—but the last time I slept for more than an hour or two was Saturday night. I'm wrecked, emotionally and physically, and try as I might, my body stubbornly continues to shut down.

The last conscious thought I have before I'm yanked under has nothing to do with Henry and Finn at all.

33 hours gone.

◆

It's after dawn when voices rouse me. The world is thick and pale outside the greenhouse, the soft gray of goose down. Inside, the air is still, compressed by the stench of illness and body odor, of dry rot and mold that I hadn't noticed only hours before. Now it's oppressive. It makes the long building feel close as a cardboard box.

I don't move at first, but watch Henry as he bends over Finn, speaking softly and moving his hands in a series of gestures that seem too intentional to make him merely a prolific hand talker.

When Finn raises a few fingers and signals back, I realize they're using a sign language of sorts, but it's like nothing I've ever seen before. Can Finn not talk? He was mumbling earlier. But perhaps the words I thought were jumbled by illness are mixed-up, regardless of whether or not he's febrile.

I want to keep watching, to observe without letting them know I'm doing exactly that, but my neck is screaming, and my legs are completely numb. Before I can shift even an inch to ease the pain, Henry says without turning toward me: "He's hungry."

How did he know I was awake? "Hungry?" I echo, pulling my legs up and rubbing the back of my neck with one hand. "He's feeling better?"

In answer, Henry shifts so that I can see Finn's face. His big brown eyes are open for the first time since I found the brothers in the greenhouse hours ago, and though they're glassy and hooded with exhaustion, his gaze is clear and lucid. He stares at me openly, his skin still porcelain white and his cheeks gaunt.

"Hi, Finn," I say giving him a smile, a small wave. "I'm Sadie."

Henry looks up at this and I realize I never told him my name. He never asked. Maybe it's a bad idea to exchange pleasantries now, to invite these wild boys even further into the waking nightmare of my life, but the truth is, my name just slipped out. We survived the night, didn't we? Henry didn't kill me in my sleep. I guess that's enough for now.

Finn waves back, an eloquent trill of his slender fingers, but doesn't say anything. Instead, he cuts his eyes to Henry and dances his hands through another series of indiscernible movements. It's graceful and mysterious, and I feel like there might be elements of ASL blended in with gestures that I'm sure are homemade. Years ago, when Peter and Carly, my best friends in Wisconsin, had a baby, they taught her the signs for *hungry*, *please*, *thank you*, and *all done*. It was such a successful experiment, they added *help, yes, book, play, sleep*, and a dozen more. Among them, *mom* and *dad*. I think I recognize those signs now—thumb tap chin twice with fingers extended and straight out, thumb tap forehead twice with fingers extended and straight out—but I can't be sure. I try to discern as much as I can while the brothers communicate silently for several seconds, but it's no use. All I can say for certain is that Finn is getting increasingly frustrated. And when Henry draws his lips into a severe line and gives his head a stiff shake, Finn crosses his arms over his chest and looks away.

"He's hungry," Henry says again.

Finn obviously said way more than that, but Henry's not about to translate for me, and perhaps that's for the best. Finn's fever has broken, and maybe now they can go back to wherever they came from. If I'm right, mom and dad factor into this story somehow, and they must be beside themselves with worry. I can convince Henry to call them. Or I'll take the brothers to Requiem in the side-by-side, or text Cleo to come and pick them up in her car.

It strikes me suddenly that as a teacher I am a mandatory reporter, and with or without Henry's blessing, I should have called the police when I found the boys in the greenhouse. What was I thinking? I *wasn't* thinking, and that's exactly the point. It was late, I was afraid, Felix was—still is, presumably—missing . . . The whole thing was a recipe for disaster. But it's not too late for me to make everything right.

"I have food," I say, dragging myself back to the present moment. One step at a time, I remind myself. I'll feed them, call for help, and turn my attention back to where it belongs: to my husband. I remember that the protein bars and raisin boxes are still in my pocket, and I pull them out now, offering them to Henry.

At first he just stares at the packets in my outstretched

hands, then he reaches across the space between us and gathers up the lot, depositing them on the blanket that covers Finn.

"What are these?" he asks, lifting a protein bar and studying the label.

"Protein bars," I begin, but Henry cuts me off with a huff.

"I can *read*," he says, his voice dripping with derision.

"They're good for you," I tell him. "I thought they'd be a quick way to get a lot of nutrients into Finn." Who are these boys? Who's never heard of ibuprofen or protein bars? I scorned the idea of them materializing from somewhere on the mountain, but that doesn't seem so impossible anymore.

Finn is already opening one of the small red raisin boxes. He peers at what's inside, then plucks out one of the dried fruits with two fingers. But before he can pop it into his mouth, he's wracked by a coughing fit that leaves him doubled over and choking. The box falls, scattering raisins everywhere.

The coughing fit is every bit as scary as it was last night. Clearly, a few hours of sleep and a couple ibuprofen have helped, but Finn is far from okay. I'd bet that his fever, though lower, is still present. Even more reason to get him out of here and into the care of someone who can provide everything he needs instead of just some musty blankets and a dirty greenhouse floor.

Guilt courses through me and isn't assuaged in the slightest when Finn finally stops coughing and leans back, giving me a weak smile. I don't know how much he remembers about last night, or what he thinks of my presence in the greenhouse now, but it seems he isn't afraid of me. For some reason, children never are.

"Forget the protein bars. I'll make some sandwiches," I say, diffusing the moment by getting to my feet. Tearing my gaze from Finn, I address myself to Henry, the alleged legal guardian.

"Finn can have another dose of ibuprofen, and maybe some of that cough syrup, too. Do you know how much he weighs?"

I haven't said anything alarming or controversial, but Henry leaps up, Finn's coughing fit immediately forgotten. "You're not going anywhere," he says, his voice gravelly and low. Threatening. "You're going to call someone; I know you are. You can't. I won't let you."

Shock must register on my face, but determination, too, because before I can take a single step away, Henry lunges. I stumble backward toward the greenhouse door, reaching behind me for the handle. Too late. He catches me by the loose fabric of my coat, yanking me toward him with a look like murder on his face. I'm astonished by this sudden turn of events, but I keep fighting, flinching away from him as I grapple for the little knife I've concealed in my coat pocket. We struggle, scuffing up the dirt of the greenhouse floor, but now that Henry has me in his grip, he doesn't seem to know what to do with me. He falters, hands pinching my upper arms, and draws a noisy, tremulous breath.

We stare at each other for a moment, chests heaving and noses just inches apart, and then Henry's eyes fill with furious tears. My face softens, I can feel it, but this makes him even angrier. He flings me away, slamming my lower back into one of the potting benches, and turns, heaving. His rage finds an outlet in the rows of nested plastic pots that still line the shelves of the greenhouse.

"Fuck!" he shouts, hurling the pots to the floor. When that proves to be unsatisfying, he grabs a whole stack of them in his hands and throws them at the glass walls. They bounce off, scattering harmlessly, and that's when he knots his hands into fists and takes aim at anything in reach. I watch him connect with a wide beam, the uneven wood instantly splitting his knuckles. He doesn't seem to register the pain. Instead of wincing, he merely reaches back to punch again, blood arcing through the air.

I throw myself at him.

Henry's hand glances off the worktop when I hit him, smearing red across the surface. My momentum spins us both in a half circle, into the center of the aisle where he can't reach anything to pummel but me. I won't let him. Before he can react or throw me off, I wrap my arms around his waist from behind and press the side of my face to the space between his shoulder blades, holding fast. He's a bit taller, but I'd guess we're nearly the same weight, and I have terror on my side.

"Get off me!" Henry screams, his voice cracking. "Let me go!"

But he can't reach me here, he can't hurt me, so I hold on for dear life, intent on stopping him from hurting himself.

Henry twists and bucks, trying to pry my arms from him as he curses and cries and spits. He's sobbing now, huge, wrenching howls torn from somewhere bone-deep and agonizingly dark. I can't begin to imagine what's happened to him to cause this much unbearable pain. I don't want to. So I squeeze my eyes shut and cling to him. As long as he's in my arms like this, we're all, for the moment, safe.

When Henry finally goes still, it's all at once, quick and clean like someone has switched off the power. He stands in the middle of the greenhouse, sweaty and bloody, and sniffs.

I'm spent, my arms trembling from the effort to hang on, and as Henry grasps my wrists to release my hold, I let him. Not because I believe the outburst is over, but because I can't hang on anymore. I almost sink to the ground when he steps away, but catch myself against a beam. I stay there gasping for breath while Henry remains frozen, his back toward me. After a few seconds, I watch him raise Felix's sweatshirt and draw it across his face, wiping his tearstained cheeks and running nose. I'm shaking, fear rattling my bones, but I can see the fight has left him like a receding tide.

"I'm sorry," Henry says, his voice ragged. But he's not talking to me. He walks to where Finn is now sitting up in the nest of blankets and pulls his brother into his chest. Suddenly, I can hear the little boy's snuffling cries, the keening of a child whose whole world has shattered. The brothers cling to each other, and I feel like I should look away. Like I'm witnessing something unimaginably intimate. Sacred.

"I'm sorry," I say, too, but I don't know what for. For the agony these boys are experiencing? For whatever brought them here? For Finn's fever, Henry's bloodied hand, my own secret desire to rid myself of them?

"I'll make sandwiches," I say again, as if the last few minutes never happened. As if I can erase the entire episode with the promise of peanut butter and jelly.

Neither of the boys look up when I leave.

CHAPTER 6

TUESDAY

Outside, the grass is dusted with frost thick as a sugar donut. It crunches beneath my feet, marking my path from the greenhouse to the side door with sets of perfect prints. It's a flannel day, all gloom and fog slung low and heavy between the trees so that my coat is soon covered with droplets. They bead up, collect, then run off in slender rivulets. When I turn back, I can barely see the greenhouse shrouded in gray.

It could be a nightmare, all of it, a strange, lucid dream that evaporates with the mist that will lift when the sun rises. But the sun will not rise today. I know that when the first raindrops hit my shoulders, light at the outset, but within seconds, so dense I jog the last few steps to the shelter of the porch.

The house seems different after the hours I spent in the greenhouse, and once over the threshold, the only thing I want to do is shower. A long, hot cleansing that would leave my skin pink and raw, my nostrils filled with the crisp scent of soap. I squeeze my eyes shut and picture Felix there, sitting on the closed lid of the toilet seat, his voice like a soundtrack as I wash my hair. He loves being in the bathroom when I shower. And I love how he grabs my towel when I turn the water off. How he wraps it around me when I step over the porcelain edge of the tub.

I rub my eyes, forcing thoughts of my husband away. I

don't have time to wallow right now. Or shower. So I toe off my boots and shed my coat in the mudroom, then head straight to the kitchen sink. After lathering my hands and arms to the elbows, I plunge my face into the still-cold stream of water. Lapping it up, I drink until my stomach hurts, and then bury my wet face in a dish towel and wish for tears. But I'm wrung dry.

When I've pulled myself together enough to keep going, I head to Felix's office and my phone. I can't resist the hope that bubbles when I realize it's charged and my screen is filled with missed messages. But none of them are from Felix. There's a string of texts and a call from Cleo, and two voicemails from numbers I don't recognize.

The first is from Chief Colin Brandt, calling to see if Felix has turned up. I'll call back later. I have nothing to report, and Chief Brandt's perfunctory tone tells me he doesn't, either. The second message is from the general manager at the Marriott Marquis in San Diego. Can I please call her back?

I do so immediately, clearing my throat while the number rings. When someone answers, I state my name, reason for calling, and request to be connected with Cynthia.

"Good morning, Mrs. Graham," a woman's polished voice greets me a moment later. I don't tell her that I'm Ms. Sheridan—it's too complicated. "I received your message this morning and have consulted our records."

"Thank you," I say, grabbing a pen and scrap of paper from Felix's desk. I need to write everything down—I don't want to miss a single word.

"Normally I don't release guest information," Cynthia says, "but since Mr. Graham did not stay with us last weekend, I decided to make an exception." There's a note of reprimand when she adds, "I understand your request was quite adamant."

She might be waiting for an apology, but I can't get past the first part of what she said. "Felix didn't stay at the Marriott?"

"No, he did not."

"Is there any—"

"The Marina District is San Diego's most exclusive neighborhood. There are dozens of fine hotels." Cynthia sounds like she's reading from a travel brochure. "Perhaps your husband booked elsewhere."

I shouldn't be so rattled, but when we hang up, the pit in my stomach sinks further. Just last night I considered the possibility that Felix didn't stay at the Marriott, but I'm dismayed that this lead is a dead end. The manager was right—there are tons of hotels near the convention center. The thought of phoning them all and begging for information about my husband is daunting to say the least.

But my next steps in the search for Felix will have to wait. If I take too long in the house, who knows what Henry will do?

As I make peanut butter and jelly sandwiches, I consider my options. I could call Cleo. It's just before nine, and although Trilogy is open, it won't be too busy just yet. But I'm still a little stung by her blasé reaction to Felix's disappearance yesterday. How would she respond to the news that I'm harboring runaways in my greenhouse? I could call Chief Brandt. Maybe ask a few open-ended questions to find out just how much trouble I could get in for helping two minors stay hidden on my property. Or I could blow this thing sky-high. Call 911 and go back to the boys, sandwiches in hand, as if nothing is wrong. Keep them occupied until the authorities arrive and let the Department of Children, Youth, and Families sort it all out.

I can't do any of those things.

There are six slices of bread on the counter before me, three spread with peanut butter and three with jelly, and as

I slap them together, I suck in a shaky breath. The raw panic that surged through Henry in the greenhouse, his almost feral instinct to protect his brother, has effectively tied my hands. I can't betray him. I just *can't*.

It would be wrong of me to turn those boys over to anyone until I know more about their situation and what—or who— they're running from. Not just because I'm afraid that Henry will grab Finn and vanish into the trees, but because I saw the look in Henry's eyes before he turned away from me just minutes ago: *desperation*. Pure and utter hopelessness and anguish and fear. Like being found is the worst thing that could possibly happen to them.

I wish for the hundredth time that Felix was here.

If I'm being honest with myself, there's a sort of wobbly balance in the way that Felix disappeared and the boys turned up. Henry and Finn aren't changelings, fairies who've slunk from the forest to take my husband's place, but he's gone and they're here and the timing is uncanny. Or maybe I'm just grasping at straws.

The rain hasn't let up when I head back to the mudroom, a canvas bag in hand. The sandwiches are carefully stacked inside, as well as more water bottles, some apples, and a sleeve of butter crackers for Finn if his stomach proves to be too sensitive for real food. A prickle of disquiet lifts the hair at the back of my neck as I pull on my boots, and I glance at the watch on my wrist to check the time. How long have I been gone? Did Henry and Finn slip away while I was busy having a breakdown, calling California, making sandwiches? Surely, they couldn't go anywhere in this deluge.

I'm halfway down the porch steps before I manage to get the umbrella popped open, and then I'm slipping on the icy grass in my rush to get back. The frost hasn't dissipated in the rain, just transformed into a thin, hard shell that fractures with each step I take. It's colder outside than I remember, or maybe I just got used to the warmth of the house. Either way, the park ranger wasn't wrong. This feels like the beginning of a significant storm system.

"Henry!" I call when I get close. I can't help myself. "Finn?"

The door to the greenhouse swings open and Henry steps aside to let me in. *Thank goodness.* He keeps his face downcast, his eyes on the ground, stubbornly refusing to meet my gaze. He's ashamed. I can feel it coming off him in waves. But I know his contrition is temporary. Anger is more palatable than shame, and Henry will soon slip back into fury to protect himself. Hopefully I can use this respite to make some progress with him.

"I brought sandwiches," I say unnecessarily. "And apples and . . ." I trail off, surveying the small building in shock.

It's only been raining for fifteen to twenty minutes, tops, but the water is seeping into every crack and crevice like we're caught in Noah's flood. It's sluicing down the inside of the warped greenhouse glass, dripping from the seams in the panels, and pooling on the floor in the far corner. I shouldn't be so surprised. No one has tended to this outbuilding in a decade or more, and the natural world found its way in. Now that I'm taking the time to notice, I can see snarls of vines that have grown up over the roof and pushed their way through fissures in the foundation.

Finn is once again lying back on the pillows in the bed Henry and I created for him, but the farthest edges of the blankets are already dark with water.

The boys can't stay here.

For a moment I battle with myself. Is it safe to invite them in? Of course it's not. But how can I do anything else?

"Come on," I say, turning to Henry. "We have to get Finn inside." I doubt that Henry will come on his own—he doesn't trust me, either—but if I make this move about Finn, he just might comply.

I can see his mouth start to form the word *no*, but when a full-body shiver makes him tremble involuntarily, he pauses. Nods.

"You carry Finn," I tell him, "and I'll get the blankets. Is there anything else?"

I think I already know the answer to this, but when Henry shakes his head, I feel a twinge of compassion all the same. They have nothing.

It hits me as we're packing up that Henry and Finn don't even have phones. I can hardly imagine a teenager without a screen in their hand, and I've spent hours with two who don't even have a single device between them.

Looping the grocery bag over my arm, I bend to gather up the blankets once Henry has lifted Finn. They're filthy and wet and will have to be washed, but we'll need them if the boys stay another night. If. Like they have anywhere else to go. Maybe these two feral young men are everything David Graham was always searching for: pretenders who have left the trees for Hemlock House. For ibuprofen and peanut butter sandwiches.

I give Henry the umbrella so that he can tent it over Finn, and then sprint to the house through the pouring rain. It's coming straight down, torrents of water that are already turning the dirt driveway into a muddy creek. I can only imagine how all this precipitation in such a short time will swell the river that runs alongside the logging road near the bottom. For a moment, I worry about being trapped on the mountain, but I shove those fears aside. It's not logical—the road is maintained and the portable cell tower on the roof ensures help is always just a phone call away. Besides, I have enough to lose sleep over. Felix is still out there somewhere.

Holding the door open for the boys, I watch Henry struggle the last few slippery steps with Finn in his arms. When they've crossed the threshold, I realize that Henry's in trouble, and I drop the blankets and reach for Finn. The young man lets me take his little brother, not because he wants to, but because he doesn't really have a choice. He's off-balance and falling, and when Finn's weight has been transferred, he hits the ground hard.

"You okay?" I ask, lowering myself to the top of the three short steps that lead from the mudroom into the kitchen. Finn is so warm cradled against my chest, I can feel him radiating heat through my coat.

"Twisted my ankle," Henry says, but before I can ask anything more, he adds: "It's fine. I'm fine."

Of course he's fine. God forbid he admits a weakness or asks for help. He can just add it to the growing list of his injuries: black eye, torn knuckles, bum ankle.

It feels weird to have the boys inside. Like I'm doing something wrong. Forbidden. Felix and I haven't really had guests out to Hemlock House, and now that I've invited the intruders in, it suddenly doesn't seem like *our* home. It seems like *Felix's*. And I'm breaking some unspoken rule. What would he say if he could see me now? Soaking wet and rocking a sick, strange child in my arms?

Realizing that I am indeed rocking—a barely perceptible side-to-side sway that I didn't even know I was doing—I stop immediately. I realize that I know exactly how my husband would respond.

My Felix has a soft spot for neglected things, a way of seeing and seeking out those who need him most. He saves beached starfish, getting his shoes wet so he can slip the echinoderms gently beneath the waves instead of hurling them into the deep. He leaves milk out for stray cats and lifts fallen nests back into trees. He befriends anyone who hovers around the edges feeling lost and alone.

Felix rescued me. And he would rescue these boys.

"Come on," I say, shifting Finn to more of a seated position on my lap. "Do you think you can walk?"

He nods, his dark curls tickling my chin, and I help him to his feet.

Henry stands, too, taking Finn's hand, and together we shuffle into the kitchen. I pull out a chair at the small breakfast table beneath the window and gesture for Finn to sit. He climbs into it, his feet barely grazing the floor, and lays his head in his arms on top of the table. Everything about him screams exhaustion and defeat. But when I glance at Henry, I realize that he is already hardening. He stands behind Finn, his fingers wrapped around the back of the chair. He wouldn't think twice about maiming or killing to protect his brother.

"What now?" Henry asks.

What now? I don't know. There's no handbook for this.

"Food," I say because it's a low bar. The most basic and necessary thing I can provide.

The grocery bag is still looped over my arm, and I place it on the table, lifting out the contents one by one. Now that the boys are here, in the kitchen, I could do better than sandwiches. My buttermilk pancakes are to die for, if Felix's opinion is to be believed, and it would be undeniably satisfying to whip up something warm and homemade on such a miserable morning. But the little kitchen feels intolerably small with the boys in it, and our next item of business is becoming painfully obvious: showers.

Henry unwraps a slightly smashed peanut butter and jelly for Finn, and when I hoist myself onto the counter opposite the small table, he takes the second chair. "Try it," he tells Finn, grabbing his own sandwich. A few enormous bites and it's gone. I had forgotten how ravenous teenage boys are. How they can eat and eat and never be full. But Finn has yet to lick a crumb. "One bite," Henry tries again. Finn doesn't even bother to shake his head where it still lays cradled in his arms.

"He's mute?" I ask. Maybe it's rude, I don't know, but this whole situation is beyond the bounds of normality.

Henry glares at me over his shoulder. Then, realizing that his back is toward me, he shifts his chair to the side so he can see both me and Finn. His gaze zips between us: keeping an eye on me, making sure Finn is okay. "You're quick," he says.

"But not deaf," I push.

At this, Finn gives his head a little wiggle. No.

"He hears just fine. And talked just fine before—" Henry stops abruptly and crosses his arms, daring me to ask more. "I don't see how it's any of your business."

"You're in my home," I tell him. "Everything about you is my business now."

"Then we'll leave." The chair legs give a high-pitched squeal on the linoleum floor when Henry pushes back to stand, but once he's on his feet, the reality of their situation registers. The kitchen is quiet but for the sound of the downpour drumming on the roof and a rhythmic tick from the old refrigerator. I chew a bite of apple slowly, waiting for him to put the pieces together.

"Finn can't go anywhere," I say, swallowing. Stating the obvious. "We both know that. And in this rain, you can't, either—at least, not on foot. But if you want to stay here, I need you to tell me the truth."

As if on cue, Finn coughs, his narrow chest convulsing as

he buries his face in his arms. The fit goes on for several seconds, long enough for Henry to cross around the table to rub his brother's back, and when it passes, they both glance up at me. Finn looks weary. Henry resigned.

"What?" he says, a challenge in that one sharp word.

I take it as an invitation. "What's your last name?"

"Smith."

A lie. Henry says it too fast, and Finn's eyes flick to him in confusion. But I don't think I'll get anywhere pressing the point, so I try another tactic. Maybe peppering him with questions will work. "Where did you come from?"

"I told you. The mountain."

"*Where* on the mountain? We're the only ones out here."

"You sure about that?"

I'm not. I know the logging road winds much deeper into the forest beyond our hidden driveway. For miles and miles according to Felix. There are even rumors that some trails lead straight into Canada, and if I'm to believe the most salacious ones, many an illicit substance has been trafficked on these forgotten paths. But it's my understanding that the road is only maintained up to our driveway, and Felix has never spoken of neighbors.

Henry can sense my uncertainty. With a smirk he says, "When it stops pouring, I'll take you there." It sounds like a threat.

This makes Finn's head jerk up. Fear darkens his eyes before Henry lays a comforting hand on his shoulder and squeezes. The slight shake of Henry's head is barely perceptible, but I'm watching him closely and I feel certain he's just assured Finn that they are *not* going back to wherever they came from. It's tiny, but it's a clue.

What are you running from? The question burns on the tip of my tongue, but I know it'll only make Henry mad, so instead I ask: "How did you end up here?"

He doesn't say anything right away, but his eyes cut to Finn's and there's a warning in them: *Don't. Don't give anything away.* "Just luck, I guess," he lies.

Somehow, Hemlock House is familiar to Henry, and the implications of that make my head spin. "Do you know Felix Graham?" I ask, even though it's an impossibility. The last time Felix was here, these boys didn't exist. Or, if Henry did, he was just a toddler.

Henry shakes his head. "Never heard of him."

That rings true. We're silent for a few moments, listening to the sound of the rain as it batters the drafty old house. A squall pounds on the roof and lashes against the windows, howling through the trees. It's a monster laying siege to this little homestead, and I wrap my arms around myself to ward off a sense of impending doom.

"Is there someone you can call?" I finally ask, raising my voice to be heard over the storm. The implications are endless: Who is worrying about you? Where are you headed? How can I help?

"No," Henry says, his voice a blade. "I'm Finn's legal guardian. There's no one to call."

I'm exasperated. "Then where are you going? What were you doing in my greenhouse?"

Henry stares at me for a second. He says, "We're meeting up with our uncle. Our ride fell through. We just need to make it to Requiem."

The truth. I can see it reflected in Finn's glassy eyes. *Finally.* "Requiem. That's a long way on foot."

Henry doesn't respond, but I can tell that this is news to him.

"About seven miles," I offer. "Four down the logging road and then another three on the highway. You take a right at the turnoff. Left will take you into the park. Eventually." I want to ask Henry if he's ever been to Requiem—it's the only town for miles and miles—but his confusion is all the answer I need.

The defeat that clouds his features is painful to see. Yes, Henry is sullen and rude, but it's clear that he loves his brother. That he's trying to do what's best for him, even if I can't begin to imagine what that might be.

"Who's your uncle? Maybe I can call him and—"

"It doesn't work like that," Henry spits.

"What doesn't work like that?" I can feel my voice rising, and I take a deep breath to calm myself down. "I'm sorry, I don't understand. If your uncle is meeting you in Requiem—"

"I don't have his number."

"Okay," I say, drawing out the word. "What about . . . ?" But I trail off when I see the furious slant of Henry's mouth, the white shine of his broken, bloody knuckles as he strangles the top slat of the ladderback chair. Things are escalating quickly in my tiny, eat-in kitchen, and unless I want to make everything exponentially worse, I have to slow down. Go one step at a time.

I stifle a sigh and say, "I'll take you. I don't have a car, but there's a Ranger outside, and I can take you down the mountain." A crack of thunder makes the antique dishes in the dining room hutch rattle and Finn jump. I add, "Maybe after it settles down a bit out there."

Henry turns his face to the window, studying the downpour that makes the forest look like a dark fantasy. The whole world is a smear of muted colors, green and blue and so much steely gray that it makes me shiver and pull my cardigan tighter around my shoulders. It's Felix's, and I barely remember putting it on. I must have done so late last night, before I fell asleep on the couch. Before the trail cam footage woke me up and I stepped through the wardrobe—or rather, the greenhouse door.

"Okay," Henry finally says, and I've almost forgotten what it is he's agreeing to. "You can drive us into Requiem."

It's a small victory, but I'll take it. "Okay," I echo. "We'll leave as soon as it lightens up a bit."

I abandon the half-eaten apple on the counter and slide to the floor. Laying the third, untouched sandwich on the table beside Henry as an offering, I go to press my wrist to Finn's forehead. He's still warm. I'd guess that his fever is climbing again, and a dart of worry slides through me. Maybe if I keep proving to Henry that I'm steady and sure, if I keep providing for their needs and showing kindness in the face of his defiance, he'll trust me enough to tell me the truth. Or, at least as much as necessary to get us through this ordeal safely. Henry's story is full of holes, and the fear that surfaces from time to time on both boys' faces scares me. If they are afraid of something or someone, I should be, too.

The rain comes hard and fast on the mountain, making it impossible to navigate in a UTV, but it also dissipates quickly. Muddy puddles and creeks that trickle where bare ground had once been, dry up as soon as the skies clear; the water soaks deep into the porous earth, leaving everything behind it rich and green. The park ranger had warned of a winter storm, but surely we'll catch a break before the snow begins to fly. The temperature must drop a long way before all this rain turns to snow.

"How about a hot shower before you go? You can clean up that hand and we'll bandage it." Henry and Finn didn't know what ibuprofen and protein bars were, but even Henry can't hide the delight that sparks behind his eyes at the mention of a hot shower. This, they understand.

"Stay here," I tell them. "I'll get some fresh towels and see if I can find any clothes that'll fit you."

"You're not taking my clothes," Henry growls.

"Just to wash them. You'll have them back before we go."

This seems to mollify him, and I stand to leave the kitchen. Chancing a touch, I slip one finger through a perfect curl at the nape of Finn's neck. "It's going to be okay," I tell him. And Henry. And myself.

I'm not sure I believe it.

BEFORE

FRIDAY, MARCH 7

**WAXING GIBBOUS MOON /
MERCURY AT GREATEST EASTERN ELONGATION**

The rain came as a total surprise. It wasn't in the forecast, at least not as a significant threat, and because Mercury could only ever be observed at twilight and it was supposed to be fifty-five degrees at dusk, Sadie had packed a picnic. She felt a bit like a suburban housewife with her hamper of ham sandwiches and cold potato salad—some fifties' throwback complete with a high ponytail and low-slung tennis shoes—but Felix never made her feel self-conscious.

Quite the opposite. After his impromptu office visit at Christmas, Felix had taken to regularly popping in on Sadie. She expanded her tea repertoire, and they sat sipping London Fog, chamomile, and, of course, peppermint, while they chatted about classes and students and life in Newcastle. Felix often thundered into her office mid-sentence, coat already sliding off his shoulders, and threw himself into the chair across from her without so much as a greeting. Sadie merely got up to turn the kettle on.

His visits were not romantic, nothing like a date at all, and their friendship blossomed without the angst of will he/won't he. *He won't*, Sadie knew, right from the start. It was enough to have a friend. More than enough. Felix was windswept and golden, a summer storm rolling across the prairie that made Sadie want to curl up in a porch swing and watch him touch the earth. But for all his unchecked enthusiasm, his long monologues about the complex chemistry between stars and the world's tragic misunderstanding of black holes, he was the furthest thing from a narcissist. Felix rambled not out of arrogance, but out of an impetuous sort of love for a cosmos he could barely begin to understand. And when he caught himself and realized that he was going on like a schoolboy, he gently wound the thread of conversation back to Sadie.

She told him far more about herself than she wanted to. It just slipped out because his questions were so guileless, his expression one of pure interest. He wanted to know her, and it was intoxicating. In a few short weeks, Felix managed to disarm all of Sadie's defenses, until she wondered if there was anyone on the planet who had ever known her like he already did.

Not her mother. Not Alice Sheridan, who sipped just enough Chablis to keep herself anesthetized and treated Sadie like the girl who lived. They both knew Alice would have preferred to keep her husband, the boy. Anyone but Sadie.

Not her friends from college or her colleagues or Peter and Carly who had grown up down the street, who knew her longer than anyone besides her mother. Sadie held people at arm's length and kept her well-tended walls high.

But Felix was breaking through. Coat abandoned on the floor of her office; arm slung over the back of one uncomfortable chair. Sometimes he propped his feet on her desk, and she couldn't even be bothered to care.

When he told her about Mercury at its greatest eastern elongation, she didn't even pause to consider that he was deftly moving their relationship out of the safe, cozy confines of her office, and into the real world.

"Mercury's orbit is closer to the sun than the Earth's," Felix said, using his balled fists as models for the planets. "That means it gets lost in the glare of the sun most of the time. But it's observable a few times a year when it reaches its greatest separation from the sun."

"Greatest eastern elongation," Sadie repeated, a quick learner and new devotee to all Felix had to teach her. She felt sometimes like an apprentice, like she was seeing the world and her place in it for the very first time under Professor Graham's thoughtful tutelage. She wanted to learn more. She wanted to know *everything*.

"Exactly." Felix drew his hands apart, increasing the gap. "It's still hard to see—less than twenty degrees above the horizon and only at twilight. But not many people can say they've seen Mercury in real life."

"Is that an invitation?"

Felix just grinned.

Now he stood at the door of her condo, the hood of his coat pulled down low over his forehead, his shoulders rounded against the rain. Even hunched over, water dripping from the lip of his cowl, he cut an elegant silhouette. His mouth was quirked to one side, dimple exaggerated as if to say: "Whatcha gonna do?" Still, Sadie couldn't help but be disappointed.

"You're kidding me." She stared beyond Felix's frame for a moment, taking in the soft, spring rain, the dark blur of sky, and the obvious dissolution of their plans. "I didn't realize . . ."

"The clouds were supposed to dissipate," Felix said, stepping over the threshold as she ushered him inside. "But I don't think that's going to happen."

Sadie felt stupid that she hadn't realized the weather had

turned. That she had instead sliced ham at her tiny kitchen island and listened to Taylor Swift's *Fearless* album like she was a lovesick teenager. She'd been in her early twenties when that record came out—too old to relate to any of the songs about high school love and candy floss romance. Definitely too old now. Sadie blushed as if Felix could take one look at her and know how she had spent the last hour in daydreams that she barely dared to admit to herself.

Easing off the tote she had slung over her shoulder with their picnic inside, she said, "Well, maybe some other time."

"Mercury will be at its greatest *western* elongation in August."

August. Sadie didn't know whether to be disappointed that their outing was canceled or excited that Felix imagined they'd still be together—still be friends—in five months.

Felix pushed his hood back, and rainwater puddled on the laminate floor. He didn't seem to notice. But he did clock her move to deposit the tote on the table and swept it from her hand. "The night's not a total write off. NASA's MESSENGER spacecraft orbited Mercury for four years before it crashed into the surface in 2015. The probe snapped over two hundred thousand pictures."

Sadie smirked. "And I suppose you have them."

"Every last one." Felix smiled back. "No, of course not. But I have *some*. The good ones. Want to see them?"

Although Felix had been to Sadie's office dozens of times, she had never been to his. The Science Department was across campus from the cluster of humanities buildings, a newer, state-of-the-art, glass-and-white-tile piece of art that was perpetually cool and empirically neutral. There were only a few carefully chosen pictures on the wall (the double helix of a strand of DNA, a complicated equation rendered in a leaning hand on an old, black chalkboard). Even the air had a filtered, blank quality. As they pushed through the main double doors and into the brightly lit building, Sadie wished they were outside in the growing dusk as planned, but a quick glance at Felix's profile revealed that he was in his glory. This was *his* space, and he was eager to share it with her.

Because it was shortly after five thirty, the science building was still buzzing with activity. Classes were wrapping up, students leaving the laboratories in pairs, either complaining about or celebrating their results on a particularly difficult chemistry experiment. A few professors paused to ask Felix a question or clarify the start time of a scheduled meeting, each of them glancing over at Sadie and then moving along when Felix acted as if her presence beside him was the most natural thing in the world. She felt uncomfortable until he pressed his fingers lightly to the small of her back, guiding her down a narrow hallway. *I've got you*, his touch promised.

Felix's office was everything Sadie imagined it would be. An explosion of color and movement and light that reflected Felix himself. There were pictures of deep space on the walls and perpetual motion machines on his desk. In one corner, he had hung a glittering mobile of the solar system, each planet carefully designed to appear as accurate and realistic as possible. Sadie looked up, and when she did, she laughed. Felix had hung a vintage poster on the ceiling that featured a retro UFO hovering over a shadowed forest with the words: THE TRUTH IS OUT THERE.

"Did I mention I'm a total dork?" Felix said, draping his damp coat over an office chair and depositing their picnic on his desk.

"I love *The X-Files*. Or I did. Twenty years ago." Sadie spun a slow circle, taking it all in. "But you're a scientist, Dr. Felix Graham. Shouldn't you find the supernatural laughable?"

"The supernatural is everything just beyond our grasp. The universe is filled with things that are outside our understanding."

"Like what?"

"I believe in infinite worlds," Felix said, crossing his arms over his chest. Watching her. "At least in theory."

Sadie felt the warm glow of Felix's attention and turned to face him. "What's that supposed to mean?"

"How complicated do you want to get?"

"I'll take the Science for Dummies version, please."

Felix laughed. "Well, there are several different theories—like the many worlds interpretation of quantum mechanics—but I think inflationary cosmology makes the most sense."

"Less science, more dummies," Sadie warned.

When Felix grinned, he did so with his whole face—eyes crinkling at the corners, dimple winking, teeth flashing so that she could see the way his left incisor twisted in just a bit. It was a perfect flaw, the kind of defect that made him all the more irresistible, and she shifted her focus to a sculpture on his desk to stop herself from staring at him.

"It's about the exponential expansion of space," Felix said, trying again. He cupped his hands together and then puffed them out slowly. "An alternative understanding of the formation of the universe that posits a brief period of accelerated expansion. Cosmic inflation predicts *many* big bangs—not just one—that create many expanding universes."

"A multiverse?" Sadie shot him a skeptical look out of the corner of her eye.

"Exactly."

"Thanks for the lesson, Spiderman."

But Felix's eyes sparkled. "Why not? I'm not a physicist, but there's so much we don't know, Sadie. The observable universe has a radius of roughly forty-six-and-a-half-*billion* light-years. Billion. Who knows what we have yet to learn?"

Sadie laughed and lifted her hands as if to say, *Enough*. "I can't comprehend it."

"Right? The Andromeda Galaxy is the nearest major galaxy to the Milky Way, and guess how many stars it contains?"

"Do I get a prize if I'm right?"

Felix regarded her, considering. "Actually, yes. I do have a prize for you."

Her eyes widened. "It better be good."

"It is."

"Ten billion," Sadie guessed. Then, seeing his face, amended her answer. "*One hundred* billion."

"Not even close."

"Five hundred billion."

Felix shook his head. "One trillion," he said.

"My next guess."

But Felix had already spun away and started rifling through his desk drawer. "Do you have any idea how much that is? A trillion is one million million. A thousand billion. A one with twelve zeros behind it."

"Felix, stop." Sadie laughed again, laying a hand on his arm. "You're going to break my brain."

"A stack of a billion dollar bills would be approximately sixty-eight miles high. But a stack of a trillion dollars would reach nearly sixty-eight thousand miles into space."

"You're making that up."

"I swear I'm not. A billion seconds is thirty-two years. A trillion is thirty-two *thousand* years."

Sadie just gaped at him, wonder sparking like electricity in the space between her body and his.

When Felix reached to take her hand, she didn't think anything of it. His fingers curled around hers and she squeezed his hand right back, tripping a little when he pulled her out of his office. But he steadied her, his hand drawing her close, and guided her deeper into the science building to a locked metal door at the very end of a long hallway.

He let go to press his fob against the sensor, and Sadie's hand felt cold without his fingers laced through hers. "You don't have a spaceship in there, do you?" she teased.

"Kind of, yeah." The lock disengaged with a satisfying click, and Felix opened the door to step inside, triggering the motion-activated lights.

Sadie followed, absorbing the large, empty room, the lab tables that had been methodically lined up against the walls, and the neat stacks of stools, four high. In the center of the laboratory, taking up most of the available floor space, was a black circle of thick fabric that had collapsed into a heap of soft peaks and valleys.

"What is that?" Sadie asked, but Felix had already grabbed an extension cord and plugged in a small blue fan. The room was filled with the whir of blowing air, and within seconds, a fat tunnel leading to the circle puffed up and began to fill the dome.

It didn't take long for Sadie to realize what she was looking at, and she couldn't suppress the little thrill that cartwheeled down her spine.

"I haven't seen one of these since elementary school," Sadie marveled when the portable planetarium was fully inflated. "It was the very best part of fourth grade."

"Our science education majors have been hosting local schools all week," Felix told her. "It's part of their practicum. I kind of forgot it was here, but since we can't see Mercury outside, maybe we can see it in the dome. And Andromeda. You know, a trillion stars."

Sadie was utterly enchanted. Something about Felix made her feel young again, childish in the most pure and happy way. His enthusiasm for life was inspiring, and when he held back the air lock for her, she eagerly crawled inside.

They lay side by side on the floor of the planetarium, and Felix transported Sadie through space. The universe that unfurled on the vault of the screen was so real, so vibrant, that she reached her fingers to trace the constellations. And when Felix maneuvered the software to make it seem as if they were standing on the moon, she marveled at the watercolor sphere that was earth. The white swirls of massive storm systems, the midnight blue of the deepest oceans, the golden veins of deserts streaking through lush, emerald rainforests.

"Thank you," Sadie said after they had deflated the dome and locked the door behind them. They were back in Felix's office, and all was quiet after the constant hum of the Starlab's artificial atmosphere. In fact, the entire science building was still and hollow; it seemed to sigh in relief at the end-of-the-week silence after a bustling Friday afternoon.

Sadie felt that way, too. Sated and content, hushed as a lullaby. Peaceful in a way she hadn't felt in years. Ever? There was something about the way Felix poured himself out that filled her right up to overflowing.

When Sadie took a step toward him, it was almost involuntary. A testament to his irrepressible gravity and the way she was drawn into his orbit against her better judgment. Felix could have turned away. She half expected him to. But he took a step toward her, and then another, until they were close enough to touch.

"Thank you," Sadie said again, and this time she wasn't talking about the Starlab. She was grateful for *all* of it: for his friendship and the joy he brought her, the way he threw wide the doors to a bigger, more beautiful understanding of the heavens and the earth than she ever thought possible.

The way he made her feel known.

Turn him into stars and form a constellation in his image, she thought, truly understanding Juliet for the very first time in her life. *His face will make the heavens so beautiful that the world will fall in love with the night.*

Sadie didn't realize she was looking down until Felix's fingers lightly touched her chin, tipping her face toward his own.

"You're welcome," he said. And then he bent his head and brushed his lips against hers.

It was a glancing touch, the merest whisper of connection, as if he wanted to give her permission to pretend it never happened at all. But that was the last thing Sadie wanted, and before he could back away, she twined her arms around his neck and pulled him close.

She kissed him hard and deep, her mouth conveying everything she didn't have the words to say. With her lips and teeth and tongue, with her nails digging into his shoulders, afraid to let go for even a moment, she said it over and over again: *I found you.*

And Felix kissed her back.

When his mouth trailed from jawline to neck and all the way down to the fragile wing of her collarbone, he whispered against her skin, "How long?"

Sadie knew exactly what he meant. "From the moment I saw you."

"Before the Hamlet quote?"

She laughed low. "Way before that."

"Me too." He pressed his nose into the hollow at the base of her throat, and then lightly ran his tongue along the bone.

Sadie shivered.

Later, after his fingers had shadowed every inch of her skin, leaving stardust in their wake, Felix coiled and uncoiled a strand of Sadie's hair. She was draped over him, head on his chest and one bare leg thrown over his thighs. He fit perfectly in her bed, in her life, and she was sure down to her marrow that she had never been, nor would she ever be, happier.

Until he spoke. "I was made for you," Felix said. It was a simple proclamation, a lover's cliché that felt all wrong coming from a man of science. Of cold, hard facts and knowable things.

"Made?" Sadie nuzzled deeper into his embrace. "I thought we exploded into being. A happy accident. The unexpected result of a physics equation in space."

Felix groaned. "You have so much of that wrong . . ."

"I guess you have a lot yet to teach me."

Shifting, Felix untangled himself from Sadie and rolled onto his side so that they were nose to nose across the pillow. "We all believe in something," he said, brushing a strand of hair from her cheek. "Even science is a sort of faith. We can't prove many things, even though plenty of evidence supports our theories. We may never know if inflationary cosmology is real or just our very best guess at why the universe is flat. In the end, we might not be able to certify any of it."

"You're losing me, Professor," Sadie said, giving him a soft kiss. It was a proposition.

But Felix pulled back. "We believe in the big bang, or that dark matter makes up roughly seventy-five percent of the universe, or that life could exist on other planets, but what's at the heart of all those theories?"

"Belief," Sadie murmured, because it was what he wanted her to say. Because it was hard to focus on his words when she was in such utter awe of *him*. She marveled at the sunburst of bronze in the very heart of his dark eyes. Sketched the fine line of his brow, his cheekbone, his jaw with a single fingertip. Fell a little deeper.

"I believe in us," Felix said, catching her hand so he could hold it against his chest. "But we're more than a theory. We're evidential. An absolute inevitability. I knew it the moment I saw you. Explain that."

"A chemical reaction?"

This time, Felix kissed Sadie, rolling her onto her back as he rose over her. Propping himself on his elbows, he brushed his lips against her forehead, the apple of each cheek, the tip of her nose, and finally, her mouth. "Something like that."

"And what about your infinite worlds, Dr. Felix Graham? Where do we fit in that theory?"

Felix laughed against her shoulder, the vibration making her tingle all over. "*Everywhere*," he said. "Sadie Sheridan, I would find you in every single one of them."

CHAPTER 7

TUESDAY

I find suitable clothes for the boys and then hustle them off to the upstairs bathroom. Finn is so weak that I don't dare leave him to his own devices, and Henry must agree because he enters the bathroom with his brother and locks the door behind them. Too late, I worry about the medicine cabinet over the sink, the neat line of amber bottles on the top shelf. Neither Felix nor I take medication regularly, but there are some old pills knocking around up there. Antibiotics that we should have finished off. Maybe even some leftover Vicodin from Felix's knee scope last spring. And drugs are just the beginning of my worries. Is there a pair of scissors in the drawer? Tweezers, a metal nail file, anything Henry could use as a weapon?

The house is filled with dangerous things, from Felix's scalpel-sharp Japanese chef's knife to the ice pick we keep in the drawer by the sink. I can't hide everything, but really, what would be the point? If Henry wanted to harm me, there are a dozen ways he could do it.

But I don't think he will. At least, I hope.

I linger just down the hallway from the closed bathroom door, waiting for the sound of the shower. Henry talks quietly to Finn, too soft for me to make out what he's saying, and when I hear the old pipes squeak and the water begin to flow, I'm grateful for the excuse to go back downstairs. I don't want to be the sort of person who eavesdrops on children, but I'm desperate to know more about these mysterious interlopers.

Back in the kitchen, I clean up the remains of our breakfast and wipe the table with a damp cloth. My movements are rote, born of routine and habit, nothing more. This is what I do: I clean up. I take care of the people around me. In this one way, my marriage with Felix is conventional, but not because of some traditional understanding of gender roles. I just like to keep the house neat, trailing after Felix as if I can map his movements by the breadcrumbs—literal and otherwise—that he leaves behind. A round stain on the countertop where he has splashed a bit of coffee over the rim of his mug. An open book on the table in the dining room, dog-eared and abandoned when a new idea snagged his attention. Thin file folders in an untidy stack on the end table beside his favorite chair; on top, an uncapped yellow highlighter, a handful of pens, a loose charging cord with no converter box.

I miss the evidence of my husband in our home. I wish I could wind back the clock and leave those hints of him all over our space. Had I known he wouldn't come back from San Diego, I wouldn't have touched a thing.

When my phone rings, a beat of adrenaline pulses high in my chest. I fumble in the back pocket of my jeans, then search the table, the counter, and finally spot the device on the windowsill above the sink. My heart drops when I realize it's not Felix; it's Cleo.

"Hey," I say, putting her on speakerphone.

"Good morning, gorgeous. How'd you survive the night?"

I know she's talking about my emotional state with Felix in absentia, but I swallow hard, willing myself to sound normal. If she only knew what my night had entailed.

"It was all right," I manage, and if my voice is thin, it's to be expected.

"I left you a message and several texts. I was about to send out the cavalry."

It wasn't several texts, but I don't correct her. "Yeah, I slept in a bit. Sorry about that."

"No worries," Cleo chirps. Then, "No news?"

I can't bring myself to answer.

"He'll turn up," Cleo rushes to fill the space left by my fear. "Have you called the hotel? Talked to any of his coworkers?"

I don't want to give Cleo an accounting of my efforts to track Felix, and I don't care to explain that he doesn't really have coworkers right now. Research partners, yes, but they are all remote, working on their own aspect of the project in different parts of the country. So I mumble a reply that could count as affirmation.

"He'll be back," Cleo assures me, all optimism and bluster. "Today's the day, I can feel it. Call me when he turns up, will you?"

"Of course." I can hear Trilogy's front doorbell jangle merrily in the background, and a moment later Cleo says goodbye.

I'm still holding my phone in one hand when a text comes through. It's Cleo again. *I'll swing by after closing with some supplies.*

She can't come here. Not with a pair of mysterious kids hiding at Hemlock House. Henry, cold and brooding; Finn, sick and quiet. Both of them total strangers with a dubious backstory. Of course, I could be en route with them to Requiem by the time she shuts down Trilogy, but that would only leave me with more to explain. *I'm all set*, I text back. *Working, actually. I'll see you soon.*

A pink heart appears almost immediately on my sent message. Cleo is pleased, no doubt, that I've set my worries aside and found a way to focus on my book. She knows how important it is to me, and how worried I am about meeting my deadline. She'll leave me alone until I reach out, ostensibly emerging from my writing cave. I feel a stab of guilt for lying to Cleo, but comfort myself with the thought that I can stop by her place once I've handed the boys off to their uncle.

Maybe I can ask her more about Felix's past and why a new side of him began to emerge when we moved to Hemlock House. Because standing alone in my shadowy kitchen, I must admit that my husband has been different since we arrived in Washington. I chalked it up to a myriad of things: his research project, being back in his boyhood home, and the inherent stress of both of us living on deadline. Never mind the isolation, the demands of the homestead, and the phantoms that lurk between these walls. But now I have to wonder if he was hiding something from me.

One night several weeks ago, I woke up to discover Felix's side of the bed empty. It was a shock, rolling over to find him gone, and though I had been in a deep sleep only a second before, the cold sheet where Felix was supposed to be, jolted me awake as forcefully as a glass of ice water to the face.

"Felix?" I whispered into the night. But even as I said his name, I knew he wasn't in our room. The space felt hollow, abandoned.

Worried that he wasn't feeling well, I tucked my robe around me and crept out onto the landing. I expected to find Felix in the bathroom, maybe searching the medicine cabinet for antacids, but the door was open, the room dark. Same with Felix and Gabi's childhood bedrooms across the hallway.

I didn't mean to creep down the stairs, but I suppose I did, avoiding all the spots that squeaked. I had learned quickly to move about Hemlock House in almost perfect silence, afraid perhaps to disturb the slumber of the ghosts that haunted the halls. I tiptoed, spoke quietly, and threw salt over my shoulder when I spilled it, trying to keep the devil away from me and my husband. From the happy little life that neither of us could quite believe was ours. Felix laughed at me, but I noticed he did the same when he thought I wasn't looking.

His absence from our room made me panic in a way that only the vacant darkness could. My husband wasn't a night owl or prone to midnight wanderings. The fact that he was not beside me was not just disorienting, it was oddly frightening and nightmarish, as if I wasn't really awake at all.

At the bottom of the stairs, I exhaled a pent-up breath when I saw a shaft of yellow light cutting beneath the frame of the closed door to Felix's office. He was here, working probably, or startled awake by an idea that he simply had to record. Never mind that it was so out of character. I could admit that there were things I was still learning about my husband.

But then I heard a voice on the other side of the shut door. Felix? If so, he didn't sound like himself. His words were fast and tight, rigid with barely contained emotion. When a second voice drifted through the door, I froze. A woman? Was someone *here*? In my shock and confusion, I hurried across the living room and the warped floorboards moaned my arrival.

I wrenched open the office door, terrified of the scene that would greet me, but the room was quiet. Felix was alone. He slowly spun his chair away from the computer and gave me a soft smile. But his cheek didn't dimple. There was no sparkle in his eyes.

"Hey," he said, rubbing his face with both hands. "What are you doing up?"

"You were gone." I didn't mean to sound accusatory, but my heart was still pumping way too fast. I was at a loss, embarrassed that I had jumped to conclusions, and only partly convinced that I had heard anything at all. I cleared my throat and hovered in the doorway. "I didn't know where you were."

"Sorry, cielito. I couldn't sleep." He put his arms out to me, and I shuffled across the space between us, sinking warily into his lap. Felix held me tight, buried his nose in my hair, inhaled deeply. "I didn't mean to scare you."

It was ridiculous, probably, to be afraid, but even pressed snug against my husband's chest, I was. Was it the lingering miasma of a bad dream I couldn't remember? Or was something off about how he seemed just a bit breathless? Over his shoulder, I could see that all the screens were black. His phone was on the desk, face down.

Did Felix put the computer to sleep when he heard my footsteps in the living room? Had he hung up his phone just in time to turn around and greet me?

I didn't want to know, and maybe that's why I didn't push him. It was two o'clock in the morning, and I was muddled and groggy. Maybe it was easier to convince myself that everything was fine than face the fact that I knew Felix was hiding something from me.

Now I wish I could have that moment back. I'd twist around in his lap, ask him what he was doing and who he was talking to. I wouldn't let him get away with some pat answer, that he was working or dealing with a rare bout of insomnia or mumbling to himself. I *knew* something was wrong. And because I was afraid to disturb the peaceful equilibrium of our too-good-to-be-true life, I let him lead me back to bed and half forgot that it had happened at all.

Forty hours gone.

Felix is really and truly a missing person now, and my heart petrifies into something cold and brittle. I have to get rid of Henry and Finn. It's illogical, but a sliver of me wonders if I can conjure my husband by evicting these intruders. Of course not. Still, I need to turn my full attention to my missing husband. I don't deserve the life I've been given. I know that. But you'd better believe I'm going to fight for it.

The boys appear in the arch between the kitchen and dining room, and I startle a bit. They didn't make a sound. Finn is leaning on his big brother, his hair damp and tousled as if Henry ran a rough towel over it but didn't bother to brush it. Maybe I should have left out a comb, deodorant, a toothbrush and some toothpaste. Still, despite my distracted oversights, he's scrubbed clean. I can smell the zest of soap mingling with Felix's favorite eucalyptus shampoo from across the room.

"Here," Henry says, drawing my attention from Finn. He, too, looks spit-polished and shiny. Like a new person. But his arms are full of their filthy clothes. "You said you have a washing machine?"

"Y-yes," I stammer, stepping forward to take the heap of rancid fabric from his arms. In truth, I should take it all straight out to the burn barrel and torch it, but Henry watches me so closely it's as if he's handed me his firstborn child. I decide not to suggest that they simply wear our clothes until more suitable ones can be found. "It's an old machine. It'll take a couple hours to wash and dry everything, but as soon as it's all done, I'll take you to Requiem." I don't add: *if the storm has let up.*

Henry seems satisfied at this, and I feel a momentary pride at how I've handled the whole bizarre situation. I've managed to shepherd us all through unscathed, more or less. I motion toward the table where I've collected a box of bandages and some antibiotic cream. "For you," I tell Henry, and when he looks confused, I clarify: "For your hand."

He glances down at his fist, at the split knuckles that are now washed clean but still oozing a bit. They'll scab over just fine, but my offerings will help, and he knows it. I just wish there was something I could do about his black eye. It's aggressively shiny, the skin tight and royal purple. It looks like it hurts.

"How's the ankle?" I ask, afraid to mention the black eye. I'm dying to know where he got it, but I feel certain he doesn't want to tell me the answer.

"Fine," he says, grabbing the box, the small tube, but he doesn't say thank you. And when Finn gives a little groan and slumps against him, Henry's hand is forgotten as his heavy brows knit together in concern.

"He needs another dose of ibuprofen," I say, taking in Finn's glassy eyes and flushed cheeks. Beneath the bright spots of color, he's pale as a sheet. "How do you feel about trying the cough syrup now, too?" But even as I say it, I change my mind. I have no idea what these boys have and haven't been exposed to, and I don't want to be responsible for an allergic reaction or some adverse effect. Finn needs a doctor, not my well-intentioned but unqualified ministrations. "Never mind. We'll let your uncle decide what to do."

This makes Henry's eyes flash, but I ignore his obvious discomfort at the mention of this enigmatic uncle. I sincerely doubt his story, but getting the boys to Requiem is a step in the right direction, whether or not there's a family member there waiting for them.

"I'll throw these in the washing machine," I tell Henry. "Take

Finn into the living room and get him settled on the couch. I'll bring a pillow and a blanket. Some medication. Maybe he can nap until it's time to leave."

Henry looks like he wants to argue, but there's nothing to argue about. So, he shoots me one last glare before turning his full attention to his brother. I watch until they're through the dining room and out of sight, then I hurry to the mudroom and drop their knot of clothes to the floor. Rummaging through the pockets, I search for anything that might give me a clue as to who they are or where they came from. A wallet, an ID, a scrap of paper, anything. But of course, Henry is too savvy for that. If there were any personal effects in their clothes, they've all been removed. Except, when I put my hand through the kangaroo pouch of Finn's sweatshirt, my finger glances across something cold and hard. When I pull it out, I realize it's a river rock, granite-colored with veins of shiny white that sparkle like quartz. Rubbing my thumb over the surface, I discover it's been worn smooth. A worry stone, then, and much beloved if the long, silky plane is any indication. Sighing, I slide it in my pocket to return to Finn.

When the laundry is running, I slip upstairs to grab a pillow and a heavy quilt. I also peek into the bathroom, glancing into every corner as if I can tell just by looking if anything is missing or out of place. The only difference I can spot is the two extra towels hung neatly over the shower curtain rod. Apparently, despite their disgusting clothing, Henry and Finn are not total slobs.

Back downstairs, I cross into the living room with an armload of things to make Finn more comfortable. "Here you go," I say, snapping the quilt loose to spread it over his legs. He's propped on the couch pillows, his dark curls still damp, but when we make eye contact, anxiety clouds his features. One hand dances through the air and points over his shoulder to where Henry is standing at the window.

The young man has drawn the curtains shut, and his body is coiled with tension as he stares through a tiny slit between the fabric and the wall.

"Someone's here," Henry murmurs, so quietly I can barely make out the words. But then they click and hope surges through me. I drop the corners of the quilt and bolt toward the front door.

Felix's name is on my lips, but before I can race out onto the porch to greet him, Henry throws himself in front of me. He grabs my upper arms and wrestles me away from the door.

"What are you doing?" I half shout, trying to writhe out of his grip.

But Henry is frantic. He pushes me back into the room, away from the little alcove that frames the front door. Away from Felix.

"No one can know that we're here," Henry says between clenched teeth. I'm staring over his shoulder, willing my husband to be parked in his usual spot, preparing to sweep me into his arms and explain everything, but there's an edge to Henry's voice that makes me look at him. The teenager's eyes are raw with panic. I realize, belatedly, that his hands on my arms are trembling.

I suck in a steadying breath and take a step back, drawing Henry off-balance. He stumbles a bit and has to squeeze tightly to keep his hold on me, making me wince. I know that his thumbs will leave bruises on the soft skin of my inner arms. I don't care. "It's okay," I say, trying to get through to Henry. "It's my husband."

But I don't know that, not for sure, and all at once Henry's fear seeps into me. I shiver. What if Henry has good reason to be afraid? "What does the car look like?" I ask, wary of the answer.

"Brown." Henry seems to realize that I'm not going to rush to the door, and he lets me go, crossing his arms over his chest awkwardly. It's a strong-man's stance, but he looks like a scared kid to me. "It's a big brown truck."

I deflate, hope plunging as quickly as it rose. "The UPS guy?"

Henry glances at Finn, one hand quieting the boy with a few intentional flicks of his fingers. "What's UPS?" he asks, yanking his gaze to me and then easing backward toward the door. Presumably to block me if I make a run for it again.

"You're joking, right?" I'm too disappointed to be kind. "It's the *delivery truck*."

I push past Henry, exasperated, fighting angry tears, and when he catches my wrist to stop me, I twist my arm quickly to break the hold. It's a simple self-defense move, but it takes him by surprise. "Don't touch me again," I whisper, biting off each word with barely contained spite. I've had just about enough of Henry.

"You can't—"

"I can do whatever I want! It's *my* house!"

A noise from the couch draws my attention to Finn, and when I see his expression, I feel instantly sick to my stomach. He's cringing away from me, his fever-bright eyes wide with fear and distrust. A second ago I wanted nothing more than to throw the boys out of my home and lock the door. But what kind of a monster would do that? Finn is sick. It's pouring outside. The mountain is hazardous even under the best of conditions. I'd be signing their death warrants.

"It's okay," I say, gathering myself. I raise one hand, palm up, toward Finn, and lift the other at Henry. I'm both surrendering and trying to keep them at bay. It's a tension we all feel. "Listen,

I won't tell him you're here. You have to trust me. You don't really have a choice."

When I turn my back on them, I half expect Henry to charge me from behind, but he holds his ground. I walk slowly to the front door, unlock it, and step outside, closing it softly behind me.

The rain is still lashing down, a torrent that is already creating slushy little rivers across the lawn. But the porch is covered, and I'm grateful for that as I stand in my socks on the chilly boards. The cold is bracing, and I inhale the damp, thick air in an effort to clear my head. *How on earth did I get myself into this mess? And where is Felix?*

The back hatch of the mid-size truck is open, the UPS logo on the side splattered with mud from the drive out to Hemlock House, no doubt. Someone carefully eases down from the storage compartment, then hurries across the grass with a medium-size box clutched tight. He takes the porch steps two at a time, rocking back on his heels when he looks up and sees me standing there.

"Holy shit," the man says, under his breath. "You scared me."

The feeling is mutual. This man is not our regular delivery guy, but some skinny stranger with faded neck tattoos and hollow, sunken eyes. He stares at me for a moment, calculating, before he holds out the box.

I take it, suddenly aware of how deeply disappointed I am. I didn't even realize until this moment that I had expected to see Douglas, the local guy. I could've asked him for help, maybe even sent the boys down the mountain with him. But the jittery stranger before me is not Douglas—I can smell the sweet rot of his oily hair and unwashed body, and when his tongue darts out to lick a sore at the corner of his mouth, I force myself not to recoil.

"My husband is inside," I lie, taking a small, measured step back. I wish I could hurry to the living room and lock the door behind me, but I need to know what's happening outside the confines of these haunted walls. I say, "How're the roads?"

The man lifts one shoulder. "Not great. And it's getting worse by the minute. This is my last delivery." He looks me up and down, then adds: "You alone up here?"

I already told him I'm not. "Felix is inside," I say forcefully, but I watch as the man's eyes flick to the UTV. No other vehicles are immediately visible, and I can practically see the wheels spinning in his head. "Thanks for this," I say dismissively, tilting the box. "Be safe out there."

"Yeah." He smiles, his lips a thin, ragged line. "You, too."

I stay rooted to the porch until he has climbed back into the UPS truck and pulled slowly back down the driveway. When he disappears into the darkness of the trees, I release a shuddering breath. It's only mid-afternoon, but it might as well be dusk, and as I shiver in the misty cold, a low rumble of thunder is preceded by a flash of lightning that illuminates the skeletal electrical poles bisecting our yard. They're bony and leaning, fragile against the onslaught. It doesn't look like it would take much to bring them down. The thought of us alone up here, without power, turns my stomach.

Back inside, I see that Henry has tucked the blanket around Finn's shoulders and removed a pillow so that he's more or less lying flat. The younger boy has fallen into a fitful sleep. Henry is sitting in Felix's favorite chair, scowling at me.

"I'm going to check on the laundry," I announce, trying to shake off the odd encounter with the UPS guy. Trying to ignore the fact that only minutes ago, Henry tried to trap me in my own home. But I'm a fast learner. I won't underestimate him—

or anyone—again. "We need to get off the mountain before it's too late."

The boys' laundry has a few minutes left on the wash cycle, so I carry the UPS package into the kitchen and set it on the breakfast table. Snagging a knife from the butcher block, I slide the blade under the packing tape, pop the flaps open, and set aside a layer of bubble film. Then I'm looking at the contents of the box, unable to make the seemingly random tableau before me make sense.

Reaching inside, I lift out the first item: a black baton with rubber grips. It's heavier than it looks, and I turn it over and over in my hands, trying to figure out why Felix ordered it. Because I certainly didn't. I press the top, the metal bottom, and feel all along the sides, but nothing happens until I give the tube a frustrated shake. In one lightning-fast snick of sound, steel shafts expand out of the baton and click into place. I know instantly what it is. A tactical weapon.

I don't know how to retract it, so I toss it on the table, frantic to know what else the box contains. There are two discreet canisters of pepper spray, small enough to be tucked into a pocket or concealed in the palm of your hand. These are nothing like the giant cylinder of bear mace, and clearly intended to be hidden. Then I find a heavy-duty Maglite, a pack of D-cell batteries, and a plastic bag full of zip ties.

Zip ties?

My mouth goes dry, and I stumble back from the table, dropping the bag on the floor.

It must be a mistake. I got the wrong package. Grabbing the box, I probe for a packing slip or something that can tell me the name of whoever purchased this bizarre and frightening collection. But there's nothing left inside except a black case the size of a pack of cigarettes. I turn it over to read: *Stun Gun.*

There's an arsenal on my kitchen table. A cache of weapons designed to incapacitate but not kill. It smacks of Felix. I imagine most people, if they felt the need to arm themselves, would simplify matters and just buy a handgun. But my husband's aversion to firearms is zealous. Only he would amass such a strange hoard of self-defense tools. I know before I close the box flap that I'll find his name on the shipping label, and I do.

What I can't begin to imagine is *why*.

CHAPTER 8

TUESDAY

My nerves are frayed and sparking like cut electrical wire by the time Henry and Finn's laundry is done. I've secreted the box of weapons under my bed upstairs. I can't deal with the implications of my husband's bizarre purchases until the boys are sorted. It's insane. *Insane* to think that Felix felt the need to arm himself. Or defend Hemlock House. Or protect me. What could he possibly be afraid of?

It strikes me as I'm lifting Henry and Finn's warm, clean clothes from the dryer that if Felix thought we were in danger, he would never leave me here. I may be a newlywed, but I know my husband. This is the man who pins me to his side when we walk dark streets, places a coaster on top of my drink when I step away from the bar, and always claims the side of the bed closest to the door. If I bristled at his chivalry in the beginning, I bask in it now. I've taken care of myself my whole life, and knowing that I can relax enough to let Felix take a shift now and then has made me soft in ways I never thought possible. No, there's no way my husband would abandon me if he thought there was a real need for those weapons. Something is preventing him from coming home.

I can feel the flutter of my heart in the notch at the base of my neck, and I put my fingers there as if to stop it. Warm skin, the velvety curve of my worn-smooth collar.

Forty-four hours gone.

After a restless nap on the couch, Finn is as alert as I've seen him. While Henry slips upstairs to change back into his clothes—now clean, but still old and tattered and nasty—I do what is necessary.

It's a mechanical impulse, hardwired inside me, to get the job done. When I was a child, I learned what my mother expected of me, and I performed my duty to the very best of my ability. Never mind that she often accused me of failure, I absorbed the lesson and adjusted as necessary. Somehow, someway, I would get it right. I would be perfect. I've always been composed and capable and responsible. A counselor once told me that perfectionism is the most paralyzing form of self-abuse, but I have never been incapacitated. I can always, *always* do what needs doing.

Right now, Finn needs food, so I microwave a bowl of leftover beef bourguignon for him and spread a slice of wholegrain bread with butter. There's a bit of milk left in the fridge, and I give him the rest of it, hoping that some calories will perk him up even more. But as he sits at the kitchen table, the stew wafting savory steam into the air, he ignores the food and stares out the window toward the trees.

"Not hungry?" I ask, sinking into the seat opposite him. Focusing on him gives me an excuse to push my fears about Felix aside.

Finn doesn't look at me but gives his head a little jiggle.

"You'll feel better if you eat something," I tell him. "You have to build up your strength."

At this, he looks down at the bowl as if seeing it for the first time. I watch as he carefully picks up a fork and spears a hunk of carrot. He twirls it around for a moment and then slides it back off the tines. This time, he pricks a cube of beef and lifts it to his lips. Licks it.

"It's good, right?"

Finn licks it again, considering, and then pops the meat into his mouth. I silently cheer.

My eyes dart to the ceiling, trying to calculate how long I have before Henry comes back. I'm dying to ask Finn some questions without his overbearing brother breathing down my neck, but I'm not sure if the younger boy will be able to answer me. I decide to risk it. While Finn digs around in the bowl for more protein, I casually ask, "How long have you and Henry been sleeping in my greenhouse?"

Finn's dark eyes flick to mine, but then he ducks his head, and his chocolate-brown curls obscure his face. Tucking another bit of beef into his mouth, he slowly raises three fingers with the opposite hand.

"Three nights?"

Finn nods.

"Including last night?"

He nods again.

I decide to keep the questions casual. Easy. "How long have you been sick, Finn?"

Two fingers this time. I breathe a sigh of relief. As ill as Finn seems, I don't think pneumonia could've settled into his lungs in such a short time. Could it? It's probably just a case of the flu or maybe bronchitis.

"How old are you?" It's a trick question, and he catches it out immediately. Finn's whole head jerks up to regard me, a hint of panic in his eyes. He holds up all ten fingers, then balls both hands into fists before offering up four more.

Fourteen. It's the same age Henry told me, but I still don't believe it. Regardless, I smile at Finn, trying to put him at ease. "I used to teach middle school," I say. "You would've fit right into my classes. Do you like football? Basketball?"

He just watches me, his expression blank.

"Maybe you're more of a video game guy," I try again. "Comics? Books?"

Finn turns his attention back to the bowl and swirls his fork through the stew.

"Hiking, then. Or hunting. Do you like to hunt, Finn?"

Finally, he gives me a little one-shouldered shrug and I rack my brain, trying to remember what people hunt out here. But hunting puts me in mind of guns and violence, and that brings me right back to the box of weapons stowed under my bed, and I just can't go there. The delivery suggests a fourth—unbearable—reason my husband might be missing: *something* is going on. Something dangerous that I know nothing about, but that Felix felt he had to prepare for. It's a chilling, impossible thought, so I shove it aside.

Disappointed in my own lack of investigative prowess and accepting that there isn't much Finn could communicate to me anyway, I let it go. "How's the soup?" I ask.

Finn seems to be gaining a little color in his cheeks, a warmth that could be a direct result of the bourguignon. He dips the bread in the broth now, then takes a careful, measured bite. It's strangely satisfying to watch him, his delicate hand holding the bread so gently it seems he's afraid it might disintegrate, his fine jaw working steady and slow. He's an attentive, thoughtful boy, I can see that just after a few moments alone with him, and there's something about his calm countenance that betrays depth. Finn is also painfully cute, and I can't stop the way he plucks at my heart. I'm astonishingly drawn to him.

I never wanted kids. Of course, I know how strange that sounds, how alien and unfathomable, so I didn't say the quiet part out loud. Instead, I'd tell well-meaning friends that I was waiting for the right person or the right time, or that I was married to my work. After all, wasn't I already a mother figure to hundreds of kids? Year in and year out, I gave up my lunch for those who forgot, listened to teary confessions of bad behavior, celebrated victories big and small, and even hugged the kids whose parents neglected them. Their artwork hung on my fridge, and when they passed me notes on the last day of school signed with *love*, I loved them right back. Didn't that make me a de facto mom?

It wasn't until I met Felix—and came to terms with the fact that my window of opportunity had likely closed—that I could fully grieve what I'd never had. *What if?* If Felix and I had fallen in love ten years earlier, what would our lives have looked like? I imagined a boy with Felix's dark hair and a girl with my honey waves. A scruffy, lovable dog. A white picket fence and—

And what? A fatal car accident that cleaved our family in two? An unconventional childhood that ended in estrangement? Neither Felix nor I had happy family experiences, so to imagine that we would have been able to pull off the American dream was pure foolishness. What did we know about family? We had each other. It was far more than enough.

But Finn, eyes dark and thickly lashed—just like Felix's—is messing with my head. I can almost picture my husband ruffling those curls, sweeping Finn up in one arm and tossing him, giggling, over his shoulder. In another life . . .

When Finn looks up and smiles at me, I smile back. He puts down the bread and points to the bowl of stew. With his right hand raised, he hovers his palm over his heart and moves it in a tight circle.

"Oh!" I say. I've nearly forgotten that I asked a question, but I'm honored that Finn is answering it. That he's trying to teach me something. "You like it? You like the stew?"

He nods and performs the sign again. I mirror his action and am rewarded with another small smile. Then, grabbing his fork, Finn snags another chunk of meat and sticks it into his mouth. Chewing, he closes his eyes and shakes his head, obviously enjoying his meal. This time, when he performs his homemade sign, he taps his chest twice with his hand at the end.

I laugh. "You *love* it."

This earns me a full, toothy grin, and I'm surprised by how my heart swings open at the sight.

"What's going on in here?"

I look up to find Henry glowering in the kitchen archway. I never even heard him come down the stairs.

"Finn is teaching me sign language," I say, my smile fading. Henry looks like he wants to strangle me with his bare hands.

"It's not sign language," Henry barks, and I watch Finn's face shut like a slammed door. The boy lowers his head, folds his hands in his lap. "Not proper sign language, anyway. Come on, Finn. You need to get dressed."

Finn slides off the chair obediently and follows his older brother out of the kitchen. It's only when Henry's back is turned that Finn chances a glance over his shoulder and gives me a furtive, secret look. Is he warning me not to disclose our conversation? To be wary of Henry? I don't know Finn well enough to interpret his gaze, and before I can respond, they're both around the corner and gone.

I push myself up from the table and take Finn's half-eaten

bowl of stew to the sink. I should probably offer Henry lunch, too, but I can't stomach the thought of him in my house for a minute longer than strictly necessary. Instead, I wrap another slice of buttered bread in wax paper and grab a banana from the counter. Henry can eat in the Ranger on the drive down the mountain. I've been more than hospitable. And I have my own misery to contend with: a missing husband, a cache of strange weapons for a battle I know nothing about.

By the time the boys return to the kitchen, I'm bundled in my winter coat and ready to go. "Here," I say, handing each of them one of Felix's heavy jackets. They're thick, down-lined flannels with hoods, and they'll keep the brothers warm and dry on our trek into town. I've never driven the UTV in a storm, and never with the weatherproof panels snapped in place. I have no idea how effective they are or how cold our trip down the mountain is going to be.

To be honest, I'm nervous. The Ranger doesn't have windshield wipers, and though the rain has slowed a bit, it's still coming down. Never mind the predictable slippery spots along the old logging road and the deep puddles that will undoubtedly make the drive treacherous. I just want to deliver my cargo and get back so I can concentrate on finding Felix.

When they're bundled and ready to go, Henry takes the banana and slice of bread with a reluctant grunt that is the furthest thing from a thank-you. He doesn't want to accept generosity from me, and I feel a little stab of spite. But this perplexing experience is almost over, and I force a tight smile at Henry because, whether I like him or not, whether I understand him or not, we do have something in common: we are both dependable. Tenaciously so.

"You're going to have to hold Finn on your lap," I tell him as we head out the back door. The porch is slippery, and water beads all along the eaves like a string of gleaming black pearls. Instinctively, I reach for Finn to steady him, but Henry shoves himself between us.

"Fine," he says, and swings Finn into his arms as if proving to me that he can take care of his brother. That he doesn't need my help. I roll my eyes but don't say anything.

The Ranger is dry inside, but cramming three warm bodies into such a small space almost immediately begins to fog the polyester. I start the engine and rub the side of my hand against the windscreen to clear away the haze.

"Where are we headed?" I ask, careful not to look at Henry. He still hasn't told me anything about who he's supposed to meet or how we'll find him.

"Requiem," he says.

I grit my teeth but don't say anything. If we get there and Henry still refuses to be forthcoming, I'll do whatever I need to do to ensure the boys are safe and provided for. I may have promised not to call anyone last night, but all bets are off now. My phone is charged and in my pocket, and I have a police officer on my recent call list.

The gate at the end of the winding drive is still swung open, waiting for Felix's eventual return. The top rail, a length of rusted metal and chipped red paint, is a gash in the drenched underbrush, pointing not toward Requiem, but deeper into the forest. I stifle a shiver. I've never been up that way, to the place where logging companies once clear-cut entire mountainsides. You can still see the scars from the highway, places where the new trees are smaller, their color a pale, juvenile green against the old, jade forests.

On the logging road, away from the homestead, I feel exposed and vulnerable. In places, the canopy meets overhead creating a dark tunnel that makes the twisting route seem plucked from some ancient folktale. It's wet and cold, ringed with mist as if a spell is being cast out of sight, and for just a moment, I understand why David Graham hunted demons. It's easy to believe they exist here.

"How far is it?" Henry asks as I give a large puddle wide berth. There's no telling how deep it is.

"The drive usually takes me just under fifteen minutes," I tell him. "But it'll take a lot longer today." I'm crawling through the hairpin curves, taking it slow as the tires chew up the soggy gravel and kick mud at the rear windshield. It's already covered in brown smears.

Out of the corner of my eye, I see Finn shift on Henry's lap and work his hands through a few motions. "How big is Requiem?" Henry asks, interpreting for his brother, I assume.

"Small. A couple hundred people or so. But it services a pretty large rural area." The truth is, I was shocked the first time we drove from Hemlock House to the coast. Between Requiem and the corridor of Interstate 5, ragtag communities dotted the landscape. Trailers and old RVs, and cabins that looked as if they had been built during the Mount Baker gold rush in the late 1800s, but then left to rot for a hundred years. These makeshift villages pimpled the bush, and the only reason I knew people lived in the hollowed-out carcasses of mobile homes and old buses parked deep in the tangled grass were the current political signs strung between trees and plastered to leaning walls. I guessed these people called Requiem home, too, and collected mail from PO boxes at the little brick post office on Main Street.

All at once it hits me that maybe Henry and Finn are from one of these settlements. Their long hair, torn clothes, and obvious neglect feel oddly reminiscent of the run-down, makeshift neighborhoods. They share the same air of unloved things.

But it's clear Henry has never been to Requiem. I don't know how they could live so close and not have ventured even once to Gus's, Timber Co., or Trilogy. An uneasy feeling churns in my stomach.

"Look out!" Henry shouts, stiffening one arm around Finn's chest and using the other to brace himself against the roll bar of the side-by-side.

I see the gulley at the last minute and yank the steering wheel to the right, slipping in a channel of sludge that spins out the back tires and whips us toward a tree. Slamming on the brakes, I fling my forearm over my head, hoping that if we crash, I can at least prevent a head injury. But we stop just in the nick of time—rocking from the abrupt, unexpected standstill—a few paltry inches from the trunk of a spruce that's almost as wide as the Ranger. It would have crushed us like a tin can.

Finn exhales a wobbly breath. Henry doesn't make a sound.

"I'm sorry," I manage, my voice shaking. "I didn't see . . . I couldn't see it." *It* being the little river that I now realize originated from a cleft in the rockface beside us and carved an absolute canyon out of the road I've driven down a hundred times. The water is running fast and several inches deep, scoring the poorly maintained road like an incision. If we had gotten stuck in it, I feel certain that we would not have made it out.

"It must be raining really hard at higher elevations," Henry says. He sounds hoarse, but not angry. In fact, I'm unnerved to detect a note of fear in his tone. "I bet the river's overflowed."

Already? I think. We missed spring in the mountains, but Felix had told me about flash floods and one unusually wet May when his family was stranded at Hemlock House for over a week after every body of water in a fifty-mile radius spilled its banks. But that had happened over the course of many days. It's only been raining for a few hours.

"We hit a rough patch," I say with more conviction than I feel. "I'll slow down, and we'll be fine. I just need you to help me keep an eye out, okay?"

Finn gives a jerky nod, and Henry shifts his brother off his lap so that they are crammed side by side, sharing the bucket seat. It looks uncomfortable, but it affords Henry a much better view. I don't argue; I need his eyes.

The rain is coming down harder again, and the temperature must have dropped because it's slushy on the polyester windscreen. I wrench open the door and slide from the cab, squelching in the muddy mess that is the only road off the mountain. Using my arm, I sweep clear the windshield, but it's a lost cause because by the time I'm done, the sleet is already collecting along the bottom edge.

"We're not going to make it," Henry mutters when I hop back in and slam the door. "It's dangerous to try."

"We will," I snap, angry at his lack of faith in me and the way it's making Finn ping-pong nervous looks between us. We shared a moment in the kitchen, and Finn *wants* to trust me, but Henry seems determined to sabotage any progress we've made. I don't know why I care. The whole point of this excursion is to extricate myself from the boys. "We'll take it slow, but we'll make it to Requiem."

It takes a bit of rocking back and forth, some steady pedal work and vigilant, incremental turns, to pull away from the divot at the base of the tree. Then I have to reverse past the growing ravine carved into the unstable gravel and hug the wrong side of the road to clear the stretch that nearly derailed us. By the time we've rounded the next curve, I'm sweating from stress and bent over the steering wheel, with my nose nearly pressed to the windscreen. I can hardly see a thing.

"This isn't safe," Henry whispers as I navigate the Ranger to straddle another gaping puddle.

"What do you want me to do, Henry? Take you back to my place? You couldn't wait to get out of there." I wince, surprised at the bite in my words, but I'm starting to panic. Henry's right, this isn't safe, but what choice do I have? My focus has to be on Felix, not a pair of strangers who carry a host of burdens I can hardly begin to guess at.

"I'm just saying that it won't do any good if—"

"I don't need you to tell me—"

"—we can't even—"

"—but there's—"

I'm so wrapped up in trying to make my voice heard over Henry's increasingly loud complaining that I don't feel Finn's hand on my arm until he pinches me, *hard*. By then it's almost too late. We're halfway around another corkscrew bend when the road itself disappears. I slam on the brakes, jerking the steering wheel to the left, away from the bluff where a section of gravel has eroded completely away, and we jolt to a stop. This time, we all spill out of the Ranger.

The logging road is gone. Or, at least, a chunk of it is. For the last mile or so, we've been hemmed in by trees on both sides, but here the mountain falls away to the west and a steep ridge cuts down to the valley below. Rocky outcroppings stand where they always have, but the places in between—the mud and foliage, the scrappy trees that had sprouted despite the severe setting—have washed away, taking a portion of the road with them. One tree has been spun upside down and is barely clinging to the cliffside with its roots in place of branches, wet soil dripping from the knotted rhizomes like dark blood. It's a world upended, strange and terrifying.

Finn is crying, a sorrowful, sniffling sound that makes me reach out instinctively and pull him to me. He doesn't fight it but throws his arms around my waist and buries his face in my side. Henry doesn't so much as blink while his brother sobs against my coat. Instead, he asks: "What now?" I can barely hear him over the steady thrum of rain.

"You were right," I say. "I shouldn't have kept going."

He looks like he wants to say something, maybe offer an olive branch of his own, but I don't give him the chance. "We need to get back inside the Ranger. You're getting soaked."

The mack jackets that I gave the boys are not fit for this weather. In my defense, I only thought they'd be running between the UTV and the toasty interior of Trilogy, not stranded at the precipice of a nonexistent gravel road in the pouring rain. Still, Finn is sick, and Henry won't be far behind if I don't get them out of the sleet. I screwed up—I let my emotions dictate my decisions—and now I have to make it right.

Back inside the Ranger, I reverse away from the jagged ledge of crumbled road, then stop to press my forehead to the steering wheel and take a few shuddering breaths. I'm unraveling at the seams, but for Finn's sake I say: "It's fine. We're okay. We'll find another way off the mountain."

"How?" Henry sounds defeated.

"There's always a way. I can—" I break off, berating myself for overlooking the easiest, most obvious answer, and dig in my pocket. *Of course.* "I can call for help."

"Who are you going to call?" Henry asks, staring at me intently, but for once he doesn't argue.

Cleo is my first instinct, though I might be better off going straight to Chief Brandt. Surely he has the resources to rescue us. But before I can share any of my plans with Henry, they fall apart. One glance at my phone screen reveals I have zero bars. No service.

Of course I don't. This has always been a dead zone, and no doubt the storm is making cellular service even spottier than usual. I sigh, tapping the useless phone against my lips for a moment while I think. I'm not comfortable enough with the terrain to try off-roading my way to the highway, even though the Ranger is built for it. Knowing my luck, I'd just get us lost, or worse, take us to a cliff edge that none of us spot until we're vaulting over the side.

"I can't call from here. We have to go back," I tell the boys, as sleet slowly ices over the windshield. I shiver, feeling the cold for the first time since we left Hemlock House. Our journey has been such a train wreck I haven't had time to think about how my fingers and toes are numb, my cheeks tingling from the icy air. Henry and Finn must be freezing.

"We can't just go back," Henry insists, but even I can tell his frustration is half-hearted. We both saw the road—or lack thereof.

"We don't have a choice. But don't worry, there's a portable cell tower at the homestead. We'll call for help." If Henry wants to argue, he must have bitten his tongue, because I don't hear a peep out of him. Maybe he realizes that the situation isn't good. That we need help. Or maybe he'll ambush me the minute we make it back to Hemlock House. Take my phone and my only connection to the outside world. But I can't think about that right now.

Instead of agonizing over Henry's silence, I make a careful turn, giving the sharp boundary of disintegrated ground wide berth, and head back the way we came. It's the only logical course of action, and because I know what I need to do, I focus on that and tamp down the dread that threatens to brim over.

Because if we can't make it down the mountain, Felix can't make it up. My husband can't come home, even if he's trying to.

CHAPTER 9

TUESDAY

It takes us twice as long to retrace our path as it did to travel to the place where the logging road has ceased to exist. I have to stop several times to clear slush from the windshield, and every time I do, the cold settles deeper into my bones. Even worse than my plummeting core temperature is the icy dread that wends its way through my veins. The nearer we get to Hemlock House, the more I come to grips with just how close we came to utter disaster. I can't think about the cavity in the earth where there was supposed to be a road without experiencing a full body shudder. The second time it happens, my teeth begin to chatter. Finn slips his arm through mine and hangs on, wordlessly passing to me what little comfort he can offer. I adore him for it.

I pull the Ranger as close to the back door as I can get, ignoring the patch of grass that Felix has coaxed to grow around the stepping stones. I can't waste my worry on frivolous things when I'm afraid Henry will make a play for my phone, when we might be cut off from civilization completely. If I could just untangle myself from the boys, everything would be so much easier. But we're stuck together now, bound by the mercurial temperament of Mother Nature—and my own inability to leave well enough alone.

In the mudroom, we shed our wet coats and soggy shoes.

I tuck my phone into the front pocket of my jeans then pull my sweater down over the bulge. If Henry wants my phone, he's going to have to work for it—and I'm scrappier than I look.

"Come on," I say, leading the boys into the kitchen. "Let's get warmed up."

Henry passes through to the living room while I turn the thermostat up and put a kettle on the stove for hot chocolate. If the boys are half as chilled as I am, it's going to take more than a warm house to stop our teeth from chattering. Just as I'm about to call out to Henry (I don't like it when I don't know what he's up to), he returns holding the quilt from the couch. He tucks it around his brother's shoulders as the smaller boy sits knees-to-chest on one of the breakfast nook chairs. Finn's eyes are glassy, polished to a sickly gleam by fever and fear.

"I turned the heater up," I tell them, turning away. I make a mental note to load the washing machine with the blankets we used in the greenhouse. We might need them. "It'll warm up in here soon."

"And then?" Henry sinks to the chair beside Finn.

"As soon as we've thawed a bit I'll call for help."

"Call who?" There's a sharp edge to his voice.

"Look, Henry. With the road washed away, we're stranded up here. I'm running low on groceries, and snow is coming. I'm not some rugged survivalist." I bark a laugh at my own incredulity. "I can't keep us safe in a blizzard."

"What if I can?" He says it quietly, tracing the whorls of wood grain on the tabletop instead of looking at me.

Something about his wary, hopeful tone tugs at a knot in my chest. Henry has been nothing but volatile, brash, and unpredictable, but I'm reminded that he's just a kid. He wants to be a big, intimidating man capable of protecting himself and his little brother, but the world has conspired against him. And I'm only adding to his troubles.

"I believe you could," I say, and though I spoke without truly considering my words, now that they're out of my mouth I know they're true. I do believe that Henry contains multitudes and could probably weather this storm better than most. He clearly understands the mountain and knows how to survive in the bush. He and Finn arrived at Hemlock House in one piece, more or less. But that's beside the point. We don't have to put ourselves in danger. We don't have to risk anything when safety is just a phone call away.

Leaving the kettle to boil, I take the chair across from the boys. For the first time since I discovered Henry and Finn in the greenhouse, I feel like Henry might be willing to listen. To see me as an ally and not a threat.

"I have no doubt you could chop wood and make a fire and hunt for food if we needed it," I say. "You're clearly very capable. But Finn is sick. And we don't know how long the storm will last or how difficult it will be to get off the mountain with the logging road washed away. It's too risky. I have to call for help, and you know it."

Finn stares at his brother, his eyes communicating something even deeper than his hands could ever express, but Henry refuses to look at him. Instead, the teenager glowers at the faded wood, his jaw working to conceal the slight tremor in his bottom lip.

"I can't let anyone take Finn away from me," he says finally, his voice a growl.

I start to ask why someone would want to take Finn away but find I don't need to. No matter what he says, Henry's not eighteen, and someone has told him how the Department of Children, Youth, and Families works. How that in the name of child welfare, the brothers might be separated while whatever sticky situation that thrust them into the forest is investigated. It must be bad. Neglect or abuse or, God forbid, a death of some sort. Murder? I twist my fingers together in my lap, trying to keep my emotions at bay. I wish Henry would let me in just a little, but it's clear that he's barely holding it together. I want him to listen to me, not blow up again, so I don't pry.

Silence stretches thin and uncomfortable, and as Finn reaches out a hand to touch his brother's elbow, I blurt: "I won't let anyone separate you." I curse myself for letting my heart take the reins. "I mean, we'll do everything we can to stop that from happening. We'll find your uncle, okay?"

Finn begins to cough, and Henry instinctively puts an arm around his brother, drawing him close. It's settled. I can see it in his eyes before he dips his head once in a barely perceptible nod. The missing road has scraped all the fight right out of him.

"I'll call my friend Cleo," I say, getting up as the kettle begins to whistle. "She'll know what to do. And maybe we can keep this all under the radar . . . I'm sure she knows a way to get us to Requiem safely, and we can stay with her until we're able to get ahold of your uncle."

I'm spinning a fantasy, but it's what we all need right now.

I don't ask if the boys want hot chocolate, just stir up two generous mugs for them and a peppermint tea for myself, and carry them all to the table. I don't have marshmallows or whipped cream, but Finn doesn't seem to mind as he curls his hands around the warm stoneware and blows the steam away.

Exhausted, I lean against the counter. My first sip of tea is a portal, and all at once I'm back in Newcastle on a snowy night before Christmas. I can hear Felix's laugh, see the glimmer in his eyes as he looks across the desk at me. I have to shake my head to dislodge the vision, and if my eyes are damp, I hope the boys chalk it up to the cold.

We drink in silence for a few minutes, and then I carefully slide my phone from my pocket. Laying it on the table—a sign of trust, an offering—I catch Henry's eye. "Cleo will help us. I'm sure of it." What I'm really saying is: *Don't be afraid, everything is going to be okay*. But Henry just drops his gaze to the swirl of chocolate in his mug. It's all the consent I need.

Tapping the screen, I unlock my phone and swipe to the call icon. But before I select Cleo from my Recents list, I realize that where I should have full bars, the screen declares *No Service*. A pinch of unease twists in my stomach, but I ignore it. Navigating to settings, I make sure my Wi-Fi and cellular data are turned on, that I'm connected to our cell tower. The carrier is listed, but it's semi-transparent. I can't select it.

"Something wrong?" Henry asks, watching me tap furiously as I try to figure out what's going on.

"A glitch," I say, pushing back from the table. "It's nothing. I'll get it worked out."

Leaving the brothers sitting at the breakfast nook, I take the stairs two at a time and drop to the edge of the bed in our room. Here, I'm almost directly below the cell booster we've bolted to the roof, as close as I can get to the signal that should easily cover a large circumference around the squat tower. But even after I power down my phone and turn it back on twice, I have nothing.

My fingers begin to tingle, and not from cold. I don't want to accept it—there must be something I've missed, a simple step that I've forgotten—but I know deep down that I've done everything right.

The landline.

I remember it with a jolt and push myself up from the bed to race back down the stairs.

"Who has a landline?" I had laughed when Felix set it up shortly after we moved in. The Graham family phone was still mounted on the wall in the kitchen, a mustard-colored base and handset from the eighties with a mismatched, extra-long cord so Gabi could take the receiver into the mudroom and shut the door for privacy when she was a teenager. I thought we'd take it down, store it in the attic or donate it to a museum or something.

But Felix grinned back at me. "*We* have a landline!" he said. "Got our old number back and everything."

"Why?"

"Because we can. Because it's more dependable than the cell tower."

I had thought it was silly at the time—and cursed the day Felix reconnected the line, because in September we started receiving actual calls. The ring jangled through the house so raucously I jumped every single time. There was never anyone on the other end the few times I lifted the receiver. Just a muffled silence and once, I thought, the sound of someone breathing. Creepy.

But now I'm elated that Felix planned ahead. That he considered this very scenario and gave us a viable plan B.

I skid into the kitchen, ignoring Henry's raised eyebrows, and lift the old-fashioned receiver. But even before it's pressed to my ear, I know. There's no dial tone. The line is dead, as vacant and useless as a relic. Of course it is. Phone lines up here are aboveground, not buried deep like they are in the Midwest. How easy it would be for a fallen tree or a strong gust of wind to interrupt service.

A sliver of dread, glittering and sharp, wedges in my chest as

I glance over my shoulder at Henry and Finn, still sitting at the table with their empty mugs before them. I feel like I've failed them when I finally admit to myself that we're completely cut off from the rest of the world.

We're trapped at Hemlock House.

◆

"Be careful up there!" I shouted when Felix climbed the roof to attach the cell antennae. It was an unseasonably warm day in May, and all the windows of the house were flung open to catch the alpine breeze. It was laced with cedar and the crisp, woody fragrance of fiddlehead ferns unfurling in the mossy shadows.

Boxes were still piled on every available surface inside, and we had spent the last few days cleaning cobwebs out of every corner, removing dusty sheets from the furniture. Hemlock House felt alien to me, like we were living on another planet, but the signal booster that Felix was installing would undoubtedly help. Just the thought of cuddling up with him to watch an episode of *Succession* or to scroll Instagram while we showed each other funny reels made me smile.

"Want to join me?" Felix's head appeared over the edge of the roof, his mouth canted in an impish grin, dimple winking. "It's the perfect place to stargaze."

I checked my watch. "It's five p.m."

"I'm sure we could think of something to do while we wait for sunset."

My husband was irresistible. I climbed the ladder, wrapping my fingers around the gutter when I got to the top, and lifted my face to his. Felix leaned over the edge to kiss me, a bright, happy smack that reminded me again of why we came. He was so radiant here. But there was an edge to his joy, an almost manic urgency that I didn't understand. Though we had come to Hemlock House to retreat, to focus and write and finish our projects, I couldn't shake the sense that Felix had a secret to-do list that kept him strung tight and ever busy. *Calm down*, I wanted to tell him. *We have all the time in the world.*

But instead of pressing it, I let him be. Maybe he needed to hustle around this place, fixing things and setting right past wrongs. Maybe his hours-long wanderings through the forests of his boyhood were an exorcism of sorts—or at least a form of therapy. And if Felix rushed to and fro, a frantic energy flickering through him, I expected him to level out eventually. To find his equilibrium at Hemlock House in a new way, as a grown man with a wife and a successful career. A life his younger self could scarcely have imagined.

There was a shushing sound, and a few gravelly bits trickled off the shingles and plinked into the gutter. Felix slid down an inch or two, his nose mashing into my cheek as he chuckled a quiet, "Whoa. Maybe it's steeper than I thought."

"Maybe I should keep my feet on solid ground—and you should hurry up."

I stayed with my hands braced on the pitched roof while Felix double-checked the bolts and made sure the cell tower was on and functioning properly. He sent me a dirty text from the apex of the house, and when it *ping*ed in my pocket, I cheered. I felt like I could spend the rest of my life alone with him and never want for another, but this connection to the outside world still felt like a lifeline.

Now, standing in the driving sleet with one arm thrown up to block my face from the bite of freezing rain, I can see that the Christmas tree–shaped antennae is completely iced over. The delicate horizontal bars have formed one solid lick of ice, and though the tower should be fully weather resistant, I can't see enough of it to know what else might have happened to cause its demise. For all I know, squirrels chewed the wire connecting it to the booster box in the house. Or the weight of the ice has cracked some vital bit of hardware.

If the roof was steep and dangerous when Felix climbed it in May, it's as accessible as the peak of Mount Everest now. The sharp plane is an absolute skating rink, scalable only with ice traction cleats and a harness—accessories we do not own.

"So?" Henry asks when I tromp back into the mudroom. He's been waiting for me, arms crossed as he leans against the doorjamb.

I want to shout at him, say something caustic and mean because I'm trembling with a terror and anger adjacent to fear. But I press my lips together, force myself to draw in a long breath. "There's something wrong with the tower."

Henry's face shifts, but I can't read his expression. Is this news a relief to him? Is he *happy* that we're cut off from civilization? But instead of gloating, he says, "I'll climb the roof. See if I can figure out what happened."

It's bravado, of course. What could he possibly know about a portable cell tower? But his kindness is unexpected. "Thank you," I manage after a moment. "That's nice of you, but you're not going up there unless you have a death wish."

"So, we're stuck."

"Looks like it." I push past him into the kitchen. Our signal booster might be defunct, but at least the electricity is working. The house is warm and still smells faintly of hot cocoa, but there's an undercurrent of must. Of sickness and decay. My nose wrinkles and I wrap my arms around myself. Finn is gone, presumably back to the couch in the living room, and I cross to the little round table to gather up the empty mugs.

"Now what?" Henry asks, following me.

Now what, indeed?

But I don't answer him. Instead, I busy my hands washing the dishes that have accumulated in the farmhouse sink. Hemlock House doesn't have a dishwasher, and though I'd bemoaned that fact when we first moved here, Felix and I grew to love the half hour we spent shoulder to shoulder cleaning up in the evenings. No phones or computer screens or distractions. Just the two of us and the gentle rhythm of our days. Often, we talked, but silence was just as good as conversation. I learned the cadence of his breath, the way he clocked every creak and moan and whisper of wind in the eaves that was the language of the old house. Felix would tilt his head, listening, and a memory would glide across his face like a phantom. At first, I asked about the ghost of a smile on his lips or the sad slant of his eyes. But he always leaned over to kiss my temple and assured me it was nothing. He'd tell me in time, I believed.

When Henry snags the flour sack towel from the handle of the fridge and comes to stand beside me, my breath catches in my throat. I don't know if tears are threatening because I'm nauseous with worry about Felix or because Henry's thoughtfulness is so unexpected. Maybe both.

Taking a plate from the shallow side of the sink, Henry carefully towels it off, then says: "We can try again tomorrow."

"I think the cell tower is done for," I tell him, lifting my shoulder to catch the tear that has slid down my cheek. I gulp a quick, fortifying breath. "And you're not going on that roof."

"I mean we can try to get down the mountain. Not on the road, obviously, but there are trails all through these woods. Maybe there's another path to the highway."

It's true that the mountain is crisscrossed with four-by-four trails, but they're not well marked. I glance at Henry's profile—

the shaggy hair, stern jawline, rough skin—and for just a moment I can see the man that he will become. He's gritty and fearless, unrelenting, and while these qualities have frustrated me from the moment I met him, they have the potential to serve him well. He could be a good man. Strong and dependable and brave.

But there is also something tragic about Henry. Something wolfish and dark. He's been hurt before, badly, and it's made him fierce. One look at the swollen, eggplant-colored skin around his eye and I can hardly blame him for being malicious. I've heard it said that hurt people hurt people, that they take their pain and unleash it on others out of spite or revenge or simply because they can, and I can see that inclination in Henry. There's a part of him that wants to rage, to tear down everything that stands in his way.

Henry is at war with himself.

And I have to be careful.

"Think you can navigate the trails?" I finally ask, turning back to the sink.

"Yes."

"You really did come from there?" I wave my sudsy hand toward the north-facing window and the forest beyond. There's nothing out there but wilderness for miles and miles.

It's Henry's turn to glance at me. He gives me a smile like a switchblade, quick and sharp. "I already told you that."

"So, what, like a Hansel and Gretel cabin in the woods?"

"Something like that."

I can tell by the way his whole body has gone tight that this line of questioning is off-limits. Okay, I can let it go. I'm discovering more about him in fits and starts, bit by bit, and for now it's the best I can hope for.

"I have a compass," I offer, suddenly convinced that trying to get to Requiem is safer than staying trapped at Hemlock House with a brooding, unpredictable Henry. "I'm learning how to use it, but I don't trust myself."

Henry exhales a derisive breath. "I can use a compass."

"What about the UTV? Can you drive the Ranger?"

He pins me with a *you've got to be kidding* look. "Obviously."

"Okay . . ." I trail off, studying the oily slick of dishwater as if my next step will be revealed in the murky swirls. But it's not like I have options. I'm stuck here, marooned at Hemlock House and utterly isolated from anyone who can help. Worst of all, *I don't know where Felix is*.

My eyes dart to the digital clock on the microwave and confirm what my gut already knew. Felix is forty-eight hours gone. My husband has been missing for two days.

"Fine. Let's do it," I say, gaze still fixed on the clock. "Tomorrow we'll try again. You can drive. You can navigate us down the mountain. If we head southwest long enough, we should eventually hit the highway."

In my peripheral vision I see Henry nod. "If it's snowing—"

"Stop," I interrupt. "I can't. I just can't think about that right now. There will be a break in the weather tomorrow and we'll make it safely to Requiem."

Henry doesn't argue.

When the dishes have all been put away, we make our way to the living room. I hope that Finn has fallen asleep again—rest is the best thing for him—but when I round the corner into the living room just a step or two behind Henry, Finn is nowhere to be seen.

"Where is he?" I ask, pinning Henry with a suspicious look. Has he been distracting me in the kitchen so that Finn could snoop through the house? To what end?

"I told him to go lay down on the couch." Unless he's a very good actor, Henry seems as confused as I am that Finn is nowhere to be seen. "Maybe he had to pee?"

Henry checks the main floor bathroom while I jog to the top of the stairs. The second floor is dark and quiet. Finn didn't come up here, and there's no way he would have wandered outside in the driving sleet. Because the house is small, there's only one other place he could be. And by the time I've made it back to the living room, it's clear that Henry has already located his brother.

A frisson of possessiveness flickers through me at the sight of Henry standing in the open door to Felix's study. That's my husband's private space, and not only is it filled with his books and notes and research, it still bears his presence. One of his flannels is draped over the wingback chair in the corner, unwashed and still smelling of woodsmoke and pine. His favorite pen is resting on a sheaf of paper beside his keyboard, a few scribbled lines the last thing he wrote before he left. Yes, I've spent time in Felix's inner sanctum since his disappearance, but that's different. I loathe the thought of Finn and Henry dragging their eyes—and God forbid, their dirty fingers—over his things.

"Hey," I call sharply. "You're not allowed in there."

Henry looks over his shoulder at me but doesn't move away from the door.

Crossing the living room in a few wide steps, I wrench open the other half of the double door and bark, "Get out. Now."

Finn turns toward me, his narrow body lithe and almost elegant as he spins on the hardwood floor. My words had an edge to them, but he seems not to have noticed as his eyes dance and his mouth pulls into a wide smile. He raises his arms and turns another circle, slower this time, pointing at all the amazing things that Felix has pinned to the walls and hung from the ceiling. There's the solar system mobile from his office at Newcastle University, and *The X-Files* poster. In a moment of silliness, Felix even peeled off the glow-in-the-dark stars that had once adorned his childhood bedroom and scattered them all around his office. They still seem to give off a faint gleam on clear nights, but maybe that's just wistful projection on our parts or a trick of the moonlight. But trinkets and sentimentality aside, the majority of wall space has been taken up by several of Felix's high-resolution printouts of brown dwarfs.

I've seen all these images a thousand times before, but the expression on Finn's face reminds me that they are awe-inspiring. A few of the posters are what Felix considers to be accurate artist's renditions, but the two pictures flanking his desk are real photographs taken by the James Webb Space Telescope. They're huge, nearly three feet by four feet, and staggeringly beautiful.

The first is a glowing red-orange orb with blazing slashes that look as if a tiger has dragged his claws across the surface of an alien planet. Finn hurries over to take my hand and then pulls me deeper into the room until we're standing together before it.

"That's a brown dwarf," I tell him, unsure if he has any understanding of astronomy at all.

"What's a brown dwarf?" Henry answers my unspoken question with another.

"I'm not a scientist," I say, wishing that Felix was here to explain. I love how my husband's whole body ignites when he talks about his work, how he becomes incandescent in his desire to make everyone he meets fall in love with the sky. But Felix is missing. Only I'm here. "A brown dwarf isn't a planet or a star. It's something in between."

"Is that for real?"

"The picture?" I ask.

"The whole thing," Henry says, waving his hands at the photo, the office, and everything it contains.

"Yes. My husband is an astronomer. He studies space. And he's currently conducting research on brown dwarfs." I hadn't planned on telling the boys anything about Felix, but I can't bring myself to drag Finn from the office when his eyes are devouring the images like candy. Moments like this are what Felix lives for. "It's real," I tell the boys. "Brown dwarfs are sometimes called failed stars. That means they start out like stars, but they don't have enough mass to burn and radiate starlight."

Henry makes a disbelieving grunt, but I'm proud that I know Felix's work enough to share this with Finn. I just hope I got it right.

"This is a star cluster," I say, leading Finn over to the second poster, a pink and purple scorch of cosmic vapor studded with twinkling points of light. "I don't remember which one. The bright points are stars, but these"—I tap near three yellow arrows that have been taped to the image—"are brown dwarfs. They're harder to see because they don't glow."

Finn looks up at me, his face radiant and open, his heart aflame. He makes a fist and then quickly splays his fingers, pulsing his hand out from his chest.

"They're beautiful, aren't they?" I know I've gotten his meaning when he grins.

"We have telescopes, too," I tell him, warming to the topic. "Several of them. When the weather clears I can . . ." But I trail off, realizing that stargazing with Finn is a ridiculous fantasy. In what world would I tip his small chin to the heavens, pointing out the glittery spill of the Milky Way?

I wish I could take the rash offer back, but Finn rushes through several more of his homespun signs, and I look to Henry for help.

The older boy is no longer loitering in the doorway, watching us with his mouth pulled into a snarl. Instead, he's wandered over to the table where Felix has collected things he loves. Found objects, pictures, mementos. Henry is holding one of the framed photographs in his hands, studying a selfie that I had taken of Felix and myself when we were falling in love. Felix is behind me, a half smile sloping the corner of his mouth, an unreadable look in his eyes. As I watch, Henry raises one finger to the dimple that puckers my husband's cheek. He touches it, and a dark expression crosses his face.

"Henry?"

The clip of my voice cuts through his reverie, and Henry's head shoots up, his eyes flashing to mine. But before I can even form a question, he drops the photo back on the table with a bang and marches out of the room.

BEFORE

SUNDAY, MAY 11

MICROMOON / MESSIER 5 IS WELL PLACED

One of the things that surprised Sadie about Felix was how seriously he took road-trip snacks. Milwaukee was only a seven-hour drive from Newcastle, and in the past Sadie had started out with a coffee, grabbed a quick lunch halfway, and then sipped on her bottle of water with a wedge of lemon until she hit the Culver's just off Interstate 94. The cheese curds and strawberry shake just hit different after a day on the road, and she found herself looking forward to it for the last hundred miles or so.

But when Sadie and Felix stopped at the Casey's on the outskirts of Newcastle to top up the tank before hitting the road, Felix almost immediately disappeared. Sadie was replacing the gas cap when he came back, arms laden with junk food like a kid who had been handed a fifty-dollar bill and left unattended.

"What have you done?" Sadie laughed when he wedged himself into the passenger seat, goodies spilling all over his lap and onto the floor.

"I got snacks." Felix shot a bewildered glance at her as he bent to retrieve a sleeve of honey-roasted peanuts and the Snickers bar that had landed near his feet.

"You're going to eat all of this?"

"Correction: *we* are going to eat all of this." Felix tore the top of a Twizzlers bag open with his teeth and held out one of the cherry-colored ropes to Sadie.

"It's barely eight. I haven't even had breakfast yet."

"What do you think this is?" Felix laughed and wagged the candy at her. "Take it. Calories don't count on road trips. Don't you know that?"

Sadie snapped an obligatory selfie before pulling out of the gas station. Felix's chin was hooked over her shoulder and licorice ropes hung from both of their mouths. She had just a few bites of Twizzlers (too rubbery) and then let Felix talk her into an old-fashioned maple-frosted donut with sprinkles. It was still a bit warm. Later there was a bag of Cheetos and tart lemonade in a glass bottle and M&M's. By the time they made it to the suburbs of Milwaukee, Sadie had a bit of a stomachache, but Felix wanted to try a ButterBurger and some custard, so they made her traditional stop. Sadie had a salad.

It felt strange to be on her home turf with Felix, and the sense of disquiet was compounded by the fact that the excursion had been last-minute. After graduation on Friday, the staff at Newcastle University seemed at loose ends, and though there was still a faculty forum and year-end grading to do, none of that started until Wednesday. It took the whole of Saturday for Felix to convince Sadie that a quick trip to see her mother was a good idea, but by Sunday afternoon they were leaning over the railing at Walker's Point, watching the boats bob in the harbor. Sadie couldn't decide if bringing Felix home was the best thing she'd ever done or the worst idea imaginable.

"She's expecting us?" Felix asked, squinting at the spring sunlight dancing on the water. He rested his forearms on the railing and gave Sadie a sidelong glance.

"I called ahead and left a message for her. Whether she remembers or not is anyone's guess."

"That's okay." Felix reached over to run one finger over Sadie's knuckles. She didn't realize she was strangling the iron bar until Felix's touch alerted her to the ache in her hands. She forced herself to loosen her grip, and Felix rewarded her with a quick kiss on the delicate bones of her wrist where her sleeve had crimped up. He told her, "I'm looking forward to meeting Alice no matter what."

Sadie sighed. "Expectation is the root of all heartache."

"Shakespeare?"

"No. But it sounds like something he'd say, doesn't it?"

Felix straightened up and pulled Sadie close, nestling her head beneath the line of his jaw. It was Sadie's favorite place to be. "I have zero expectations. I just want to meet the woman who gave birth to you."

It was a pretty apt assessment of Alice's impact on Sadie's life. *The woman who gave birth to you.* A *set it and forget it* sort of mother. There must have been hands-on parenting when Sadie was very little—moments of tenderness and connection and love—but the only mother she remembered was a woman carved out by loss, empty and aching and unable to see that even in the face of incomprehensible tragedy, her daughter still needed a mom.

"I parented myself," Sadie mumbled against Felix's chest. "Maybe you could just interrogate me about my childhood, and we could call it good?"

"This is not an interrogation." Felix took Sadie by the shoulders so he could hold her at arm's length. "It's an exploration. I want to meet her, Sadie. She's a part of you, and I don't want to miss the chance to know her."

The fact that time was running out was left unsaid. Swallowing was becoming increasingly difficult for Alice, and as a result she was losing weight fast. "You could pick her up and carry her in your arms like a child," one of the nurses told Sadie the last time she called. "You could hold her in your lap and rock her."

Sadie couldn't remember Alice ever doing that for her—pulling little ponytailed Sadie onto her lap for snuggles—and the reversal felt cruel. Cruel because Alice had known what a good mother should do, but she could rarely bring herself to do it. Her attempts at nurturing were half-hearted and more often than not, left undone. A box of devil's food mix languishing in the pantry that was supposed to be for Sadie's birthday cake. A pile of random books from the library that Sadie thumbed through again and again, making up the stories as she went, since Alice never took the time to read them to her. A Christmas present in a plastic Walmart bag on the counter because Alice bought a doll but forgot to buy wrapping paper or a Christmas tree to tuck the gift under.

It was cruel because, even now, healthy and successful and dating a man who felt like a daydream, Sadie wanted to do exactly that. She wanted to wrap her mother up and rock her like a baby. Tell her, *I loved you anyway.*

"Okay." Sadie tried to sound more confident than she felt. "Let's do this."

Alice Sheridan lived at Valley Rest Senior Care Home in the locked and secured memory care facility. It was a beautiful campus of redbrick buildings in a wooded neighborhood in one of Milwaukee's more exclusive suburbs. The monthly cost was enough to make Sadie hyperventilate, but her father had been a private financial advisor and had left his wife with a sizeable life insurance policy that Alice more or less ignored while it collected interest in the bank. Alice and Sadie never took vacations or bought new cars or wore expensive clothes. They never moved out of the small, classic colonial that Sadie had lived in since birth. And after Alice took several months' bereavement leave from her job as the office manager for a pair of endodontists, they gratefully took her back because no one else understood their billing codes and filing system. The Sheridan girls were fine, at least financially, and when it became obvious that Alice needed full-time care, Sadie spared no expense.

Felix whistled low as they drove the tree-lined drive to the state-of-the-art facility. The grounds were elegant, the buildings newish but designed to look historic. There was a fountain with copper peacocks and bespoke marble stairs, and all the employees wore the same plum uniforms with crisp, straight lines. In short, it was the sort of place a very wealthy woman would live out her days, and Sadie was uncomfortably aware of how confused Felix must be. Her cheap condo and Target clothes had not prepared him for this. His family had been land-rich, but empirically poor. Goodwill clothes and ramen suppers and kitchen-chair haircuts with his mother wielding the scissors.

"We're not rich," Sadie said, pointing Felix to the hidden parking lot on the far side of the main building, but found she didn't have the energy to explain further. She would, someday. For now, she just had to get through the next hour or two.

They signed in, were buzzed through the locked and alarmed doors—a precaution for residents who were often confused and prone to wandering off—and wound through the courtyard filled with live trees and a tiny, sedate pond, to the hall where Alice's room was third on the right.

Sadie paused before the closed door, her gaze determinedly fixed on the brass nameplate. "She'll probably think we work here," Sadie said. "It's more than likely she won't remember me, and she'll treat you with suspicion. Men are not to be trusted in Alice Sheridan's world. They leave."

But Felix wasn't deterred. He turned Sadie gently toward him and cupped her face in his hands. Pressing a chaste kiss to her mouth, he said: "It's fine. Whatever happens is fine. I love you. That's all that matters."

For one surreal, shimmering second, time froze. Sadie froze. But then she could feel the rough skin of his thumbs on her cheeks, his warm breath in her hair. They were both rumpled and tired, wilted from long hours in the car, but she found she didn't want fanfare anyway. Felix had said "I love you" for the first time in the most straightforward, unequivocal way, and it was perfect. She didn't need a confetti cannon or candlelight, this right here was a gritty, dirty, real-life sort of love. The kind that could withstand the ugly truth of fear and uncertainty and her hidden, secret self.

Somewhere, a television was tuned to *Jeopardy!* and Ken Jennings's voice created a quiet soundtrack as Sadie stared up at Felix. The air smelled faintly of cooked vegetables and urine, and Sadie had dark shadows beneath her eyes, and a rumble of indigestion. But it was the most extraordinary moment of her life, because she knew beyond a shadow of a doubt that she loved Felix, too. She felt like she always had.

"I love you," she said, and the words tasted as rich and decadent as dark chocolate.

Felix grinned. "I know."

After that, it felt easier to rap on Alice's door and then step into her single bedroom apartment. "Hey, Mom," Sadie called, her fingers twined through Felix's, but there was no answer from the old woman.

From the threshold, Sadie could see that Alice was not in her favorite spot: propped in an oversized chair near the window with a view of the carefully maintained grounds. It was getting dark, and Sadie and Felix were reflected in the pane of glass, a mismatched pair. He, tall and broad, black-haired and brown-eyed, with skin the color of sunbaked earth. She, small and slight and blond, with mossy eyes and creamy skin. Sadie loved the view, the vignette of the two of them framed by gauzy curtains, and she pressed herself into his side for just a moment.

But then there was a sound from the bedroom, and Sadie realized that Alice wasn't in the community dining room or somewhere else on the grounds like she initially thought. For some reason, this knowledge hit her with the force of a slap, and she squeezed Felix's hand tighter. For Alice to be in the bedroom and not propped in her favorite chair by the window was telling, a subtle but unalterable indication that her disease had progressed to another stage. Alice's primary physician had warned Sadie about this and tried to prepare her for the beginning of the end. A near total loss of language. The inability to perform even the most basic motor functions. Confinement to her bed. Had it happened already?

Sadie pulled away from Felix, hurrying across the sitting room to the half-closed door of Alice's bedroom. Pushing it open, she found a nurse in aubergine scrubs with her back turned as she fiddled with the bags on an IV cart. On the bed before her, Alice lay still and pale as a corpse.

Something in the air shifted, and the nurse spun around, drawing a tiny, wireless headphone from one ear while she did. "Oh!" she exclaimed, pocketing the device. "I'm so sorry. I didn't realize Alice was expecting visitors."

Sadie opened her mouth and closed it again.

"You must be Alice's daughter. I'm Remy, one of the hospice nurses."

Hospice? Sadie knew it was coming, but she hadn't realized the transition had already been made. She thought of the recent voicemails that she hadn't bothered to listen to. Apparently, they weren't just run-of-the-mill updates.

"Alice had a really good day today," Remy continued, then

directed her attention to where Alice lay curled in the bed. The old woman was so small she looked like a child beneath the pale-yellow blanket. Remy gently lifted one gnarled hand and patted it. "You had a good day, didn't you, Alice? Look, you have visitors. It's Sadie."

Of course Remy knew her name. And where she lived and how often she visited or called. It was part of the comprehensive care package at Valley Rest, and Sadie shriveled at the thought of this stranger knowing all about her negligence. She was a terrible daughter. Ungrateful and distant and cold. Sadie should never have moved to Newcastle when Alice was so obviously declining, in need of family nearby to care for her. She never should have tried to start a new life, make friends, fall in love.

Tentatively, Sadie took a step forward, and then when Remy made room for her beside the raised bedrail, another.

"I'm sure Alice would like some time alone with you," Remy told her. "Everything is fine. I just administered her meds and she's comfortable. I'll give you all some space."

Don't! The word was a quiet scream, a split second of terror that made a tremor billow through Sadie's body. But it was too late. Remy had already slipped past Felix with a soft smile and was out the door. In the sudden, deafening silence Sadie could hear the mechanical blip of the machine that Alice was hooked up to, and the irregular, wheezing breath of her dying mother.

When Felix came to stand beside her, Sadie felt herself stiffen against his embrace, assured of her own unworthiness in the face of his so recently professed love. But Felix only held her tighter.

"Hello," he said, reaching one hand down to Alice's, where it lay inert on the thin blanket. He covered her knobby fingers with the warmth of his wide palm. "I'm Felix Graham. It's so nice to meet you."

If Alice understood what he said or knew who was standing beside her, she made no indication. Her head was angled toward the window and her eyes were at half-mast, lids heavy and unblinking. Sadie couldn't tell if she was awake or not. But she was painfully aware of how much her mother had aged in the weeks between her last visit and now. Alice's fine hair had been brushed into a white cloud that floated ethereally around the pleats of her high forehead, and her gaunt face was etched in shadows. Her mouth moved, slowly, as if she was whispering something to herself.

"Alice?" Sadie tried, leaning over the bedrail. And then, when that didn't work, "Mom?"

Still nothing.

Sadie was gripped by a longing for a different life, a relationship with Alice that would allow her to lower the side of the bed and curl up beside her mother. But that reality was as distant as a world in which her father hadn't been T-boned in an intersection by a woman who had been texting and driving. She thought for a moment of that stranger and hated her with a blinding, viscous fury. One moment of distraction, and the trajectory of Sadie's life had hurtled off into space.

"Is there a world in which the accident never happened?" Sadie said it so quietly she wasn't sure that Felix had heard, but when he kissed the crown of her head, she knew he had. "I'm sorry. I wouldn't change a thing, but—"

"Hey," Felix stopped her. "I understand."

She knew he did. They were uniquely torn between what might have been and what could be, and just because Felix had already grieved the death of his parents and the loss of his sister didn't mean that he couldn't remember the ache of it. He hadn't told her much about his own broken past, but Sadie could feel the throb behind his words whenever David and Lucia came up. Or worse, Gabi. His sister was so precious a memory, Felix hardly spoke her name. It was as if she was a black hole, and he didn't dare to get too close for fear of being swallowed whole.

And here they were, together in a world that wouldn't exist if they weren't both the walking wounded. Sadie, trying to free herself from a sadness that had robbed her not just of a father and brother, but of everything else, too. And Felix putting distance between himself and the phantoms his father chased, the striving that led his mother to an early grave, and the abandonment of his only sister. He missed her so fiercely Sadie could see panic etch itself across his features whenever she came up in conversation. Gabi was a bridge too far, a holy relic that Felix treated with reverence and awe—and not a little fear.

Staring down at Alice, at the hollow shell of a woman that she had become, Sadie could see the end in sight for them both. A clean break, a new beginning, a way to leave it all behind and start over new. Felix was her tabula rasa, as fresh and filled with promise as a moonrise, and when Alice breathed her last breath, they could make a new world. One in which they loved each other, and whatever had come before didn't matter anymore. Sadie promised herself in that moment that she wouldn't press Felix for information, she wouldn't rake over old wounds trying to resurrect a part of him that had withered and died. And as she reached to wrap one hand lightly around her mother's brittle wrist, she knew that Felix would do the same for her. He was bearing witness to the slow dissolution of her childhood hopes and dreams, the final, bittersweet letting go.

They stayed until the stars came out and Remy returned to settle Alice down for the night. Though Sadie thought it was absurd to pretend that anything would change for her mother as a result of the bedtime routine. For the entirety of their visit, Alice remained impenetrable. Her breath erratic, her dry lips mouthing silent words. Sadie pretended that it was a monologue of all the things that her mother had never said. "Good job" and "I'm so proud of you" and "I love that you're mine." But in a way it didn't matter anymore.

Once, Alice turned her head on the pillow and seemed to raise her eyes to Sadie's face, but her cloudy gaze was as empty as a swirl of blue marble. "Goodbye," Sadie said then, and kissed one papery cheek in benediction. It was an act of grace. Of forgiveness.

Outside, the spring sky was clear and dark, pinpricked by stars.

"It looks like a fanous," Sadie said, gazing up. Her relationship with Felix had taught her to look to the sky, always, and the spectacle above them seemed like a gift after the sad hours they had endured.

"Fanous?" Felix wove his fingers through hers and tugged her away from the car toward a sloping hill, an apron of fresh-cut grass. Just enough room to lie down.

"An ancient Egyptian-style lamp. You know, the ones with the intricate patterns? The light punches through the tin like stars at night."

Felix hummed his approval and pulled Sadie down to the ground. They lay back together, Felix's arm beneath Sadie's head, and breathed deep in the darkness. The grass was still warm, the air just starting to cool. It felt fresh and welcome after the long hours in Alice's fusty, little room.

There were a dozen things Sadie wanted to say. Confessions and thank-yous and promises that she would spend the rest of her life trying to keep. But when she opened her mouth to speak, all the words spilled out and seeped into the ground.

"Tell me about the sky," Sadie said instead.

And though they didn't have a telescope or even binoculars,

Felix painted a picture of Messier 5 for her. It was "well placed," as in, it was in a good position for amateur viewing, and, according to Felix, a colorful and popular globular cluster for astronomy enthusiasts.

"Stars in globular clusters form in the same stellar nursery and grow old together," Felix said.

Sadie's heart echoed *grow old together*, but she just nestled her head deeper into the crook of his arm.

"Messier 5 is one of the oldest in the Milky Way. If you look there," Felix pointed toward the Serpens Caput, "you might be able to see what appears to be a faint-looking star."

"I think I see it."

"You don't," he said, but not unkindly. "At least, not really. And if you did, it's not a star—it's hundreds of thousands of stars, and they're billions of years old. If you could see Messier 5, it would blow your mind. The Hubble photos are . . . " At a loss for words, Felix trailed off and gave a low, awed whistle.

"Tell me," Sadie said. "Describe to me what it looks like."

"Okay," Felix drew out the word slowly, thoughtfully, then began. "An explosion of light. An entire jar of glitter upturned. Blue and yellow and white sparkles so densely crammed together you can hardly see the black between them."

Sadie sighed, and she could feel Felix tilt his head toward hers, press his cheek against her hair.

"It looks like a thousand Egyptian lanterns," he said. "All lit up at once. Like a celebration of love and light and life."

His words were enough. So vibrant and beautiful, Sadie felt tears trickle down her temples and drip into her hair. She closed her eyes and, studded like diamonds on the black veil of her eyelids, she swore she could see it all.

CHAPTER 10

WEDNESDAY

The house is quiet as I stand on the landing in near total darkness. It's past midnight and sleet is battering the windows, the wind howling through the forest, but behind Felix's childhood bedroom door, I can make out the sound of a soft, rhythmic snore. I just don't know if Henry snores or Finn. Finn is sick, but I hope it's Henry and that he's finally, blessedly asleep. I need a few hours when I'm not looking over my shoulder, worrying about him.

After fleeing from Felix's office, Henry fixated on bringing some firewood inside for the potbellied stove in the corner of the living room. I use the cast-iron monstrosity as nothing more than a good place to stack extra books, but Henry poked around inside, tested the flue, and eventually proclaimed it was in working order.

"We've never used it," I told him. "We've been here since late May and haven't so much as opened the firebox."

He leveled a haughty look at me. "You haven't needed to."

"Exactly," I said. "We don't need to because we have central heating."

"And what if the electricity goes out?"

His words slowly settled in my chest. Henry had a point. Like the landline, the electrical wires were aboveground on the mountain, marching through the trees like a string of hikers tethered together in a storm. They seemed fragile to me, unreliable, and I reluctantly pointed Henry in the direction of the shed and the pile of stacked wood covered with tarps nearby. The axe was stuck in the chopping block beside it. A part of me couldn't believe I was willingly offering Henry access to a weapon, but if the electricity really did go out, we would need that firewood. Once again, I found I had no choice but to trust him.

It was over an hour later that he stomped back into the mudroom, arms laden with dry, splintered wood. I helped him stack it beside the stove and moved my piles of books and a sad-looking houseplant to the coffee table in case we needed to start a fire. After that, there was really nothing for us to do. Finn languished on the couch, pale and coughing, his condition deteriorating as the night went on. I plied him with sips of cool water and tried to make him comfortable, but he shivered and seemed not to notice my ministrations, his little body throwing off heat like a radiator.

Henry kept watch from Felix's chair, and I curled up on the far end of the couch with Finn's feet in my lap. I hadn't expected the boy to treat me so familiarly, but when I eased myself into the corner, he instantly scooted down to press his feet against my thigh. I melted a little, even though it likely had nothing to do with me—Finn needed comfort in whatever form he could get it. So, I stayed put, staring at the same page in a dog-eared novel, while I chewed my fingernails to the quick and stole glances at Henry. Once, I caught him staring back at me and realized we were both surreptitiously analyzing each other.

Now, I pause outside the bedroom door and pray that Henry is out cold. The last thing I want to do is wake him up and be interrogated about why I'm creeping around after midnight like a burglar in my own home. Hemlock House is small, and it's not easy to move without alerting everyone present to exactly where you are and what you're doing.

I've stuck the brothers in Felix's old room for the night because it has a bunk bed and I want them as contained as possible. Besides, the door squeaks, and if either one of them leaves the room in the night, I'll know.

I'd like to tear apart Felix's bedroom, something that has never once occurred to me to do. When my husband closed the doors on the rooms we wouldn't use, I wasn't suspicious. Why would I be? We were temporary interlopers at Hemlock House—it wasn't our *home*. I burrowed into our shared spaces— our bedroom and bathroom, the entire main floor—and never gave the extra bedrooms or attic a second thought.

My avoidance isn't just disinterest; I have to admit now I'm also superstitious. Afraid of troubling the silence. The whole place feels eerily abandoned, deserted mid-sentence as if crowded with words that will never be spoken. Over two decades ago, the homestead was drained of all life in quick succession: first Felix (a full ride to Oregon State for applied physics), then Lucia (a brain aneurysm during Felix's first semester), next Gabi to places unknown (Felix was reticent to say anything at all about his enigmatic sister), and finally David (late-stage pancreatic cancer). And all that loss has left behind the faint stench of suppression, of a rough hand pressed tight against an open, crying mouth.

But what choice do I have? Maybe there are clues about my husband's whereabouts contained in the artifacts of his past.

Since the boys are sleeping in Felix's room, I start with Gabi's. My cell phone is charging in my room, so I use a small penlight that I keep in my nightstand drawer to illuminate the dark recesses of the unfamiliar space. I've only ever been in here once or twice before, and I don't know where the floorboards creak or where old nails have started to work their way out of the narrow planks. I step cautiously to the center of the room and pause, straining to hear movement from next door.

Nothing. I allow myself a shallow exhale, then turn my attention to Gabi's haven. The walls are painted white, just like the rest of the house, but there are peeling posters all over the walls. Nineties rock bands—Pearl Jam, Nirvana, Smashing Pumpkins—and a real stop sign propped in one corner that she must have stolen from a worksite. Her bed is roughly made, the sheet hanging lower than the comforter, everything clearly unwashed. My heartbeat stutters when I realize that her DNA is probably still all over the rumpled pillow.

This little glimpse into Gabi's teenage world feels almost voyeuristic. I don't know much about my husband's sister. Once, they were best friends. Now they're estranged. Gabi's living somewhere in Washington (last Felix knew). She had a baby shortly after David died. That's all I know. It's not much, and I regret not pressing Felix more. Maybe I should have made an issue of it, reminded him that Gabi and her child are our last living relatives and convinced him that we should try to repair whatever had been broken between them.

I'm grasping at straws. I know that. But I can't shake the memory of the look on Henry's face as he studied the picture of me and Felix in the office only hours ago. His expression was one of shock and horror. But also, something that looked a lot like relief.

What if Felix's disappearance has nothing to do with the Planetary Sciences Symposium and everything to do with the appearance of Henry and Finn? What if I've been looking everywhere but exactly where I should focus my attention? Right here. The idea is chrome-bright and blinding—I can't look at it straight on because if it's true, it means that I don't really know my husband at all.

Beyond the posters on the wall and the wrinkled bed, there's not much else in Gabi's room. She must have taken her personal effects with her when she left, and after I open the closet and find it empty, I know my hunch is right.

All the same, I pull out the spindly chair at a desk beneath the one window. There's only a sheer curtain over the thin glass pane, and I can feel the cold seeping in around the edges. I reach to push back the fabric and look out into the night, but everything is black and threatening, and I can't see beyond the streams of icy water that course down the glass. My own reflection is a colorless blur.

When a hulking shadow darkens the other side of the window, I nearly topple over backward. My grip on the curtain is the only thing that keeps me from crashing to the floor, and I quickly resettle my weight, slamming the chair legs in the process. The sharp smack is shocking in the silence, a gunshot of sound that kicks my heart into a gallop.

What did I see? The curtain is once again in place, rippling gently, and I blink hard a few times before standing up and forcing myself to pull it back again.

There's nothing there.

Of course not. What did I expect? A monster? A witch on a broomstick with sunken eyes and gnarled fingers pointed right at me? Maybe, I'm afraid of something much more ordinary: whoever or whatever Henry and Finn are running from. But I'm on the second story. The shadow I thought I saw was nothing more than a trick of the darkness and my overactive imagination.

I make myself sit back down and resume my search. I try

Gabi's desk drawers, but they're empty. Just a handful of old paperclips and the half nub of a worn-down pencil knocking around in the corners. I realize that I had hoped to find a journal or something juicy. Maybe one of David's composition notebooks that Gabi had claimed and doodled all over before confessing the darkest secrets of the Graham family. No such luck.

With a sigh, I click out my penlight and decide I should try to get some sleep. Wrapping my hands around the edge of the desk, I quietly ease back the chair so I can stand. But in the moment after I let go, my mind registers that something about the desk felt strange beneath my thumbs. Immediately, I begin to run my fingers over the wood, hoping for a secret drawer or hidden compartment that might contain some of the answers I'm desperate for. There's nothing of the sort. Still, something feels off about the underside of the desktop. When I brush my hands over the surface, it's rough and scored with ridges that shouldn't be there.

Standing, I carefully lift the chair away and flip the flashlight back on. Then I sit on the floor and shimmy beneath Gabi's small desk. Turning the light to the underside of the desktop, I illuminate the pockmarked surface. It takes me a few seconds to understand what I'm looking at, but when I trace my finger over some of the notches, I know: I've found an archeological site of Gabi's teenage obsessions. She has used a sharp object (a piece of wire? a pocketknife?) to carve words into the flat underbelly of her desk, and the etchings stretch from edge to edge across every square inch. In some places, she's filled the score marks with colored pen, casting them into sharp relief like 3-D graffiti.

My heart bottoms out, a sickening freefall.

Gabi hasn't traced song lyrics or curse words or doodles on

her desk. There's only one word repeated over and over and over again. An addiction, a compulsion, an incantation that I can hear her whispering in a round.

A conjuring.

Ben.

◆

Before I even open my eyes in the morning, I know two things. First, the rain turned to snow in the night. The air has that inexplicable snowy quality, cottony and muted, like I'm in a vacuum. And that's when I realize the second thing: the house, too, is eerily still. Not a single wisp of noise. Henry was right—the electricity is out.

I can feel it then, the encroaching cold. I'm bundled beneath a down comforter and wearing flannel pajamas, but my cheeks are frozen, my nose numb. Apparently, the temperature drops quickly in this poorly insulated house.

The clock says it's 6:56 a.m., and I'm grateful for the few hours of rest I managed, even though my heart and mind are still in knots. Henry and Finn . . . And *Ben.* Who on earth is Ben? I want to put my formidable research skills to good use. To fall down online rabbit holes in my search for more information about the enigmatic men suddenly thrust into my life. To tear apart the house, foraging for more clues about the boy whose name Gabi had once carved into the underside of her desk like the words to an evil hex.

And Felix. I roll to face his side of the bed. Sheets flat, pillow smooth. I feel his absence like a phantom limb, prickling and raw with pain I can do nothing to ease. My husband has been missing for sixty hours, give or take. Two and half days. It feels like an eternity.

There's a thump across the hallway, then footsteps and a

low, hushed voice murmuring in the uncanny quiet. Henry and Finn are up, probably half-frozen and confused about the bitter cold. We were like the proverbial frogs being slowly boiled all night long, except in reverse.

Focusing on the matter at hand, I throw back the covers and wince as my bare feet touch the freezing hardwood floor. I need thick socks, a heavy cardigan. I'd even take a stocking cap and mittens at this point, and I thrill a little at the thought of a hot cup of coffee. The range is gas, and I'm guessing that still works just fine. I can boil water and use the pour over. Thank goodness for small mercies.

Grabbing a pair of wool socks from my drawer, I swing open the bedroom door just as Henry does the same across the hall. His hair is matted down on one side and there are deep pillow creases in his cheek. Although he's taller and broader than me, he looks like a little boy, and my heart softens involuntarily at the sight.

"Good morning," I say, a wry, half smile lifting one corner of my mouth. "Did you sleep okay?"

"I was right," Henry snaps, ignoring me, and my goodwill toward him dissipates.

"Yes, you were. Good thing you split all that wood."

Finn appears behind him, peeking around Henry's bare arm. I realize with a start that they're both wearing nothing but T-shirts and thin pajama pants. Henry doesn't seem to notice the cold, but Finn is shivering visibly.

"You must be frozen solid," I say, and wave Finn over. "Let's find you some warmer clothes."

Finn slips between his brother and the doorframe, and hurries across the hall into my bedroom. I watch as Henry's face falls, but he rights his sour expression a moment later, and I'm left to wonder if he is hurt by Finn's easy trust of me or if I'm just imagining it.

"Come on," I say, stepping aside to make room for him, too. "My husband has a closet full of warm clothes. You can pick out whatever you'd like."

"I'm fine," Henry insists. He walks barefoot into the hallway and starts down the stairs. "I'll get a fire going."

I think he's crazy, and obnoxiously stubborn, but what am I supposed to do? Chase him with a pair of socks and try to wrestle them onto him? The thought makes a quick grin flit across my face and Finn smiles back at me, a mischievous glint in his eye. For just a moment, we feel like co-conspirators sharing a laugh at Henry's expense. But that's not a good move. I have no desire to come between the brothers or engender doubt and mistrust.

"Your brother is really tough," I tell Finn, as a whole-body tremor shakes me. "I can't imagine going downstairs without a sweatshirt or socks. I feel like an ice cube."

He nods vigorously, and I lead him over to the dresser where I find him a pair of knee-length, wool hiking socks plus a second pair for Henry. In the closet, he chooses one of my sweaters—a unisex charcoal-gray knit that he pulls right over the T-shirt and pajama pants he wore to bed—and I hand him one of Felix's Patagonia fleeces.

"For your brother," I say. "Can you take these down to him?"

Finn presses the clothes to his chest and turns to go, but when I lift my own jeans from the floor and feel a slight bulge, I stop him. "Wait," I say, remembering. I stick my hand inside the pocket of my pants. "I think this is yours."

I had gotten used to the weight of the worry stone and forgot about giving it to Finn yesterday. When he sees the smooth rock in my hand, his whole face lights up and he races across the space between us to snatch it out of my palm. It's beloved, then, even more significant than I'd imagined, and I'm grateful I'm able to return it to him.

Finn stares at the stone for a moment, then he looks up at me and makes the sign for "thank you" in American Sign Language. This one I know well, and I can even sign back "you're welcome." I expect him to leave then, but Finn doesn't turn to go. Instead, he stutter-steps back and forth as if trying to decide what to do. Suddenly, he lunges forward and throws his arms around my waist. His cheek is pressed against my chest, his curls tickling my chin, but before I can think of what to do, how to respond, he's gone.

I'm left trembling in the middle of my bedroom, and not because of the cold. For just a heartbeat, I can see the world as it might have been. Not just my extraordinary husband, this beautiful life we've built. A *family*.

By the time I join the boys downstairs, Henry has a fire roaring in the potbellied stove. The door is propped open, and the flames look dangerous, but the flue is indeed working and there is no smoke in the room. Just the pleasant scent of a cedar fire and a growing, dry warmth radiating out from the corner.

"Thank you," I say sincerely as I come to stand before the blaze. "I don't think I would have been able to do this on my own."

It's true. Now that we're here, a ragtag trio of unwitting survivalists, I can't imagine how I could've handled this situation alone. I picture barreling down the mountain in the Ranger by myself and pitching right over the side of the crevasse. Finn had alerted me to the landslide. Would I have seen it? A shudder ripples through me.

Henry doesn't acknowledge my gratitude, but says, "There's not much of it. The wood, I mean."

"Felix was going to order a cord from Timber Co., but . . ." I trail off, realizing that it doesn't matter what Felix was going to do. It's too late now. "How much?" I ask instead.

"A few bundles."

I stare at the hot belly of the stove. It looks like there's an entire bundle of wood inside it now. And it's burning fast, the edges of the split logs already blackening to ash.

The silence between us is thick with everything unsaid. I can tell that Henry and I are both trying to spare Finn the weight of our worry, but the fact that we only have a day or two worth of wood is concerning. As I watch, Henry steps over to the bay window in the living room and pulls back the curtains. Beyond the porch, the world is indeed flocked in white. It's just an inch or two, but the snow is coming down thick and relentless. If Felix were here, if we were huddled together before the fire with mugs of coffee in hand, it would be postcard perfect. We would read together and have long conversations and make love in the warm glow of the flickering flames as the world sank into sleep outside.

But it's hard to see any beauty in the snow this morning.

"Finn, how are you feeling?" I wave him over and press my palm to his forehead. He definitely still has a fever, but it's lower than last night. Moving my hand to his back, I hold my breath while he takes a few wheezy inhales. I can feel the rasp and rumble of air in his lungs. "Is he asthmatic?" I ask Henry.

The older boy looks confused. "I don't think so."

"Does he struggle to breathe sometimes? Like, does the air whistle in his lungs? Does he get winded easily?"

Henry's eyes go wide, and he gives me a tight, barely perceptible nod.

If Finn is asthmatic—and if he's had any previous lung infections, which I highly suspect he has—a simple cold or flu can escalate quickly. And be deadly. "We have to leave soon," I say, "before the snow gets much deeper."

Henry's eyes flash to mine, and I can see him making calculations, just like I am. Maybe trying to make it to the highway *isn't* the best idea. But if we don't go now, and the storm gets worse, who knows how long we'll be trapped up here? Finn's cough and persistent fever are concerning, and there are so many unknowns. What if the pipes freeze? What if the snow gets so deep it's days before travel is possible? What if we run out of firewood?

"It's got to be solid ice beneath the snow." Henry turns from the window, and I can see that his brows are drawn together, his expression serious. He agrees we have to go. "Do you have snow chains for the Ranger?"

"I think so? Honestly, I don't know. But you can check the shed."

Any warmth that has comforted me this morning, from Finn's unexpected hug to the fire smoldering merrily in the stove, fades away as the reality of our situation hits full force. Finding our way off the mountain in these conditions is going to be dangerous, but I don't think we have a choice. I wish for the hundredth time that I could just phone Cleo. The last time we texted, I told her that I was in work mode; will she try to get ahold of me anyway? And if she does and I don't respond, will she worry enough to send help?

I doubt it. Even back in the Midwest, the general consensus during storms of any kind is: hunker down. Cleo believes that I'm safe up here. I told her I had plenty of food and there's no reason to suspect that my situation has deteriorated—or that I'm worried about a sick child in my care. How long might the storm last? And how long will it take anyone to realize that I'm stuck up here once it's over?

I'm hit with a wave of loneliness so immense I have to swallow back a sob. I'd be furious with Felix for abandoning me if I didn't miss him so much. If I wasn't sick with worry about where he is and why. Even though I know it's ridiculous, I felt closer to him when the *possibility* of connecting was still on the table. At any moment he could have called, texted, or pulled down our driveway in his Jeep. But now, my husband may as well be on another planet. In another world. For just a moment, I remember Felix's description of the theory of inflationary cosmology and it's as if I'm stuck in a work of speculative fiction. Like I'm Meg Murry in *A Wrinkle in Time* and Felix is out in the universe somewhere, waiting for me to wise up and come rescue him.

But my current situation is much more temporal.

"Chains," I say absently, trying to ground myself. "Boots, coats, something hot in a carafe . . . "

"I'll go check the shed," Henry says. "Those boots by the back door . . . ?"

"They're yours. Take them. I hope they fit."

The next half hour is a blur of activity. Henry disappears to look for tire chains while I gather boots, gloves, and hats, and then grab the blankets from the dryer. Even bundled in multiple layers, I know we'll get cold in the Ranger, and I have no idea how long we'll be out in the snowstorm.

While I boil some water for instant oatmeal so we can have something warm in our bellies before we head off, Finn stands by the kitchen window and watches the snow blanket the trees. Without looking, I know he's staring at the path that he and Henry took through the blackberry brambles to the greenhouse. It feels like a lifetime ago when I first saw them on the video feed in Felix's office. And yet I still know next to nothing about them.

"What's out there?" I ask, not expecting a reply.

But Finn absently lifts one hand to the corner of his mouth. His fingers and thumb form a loose O, and when he brings the shape from his jaw to his cheekbone, I realize that he's making the sign for *home*.

"Maybe I should call you Mowgli," I say, but he doesn't respond. I don't know if he isn't familiar with *The Jungle Book*, or if he just doesn't feel like talking.

I mix up three bowls of brown sugar and cinnamon oatmeal and hand one to Finn. "Eat up," I tell him, forcing a smile.

"Sadie?" The sound of my name makes me whip my head around. There's something about the way Henry calls from the open mudroom door that puts me in mind of Felix, and my heart does a sad little flutter. Henry has never called me by my name before now. "Can I get a hand?"

"Back in a minute," I tell Finn, but he's still staring at the trees.

In the mudroom, I step into my boots and shrug on a winter parka. I've laid gloves out on the top of the washing machine and I grab a pair, assuming that Henry needs help with the chains I hope he found in the shed. But when I step out onto the porch, Henry is standing beside the door, leaning against the house and watching the snow fall. I can see that all four tires of the side-by-side are now—thankfully—encased in chains.

"Hey," I say, crossing my arms over my chest to ward off the cold. I haven't stopped shivering since I woke up. "Need a hand?"

"I have a question." Henry pushes off the house and comes to stand before me. Staring down at me he asks, "Where is your husband?"

His words land like a blow. "Excuse me?"

"Your husband. The guy in the picture. The guy whose boots I'm wearing." Henry lifts one foot and stomps it back down.

"I don't see how that's any of your business."

"Is he dead or something?"

I just gape. How dare he? After a moment or two of opening and closing my mouth, I manage, "He's at a conference."

"How long has he been gone?"

"That's not any of your business."

"I just want to know. When's he coming back?"

The hurt and anger that has been coiling behind my ribs strikes suddenly. "Where is your mom, Henry? Your dad? Where are the people who are supposed to be keeping *you* safe?"

He looks as if I've slapped him.

"I'm sorry," I say quickly, because tears have sprung to his eyes. They shimmer along his lashes until he swipes them away furiously with the heel of his hand.

"You're a real bitch," he spits, and then turns on his heel to head back out into the storm.

I watch as he trudges through the deepening snow toward the shed. I don't think there's anything left for him to do, nothing that needs to be fixed or prepared on the Ranger before we leave, but I don't blame him for needing a minute alone. He had no right to interrogate me about Felix, and no way of knowing the raw ache his questions would inflame. But I can admit that it was cruel of me to turn on him. I have to remind myself for the hundredth time that for all his bluster and bravado, Henry is just a kid.

And somehow it has become my responsibility to keep him and Finn safe. To get them off the mountain and into the hands of someone—*anyone*—who can untangle the tragedy of whatever happened to them. Clearly, I'm not up to the task.

CHAPTER 11

WEDNESDAY

My hips are slimmer than Henry's, so cramming into the passenger seat of the Ranger with Finn isn't too much of a chore. I put him in the middle, near his brother, and prop my back against the door. Then I drape blankets over us, tucking them in around Finn's legs and pulling them up to his chest. It's still cold, and the interior of the side-by-side is so drafty it smells almost overwhelmingly of exhaust as we idle in the falling snow. I want to ask Henry if something is wrong with the vehicle, but he's still not speaking to me. I'm sure the fumes will dissipate once we get moving.

The only things in the cab besides the three of us are a carafe of peppermint tea and the extra blankets—the only two items I could think of that might keep us warm. But the dump bed has a hard top, so we stored a few supplies in the back, too. There's a first aid kit, an extra jerry can of fuel, and some food and water. Henry insisted on filling any remaining space with wood. As he came around the shed with armload after armload of split cedar, I wanted to tell him that he was wasting his time. Because, let's be honest, if we need to build a fire on the mountain in this weather, we're done for. But I held my tongue and shut the tailgate myself when the last log was in place.

Now, as we drive away from Hemlock House, I can't help but look over my shoulder. From here—the south side of the property as Henry picks up the UTV track beside the small stable—everything looks ominous. The farmhouse seems dirty through the veil of the storm, and I realize a few of the black shutters are hanging crooked from rusty nails. The dark backdrop of the trees and clumps of overlong grass still peeking through the snow make the homestead appear downright Dickensian.

"I have some good memories of this place," Felix had told me when we first moved back. It was a warm, early summer day, and the air felt so fresh and clean it almost hurt to breathe it in. It was a welcome change from the stale, dusty interior of the house and the deep cleaning we had undertaken.

"Like what?" I asked, hooking one leg over his where we sat side-by-side on the bottom step of the porch. We were both in shorts and filthy T-shirts, and my hair was tucked beneath a knotted handkerchief.

"Days like this." Felix cupped my bare calf and absently rubbed the tender skin behind my knee with his thumb. "When we were kids, Gabi and I made a trail through the trees and built a hideout in the exposed roots of an old spruce."

"Still there?" I asked.

"Nah."

"What else?"

Felix smiled a little, his gaze unfocused as he remembered a life I knew nothing about. We were touching, he there and I here, but we were apart somehow. He said, "We played in the creek and used sticks as swords and ate blackberries until we got stomachaches. Once, we followed deer tracks so far into the forest we almost got lost, and the only thing that led us back was a tendril of smoke rising through the trees from the leaves my mom was burning in the barrel."

"Sounds dreamy." I sighed, glad to hear even a bit about his childhood. This place was a ghost town, but not every shadow was menacing.

Felix thought about my words for a moment. "I guess it was. We grew up free-range, you know? My mom would pack us a couple of sandwiches in the morning and send us on our way."

I bit the inside of my cheek at the thought of Alice doing anything like that for me. I was usually the one who took care of her. Who packed her lunches and took the hamper out of the closet in her bedroom to wash the clothes that she had left too long. I could still smell the sour-sweet tang of her work shirts. The distinctly Alice odor of her sweat.

"You and Gabi were close?" Felix rarely mentioned his sister by name, and I hoped my wistful tone was lost on him. I wanted to keep him talking.

He shrugged. "We used to be."

"That must've been nice."

"It was."

There was a tiny, secret smile on Felix's lips, and I felt an unwelcome squeeze of jealousy that there were things about his past I didn't know. I had no right to be greedy, to long for more information about his family of origin since I held my own sad stories close to my chest. But being at Hemlock House, in the place where some of his most significant and formative experiences took place, shifted things. I felt off-kilter, like I was grasping for purchase and suddenly Felix wasn't my steady ground. He was different here. Chaotic somehow. In a moment he could go from almost giddy with excitement to pensive and quiet. And when I tucked myself against him, asked what he was thinking, he was quick with a kiss and a canned response: "Nothing." Both seemed dismissive.

Because I was feeling vulnerable, maybe even just a bit fragile, I pressed him. "What happened between you and Gabi?"

It was the wrong question to ask. Felix's eyes glazed over and he untangled himself from the weight of my leg so he could stand. "She changed," he said simply. It wasn't much, but it was more than I expected him to share, and I tucked the nugget of insight away as he turned to go. "There's a shutter loose," he said, pointing to one of the upstairs windows and transforming once again into the dependable, levelheaded man of the house instead of the adventurous little boy he used to be. "I'm going to find a ladder and fix it."

But it's obvious now that he never did.

Hemlock House disappears from view as I point Henry to the barely visible, two-track trail that leads away from the homestead and we're swallowed up by the trees. Something about leaving under these conditions seems irrevocable, and I wish for a moment that I would've taken more things with me. My computer and some of Felix's files. Maybe David's two composition notebooks that I found hidden away. I can't help feeling like there must be clues about why Felix disappeared everywhere. Like I'm missing something very important. And now that we're gone, I don't know when I'll be back.

Finn is holding a battered atlas in his hands, folded so that our section of Washington State is exposed. Tapping the map to get his attention, I motion for it and Finn hands it over. Henry has marked a route of sorts on the thin paper, but the truth is the wilderness around us isn't even close to being accurately depicted. We have no idea where the elevation changes or how long it might take us to wend our way down. The highway is south, and, theoretically speaking, if we keep heading in that direction, we'll eventually hit it. From there, getting to Requiem will feel like a walk in the park. But there are no guarantees that we'll find our way.

We make slow progress, following a track that David Graham charted through the trees over thirty years ago. The twisting arteries of his personal wilderness highway system have faded over the decades, but his years of trekking back and forth have created a well-worn path through the trees that cannot be completely erased. Of course, there are new saplings that have sprung up, and the wild has encroached in irreversible ways, but the suggestion of a route seems discernible. Like we're following the lingering tone of an echo. And Felix has spent many hours since we moved here rediscovering them all, deepening the grooves that have filled in over time. I just don't know how far he got—or how far the winding routes go.

"How is it?" I ask after a while, directing my question at Henry.

"Fine." His response surprises me. I guess we're on speaking terms again. Or at the very least he's decided that we'll need to work as a team to get off the mountain.

"Good." I brace myself against the shallow dashboard as we do a slow-motion skid around a corner, narrowly skirting a boulder the size of a compact vehicle.

"It's slushy, but slippery, too," Henry mumbles.

If I didn't know better, I would think he was apologizing for the near collision, and I make a little grunt of agreement. The truth is, Henry's a fine driver. Capable and conscientious. Always looking around the next bend and taking it much slower than I thought he would. Against my better judgment, I relax just a tad and discover I'm grateful that he's behind the wheel and not me. This whole odyssey is far beyond my comfort zone.

We seem to be making decent progress, even if Henry has to pause every so often to check the compass and make sure that we're still heading south-southeast. We are, at least mostly, and whenever we hit a fork that splits the makeshift road in two, Henry always chooses the one that keeps us moving in the right direction. But the trajectory is not necessarily downhill, and before half an hour has passed, I'm hopelessly lost. I feel like Gretel in the Black Forest leaving breadcrumbs all along the way. And just like those useless crumbs, when I look over my shoulder, I can see that our tracks in the snow are quickly filling in. If we must retrace our steps, I pray Henry knows the way.

Finn is slumped against me, his head on my shoulder, and without thinking, I drop my cheek to his forehead. It's burning. I can't tell if his skin feels hot because I'm so bitterly cold or if his fever has spiked again. It's been so unpredictable, so up and down that I worry any progress he's made isn't really progress at all—medication and rest has merely masked the symptoms of an underlying raging infection. All the more reason for us to keep going.

When Henry pulls to a stop in a small clearing between a sentinel of trees after nearly an hour of progress, at first, I'm annoyed. "Something wrong?" I whisper, because I can tell by the rhythm of Finn's breath on my neck that he's asleep—or nearly.

But Henry doesn't say anything. Instead, he points.

I peer through the gray, trying to make out what he wants me to see. Here, protected beneath the canopy of trees, the snowfall seems less intense, but the swirling flakes still form streams and eddies that flow like water and sometimes obscure the windscreen completely. A gust of wind momentarily blinds me, but when the whiteout clears, I catch a glimpse of what Henry is pointing at.

Antlers. A perfect pair of ghostly antlers—seven points at least—strangely illuminated in the dusky glow of the Ranger's headlights. They're eye level and seem to be hovering in the tree directly in front of us. *Impossible.*

My heart judders. "What on earth . . . ?"

Henry is already getting out. His door slams before I can stop him, and the sound startles Finn.

"Shhh," I murmur, pulling the blanket up to his neck. "Close your eyes, Finn. Henry and I have to check something out a minute."

Finn makes an unintelligible noise and slumps his head against the back of the seat as I ease myself out from under him. Somehow, he's managed to half crawl into my lap, but extricating myself doesn't do much to rouse him. I slip out the passenger door and shut it gently behind me.

The moment my feet hit the ground I realize just how numb they are. I can hardly feel my toes, and the frozen earth beneath my boots only makes the ache worse. A surge of panic rises like bile in the back of my throat. What have we done? What are we doing out here? It seems obscenely irresponsible to have dragged Henry and Finn—a sick child!—into the very eye of the storm. I would swear the snow is falling heavier now than it was when we left.

"Sadie!" Henry's voice is whipped away by the wind, but it's enough to ground me back in reality. We're here now, and the only way out is through, so I hurry over to where he's standing in front of an enormous tree.

"I don't understand," I say, when I'm close enough to see that I was right—there are deer antlers suspended in the tree.

"They've been screwed into the trunk." Henry has to half shout over the howl of the wind. His eyes are wild, his expression pure horror.

The set of antlers is still attached to a hunk of scalp that has been cut clean off what I can only presume was a hunting kill, the fur matted and macabre. My stomach flips, thinking about the knife that split the buck's skull. The axe? Whatever it was, it was sharp. Fatal.

"Look." Henry pulls off a glove to expose one hand and scrapes at the bone with his fingernail. Bits of yellowish-green flakes peel off.

"Moss?" I ask.

He shakes his head, a jerky, frantic movement. "Paint."

I rub my mitten against a point, and more of the sticky material strips off. There's something about it that doesn't seem quite right. The sickly-green gleam, the unusually thick consistency. "It's glow-in-the-dark," I say suddenly, raising my voice so I can be heard over the wail of the wind.

Henry shoots me a sharp look. "I know."

How? I wonder, but I don't ask. Henry feels locked and loaded, his body pulsing with a furious revulsion. Yes, the thought of coming across the faint, spectral shine of these remains in the middle of nowhere gives me the creeps, but Henry's reaction feels extreme.

Who would do this? And why? But I find I already know the answer to at least one of the questions. Or I think I do. David. If Felix's stories are to be believed, this is exactly the sort of thing that his father would have done. Stripped a kill of its antlers and then hung them in the tree as some sort of warning. An omen, perhaps, to keep trespassers away—or to lure spirits in. I shudder.

"Let's go," I say, tugging at Henry's coat sleeve.

But he's no longer paying attention to me or the tableau before us. Instead, he's turning a slow circle, staring off into the endless procession of trees that surround us. I feel utterly disoriented for a moment, lost in this wilderness that has transformed into a labyrinth. I don't know which way we came from or where we're going, and I have to repress the urge to take Henry by the arm, just so I have something to hang on to.

When he steps away, I stumble after him, and it's only when

I raise my eyes to follow his gaze that I see it: another pair of antlers. This set is higher in the tree before us, and bigger. The scalp has a loose, jagged edge, a flap of moth-eaten, desiccated flesh that flutters in the relentless wind. My breath comes high and quick as my gaze darts around and I realize that there are antlers hung from *every* tree.

Dozens of them, all shapes and sizes, screwed into the bark at monstrous, leering angles. We're standing in a graveyard. A summoning circle.

"Let's go!" This time it's Henry who shouts it, and he throws one arm roughly around my waist to yank me back to the Ranger. Thick snow has settled on the passenger door in the few minutes that we've been in the clearing, and I frantically brush it away to find the sunken handle. My gloved fingers are stiff and ineffectual, but I finally gain purchase and rip it open. I can't stand to be in this evil place for another second, and Henry must feel the same because he punches the gas before my door is even fully closed.

In the cab, I shush Finn and pull him against me, wrapping both my arms around his slight frame. He doesn't even seem to realize that we were gone, and sinks into me, his hot head tucked beneath my chin as I tremble against him.

"What was that?" I ask, my voice sounding ragged and thin.

Henry ignores my question. "It's sick."

I agree. If David did that, he wasn't just unique, he was disturbed. There was something wicked about that place, an oily menace that feels as if it seeped into my pores and now lingers odor-like in the close air of the cab. I want to take a scalding shower and wash the residue of it from my skin. I wish I could scrub my soul. I'm grateful that Finn didn't witness it, and I hold him a little tighter, unconcerned about how Henry will react.

"Where are we going?" As the dread begins to fade, I realize that something feels off about our direction.

"Back."

"Henry!" The disappointment is almost overwhelming. Scared or not, we have to keep going. "Turn around," I tell him. "Finn's fever is climbing again, and this snow isn't letting up."

"Exactly," he says, gesturing to the path between the trees. It's barely discernible now, so snow-covered that I hadn't even realized we were retracing our steps. I look at the stern set of Henry's profile, and he must feel my gaze because he says: "If we don't go back now, we might not be able to."

He's right, but that doesn't stop the tears that spring to my eyes. I feel so hopeless. Like I'm tied to the tracks and a train is barreling down the line. I wish we would have never come across the antlers—we would've kept going.

And gotten stuck in a blizzard.

All at once I can picture it: the three of us stranded out here as the snow continues to ravage the mountain. It's our bones I see, picked clean and bleached white come spring. An improbable tangle of limbs and stories that will never be told. I know we have to return, but Hemlock House doesn't just feel haunted anymore, it feels like a tomb. And we're going back to inter ourselves.

Every fiber of my being cries out for my husband. If only he were here. If only he had come home on Sunday like he was supposed to.

If only he had never left at all.

✦

Henry stops more frequently on the way back and carefully examines the compass I've given him. He turns it this way and that, and a few times he even steps out of the side-by-side to examine the trail and squint off into the trees. There's not much to see, and once, when an almighty gust tosses a powder keg of snow, he disappears completely. For just a moment, Finn and I are left behind. Trapped in a white, icy grave. Seconds later, when the dark silhouette of Henry reappears, I feel a surge of affection for him so strong it stings.

As he climbs back into the Ranger, his movements labored and heavy, I know we're lost.

"How long?" I ask.

"Since we left the trail?"

I nod, and even though Henry doesn't look at me, he must sense the movement. He says, "Only fifteen minutes or so. I think."

Pressing Finn's head to my chest, I swivel around trying to see where we came from and how we might retrace our steps.

"We can't go back." Henry puffs a frustrated breath. "And we can't just head north—the homestead is a much smaller target than a highway."

I think of the long stretch of road we were aiming for and then the little cluster of buildings that comprise Hemlock House. It's just a tiny speck somewhere in the wilderness. Our chances of finding it without the benefit of David's old trail system are beyond slim.

Panic thrums beneath my skin, a furious drumbeat that for the first time in hours makes me feel hot. I got Henry and Finn into this mess. It's my job to get them out.

"Stay put," I say, twisting out from underneath Finn.

"Where are you going?"

"We can't be too far from the homestead. There must be a whole grid of trails nearby, and I know from riding a few of them with Felix that there are markings all along the way." Not many, and David didn't bother with reflective metal trail signs like he probably should have, but I've seen lengths of pale orange fabric tied on low-hanging branches at intersections or after a particularly long, uninterrupted stretch. Just a little token of civilization in the midst of this great unknown. "If I find one, we can get back on track."

"So, we'll drive slow and look for them," Henry says, a note of desperation in his voice. "You can't go running around out there."

"You worried about me?"

Henry glares at me, which was exactly what I wanted. Better for him to feel incensed than defeated.

"You know we'll never be able to see a ribbon from here," I say, wrenching open the door before he can argue further. "It's the only way."

Finn looks straight at me as I ease the door shut, his eyes clear for just a moment. He doesn't look scared, he looks trusting, as if he knows that even though we're trapped in a precarious situation, I'll keep him safe. It feels misplaced.

Outside of the protection of the cab, the wind howls like a banshee and whips snow in my face. Within seconds, my damp eyelashes are crusted in ice particles and my lips feel dry and cracked. I wish for a balaclava, a pair of snow goggles. But I comfort myself with thoughts of the fire that Henry let smolder in the inviolable cast-iron stove, and trudge forward through the deepening snow. Henry has no choice but to follow in the Ranger at a snail's pace several feet behind me.

At first, I stumble from tree to tree, steadying myself against the thick trunks and searching for any evidence of human interference—one of the tattered ribbons, a nail, anything that might be a clue that we're headed in the right direction. But when several minutes pass and I see nothing of the sort, I realize that this may be a doomed endeavor. Instead of focusing so narrowly on the individual trees, I start to scan the area, hoping for a glimpse of something—*anything*—that stands out against the unrelenting sea of white around me.

When a splash of red appears in the distance, I blink and then blink again, sure that my eyes are playing tricks on me. The world has become unyieldingly monochrome, and the interruption materializes like an oasis in the desert. A mirage, nothing more. But in moments when the snow parts like a veil, the color remains, a stain that only seems to intensify the more I stare at it.

Something breaks inside of me, a splintering that began when I first looked at the clock several nights ago and wondered why Felix wasn't home from the airport yet. I remember the morning he left, his freshly shaven face, the weight in his eyes that suddenly seems like a crucial detail I missed. He was burdened the morning he left, preoccupied with something.

He was wearing his favorite red sweater.

I'm running before I have time to stop and think about what I'm doing. My whole body is pulsing with one thought: *Felix*. My husband, here all along. An apparition in a red sweater beneath a universe of falling snow.

It isn't until I've nearly stumbled over the specter that I understand I've made a terrible mistake.

Yes, there is crimson amid the snow. A vibrant spill of it, as bright and garish as a sacrifice. But it's not Felix's sweater, or anything that might offer me comfort or hope. Instead, a carcass is split open on the ground.

Fur and hooves, a rib cage fanned open like a fragile, broken instrument. Snow wreaths the limbs but melts in the still-warm cavity that gapes open, stinking and ripe. It's nearly empty, the tender organs devoured, the tough hide left for scavengers.

He grabs me from behind, and my scream is swallowed

by the wind. But Henry is undeterred as he drags me backward, away from the carnage. "Come on!" he shouts, twisting me around and jerking me in the direction of the Ranger. At least, I think that's where we're headed; I can't see it anymore. And then he's taking me by the wrist and we're running as best we can. Tripping and stumbling and holding each other up until the black shape of the UTV looms directly ahead and the kill is left behind for burial by snowstorm. We only stop when we can fling ourselves at the icy, unyielding side of the Ranger. I'm leaning against it, catching my breath when Henry whirls on me.

"What were you thinking?" he growls, biting off each word with such fury it would frighten me if I wasn't so numb.

I can't respond. Words seem just out of reach, a luxury I can't afford when everything inside of me just wants to give up.

Henry must realize I'm in no shape to fight—that we're all clinging on by a very thin thread—because as quickly as his anger flares, it fades. He drags one gloved hand across his face and sighs. "You shouldn't have done that. We have to stick together. We could've . . ."

He trails off, but there are a half dozen ways to finish that grim sentence. We could've gotten separated from each other. Or lost. If Henry and I didn't find our way back to the Ranger, what would have happened to Finn? For a moment I feel like I'm going to throw up, but I swallow down the bile in my throat. Henry is right, I shouldn't have run off. It was selfish and stupid.

"I'm sorry," I say. "I thought I saw something." *Felix*. I thought for just a moment that my husband was closer than I could have ever imagined. And I'd be lying if I didn't say that the residue of his presence still clings to me now.

I feel him.

But maybe that's just a cocktail of hypothermia and longing.

Or trauma from the gruesome tableau laid out like an offering on the forest floor.

Henry doesn't accept my apology, but he does offer an explanation. "The work of wolves," he tells me simply. "There aren't many, but they're here. Sometimes they take what they want and leave the rest for scavengers."

Somehow, this makes me feel marginally better. The natural way of things is a much more palatable explanation than poachers—or something even darker. My mind is playing tricks on me out here, and I wish, not for the first time, that we had never left Hemlock House.

"Let's get out of here," Henry says, shielding his face from a gust of wind that whirls a funnel of snow at his head. "I found a trail marker."

It's just enough hope to keep me going.

CHAPTER 12

WEDNESDAY

It takes us nearly two hours, but we somehow manage to find our way back. We lose the trail again and again, only to catch a glimpse of orange through the blizzard, as if something (someone?) is leading us through. With Henry setting a course for north-northeast, we crisscross our way through the forest and eventually stumble upon a landmark I recognize.

"Go left!" I blurt, reaching across Finn to grab Henry's arm.

"But the path leads—"

"Trust me. Those boulders point the way to the creek, and if we take a left here, we'll emerge between the stable and the greenhouse. It's not far—maybe a quarter mile?"

Henry glances over at me, wavering, but he must see the certainty in my eyes because he does as I ask. Several minutes later the leaning stable of the homestead appears between the snarl of trees like a vision. Henry catches my eye over Finn's head, and something powerful passes between us. Relief and gratitude after the stress of the last few hours, but it's more than that. We're connected now, bonded by this crazy ordeal and the knowledge that we could have died out on the mountain. I find I'm proud of us. Proud of Henry.

"You're going to have to carry him," I say when Henry has parked and shut off the Ranger. Finn is fully slumped against me, and his hot head pressed against my neck is damp with sweat. Now that we're safe—or at least in a place where we can get warm—a new kind of fear slinks in. We survived our ill-advised attempt to off-road our way to Requiem, but our situation is still perilous, to say the least. And I'm so worried about Finn my chest aches.

Inside, protected from the wind and driving snow, it feels like a sauna. Henry and I kick off our ice-crusted boots and make a beeline for the living room. It's warmer in here, the heat of this morning's fire still radiating from the black belly of the cast-iron stove, and goose bumps race across my skin. Thawing will be painful, and I already know that my fingers and toes will burn as they come back to life.

But none of that matters now. Henry lays Finn down on the couch and goes to stoke the fire while I get the boy settled. We agree to this wordlessly, our actions quick and decisive, intended to be as efficient and productive as possible. We instinctively know what to do, and while Henry throws more logs on the still-smoldering coals, I help Finn out of his damp coat.

"Hey, Finn," I say quietly, sliding down the coat zipper and then easing his arms out one by one. Finn's eyes flutter, but he doesn't respond. His limbs are limp and toneless, his wrists catching awkwardly in the sleeves of the heavy parka. I feel like I'm undressing a baby, and I have to repress the urge to kiss his pale forehead.

Behind me, Henry pokes at the fire and determinedly ignores my ministrations. He's worried about Finn. It's evident in the tight set of his shoulders, his quick, shallow breath. I want to assure him that everything is going to be just fine, but the words taste like dust on my tongue. Instead of offering insincere assurances, I say true things as I peel off Finn's hat and gloves and settle the blankets over him.

"We made it back to Hemlock House," I tell him. "Henry's

getting a fire going and we'll be nice and toasty in no time. If we run out of wood, we'll burn the coffee table. And the kitchen chairs and the boxes in the cellar!" I force a laugh, and it sounds manic even to my own ears. Finn stirs a little, his fingertips twitching. I don't think he's unconscious, just drifting in and out, sleepy and sick and probably in desperate need of IV fluids and some hard-hitting antibiotics. Neither of which I can offer him.

"We'll get you some medicine," I continue, thinking about what I can do. "And food and water. You'll feel better soon."

That last part seems like a bit of a white lie. Finn has definitely taken a turn for the worse. He's pale and wheezy, and his cheeks are clammy against the back of my hand. When he breathes, the fine tendons in his neck stretch taut as violin strings. I know we've just clawed our way to shelter, but a part of me is already eager to try again. Finn needs help.

"We need some extra pillows," I tell Henry. "Something to prop him up a bit. And it's time to try an expectorant. Does Finn have any known allergies to medications?"

"What? What do you mean?" Henry turns from the fire, his expression at once anxious and defensive. After the heroics of his masterful navigation through the woods, he looks impossibly young and frightened. I get it. The fear of a blizzard can't hold a candle to the dread that looking at Finn stirs up. And Henry doesn't want to admit that he has no idea what an expectorant is. Or maybe even a medical allergy. It's a big ask.

I give him a soft smile. "I just need to know if he has ever taken medication and had a bad reaction. A rash, trouble breathing, anything out of the ordinary."

"I don't know. I don't think so."

"Okay. With your permission, I would like to give Finn some

cough syrup. It will help loosen up the mucus in his lungs. I'm afraid he's having a hard time breathing."

Henry wavers, but after a few seconds he stands a little straighter and says, "Let's try it."

"Good. I'll get the medicine. Would you grab some pillows from upstairs?"

I think we're both grateful to have a specific way to help Finn, because Henry all but bounds from the room. In the kitchen, I find the ibuprofen and cough syrup and fill a glass with orange juice from the nearly empty jug in the fridge. Even though the electricity has been out for hours, the interior of the refrigerator is still cold. I cast a glance at the freezer, knowing I should probably empty it before everything starts to melt. But that's a problem for later.

Back in the living room, I wrap my arms around Finn and lift his torso so that Henry can slide a pair of pillows beneath him. "He'll be able to breathe easier if he's not lying flat on his back," I tell Henry. Then I hand him the small cup of purple cough syrup. "Finn will take it better from you."

I perch on the edge of the coffee table and watch as Henry sits beside his brother and touches his face.

"Finn," he says, his voice uncharacteristically gentle. "Finny-Boy, Finnigan Begin-Again, Finn Thomas . . . Come on, Finn. Wake up."

Whether it's the sound of his brother's voice or the brush of his calloused finger along his cheek, Finn does as he's told.

"Oh, hey." Henry smiles. "There you are. Hi, bud."

My heart pinches at the way Finn's face lights up at the sight of his brother. For just a moment his rich golden-brown eyes sparkle, and then they drift closed again.

"Stay with me, Finn." Henry lightly taps his brother's cheek with his fingers. "You gotta take this stuff. It'll make you feel better."

"It tastes gross," I tell him. "But there's some juice here to chase it."

"Aw, man." Henry sniffs it and pulls a face. "It's disgusting. You can't take it, Finn. It'll make you throw up. Projectile vomit all over the place—all over *me*. And that's a no-go. I've changed my mind. No medicine."

The corner of Finn's mouth quirks as he struggles to open his eyes and keep them open. Henry is gagging now, smelling the cough syrup and then pulling exaggerated faces that elicit a breathy little half laugh from Finn. I'm elated—until the laugh ends in a coughing fit.

I lean forward to prop Finn up even more, lifting his head so that the weight of gravity on his own chest doesn't make matters worse. With my hand on his back as he rasps and hacks, I can feel the deep, unsettling rumble of his lungs. It's terrifying.

When the fit passes, Finn has been roused enough to swallow the cough medicine, a couple ibuprofen, and a few sips of orange juice. I keep encouraging Henry to tip just a bit more juice into his brother's mouth, because I'm not sure when we'll get another chance to hydrate Finn, but the boy slumps back after barely an inch is gone. I try to reassure myself it's better than nothing.

Henry hands me the glass as he pulls the blankets back up over Finn. Then he glances at me, and I find myself raising one hand for a high five. It's a bizarre, instinctual move—a remnant from my middle school teaching days, no doubt—and for a second, I'm mortified. But then Henry's mouth pulls into a tight line that could be interpreted as a smile, and he gives my hand a soft slap. I can't stop the grin that blooms. True, our situation couldn't possibly get much worse, but we survived the storm and managed to dose Finn.

I'll take whatever wins I can get.

◆

When I was a little girl, I attended the church in our Milwaukee neighborhood. My mother had once been a devout Lutheran, but after my dad and brother died, she said God had abandoned her. I wasn't old enough to know anything at all about religion, but when our next-door neighbors offered to take me off her hands on Sunday mornings, she gratefully accepted—any beef she had with the Almighty did not extend to me.

I loved church. It was a small, nondenominational Bible church with red Kool-Aid and watery coffee on a table near the entrance, and a Sunday school teacher who smelled of roses. She used to draw me close when she read the Bible story, letting me look at the pictures before she turned the book around for the rest of the circle to see. Looking back, I realize that she must have felt sorry for me, a pint-size charity case with unbrushed hair.

One day, after she read the story of Jonah and the Whale, she asked what we had learned from Jonah's adventures. The rest of the kids, who had been born and raised in church, gave answers straight from the textbook. Jonah learned about the importance of obedience, trust, faithfulness. But I was stuck on the final scene when Jonah went out of Nineveh and threw himself a pity party.

"God gave him a nap and a snack," I said, almost without thinking.

There was a sort of stunned silence for a moment. And then that sweet Sunday school teacher hugged me close. "Aren't you clever?" She laughed, but it was a happy, delighted sound, not mocking as I feared it would be. "Sometimes a little nap and a snack fix everything."

It's the only lesson that really stuck with me, and a philosophy I still cling to today—a biblical mandate for the not-so-surprising benefits of sleep and food. And after Finn is settled and safe, I gather the necessary elements for myself and Henry: the down comforters from our beds upstairs, more pillows. In the kitchen I find some cheddar cheese and multigrain crackers, then grab the rest of the orange juice, the last apple, and a jar of crunchy peanut butter.

Henry and I eat on the floor in front of the stove, voraciously. Apparently, a dangerous experience gives you an appetite, because we polish off the cheese and crackers in no time, then cut up the apple and slather the wedges in peanut butter. When the apple is gone, we take turns using the sides of our thumbs to scoop even more peanut butter straight off the knife and eat it plain. I feel full for the first time in days.

By the time we're done with our makeshift picnic, we're more or less comfortable, and unbearably exhausted. Henry keeps trying to swallow his yawns, but it's no use, and after I assure him that some rest would do us all good, he rolls over and falls asleep almost instantly.

I'm weary down to my bones, but though I try to close my eyes and let the crackle of the fire soothe me, I can't drift off. Maybe it's because I feel responsible for Henry and Finn. Or guilty about trying to off-road in a blizzard. My mind is stuck in overdrive, revving between thoughts of Felix and these mysterious brothers and all the secrets that seem to hide behind every corner in Hemlock House. It's an elaborate puzzle, and I simply can't stand back far enough to get some perspective.

Finn Thomas. Henry had broken out several nicknames, trying to wake Finn, but that one felt real. Is Thomas his middle name?

Last name? I wish I could type in a few internet searches while the boys sleep, and I slide my phone out of my back pocket to try. It's little more than a hope and a prayer, and when I find that I still have no reception, I'm not surprised. Just disappointed.

Since I can't sleep and it seems the brothers are both out cold, I quietly sneak out from beneath my duvet and tiptoe across the living room floor. I don't want to wake them, but right now feels like the perfect chance to snoop through Felix's childhood bedroom.

Upstairs it's much colder. The window on the landing is starting to crust over with hoarfrost, a rime of ice particles that fan across the glass in exquisite, perfectly symmetrical patterns. How is it possible that just a few days ago I was working outside with my sleeves rolled up? I feel like I've stepped through the wardrobe in more ways than one. As I'm watching, a gust of wind blasts against the window and the whole house moans. It's a reminder of how small I am. How fragile.

Felix's old bedroom feels more compact than Gabi's. Darker. There's a bunk bed pushed against one wall and a low cabinet along the other. No desk or sitting area—there simply isn't room for it—but beneath the dormer is a quaint, built-in window seat with room for one. I turn a slow circle in the center of the room, then sink to the flat, wooden bench and wrap my arms around myself to ward off the cold.

I can picture Felix here as a boy. I've seen a few pictures. Long limbs, shaggy hair, that one perfect dimple. It was more pronounced when his cheeks were rounded with youth. Even at a young age, there was a wise glint in his eye, a sparkle that somehow belied both his intelligence and that curious, intoxicating spark that still makes him irresistible. I wish I could have known him when he was just a kid. I think I would have loved him even then. Maybe *especially* then.

"Felix, Felix," I whisper. I'm hoping, maybe, that I can summon him. My voice a signal through time and space that will alert him to the fact that I need him. Now and always. But the room remains still and empty.

So, I push myself up and open every drawer in the cabinet. It doesn't take me long to realize that Felix's childhood space is very different from Gabi's. The drawers aren't empty, but half-full of dusty old items left behind and forgotten. Grayish socks balled together, a few pairs of boxers, T-shirts worn thin and in a size that would never fit Felix today. I can almost picture him getting ready for college, packing his favorite things and leaving the rest behind. He didn't know that when he left for Oregon State, he would never live at home again.

I rifle through everything like a cop with a search warrant, unconcerned about making a mess. In the closet I find some worn-out tennis shoes, an old pack of gum, and a cheap, empty wallet, but nothing that might tell me more about my husband, his family, or Hemlock House.

Why didn't Felix want me in here?

I can't quite bring myself to go back downstairs, even though I'm starting to shiver and my fingers feel numb. Blowing into my cupped hands, I pace the floor, squinting in the dim, ashy light that filters in through the window.

And that's when it hits me. Spinning toward the chest of drawers, I yank the top one open. Socks, underwear, T-shirts. When I search the second drawer, I find more of the same, but the brands and styles are different. I grab a T-shirt from each drawer and find the tag, confirming that they're different sizes, too. It's as if two people lived in this room. Not one.

Looking with fresh eyes, I can see that there's two of everything. The closet is loosely divided in half and the shoes on the floor are elevens (Felix's size) and nines. There are even two beds. Why did Felix need a bunk bed?

Henry and Finn slept here last night and the beds are unmade, the sheets wrinkled and bunched. Because we pulled the duvets off to keep ourselves warm in the power outage, it's easy for me to strip the bedding and search every inch for something that might offer a scrap of information about why it appears that Felix shared his room. My husband doesn't have a brother.

I've almost given up when I feel something on the inside edge of the top bunk. There's a gap between the mattress and the two-by-four that runs the length of the bed, and pressed into the wood are a handful of round-headed brass tacks. The thin crevice is the perfect place to hide secret things or maybe stash photos that Felix didn't want his mother to see. But only one tack is holding something in place.

A flush of excitement warms my cheeks as I slide the metal from the wood. The paper it's pinning in place feels thick and brittle, and I move slowly, not wanting to damage it in any way.

When the paper is loose, I hop down from the bunk bed and hurry over to the window seat where pallid daylight casts an eerie glow. I'm holding a photograph. A faded square with frayed edges that has obviously been well-loved. Someone looked at this picture often, his or her fingers tracing the corners and maybe smoothing the faces of the people who had once grinned for the camera. Two people stand in the frame, a boy with a mop of sandy-blond hair that falls nearly to his collar, and a girl with a long, dark braid. The girl is Gabi. Maybe sixteen or seventeen years old, her limbs lean and tanned, her eyes glinting at whoever was taking the photo. She's wearing a pair of cut-off jean shorts over a red, one-piece swimming suit that, while modest, does nothing to hide her curves. Gabi looks gorgeous, and it's no surprise that the boy with his arm around her waist is staring at her instead of the camera. His feelings are splayed across his face, plain as a billboard: love and lust and longing. It almost hurts to look at him.

It's a sweet photograph, a snapshot that could have been taken at any beach along the Washington coast. The water is the color of slate, the sky a mix of sun and high, white clouds, a breeze scattering the loose hairs around Gabi's face. They both look happy. At ease with each other. Who's the boy?

He's attractive, in a way. A bit too thin, maybe, his jawline chiseled and just this side of gaunt. But there's something confident about his hand at Gabi's waist, the slight pressure of it that scoops her hip toward his. "Mine," he seems to say, his body language possessive, his head tilted as if he would like to press his lips to the high arch of her pretty forehead. For some reason, it fills me with dismay.

And that's when I realize there's another arm around Gabi—a hand reaching from her other side. One-third of the photograph has been folded over, a crease so clean and neat I hadn't even noticed it. But when I peel the flap back to its original position, the picture is complete. Gabi in the middle with the blond boy on her right and Felix on her left.

The sight of Felix on the cusp of manhood (eighteen? nineteen?) is enough to undo me. A bad haircut, a bare, skinny chest. His collarbones jut out, and he's awkward, unsmiling, his mouth half-open as if he is about to say something to the photographer.

The only person smiling is Gabi.

The photograph is a case study, a complicated story played out in the postures and facial expressions of the three subjects. Gabi, happy and oblivious. The blond boy, drawing her to him. And Felix, wishing it all away.

I'm glad to have found the picture, but it's useless without context, a story. It doesn't help me understand why Felix—

gently but unswervingly—closed off rooms in Hemlock House. It doesn't explain why Cleo called him flighty and seemed unconcerned about his disappearance. And it doesn't offer one meaningful insight into where my husband might be now. And how Henry and Finn fit into it all. Because I'm becoming more and more convinced that they do.

I gently fold the photo again, tucking Felix against the back so that he is alone, facing away. I want to show it to him, ask him a dozen questions about what his life was like when there were no lines around his eyes and his hair wasn't threaded through with gray. He suddenly feels like a stranger to me, and I hate it. I want to know him—every part.

I slide the photograph into my back pocket and then think better of it. Stepping onto the bottom bunk, I replace the photo where I found it, being sure to locate the old hole in the paper with the tack so that I don't mar their beautiful faces. It feels like the picture belongs here, in this dark and secret space. Tucked away for decades now, as if whoever put it there had something to hide. And maybe I don't want to know about it after all.

BEFORE

WEDNESDAY, AUGUST 13

WANING GIBBOUS MOON / PERSEIDS METEOR SHOWER / MOON AT PERIGEE

August was long and hot, so humid that Sadie discovered she was actually a curly girl. Alice had passed away in early June—only a couple of weeks after Sadie and Felix visited—and following the small funeral and the settling of Alice's estate, Sadie found that she didn't much care about things that had once seemed so important to her. She let her hair go natural, lived in running shorts and old T-shirts, and nearly stopped wearing makeup altogether. Because she didn't even have the bandwidth to care about how Felix felt about her sudden transformation, she was surprised when he commented on it one day.

"I love it," he said, wrapping the heft of her unruly waves around one of his fists. He tugged her head back gently and kissed the warm skin of her exposed neck.

"My hair?" Sadie gripped his shoulders as he tipped her even farther.

"The hair, your bare skin, all of it."

Pushing Felix away, Sadie sank into one of the wicker chairs in her postcard-size backyard and stretched out her arms to study them. They were tanned from long morning walks in the hot, Iowa sun and afternoons spent in this exact spot, writing lesson plans on the cheap outdoor table Felix had picked up on clearance from Walmart. But her limbs were also dotted with freckles and sunspots, the skin of a middle-aged woman. It surprised her. In her heart she was forever young: a little girl wishing her mother would bring her close, a teenager longing to be pretty, a woman coming into her own in a world that assured her she wasn't quite right. And here she was, past forty, and just beginning to figure herself out. For a moment, Sadie wished she could rewind the clock and do it all over again. Live her twenties and thirties knowing what she knew now. But then Felix winked at her before turning to lift the lid of the charcoal grill, and her life in this moment—her job, the manuscript she was working on, and Felix, flipping hamburgers as he hummed a tune she couldn't quite place—was more than she deserved.

"I'm old," she told him. "I'm wrinkled and graying and probably perimenopausal."

"Bring it." Felix grinned over his shoulder.

"But you missed the best parts. I was perfect when I was twenty-five and I didn't even know it. Youth is wasted on the young."

"I wouldn't change a thing." Burgers flipped, Felix replaced the lid and came to sit opposite Sadie. He reached across the table and drew a finger from one side of her forehead to the other. "I love this line best."

"Stop it." She slapped his hand away, but a smile played on her lips. "You're no spring chicken, either."

"And hallelujah for that." Felix looked thoughtful. "Come on, Sadie. This isn't you. I'm sure I would have loved you at twenty-five, but we're grown-ups now. We know who we are and what we want. We don't have to preen or pretend. And this"—he circled one hand before him, indicating the whole of her—"is perfect. This is Sadie in her natural element. Sadie undone. You're wilding."

"Wilding," Sadie repeated, laughing.

"Returning to your natural state. Behaving in an unrestrained, organic manner."

"Thanks, Mr. Merriam-Webster," Sadie said. "I just stopped straightening my hair. It's hardly a manifesto."

But Felix was shaking his head. "It started when Alice died," he told her. "You are becoming the woman you were always meant to be."

Maybe he was right. At least a little bit. It was true that Sadie didn't see her mother often in her waning years, and Alice's influence over her life was certainly less than it had ever been, but just knowing that her mother existed in the world, thinking about Sadie and disapproving of her choices and decisions, was a burden that Sadie hadn't even realized she carried. Alice had straightened Sadie's hair when she was a child, so Sadie continued doing it for thirty years. Alice told her that her complexion was sallow, so Sadie never dreamed of leaving the house without blush. Alice complained that she was too loud or too quiet, too mousy or too bold, a show-off for getting an A+ on her English literature paper or "not college material" for only managing a C on her chemistry final. Too much and not enough, all at the same time, and never exactly who she was supposed to be.

"It's kind of pathetic, isn't it?" Sadie finally said, ruefully. "That it took me so long to figure it out."

"Stop doing that to yourself. Life doesn't come with a handbook. You're just on time. *We're* just on time."

Felix was right. The evening was perfect, and they were perfect. Her hair, tangled from the wind and kinking a little crazily over shoulders, his forehead just a bit sunburnt and peeling at the hairline. The burgers were charred when they finally got around to eating them, and the tomato overripe. Sadie had a mosquito bite behind her knee that itched so badly it nearly drove her mad, but it—all of it—was everything she ever wanted.

✦

It was a bad night for watching a meteor shower. The moon was not just waning gibbous—almost full and bright enough to fade the stars—it was near to perigee, the point when it orbited closest to earth and was therefore huge and luminous in the night sky. Sadie tried to beg out of their planned viewing on the roof of the science building at Newcastle, but Felix was uncharacteristically insistent.

"For me?" he finally asked, one degree shy of begging, and made his brown eyes wide and beseeching.

"Don't do that," Sadie moaned. "We're the grown-ups, remember? We don't pull out puppy eyes to coerce each other."

But it worked, and they biked to Newcastle after midnight along abandoned streets that thrummed with the song of summer cicadas.

On the roof, through a door in the sticky, teeming greenhouse, they were at the highest point in Newcastle. The science building was on the edge of campus on the farthest perimeter of town, and cornfields stretched uninterrupted before them. No streetlamps obscured their view, and with a thigh-high brick wall around the flat rooftop, even if someone had been watching them from below, they would not have been able to see a thing. So, Felix drew Sadie into his arms and kissed her long and slow, his fingers tracing the dip of her spine beneath her T-shirt and his teeth nibbling her lips, her jawline, her earlobe.

"I thought we were here to watch the meteor shower," Sadie

gasped when it became apparent Felix had other activities in mind.

"Marry me," he said in response.

That stopped her cold. Marry me? Marriage was something Sadie had long ago accepted would never happen for her. She'd stopped dreaming about children and grandchildren, someone to grow old with. Or maybe she had never dreamed of those things. If love always ends in death—and it always, *always* will—why love singularly at all? Sadie loved her students in a way, and felt safe in the familiar pattern of their coming and going, wave after wave on the beach where she was steady, immovable ground. She loved her late mother and what might have been. She loved classic literature and a perfect turn of phrase and a book that made her forget where she was. But this? Tethering herself to Felix? Trusting that he would be there when she woke up in the morning and curl up beside her at night? Merging their homes and their bank accounts and their schedules and their lives?

"Why?" she asked, the question popping out of her as Felix continued to trail kisses along her cheekbone.

Because I love you was the obvious answer. But that's not what Felix said. He wasn't startled by her reticence or hurt that she didn't scream yes. He simply tightened his grip on her waist and drew her even closer. "Because you're the most fascinating woman I've ever met, and I want to spend the rest of my life trying to figure you out."

"I'm a colossal bore." Sadie laughed.

Felix pulled back, offended. "How dare you. You're brilliant and focused and kind. I've seen you with your students, and they adore you. You create entire worlds in that crazy little brain of yours, and then translate them onto paper so beautifully it makes me want to weep. You've practically memorized

Shakespeare's entire canon, and yet there's still room for more, so you're learning all about relativity. For me."

"It's like a foreign language," Sadie complained. "I don't understand a thing."

Felix pressed a finger over her mouth. "Shush. I was talking. You do this thing when you're really concentrating where you wrinkle your nose as if trying to cast a spell, and when you finally work out the problem, you grin at yourself."

"I do not."

"You absolutely do."

"But—"

"Still not done. You're methodical and organized and careful. I admire the way you never drop a ball, and always stick with a problem until you've figured out the solve. You're really good at taking care of things, Sadie, and I think that's because no one has ever taken care of you."

Sadie felt the tears then, not because Felix was in love with her and wanted to marry her, but because he saw her. He knew her in a way no one else ever had. It was a naked, exposed feeling, as if everything that hid and sheltered and protected her had been stripped away. But instead of being repulsed by what he saw, Felix leaned in. He wanted more.

"I know you don't need me, Sadie." Felix's fingers kneaded her skin gently, the only indication that he was nervous. "You're perfectly fine on your own. But I hope that you want me enough to say yes. I plan to spend the rest of my life trying to unravel you."

She didn't say yes, not exactly, but she did stand on her tiptoes and kiss him. And when she paused to catch her breath, Felix slipped a simple woven band on her finger. There were tiny blue sapphires set in the golden twists, and when Sadie tilted her hand, they sparkled and danced like the night sky.

A couple of weeks later, before the fall semester began, she said "I do."

Felix and Sadie were supposed to get married on the roof of the science building beneath the stars, but a thunderstorm rolled in the afternoon of the wedding, and severe weather warnings forced them to hold the ceremony in the greenhouse instead.

The glass building was hot and lush with the scent of earth and evolution. Tropical flowers that had no business blooming in Iowa hung from disheveled vines in a scandal of reds and pinks so vibrant they seemed indecent. There was hardly room to move among the riot of green, but they cleared a space before a wall of yellow-throated hibiscus and said their vows while the rain coursed down the foggy panes.

Dr. Anthony Becker, the head of the theology department, performed the ceremony, and a few of Sadie and Felix's colleagues were in attendance. They kept it small on purpose, both because there was little room on the rooftop for guests—and even less in the greenhouse—and because they wanted it that way. Their marriage felt set apart somehow, almost holy, and if they could have accomplished it alone, they would have done so in a heartbeat.

But the handful of friends that attended them turned out to be a blessing. Marin, Anthony's wife, brought a few bottles of expensive sparkling rosé, a vintage she had shipped all the way from the south of France. "It's the perfect occasion," she assured them over and over, as the chilled wine shimmered on their tongues.

Another coworker brought a homemade pavlova filled with fresh lemon curd and topped with raspberries that had ripened in her own backyard. There was music from a Bluetooth speaker, and with the Christmas lights that Felix had strung from tree to tree, it was a true celebration. Lightning split the sky above them like a fissure in time and space, the light of another world breaking through for just a moment before slipping away again into oblivion.

Sadie laid her head on Felix's shoulder and danced.

If she had been a younger woman, perhaps Sadie would have imagined that this union was an undoing. A way to make amends for all that had come before, a fixing of what had been so grievously broken. But she knew better than to wish the past away. All her days had formed her into the person that Felix now held close, and there was a certain unknowable grace in that. A sacred mystery. As if where they had once been and where they would someday be, were one and the same: a theory of relativity and a poem without a beginning or end. A uniform movement of translation. Letter by letter, line by line, forever and ever. Amen.

CHAPTER 13

THURSDAY

The night is cold and dark. The wind howls over the mountain and makes the forest cry, a wailing that winds its way inside my dreams and twists them into nightmares. I don't sleep much. With Finn on one side and Henry on the other, I feel hemmed in by fear, crushed by a responsibility that I didn't ask for and don't know how to manage.

Around three a.m., I get up to throw a few more logs on the fire and try not to panic at the fact that there is only a small pile left beside the cast-iron stove. Henry assured me that there is another load beside the shed, but there's no denying that we are running out of firewood. As I huddle under my down comforter—the hardwood floor making my entire body stiff and sore—I pray that it will last beyond what is reasonable or fair to expect. We need a miracle.

At some point, I must drift off, because when I wake, the morning light is thin and milky beyond the sheer curtains in the living room. For a few seconds I don't know where I am or what's happening. I enjoy an empty moment of near peace before it all comes back in a rush, and I push myself to a cross-legged sitting position. Henry is already up, staring out the window.

"It stopped," he says, and there's no wonder in his voice, only a sense of finality.

"That's good, right?" I run a finger beneath my eyes and yawn. Then I reach over to where Finn lays curled on his side on the couch, his hair matted and his skin still flushed with fever. I touch his cheek gently, wondering if he'll stir, but he doesn't. Finn is breathing, and for now, I have to content myself with knowing he's stable. "How deep is it?"

Henry squints at the snow, estimating. "Five inches? Maybe six. Deeper in some spots because it drifted. There was a lot of wind—that's unusual around here."

He lets the curtain fall back into place and then paces the living room floor, his arms wrapped tight around his chest to ward off the chill. The fire throws off a decent amount of heat when we're near it, but the warmth doesn't radiate far into the room. Most of it belches out the chimney and evaporates into the atmosphere above the roof. I'm sure that at one time there were vents that helped distribute the heat from the stove throughout Hemlock House, but they must've been boarded up when central heating was added. We have this one little cocoon of warmth, no more. I'm once again convinced of our only course of action: we have to try to get off the mountain. Again.

The clock on the side table says it's just shy of seven o'clock, and I wonder how long it has been since the last snow fell. I push myself up against the coffee table, my hips and shoulders protesting at my choice of sleeping arrangements for the night. We should have dragged the mattresses from upstairs into the living room, but it's too late for regrets. I'll live, though I wish Felix was here to dig his knuckles into my aching muscles. He knows just how to work out all the kinks.

"I need to go to the cellar," I say, more to myself than Henry, but the strangled sound he makes, whips my head around. "What?"

"Why?" He answers my question with one of his own.

"Because there's a case of soup down there and I think we're going to need it."

An unreadable expression crosses his face, and as I watch, he squeezes his eyes shut for just a moment. I watch his Adam's apple bob as he swallows. "Okay," he says eventually. "I'll get the shovel."

"Shovel?" I stand slowly, stretching. "There's a hatch in the mudroom floor. Unless the roof was torn off while we were sleeping, I don't think a shovel will be necessary."

Henry nods a bit jerkily, then shakes out his arms and bounces lightly on the balls of his feet, a fighter trying to shed adrenaline. He's acting strangely, but I'm too tired to interrogate him, so I shuffle out of the room without a backward glance.

Kicking the rug out of the way to expose the cellar door, I bend and yank the recessed steel ring. It's so cold it burns, the metal singeing my skin so convincingly, I feel as if I've been branded. I gasp a little but hang on, tugging the heavy plane of the door until it's propped fully open.

In my sleepy, problem-solving state, I had forgotten how much I loathe the cellar. It's a long, narrow box carved into the earth and lined with creaky wooden shelves that Lucia Graham once stocked with jars of canned peaches and pears, applesauce and blackberry jam. All those lovely things are long gone, and in their place spiders and rats and nightmares have moved in. At least, staring down into the gaping mouth of the cellar, that's what I imagine is down there.

"Banker's boxes," I remind myself, cataloging the truth so that I won't lose my nerve. "Old books and family artifacts and *soup*."

But when I ease down the ladder, it feels as if something sinister is pulling me beneath the house, cold fingers pressing under the cuffs of my pajama pants and circling the gap between the fabric at my waist. The second my foot touches the dirt floor, I fumble for the vacuum-packed box of tomato soup that I know is on the nearest shelf and heave it up onto the mudroom floor. It lands with a crash, and I scramble back up the ladder, letting the hatch door slam down the second I'm clear.

If Henry heard the racket in the mudroom, he doesn't let on when I hurry back to warm myself by the fire.

"There's a case of tomato soup on the counter," I tell him. "We're not going to starve." It's a bad attempt at a joke, and Henry doesn't laugh. He hasn't moved since I left the room.

"Okay," he says, eyes fixed on Finn's still-sleeping form.

I flick my gaze between the brothers for a moment, then say, "I have a plan." I hope I sound casual, calm.

"What kind of a plan?" He crouches down and sticks the poker into the belly of the stove, kicking up an explosion of sparks. The fire is, predictably, almost out.

I take a deep breath, knowing that what I'm about to say will not sit well with Henry. "I'm going to try the logging road."

"We did that. It's washed out."

"I'll go the other way."

"Up the mountain?" Henry glances over his shoulder at me, his expression guarded. Cynical. "That's the wrong direction."

"It might not be. The forest access roads are a tangle of arteries in and out. I might find another path down."

Henry sits back on his haunches, considering. We both know that deep snow and unexpected pockets of gullies and drifts will make navigating David's old trails nearly impossible. Still, it takes a few tense heartbeats of silence for Henry to acknowledge that my idea is worth exploring. When he gives a terse nod, I breathe a sigh of relief. He knows the terrain so much better than I do; I'm grateful that he thinks I may be on to something.

"Okay," he agrees. "Let's give Finn another dose of medicine and get everyone bundled up. We'll need—"

"Henry," I interrupt, holding up my hand as if to staunch the flow of his words. He missed the subject of all those verbs: I'm *going to try*. I'll *go*. I *might find*. "I'm going alone."

At first his face remains blank and unreadable. Then his eyes flash and the corner of his mouth pulls up in a sneer. "No, you're not."

"Yes, I am. It's the only way that makes sense. Finn can't travel—not crammed into the Ranger with no heat for God knows how long. And he can't stay here alone."

"Then I'll go."

"No," I say again, and there's heat in the word. He's a minor, I'm sure of it, and I refuse to put him in danger. Whether he likes it or not, I'm in charge. Besides, I'm just going to drive up the logging road. See if there is another way off the mountain. "I can get help. I have friends in Requiem who will know exactly what to do. And I'll take my phone. I still have a bit of charge left, and maybe I'll get reception somewhere. Even if I can't find my way down, I might be able to call for help."

Henry holds his tongue, frustrated but considering, and I play my final card. "Finn needs you," I tell him. "I'm a stranger and he's suffering. He needs his brother."

I know I've won when Henry jumps up and stalks out of the room. He can't argue with me, so he's abandoning the fight altogether. I had hoped for a bit of support, but this is better than a brawl, and I force myself to be grateful.

Upstairs, I brush my teeth and wash my face in the ice-cold water that the sink still dutifully pumps out. I'm sure the pipes are slowly freezing and that the luxury of running water won't last much longer, but hopefully help will be on the way before things get too dire. It's as I'm toweling off that I remember the generator. Felix showed it to me when we first moved in, a portable machine about the size of a riding lawn mower that was covered in cobwebs in the very back of the small stable. I had forgotten all about it, probably because I don't know the first thing about using a generator, but maybe Henry can get it up and running.

By the time I get back to the living room, as cleaned up as I can get and wearing a fresh set of warm clothes, Henry is waiting for me.

"I filled the gas tank for you," he says gruffly.

I'm touched that he would do that for me, but when his gaze lands on Finn, I know I'm reading too much into Henry's gesture. It wasn't for me. But making this work is the best chance we all have.

"Snow will accumulate on the leeward side—away from the wind—so you might have to do some zigzagging," Henry tells me. "If there are really deep drifts, just make sure you have ground clearance. If you don't, and you can't get through, *turn around*." He bites off the last two words and glares at me for added effect.

I get the point: don't do anything dumb and get irreparably stuck. If I do, we're all in trouble. "Got it," I say, taking him seriously. "Anything else?"

"Do you know how to use the winch?"

The look on my face makes him roll his eyes, but instead of berating me, he says: "I'll show you."

Before we head out, I crouch down by Finn and take his face in my hands. "I'm going to get you some help, buddy." His eyes don't so much as flicker, but his breathing is even, if a bit shallow. I brush a quick kiss against his forehead, not caring if Henry is watching or if my familiarity upsets him. Whether these boys are complete strangers or not, we've lived through something together, and I care about them. Them? Of course, Finn is easy to love, but as I probe my feelings, I realize that I do care about Henry, too. I want to see them both safe and well. And I'm going to make that happen.

Henry has his marching orders for Finn (ibuprofen every four hours, cough medicine every six, and as much water as the boy will tolerate), and it's time for him to share his side-by-side expertise.

The morning is ashen and still, low-hanging clouds crowding a pewter sky. The air feels like a pent-up breath, a brief pause before a heavy exhale.

"There's more coming, isn't there?"

It's a rhetorical question, but Henry answers anyway. "Soon," he says.

I stare at him openly as he tromps through the snow in Felix's boots, his eyes fixed upward. "How do you know that?" I ask.

"Can't you feel it?" He lifts his arms, palms up. "The air is so heavy. It's giving me a headache."

I don't know the first thing about drops in barometric pressure and their effect on humans, but somehow, I believe Henry when he says he can feel the weather. This strange boy—who wondered at a UPS truck—is so in tune with the natural world he can tell me that more snow is coming without the aid of a meteorologist or a forecast. He's an enigma, to say the least.

For the next ten minutes, Henry gives me a tutorial on the winch, and then offers up as much advice as he can on plowing through deep drifts. Finally, he says, "When it starts to snow, turn back, no matter where you are. You'll be able to follow the tracks home. But once the storm starts up again . . ."

He trails off and I can hear the note of anxiety in his voice. I understand. If I get lost out there, he and Finn are completely stuck. And who knows what will happen if Finn doesn't get the care he needs? Beyond his obvious illness, I'm afraid he's also dehydrated. I can't remember the last time he asked Henry to help him to the bathroom.

"I don't like you going that way." Henry's expression is intense but unreadable. He opens his mouth as if he's about to say something else but thinks better of it and snaps his jaw shut with a click. I watch as he wrestles with himself for a moment, then squeezes his eyes shut and says quickly, "Don't trust anyone you meet. Just find a way to Requiem."

I almost laugh. "There's no one up there," I assure him. "We're the only ones crazy enough to live out this far." But a needle of alarm pierces my chest all the same. I wonder again where Henry and Finn came from. What they know about this mountain and the ghosts that haunt it.

"I'll be careful," I assure him, pasting a brave half smile over my dread. "And hopefully I'll be back soon with help." I leave it vague, because I don't know what help might look like. An ambulance can't make it to Hemlock House on unplowed roads, and I doubt a helicopter can fly in a blizzard. But somehow, some way, someone knows what to do. I just have to find them.

I leave Henry with instructions on how to find the backup generator, and the relief that floods his eyes at the thought of having a task is briefly gratifying.

"I'm on it," he says, his shoulders set in a solemn line.

We don't say goodbye, just take off in opposite directions toward what I'm afraid are doomed endeavors.

◆

It's a different world heading up the mountain instead of down. Although it's a bit misleading to call the northern path "up." The truth is, our mountain rolls into another and then another, and it's not nearly as cut-and-dried as a child's drawing would suggest. The road wends up hills and down shallow valleys, skirting drop-offs and jagging around unexpected bends as the rugged topography requires. Still, I'm climbing, if the changes in vegetation can be trusted. I'm far from the timberline, but the trees are different here, thinner and more spread out, with less dense ground cover. There is also more snow.

Half an hour from Hemlock House, I feel disoriented and completely lost, though I know that there is only one path back and the brawny tires of the Ranger have clearly marked the way. But the world is wreathed in shades of gray, the clouds and the drifts of newly fallen snow cut from the same faded bolt of cloth. I could go mad out here, alone in the wide, wild world, and I long for the meager comfort of the stove and the boys.

When the snow begins to fall, it's so light at first that I hardly notice it. The flakes are barely a whisper, feather-fine and a perfect match to the rest of the terrain. But it clings to the windshield, a stubborn reminder that this storm isn't over yet, even if we enjoyed a momentary reprieve. I pull to a stop, the growl of the waiting engine almost absurdly loud in the eerie hush all around, and bury my face in my hands.

I don't want to go back. Not without good news. The thought of returning to Hemlock House only to watch Finn steadily decline is enough to make my empty stomach revolt, and I throw open the door of the Ranger to dry heave. When the moment has passed, I yank my phone out of my pocket and hold it up, yearning for even a single bar. Just one. But I've checked my reception multiple times along the way and haven't had so much as a hint of coverage. It's the same here, at the apex of my progress: nothing.

In the few minutes that I've been stopped on the logging road, the snowfall has already increased. Thankfully, the wind hasn't picked up, and it's coming down straight and even, like a heavy sifting of fine sugar. It seems innocent enough, but I promised Henry I would come back when it began to snow, and I battle with myself for a few moments, looking forward and then back. Weighing. Deciding.

Up ahead, there's a hairpin curve around a jagged rock formation, and I decide to make it my turning point. If there is nothing around the bend—a fork in the road, a sign pointing the way to civilization, a cell signal, *anything*—I'll go back. Return to Hemlock House, regroup, pray for grace.

But something feels different even before I reach the snake in the road. It's a gasp of recognition, a single heartbeat that thuds out of rhythm and makes every hair on my body stand up. I'm both ready for it and totally blindsided when I twist around the hook of the narrow road and see it: Felix's Jeep.

For just a moment, my vision goes black, blurred by shock and doubt and the impossibility of the scene before me. But then I blink, and it passes, and I can't deny what my eyes already know is true. Pulled to the side of the gravel road—buried in six inches of snow and angled toward home—is Felix's midnight-blue Jeep Wrangler.

One week.

My husband has been gone for a week, and my blood runs cold and sluggish at the thought of him trying to make his way home to me.

I don't know how long I sit in the side-by-side, staring at the apparition before me, but it's long enough for fresh snow to dust the windscreen. When I yank myself back to reality, I realize that I'm hyperventilating, breathing so fast that my fingers are tingling, and not from the cold. If I thought I was afraid before, it's nothing compared to the raw horror I feel at the sight of Felix's Jeep. Because if Felix is okay, if he is perfectly fine and safe somewhere, there is no logical explanation for his car to be *here*. Just a few miles from home. On a stretch of abandoned logging road that he has never—to the best of my knowledge—explored as long as we've been living at Hemlock House.

Why?

How long has the Jeep been parked here? Since last Thursday? Just a couple of days? If Felix was headed home—if he found the road washed out and had to navigate another way—why stop here? And if the Jeep broke down, why didn't he just walk home? We're miles from the homestead, but he could've made it. *Not in the storm*, I think, my heart hitching.

I realize I'm crying when the warm tracks of tears burn my frozen cheeks. The windshield of the Jeep is covered in snow, and I can't see inside. I want to throw open the driver's side door, but I'm terrified of what I'll find there. Felix slumped over the steering wheel, his body stiff and frigid. Felix alive, but barely—frostbitten and half-starved and fading. Felix gone.

The deep snow drags at my boots as I wade through the space between the Ranger and the Jeep. Overhead, a sheer rock face looms thirty feet into the air before ending in a craggy outcropping that's covered in hearty brush, roots digging clear through the volcanic rock and braided in mossy, ice-covered tendrils. In some obscure, still-functioning portion of my brain, I feel like the heroine in some tragedy, adventuring through the forest only to find that it's too late. *Ill met by moonlight*, I think, but it's daybreak, and this is no high comedy. I never deserved happiness—and certainly not the extravagance of what I shared with Felix—and suddenly this moment feels like it was predestined. An inevitability since the moment I fell in love on the football field in Newcastle.

The driver's side of the Jeep is nearly flush with the rocky cliff face, so I hurry to the passenger side. Snow has drifted all along the vehicle, creating a deep crest of white against the doors. Henry put a small, collapsible shovel in the back of the side-by-side for me, but I don't want to take the time to go back and get it, so I just start digging with my hands. Because I'm not careful, snow slips between the cuffs of my coat and my gloves, and in seconds it's packed into place and burning my wrists like fire. I'm a woman possessed, scooping and kicking and attacking the snow as if it alone is responsible for the agony of the last several days, and by the time I've cleared enough space to wedge open the front passenger door, I'm panting and spent.

A wordless cry, a wish. A bone-deep supplication. Then I try the door. It's unlocked, the handle clicks, but the door doesn't budge. It's frozen shut, I realize, and the thick layer of rippled ice obscuring the window is proof of what I'm facing. I need a chisel, warm water, a hair dryer. A dozen different tools would do, but I don't have access to any of them, so I yank the door instead. Like a madwoman, I pull and jerk and throw my entire body weight into wrenching the handle as far as it will go, as if I can open the door by willpower alone.

When the front passenger door finally gives, I'm not ready for it, and tumble backward into the snow. My wrist tweaks painfully as it breaks my fall, but before I can even assess the damage, I'm back on my feet and thrusting my upper body into the Jeep.

It's empty.

The keys are in the ignition. Felix's backpack and duffel are crammed into the footwell of the passenger seat. His cell phone is in the cupholder. All his personal effects, the things he left Hemlock House with, are right here. It's as if he left me nearly a week ago, drove a few miles up the mountain, and disappeared into thin air.

I want to touch his things. To unzip his backpack and lift out the yellow legal pad that he makes all his lists on—from grocery to honey-do to next steps in his research grant applications—and grab his phone to see if there is any charge left. But I'm vaguely aware that Felix's Jeep could be a crime scene. It could contain clues about where he went and why, and I am not a private detective. I look at my gloves, suddenly grateful that I'm wearing them, and slowly lift my hands from the passenger seat.

It hits me then: the scent. I hadn't noticed it before because I was so focused on Felix's things. But now it's unmistakable, an acrid tang like cold copper pipes. Like drinking from the garden hose when I was a kid, the metal end burbling mineral-rich groundwater.

My subconscious clocks it long before I realize what it is, and my heart begins to pound in response. I press farther into the vehicle and force myself to look over the headrests to the back seat.

She's lying on her side, one arm dangling off the bench seat and the other tucked beneath a stained wool blanket. Her eyes are half-open in a weary, defeated gaze, but whatever she is looking at is not of this world.

It's clear that she's been dead for a while. Her skin is bluish and mannequin-smooth, like she's a cruel caricature of a person and not real at all. But I know she is. Her blood is poured all over the back seat of my husband's Jeep, and I can nearly taste its earthy, metallic edge.

I would throw up if there was anything in my stomach to expel, but instead I reel back, hitting my head on the doorframe and crumpling to the ground beside the Jeep. I lay there for a few minutes, my head spinning in pain and disbelief as I try to grab reality with both hands. This can't be happening. It can't possibly be real. Felix gone, and in his place, a dead woman with eyes as rich and brown as his. A smattering of pale freckles across her cheeks. Jawline sharp as cut glass.

I wonder if she has a single dimple when she smiles, just like her brother.

CHAPTER 14

THURSDAY

The trip back to Hemlock House passes in a daze. I don't know how long I've been gone, or how much snow has fallen in my absence, but when I pull in sight of the front porch, I find that Henry is already waiting for me there. He's bundled in Felix's winter coat and boots, his black stocking cap pulled low over his dirty-blond hair, just like the very first time I saw him on the monitor in Felix's office. Henry looks as if he's been waiting for me all along, but that's impossible.

"How's Finn?" I ask immediately when he strides down the porch steps to open my door. The words taste like ashes in my mouth, and my heart is pounding wildly, but I've rehearsed this simple line over and over on the drive down. It's the most obvious question I could ask upon returning, and I can't risk letting Henry know that something is wrong. He can't know what I found. Not yet.

"There's something wrong with the generator," he says, ignoring my question. "I think the problem is—"

"Don't worry about that." I inwardly curse the way my voice wobbles. "It's not important."

It's the wrong thing to say. Henry reaches for my arm, then thinks better of it and demands: "What did you find?"

I planned to be poised, but already I'm fraying at the edges and hot tears spill down my cheeks. Maybe I've been crying all along. I force myself to ask again: "How's Finn?"

Henry stares at me, wary, snow slowly accumulating on the dark weave of his hat. "He's okay," he says after a moment, backing down. "He woke up a while ago and I gave him some more meds."

"Water?"

"He drank a bit."

I give a shaky nod. Somehow this outer display of control helps to quiet the cacophony inside—or at least turn the volume down a bit.

"What happened?" Henry asks. "Why are you crying?"

It's an impossible question to answer. I've had the drive back to muddle it through, trying to put the pieces together, but the picture is so fuzzy and indistinct I can't make anything come into focus.

"What's your uncle's name?" It slips out unbidden, and I'm as surprised as Henry seems to be. But I'm not asking a question so much as giving an ultimatum, and we both know it. He studies me for a few seconds, measuring his secrets against the quandary we find ourselves in. We've been thrust together for better or worse, and I can see the moment that he accepts our fates are now tied. He blinks, and when his eyes open it's as if he's a different person. Realer somehow. But also more afraid.

Finally, quietly, he admits: "Felix Graham."

The earth fractures beneath me and spits me out in one of my husband's infinite universes. Henry is my nephew. Finn is, too.

And I have to tell them that their mother is dead.

I spin away from Henry and stalk across the yard and then back again, my hands knotted in my hair. I want to crawl outside of this splintered reality and find my way to Thursday morning when Felix bent over our bed to kiss me goodbye. Was that just a week ago? I'd grab hold of him, make him stay. Do anything to prevent the series of events that have led me to this moment in the middle of a storm with a boy who attacked me in my own greenhouse before he realized that we belong to each other. Somehow.

"How long have you known?" I demand, marching back and taking him by the shoulders. "Did you come here looking for him?"

Henry doesn't shrug me off, and in a way that scares me more than if he would rage and fight back. I need that Henry right now. The fierce one. "I didn't know," he says. "Not at first, anyway."

"The picture?" I guess, remembering the night that he studied the photograph in Felix's office. His strange reaction.

He nods.

"Why didn't you say anything? Why didn't you tell me when you figured it out?"

Henry ducks his head, pulls the stocking cap over his eyes before thrusting it back. "She didn't say anything about you."

She. Gabi. My mind twitches to her ruined body on the back seat of Felix's Jeep, and I swipe furiously at the tears freezing on my cheeks. "Oh my God." The words wisp out, a plea.

"What happened out there, Sadie?" Henry has never sounded more like a child, but I can't bring myself to meet his gaze.

"You have to tell me everything," I say instead. "Who you are and why you're here and how it is that you don't know your own uncle." But that's a cruel thing to say. I know that Felix and Henry have never met. That whatever had fractured between brother and sister had thrust them so far apart they stopped speaking decades ago. I don't think Felix knows that Finn even exists.

"I'm Henry Abbott." He says it quickly, like ripping off a bandage. He's stomping his feet against the growing cold, rubbing his gloved hands together. The snow is piling up on his shoulders, his dark hat is flocked winter white. "Finn is my brother, and we're here because our mother sent us here."

"Why?"

"Because he was going to kill us."

◆

We stumble inside, half-frozen and in shock. Henry knows that I'm not okay, and he absorbs my panicked energy like a sponge. After a quick check on Finn (he's sleeping, his breathing tight and shallow), I drag Henry upstairs. I'm numb when I reach for the photo hidden on the top bunk and hand it over with trembling fingers.

Henry studies the picture, his gaze glued to his mother.

"I've never seen them like this," Henry says, confirming what I already guessed to be true. "They look so young. So happy."

"Who is he?"

"My father. Benjamin Abbott."

Ben. The name scrawled over and over on the underside of Gabi's desk.

I realize that in the picture, Gabi and Ben are about the same age that Henry is now. It's shocking to me that I didn't see the resemblance between Henry and his father when I first found the photo. They have the same flop of tawny hair, the same narrow face and long, straight nose. But I wasn't looking for similarities. How could I possibly have guessed?

And Finn. His nearly black hair, those moody, quicksilver eyes. I haven't seen him smile authentically enough to know if he has Felix's characteristic dimple, but I wouldn't be surprised if he did. For days I've been looking at a version of my husband as a child, and I didn't even know it.

Henry rubs his thumb over their faces in the picture. "They were kind of siblings, you know? I mean, they lived together when they were kids. Here, I guess." He looks around the room as if seeing it for the first time. I know he's imagining his father here, sleeping in the same bed where Henry himself spent a single night. A shiver ripples through him and his jaw hardens, but I don't know if it's because he's cold or angry. Maybe both.

I decide not to tell him that the drawers are still filled with his father's clothes, with remnants of his life here. "I didn't know that," I say instead. "I've never heard the name Benjamin Abbott before today, and I didn't know the Grahams took him in for a season."

Henry sniffs hard and then shoves the photo into my hands as if he can't bear to touch it for another second. But when I unfold the flap and show him Felix with his arm around Gabi, Henry reaches for it again. He holds the yellowing paper close, studying the tableau. His mother in the middle, her brother on one side, Ben on the other.

"He looks like her," Henry says of Felix, and it's true. "Finn, too. I look like *him*."

I can tell that Henry is a second away from crumpling the photo, so I gently slip it from his grasp and tuck it in my pocket. But his aggression needs an outlet, and I watch as Henry pulls at the bindings wrapped over his knuckles, dragging the edges down to soak up the dots of fresh blood. The greenhouse feels like a lifetime away—I can hardly remember the boy who terrified me. Who ripped up his fist on the wooden counters and would've probably punched through the glass and torn an artery if I hadn't stopped him.

There is so much I don't know, but this is not the time for an interrogation. I try to distill my questions down to the essentials and come up with: "What happened?"

Henry juts out his chin a little, then paces the room while he starts at the very beginning. He spins a dark fairy tale about a cabin in the woods and a monster who rules his terrible kingdom with an iron fist and fear. And as Henry talks and talks, circling the room like a caged animal, I piece together a narrative that chills me to the bone.

Beautiful, brave, big-hearted Gabi fell in love with a broken boy who had been abandoned by his own family and welcomed as a Graham. When Lucia discovered Ben walking home from football practice on a freezing fall day—a four-mile trek to the condemned house where he lived with his addicted mother and her on-again, off-again dealer boyfriend—she scooped him up and took him to Hemlock House. It was supposed to be a one-night thing, a chance for Ben to get a hot meal in his belly and an uninterrupted sleep, but that first night turned into a second and then a third. He didn't leave until the summer after his high school graduation—the same year as Felix—and no one at his so-called home ever missed him.

Maybe it was love at first sight, but I suspect Gabi's attraction was more of a gradual thing. Reading between the lines of Henry's frenzied account, Ben was a summer storm, dangerous and unpredictable, but wounded in his own devastating way. That mix of vulnerability and quiet cruelty was trademark Bad Boy, and I wince a little, imagining teenage Gabi falling incrementally for a man she believed she could fix.

Felix would have hated that. My husband is not one to suffer fools, and judging by his expression in the vintage photograph, I can only assume that he loathed Benjamin Abbott and the way he was manipulating Gabi.

"Ben's very convincing," Henry says wryly.

The boy pauses for a moment, swaying in the center of the

room, and I study him. His black eye is just starting to yellow at the edges, and the swelling is going down. The purple is less knight errant, more simply tragic. He's just another kid with an injury that, in a different context, he would try to pass off as an accident. *I fell down the stairs. I bumped into a door. I'm so clumsy.* Take your pick.

But Henry doesn't have to deflect now. It's a straight line from exploiting your quasi-foster sister to a twisted, abusive relationship, and even as I recoil at how deeply unwell Benjamin Abbott clearly is, my rage is stoked. Henry doesn't know exactly when Ben moved their little family to a cabin on the far side of the mountain—he was too young to remember a life before the wilderness—but he knows that his existence up until this point has been *wrong*.

Homeschool in the cabin. A rainwater collection system for showers. Dinners by candlelight. And always, the threat of Ben's fists. Of his collection of knives, kept sharp on the whetstone and glinting from his belt. Of the small armory that Ben oiled nightly so everything would be in perfect working condition for the day that he would have to take up arms against his own government.

"It never came," Henry says, glancing out the window at the ragged swirl of snow outside.

"What never came?"

"The civil war."

I'm not sure how to respond. "There isn't going to be a civil war," I tell him eventually. "It's okay. Everything is okay."

He nods. Sighs.

I chance a touch and lay my hand on his shoulder. Henry doesn't shrug it off. "Why are you here?" I ask him. "Why now?"

"Escape," he says, a maniacal sheen in his eyes. "We were

going to get out. Did I tell you about the root cellar? About how Ben locked us down there when he went to Bellingham every month for supplies?"

My hand slips off Henry's shoulder and I take an involuntary step back. Suddenly his reaction to my quest for soup this morning makes perfect sense. I feel hot tears form behind my eyes as I remember how terrified I was to spend just a few seconds underground. I open my mouth, but no words come out.

"Mom got brave. She snuck a crowbar into the cellar. On Friday morning when he left for the city, she slipped it out from behind a loose board in the shelving unit and told me to get to work."

I picture Gabi, Henry, and Finn in a coffin-size room dug into the earth. Dirt floor, sagging walls. It's like something out of a horror movie, not real life, but the evidence of Ben's crimes is before me. Henry's haunted eyes. Finn's silence. Is that why he doesn't speak? Because he was imprisoned in the ground by the man who was supposed to love and protect him?

Henry tells me about breaking out through the wooden hatch door. How he swung the crowbar at the boards and hacked away until the handle was revealed. Then wedged the straight end through the steel padlock and used his body weight as leverage to snap the shank. They all shouted and laughed because they had heard Ben's truck drive away, and trips to the store always took hours if not days. They had all the time in the world. And Gabi had a plan.

"There's a house at the edge of a border town," Gabi told her boys. "With a tire swing and little creek out back."

"How?" Henry asked, suspicious. "How do we have a house? How will we get there?"

But she smiled a secret smile and just said, "An angel."

Felix, I think, though I have no idea how. Did he know all along that Gabi was here? Is that why we came to Hemlock House? Or was it some sort of divine coincidence, a twist of fate that brought us to this moment where my nephew stands before me, fists clenching and unclenching as he recounts an impossible tale?

"But Ben never left," I guess, and Henry shudders in confirmation.

"Or he came back because he had forgotten something," he says. "We were making such a racket we didn't hear a thing. But when we'd all climbed out of the cellar, he was there."

I touch a finger to my own eye, indicating Henry's shiner, and he nods. I'm guessing if I could lift his shirt I'd find more bruises. A part of me wants to press him for details, but it doesn't really matter. There was violence. Gabi threw herself at her husband, stepping between her children and the man who would kill them, and told her boys to *run*.

And because all the world's a stage and everyone has their exits and entrances, Henry and Finn ended up in the greenhouse, and Gabi is dead in the back seat of the Jeep.

Felix was their getaway. It was just a matter of timing: all he had to do was wait and watch until Ben left for his planned supply run, then spirit Gabi and the boys away when they came hiking through the trees. Since he left Hemlock House on Thursday and the attempted escape took place on Friday, he must have used the day between to attend to the details of Gabi's plan. If there was a house on a border town with a tire swing and a bubbling creek, I believe Felix was the person who set it up. I can picture my husband carefully crafting a new life for his sister and her sons. In my mind's eye I see him grinning over the console at Gabi, one dimple puncturing his cheek.

I pitch forward and Henry catches me by the shoulders, preventing me from collapse. He hangs on until I've stopped swaying, his fingers pinching my skin as if I'm holding him up instead of the other way around. "What did you find out there?" he asks, dread shading his voice.

But I ignore him. "I need a drink," I say as my head swims. "I think I'm dehydrated."

We make our way downstairs together, Henry shadowing my steps so closely it's uncomfortable. But I recognize that need for proximity, for someone to just be near, and I let him crowd me, then accept the glass of water that he proffers once we're in the kitchen. The water from the tap is ice-cold and fortifying, and I guzzle it all before refilling the glass and drinking it gone again.

"How did you know to come here?" I ask him, my voice low in case Finn has woken up and can hear us from the living room. I sincerely doubt it, but Henry answers me in a near whisper.

"We came here to find Felix. For years, Mom's been telling us about a house in the woods." He squeezes his eyes shut, seemingly trying to remember her exact words: "'Over the far ridge at the place where the peaks seem to meet, and the sun pours into the valley like a cup of cream in the morning.'"

Like cream. Rich and sweet. I can hardly imagine Hemlock House as anything other than ghostly and echoing. But Gabi's instructions are nearly a poem; they make it sound like Henry and Finn were running to a haven. To a place where they would be wrapped up and kept warm. Safe. And wasn't that exactly what the Grahams offered Ben? A sanctuary. And then he destroyed it.

Henry continues: "If we couldn't find the homestead, we were supposed to go to Requiem. Get help."

But they did find Hemlock House. Except instead of Felix—their uncle, a man who looked like their mother and would help them—they found a stranger. A woman who was suspicious and thought they were dangerous. I rub my forehead with my fingers and try to swallow the guilt that lodges in the back of my throat.

It's not just remorse that chokes me. It's also betrayal. Henry's story is wrenching, but I find that underneath my shock and horror, I'm beginning to wrestle with the ugly truth that my husband hid things from me. No, he *lied* to me. My heart thuds painfully as I cast about the kitchen. And that's when I see it: the landline. I remember the phone calls with no one on the other end. The night I found Felix in his office, talking on the telephone with the sound of a strange woman's voice emanating from behind the closed door. There's a second phone jack in that room, a second rotary on an old side table by Felix's favorite chair. My breath hitches as the *how* of it all clicks into place.

"Did your mother have access to a phone?" I ask Henry.

He gives a tight jerk of his head. "He'd kill her if she touched his. She wouldn't dare."

But maybe she would. Maybe she *did*.

"Your place, it's up the logging road, isn't it? That's why you didn't want me to go that way."

Henry gives an uncertain nod. I can tell my seemingly unconnected questions are giving him whiplash.

"How far is it? Between Hemlock House and your cabin, I mean."

Henry pauses, hesitant. But there's nothing to hide now, and after a moment he says: "As the crow flies, three miles, give or take. On the logging road, five miles, maybe a bit more. I don't really know for sure because I've never been beyond the pass. Not far at least. Benjamin took me there once."

"The pass?"

"It's a crevasse in a low cliff that leads to our cabin. You can't see it from the road, but it's there, behind an S-curve and hidden by brush. It's the only way in or out unless you're an accomplished hiker and know exactly where you're going."

I would bet my mother's entire unwanted fortune that the curve where I found Felix's Jeep parked is the place that Henry is describing. Felix went there to collect his sister and her sons, and then what? Ben came back unexpectedly and threw everything into chaos. Gabi sent her boys into the woods, and Felix . . .

Felix is a terrifying blank space, a question mark that torments me. I want to pound my fists into his chest and ask him why he did this, why he didn't feel like he could trust me with the truth. I would have helped—I *am* helping. We're all tangled up in this together, whether he wanted to let me in or not.

I thought we were different.

"What are we going to do?" Henry sounds like a little boy, and my heart splinters. "She's back there, Sadie. She's there with him, and I just left her . . . " His voice cracks, and I realize how close he is to a total breakdown.

"Don't say that," I say quickly. "You did what you had to do. You kept Finn safe. Henry, you may have saved his life."

He blinks at me, unseeing, and I watch as he wars with himself. Henry knows I'm right, but I can't begin to imagine what it cost him to leave Gabi and flee.

Somehow, I will have to tell him that his mother is dead. That his uncle is missing. That we're still trapped at Hemlock House with no way out and no way to protect ourselves if Ben Abbott decides to come hunting for his sons.

But all those vile words are stuck in my throat, cemented in with horror and unshed tears. Instead of trying to force them out and annihilating the world as Henry knows it, I just put out my arms. It's a bit of a surprise when Henry steps into them, but he is warm and solid against me, a messy, imperfect fit. When he buries his face in my shoulder, I put my hand to the back of his warm head and hold on tight.

CHAPTER 15

THURSDAY

I don't tell Henry about his mother because I can't bring myself to do it. It's cowardly and unforgivable, but when I measure the weight of everything that he and Finn have endured—and balance it against the strength that they will need for whatever lies ahead—I simply can't destroy him by sharing what I discovered in Felix's Jeep. That day will come, but not quite yet.

When Henry calms down a bit, we go to check on Finn. I'm surprised to discover that he's awake, staring at the ceiling.

"Hey," I say, forcing a wobbly smile and sitting on the edge of the coffee table. "How are you feeling?"

Finn's gaze rolls to meet mine, and I find that his eyes are clouded and confused. He looks exhausted, his lips chapped so badly they're cracked at the corners. I'm frightened by his downturn, but the vise grip on my heart loosens by a single degree when Finn pulls one arm out from beneath the blanket and gives me the universal so-so sign. He tilts his hand back and forth a few times, and then I reach out and grab it, pressing it gently between both of my palms.

"It's good to see you awake," I tell him as Henry sits beside me. He squeezes Finn's leg beneath the blanket and taps something out with his fingers that makes one side of Finn's mouth quirk up in a half smile. He winces as a bright dot of blood pricks at the edge, and I use my thumb to wipe it away.

I wish I could smile back, but my mind is stuck in a loop, conjuring a dungeon carved into the forest floor. A trio of figures huddling in the dark, talking to one another with touch because it's simply too terrifying speak. The place stinks of urine and fear. Of black earth and old bones. I understand why Finn lost his voice.

I've been scared from the moment I drove around the corner on the logging road and saw Felix's Jeep in a place where it simply did not belong. Actually, long before that. From the moment I saw Henry's ghostly figure on the antiquated trail cam. It strikes me that maybe Felix replaced the cameras without telling me, maybe he wanted to see what was moving about Hemlock House. I feel a spark of anger, and I fan that single, tiny flame.

"Hungry?" I drag my attention back to the boy before me and deflate just a bit when he gives his head an almost imperceptible shake. "Let's try something anyway, okay? Maybe some soup?" We're practically swimming in tomato soup and I hope I can convince him to take a few bites at least.

Henry slides into my spot when I head for the kitchen, and I can hear the low rumble of his voice as he talks softly to Finn. I marvel at the deep love he has for his little brother, and the selfless way he shoves all his own fears and emotions aside to coax a laugh from the sick boy. Finn's brief giggle is faint and wheezy, but it's music to my ears all the same.

I'm pouring steaming soup into two bowls when Henry comes into the kitchen. "I added the last of the logs," he tells me. "The fire will be out in a few hours."

"Then I'm going to need you to make firewood out of something in the house. Nothing painted or with a high-gloss varnish.

The fumes wouldn't be safe. But the bunk bed upstairs is untreated, I think. It'll work."

Henry is giving me a strange look, and I realize that I'm talking too high and fast, and sloshing hot soup all over the counter. I can see in his eyes the moment he clocks that there are only two bowls. "Sadie," he says, his voice a warning.

"I'm going back," I tell him.

"Back where? What are you talking about?"

I put down the spoon because my hand is still shaking and it's clicking against the side of the bowl. "I found Felix's car," I tell him. "Parked on the road near the spot where I think the path to your cabin must be."

Henry looks stunned, as if he can't quite process what I'm saying. "But if Felix's car is there . . . "

"Yeah," I exhale. "I think he was trying to help you."

"Mom's angel." Henry grasps for an explanation that's just out of reach. "But if he's at the cabin . . . " He pins me with an anguished look. "They're okay, right?"

I press a fist to my mouth for a moment, trapping the sobs inside. I can't answer his question, and I hope he simply chalks it up to concern for Felix's well-being. Spinning back to the counter, I snag a pair of spoons, stick them into the bowls of soup, and pass the whole lot to Henry. There's one for each hand, and he only accepts the offering because of Finn. If it were just the two of us, he'd be spoiling for a fight. He'd never let me get away with this.

"You have to stay here," I tell him, my voice hoarse with unshed tears. "Finn can't be left alone."

"And you can't go back." Henry glares at me. "If Felix is there—if my mom is still there—it means they didn't get out."

"I know."

"But you don't know him," Henry mutters, teeth clenched.

His tone is low and dangerous, his eyes imploring. "He hunts. He has knives and hatchets. A bow and arrows. Sadie, he has so many guns. An elk rifle for hunting big game, a .22 for the small stuff, several handguns . . ."

My heart stutters, but the information doesn't change anything. Felix wasn't crumpled in the back of the Jeep with Gabi, and that means there's at least a chance that he's alive. Maybe wounded or trapped or in need of help. And if that's the case, I can't leave him there. Not if he needs me. Not if there's anything at all that I can do. I can feel the clock ticking, a metronome keeping time beneath my skin. We can't wait for the storm to pass or for someone to discover that we're trapped up here. It'll be too late. I'm convinced of that.

"I won't do anything stupid," I say, trying to sound calm and capable. Resolute. "I'm a big girl, Henry, and I can take care of myself. I just want to get the lay of the land. Figure out if they're still at the cabin and if everything is okay."

Everything is not okay—and we both know it—but Henry just stares at me, fuming. Or maybe there's more behind his eyes. Worry, concern. I'd be touched if I wasn't beside myself with foreboding. I feel sanded down to the bone, raw and tender to the touch.

"I'll be careful," I promise. "I've already created a path, and it's not snowing too hard. I'll be there and back in no time. Before sunset."

That gives me four hours, give or take. But to be honest, I can't see myself returning triumphant in the span of the afternoon. Everything beyond retracing my steps deeper into the forest is a nebulous, black nothingness. As dark and unknowable as deepest space. I have no idea what I'm going to do other than run blindly after my husband.

"Fine," Henry finally says, still clutching the bowls. "*Go*."

When he turns his back on me, I lay one hand on his shoulder. "I need your help, Henry. I can make it back to Felix's Jeep, but after that, I don't know where I'm going."

I can tell that he considers withholding this information from me in a misguided effort to make me stay. His shoulder is rock-hard beneath my palm, his jaw tight. But even if he refuses to help, I'll still go. I'll find a way.

"Please?"

Henry shrugs me off. But he says, "You'll know you've come to the right place when the ridge on the mountain side of the road looms over you. It looks like it might collapse."

I nod and think of the spot where Felix's Jeep has been abandoned. There had been a cliff, but did it feel ominous? I had been so focused on finding evidence of my husband that the rest of the world had disappeared. But it's got to be the same place. I'm sure of it. "And how will I find the path?"

"You can't see it unless you're up against the rock face. But when you're close, it looks like the cliff was dropped, and it cracked open. The split is just wide enough to fit the Ranger, but you won't get it through in this snow. You'll have to go the rest of the way on foot."

On foot. I swallow hard. I'm not a confident hiker, and certainly not in these conditions. But I push down any misgivings and ask, "Where's the cabin?"

"Maybe three-quarters of a mile beyond that, due east. A mile at most." Henry seems resigned. "You'll need to take the compass, or you'll never find it. It's easy to get twisted around—the trees all look the same after a while."

Don't I know it. But due east should be easy enough. I think I can hold that line. I'm grateful that Henry has given in so easily, and that I don't have to waste even more time arguing with him about the merits of this ill-advised rescue attempt. Is it even that? I can't imagine finding Felix in some desperate situation, throwing him over my shoulder, and hiking back out like some modern day, Shakespeare-quoting Wonder Woman. The thought almost coaxes the whisper of a smile to my lips.

"Thank you," I tell Henry seriously. But I stop short of assuring him that everything will be okay. I'm well aware that it may never be okay again.

✦

When it's time for me to leave, Henry is nowhere to be found. Finn hears me calling for his brother from the dining room and waves to get my attention. Jabbing a finger at the ceiling, he attempts to roll his eyes. He's groggy and fading fast, but I get the message. Henry's avoiding me.

"He's still mad?" I ask, coming to run my fingers through Finn's hair. It's a surprisingly familiar gesture, but it feels natural. I know the bond we've formed is the result of forced proximity and trauma—and when this is all over, we'll have to work hard to extricate ourselves from the fragile affinity these days have engendered—but the love I feel for him in this moment is fierce and real. "Don't worry," I say. "I'll be back soon. And Henry will get over it."

Finn nods a little, the movement twitchy and uncertain somehow. He won't meet my gaze, and when I hook my finger beneath his chin to try and make him look at me, he pulls away and turns his face into the pillow.

"Hey, what's wrong?" I wish I could sink to the couch beside him and give Finn my full attention, but I'm already half gone. And even if I did have the time and capacity to engage him, I couldn't begin to fix what's broken in his world. Instead, I say, "We'll talk when I get back. I have to go, okay? Tell Henry I said goodbye."

Finn doesn't respond. He doesn't move at all.

I'm torn as I turn to go, but I can't even conceive of a world in which I don't at least try to find my husband. *It'll be okay*, I assure myself again and sling the rucksack I've packed over one shoulder. I don't look back.

In the Ranger, I deposit the bag on the passenger seat and feel a swell of gratitude for Felix's perplexing foresight. The baton and mace that he ordered are tucked inside, as is the stun gun, though I'm not convinced I'd dare to deploy it. It's not a taser, and from what I understand, I would have to be in very close proximity to use it. Close enough to touch. I have no intent of getting within arm's reach of Benjamin Abbott—or anyone else who might be lurking in the woods. But if I can lay eyes on Felix, any risk will have been well worth it.

Of course, I understand that there is a very real possibility that Felix's fate has already been determined. If Gabi is dead by Ben's hand, I can't think of any reason why Ben wouldn't get rid of Felix, too. But hope is a reckless thing, as risky and unpredictable as diving headlong, and I've already flung myself over the edge. If there is any chance that my husband is alive, I'll do everything I can to bring him home.

It snows steadily on the way back to the place where Felix's Jeep was abandoned, but I hardly notice it. The world is gray and quiet, the mountain a sweeping potter's field that harbors the dead. I can't help but wonder about the bodies buried in these woods: the Indigenous tribes that called Washington home long before settlers came bearing guns and disease, the colonizers who knew nothing about the savage land, the miners who came during the Mount Baker gold rush to eagerly stake their claim. Surely this mountain is rife with hunters and hikers and homesteaders, peppered with tiny graveyards like the one in a clearing near Hemlock House that I have never visited.

Felix once told me that the Graham family plot contains sixteen bodies—sons and daughters and more distant relatives who didn't survive his great-grandfather's scheme to tame the mountain. Alastair Graham was lured to Washington in the late 1800s by the promise of cheap land and stayed because he was as headstrong as the mules that plowed his gardens. When others moved on, the Grahams clung on, and Hemlock House remains the only original homestead in the swath of wilderness between the border of the North Cascades and Requiem.

Except that it's not.

I believe Henry. There is another cabin on this mountain.

When I reach the Jeep, I carefully maneuver around it, keeping my gaze fixed forward so I don't have to confront the awful truth of what it contains. *Gabi*, my heart groans, mourning for a woman I never knew and the grief that her loss will unleash on Henry and Finn. On Felix. But I tamp down the horror that threatens to choke me and leave Gabriella Graham to her ancestors. For now.

Pulling the Ranger near the rock face—and as far from the Jeep as I can manage—I kill the engine and sit in the cold interior for a moment catching my breath. I'm heaving as if I've run a marathon, even though I've done nothing more arduous than steer for the last twenty minutes or so. A single tear would slice me wide open, but crying is a luxury I can't afford, so I swallow hard, grab the pack, and wrench open the door.

Almost immediately, snow begins to collect on the dark sleeves of my coat. On the ground, it's soft and deep, pooling around my waterproof boots and promising a difficult trek. When I take a step, my footprints backfill with slush and water, and it hits me that the snow won't last. When this is all over, the bridal veil will melt, leaving behind a dirty, winter world.

Did Henry say the cabin was a half mile due east? Three-quarters? It feels like an impossible journey from here, and I haven't even found the split in the rock. Yanking the straps of the pack tight, I settle it onto my shoulders and take off. But I haven't made it five steps when an unexpected burst of sound stops me short. A sharp, metallic bang ricochets unnaturally off the cliff face, then echoes again and again. The fourth time it rings out, it's accompanied by someone shouting my name.

"Sadie! Come on, Sadie! Let me out!"

My heart sinks. "No," I whisper, but he's still pounding away, and I have no choice but to hurry through the snow to the back of the Ranger.

When I release the tailgate, Henry all but tumbles out, his arms and legs unknotting. How long has he been sandwiched in the dump bed? And when did he tuck himself back there?

"What are you doing here?" I demand, silently cursing myself for believing that Henry would give up so easily.

"The same thing you are."

"How? How did you fit in there?" The dump bed is shallow, requiring Henry to be a contortionist. Never mind the fact that he was surrounded by hard plastic and metal as I bumped along the mountain road. It must've been absolutely miserable.

Henry works at his neck with the heels of his palms and indicates a corner of the back cover that's slightly ajar. He must have snaked a hand through and shut the tailgate himself. I regret that it never even crossed my mind to check.

"You shouldn't have come," I say, despairing. Felix's Jeep is behind us, closer to Hemlock House and less than thirty feet from where we stand. I'm frantic at the thought of Henry wanting to investigate, of what I'll have to do to stop him if he decides to take a peek. Nausea forces me to take shallow, guilty breaths.

But Henry seems wholly unconcerned about my husband's

Jeep and the terrible secret it contains. He just leans against the tailgate to shake out what I assume is a sleeping leg. "You'll never find it without me."

"You said due east! I'm not completely helpless. I can handle a little hike."

"It's harder than you think." Rising to his full height so that he's looking down at me, he adds: "And if you haven't noticed, we're in the middle of a storm. Just because you're too stubborn to admit it doesn't mean you don't need help."

"What about Finn?" Henry's eyes harden and I realize that I'm shouting. A cocktail of fear and fury is bubbling in my veins, but for once he doesn't engage. Instead, he turns away and sets off in the direction of the rock face. Away from the Jeep.

"He'll be fine," Henry calls over his shoulder. "I talked to him while you were upstairs. I promised we'd be back in no time."

I jog after him, weak with relief and hating myself, but the slushy snow drags at my feet and slows me down. I'm still several paces behind when I call: "And what if we're not?"

Henry pauses, and I can't tell if he's waiting for me or considering the question. Maybe both. But it's foolish to pretend that this ill-advised reconnaissance mission is safe or smart, and finally Henry relents. He turns to face me. "Look. We're doing this my way. I know Benjamin. I know the area. If you won't agree to my terms, I won't take you to the cabin."

I bite the inside of my lip, considering. I'm the grown-up here, and I want to be the one to call the shots, but Henry has a point. "Fine," I say crisply.

"Fine," he parrots, and takes off again. I scramble to keep up. "There's an outbuilding maybe fifty yards from the cabin. You're going to stay there and *stay hidden*." Henry shoots me a glare over his shoulder to make sure I've gotten the point.

"Stay there, stay hidden," I repeat, but there's heat behind my words. Unfortunately, he doesn't seem to notice. Pushing a frustrated exhale between my lips, I say, "And if anything happens—"

"You go straight back to Finn," Henry interrupts. "Don't worry about me, I can take care of myself."

I do worry about him, more than he could ever guess, but this sullen teenager has tied my hands. Maybe my sense of control was an illusion all along. And Henry has a point: we can't just abandon Finn to his own devices. "Fine," I agree reluctantly. "But you have to promise you won't *do* anything. Take a look around and get out."

Henry doesn't respond.

My hand shoots out and snags his sleeve, dragging him to a stop. "Promise me," I demand, twisting him around to face me. I search his eyes, looking for any indication that he can't handle this, that he's lying to me and has a plan beyond what we've agreed to. I can't read his expression.

"Yeah," Henry says after a moment. "Sure. Okay."

"We can't fix this alone. You know that, right? We're just here to check everything out." *To find Felix*, my heart whispers.

"To find my mom," Henry says, and I die a little inside.

I'm afraid he expects a response from me, but instead he yanks his arm away and takes off at a clip. He's not jogging, not exactly, but before I can take a single step after him, he tucks between a split in the smooth expanse of stone and disappears. I hurry to follow him into the shadowed cleft in the mountainside.

All at once, the world falls away. The crevasse is a natural wonder, a small slot canyon that looks as if two pieces of a perfectly matched puzzle have been drawn slightly apart. The ground is patchy with snow, and although thirty feet above our heads the top is open to the sky, between the sheer rock walls it's darker and stiller than I expected it would be. It's also smaller. I think Henry's wrong—I'm not sure the Ranger could pass through here because in places I can spread my arms and nearly touch both sides—and I wrestle an uncharacteristic claustrophobia as the canyon stretches on. Henry keeps vanishing around shadowed, silent corners, and although I know that he's only a bit ahead of me, I struggle to keep up. To keep him in my sight.

At any other time, I would find this place extraordinary. A well-kept secret. A gateway to another world. But we're not here to sightsee, and in a few interminable minutes, when I can finally spot the slow descent of the ridge coming to an end, relief floods through me.

The forest on the far side of the split in the earth doesn't look any different from the woodlands surrounding Hemlock House. But it *feels* different. Colder. Close somehow. Thick with the stench of a seclusion so absolute it tastes like exile. Tall trees cut the afternoon into ribbons, and a fist grips my heart and squeezes hard. I hate this place. And though I know I'm probably just reacting to the stories that Henry told me, I feel like I'm walking on unholy ground.

"Here," I say, fumbling in my pocket to offer Henry the compass. But when I look up, the instrument nestled in the palm of my outstretched hand, he's already striding away.

Henry ducks his head against the snow and takes long, purposeful steps. His feet know the way. He's going home.

BEFORE

SUNDAY, JUNE 21

SUMMER SOLSTICE

To Sadie, born and raised in the Midwest, June had always been synonymous with summer. With rising temps and sunny days. With her favorite strawberry ice cream and trips to Lake Michigan, where in the afternoon the sand was hot on the surface and cool underneath, damp and heavy when she dug in her toes. She had tan lines already, and a sprinkling of freckles across her sun-kissed cheeks. By mid-month, her hair was brightening to white gold.

But June in the Cascades wasn't summer at all. It was cool and wet, wreathed with fog in the morning that sometimes never evaporated but settled in low places like steam skimmed from a pot of boiling witch's brew. Sadie was perpetually cold, unused to the way the damp air crept in between every seam and chilled her to the bone. Those first few bewildering weeks, her heart curled still and numb in her chest, hibernating out of season.

Felix, on the other hand, was home. He rose early and hiked into the forest with nothing but a canteen and a sickle. Sometimes, Sadie woke just in time to peer out their bedroom window and watch him disappear into the trees, the wooden handle of the hooked weapon grasped loosely in his fist. She hated the oversized knife and its razor-sharp edge, even though she knew it was just a tool.

Decades ago, David Graham had cut trails all over the mountain, and when Felix and Sadie reclaimed Hemlock House, Felix had set his mind to clearing them. Why, Sadie wasn't entirely sure. Their stay on the mountain was supposed to be temporary, and Felix openly admitted that his father's paths through the trees serviced nothing but David Graham's own dark fantasies. He was hunting Sasquatch and mapping thin places, creating tabernacles out of nothing but towering firs and his own overactive imagination. Still, Felix spread his father's homemade maps across the table in the kitchen nook and pored over them as if they charted the way to buried treasure.

"Why?" Sadie asked when Felix came home around noon after several consecutive days spent clearing the trails. He was carefully wiping the sickle on a length of stained cloth that he had found hanging on a nail in the shed. His boots were caked in mud, his jeans soaked through from the knees down. But he'd rolled the sleeves on his flannel and pushed them past his elbows, and his ropey forearms were beaded with sweat even though it was barely fifty degrees.

"Excuse me?" Felix turned, his face half lit from the milky sun that poured in through the open shed door, but he kept his focus on the blade.

"Why are you doing this?"

Felix's brow furrowed. "Wiping the blade? It'll rust if I don't."

"No, why are you clearing your dad's trails? What's the point?" Sadie propped one hip on the doorframe of the shed and crossed her arms over her chest. Her nose crinkled at the scent of woods that clung to her husband from his morning expedition: moss and the sharp, green zest of crushed ferns.

She had to admit, it was kind of sexy, this alter ego. Her nerdy scientist husband stalking into the forest every day like some lumberjack. But it was also hard to square the man she knew with this stranger, and misgiving thrummed just beneath her skin. Felix hadn't even unpacked his telescopes yet, and when he carefully hung the sickle on a hook and wiped his hands on the dirty, checkered cloth, Sadie caught a whiff of decay. From the forest, of course. Rotting logs and decomposing leaves and the musty, rich aroma of dead and dying things.

"I don't know," Felix said, taking a step toward her. "I guess because in some ways I've really missed this place."

"Hemlock House?"

He winced, gave his head a single shake. "The mountain. I grew up here. I became interested in astronomy here."

Sadie remembered their first night at Hemlock House, the whelping foxes and the spill of stars in the midnight sky. Felix had been more himself then, more the man she married. She wanted to remind him that he had barely glanced at his research project since they arrived. Instead, he'd spent most days disappearing into the forest for hours on end. But there was something vulnerable in the way the fingers of his right hand pedaled at his side as if he wanted to reach for her but didn't dare.

"I just miss you, I guess," Sadie said, stepping close so she could still his hand with her own. She laced her fingers through his and turned her face up to wait for the kiss that he dutifully pressed to her lips. A chaste peck, but Sadie pushed to her tiptoes and found his mouth again, insistent, hungry for the man who had not so long ago given her the full weight of his staggering attention.

At first, Felix stiffened in surprise, then he softened and

kissed her back, untangling his hands from hers so that he could wrap his arms around her and pull her close. In a moment, they were breathless, and Sadie felt relief warm her from the inside out. She laughed against her husband's mouth and said: "Come upstairs with me."

Felix pulled away. The space where he'd been was instantly cool, a sudden breeze making Sadie shiver.

"I can't right now," Felix said, and though there was genuine regret in his voice, he was already ducking past her out of the shed. "I've made it to a junction, and I want to get as far as I can before it rains tomorrow."

On any other day, knowing that there was more rain in the forecast would have depressed Sadie to no end. But she didn't need any help in that department with her lips still flushed and her skin tingling from their all-too-short kiss. Felix had never dismissed her like that before. "Okay," she managed a little thickly.

"Hey," Felix turned back, cupped her cheek in his hand. "Let's do something special tonight. Maybe drive into town. Go to that Rye place. I hear they have food trucks there on the weekends."

Sadie managed a smile, a lopsided, wistful thing, and then Felix gave her chin a squeeze and left. He jumped into the Ranger and took off into the trees. He didn't look back.

✦

Nobody got dressed up in Requiem, but Felix did shower and change into clean clothes before meeting Sadie on the porch that night. The wilderness had been washed away, and in its place, Sadie could smell the essence of her husband again. She tipped the amber bottle of her half-gone beer in salute when he leaned against the porch rail across from her. Even wrapped in a blanket, Sadie was cold, but Felix was wearing a T-shirt, a jacket for later bunched in his fist.

"I'm sorry about earlier," he said, unprompted. Maybe he was responding to the look on her face, the set of her jaw as she threw back another swallow.

"It's okay."

"It's not." Felix seemed to wrestle with himself for a beat, gazing off into the trees before centering his attention on Sadie. Then he crouched down before her, resting both hands on the arms of the Adirondack chair so that she was trapped. "I know I've been busy and distracted. It hasn't been fair to you. I dragged you across the county, took you away from a community that you loved, and more or less left you alone in the middle of nowhere."

Tears pricked the back of Sadie's eyelids because everything he said was true. She took another swig of her beer to cover up the fact that she was one kind word away from crying for real. Moving to Hemlock House had been unimaginably hard—worse than she had expected. And with Felix acting aloof and even secretive, Sadie wasn't sure she had ever felt more alone in her life. Having Felix's love and attention, his sincere interest and careful notice of her, and then losing it, was far worse than if she had never fallen in love with him at all.

Felix ducked his head for a moment, took a deep breath. "This isn't an excuse, but it's hard for me to be here, too."

Sadie's laugh was brisk and sharp. "I can tell it's been a real nightmare."

"I deserve that. And I haven't been totally honest with you."

There was a second of pure nothingness, the moment before

impact when Sadie felt every muscle in her body tense. Here it was: a confession that would change everything. That would confirm what she always knew to be true. Love was a fickle, unpredictable, dangerous thing.

"I hate it here," Felix whispered. "This house. The memories it contains. My parents didn't love each other. My father was insane. Gabi was all I had until . . . " Felix rubbed his hand across his mouth. "Until I lost her. I thought it would be good to come back, you know, reclaim this part of who I am. I've been running for years."

Sadie put down her beer and covered Felix's warm hands with her cold ones. Running was something she understood well. "Then let's go. We don't have to stay here. We can go back to Newcastle or find somewhere else to enjoy our sabbatical. Maybe somewhere warm?"

Her half-hearted attempt at a joke didn't land, and Felix went to his knees on the porch and draped himself across her lap. There was nothing for Sadie to do but stroke his head, raking her fingernails through his dark hair the way she knew he liked. She had been angry only seconds before, but this was a side of Felix she had never seen. It undid her.

"I think I'm supposed to be here," Felix said, and Sadie could feel the burden of his exhale.

"Why?"

He thought about it for a long minute. "Because I haven't forgiven any of them."

"What about Gabi?" Sadie asked. "We could find her, Felix. She's the only family we have left."

We. The instant the word had left her mouth, Sadie wished she could take it back. But she and Felix were one. They'd made that exact promise when they said their vows, and she found that her heart longed for Gabi, too. It was illogical, maybe, but born from her own ache for family and the way that she couldn't help but love everything Felix loved. She wanted this for him. For herself, too.

"No," Felix said.

"What do you mean, no?" This time, the laugh in Sadie's voice was teasing. "We could find her, I'm sure we could. Everyone is online these days, or if she changed her name or something, we could hire a private detective. She's your sister, Felix. She has a *child*. You don't even know if you have a niece or nephew. We could—"

"Stop." Felix jerked upright, surprising Sadie with the vehemence of that one word. "Just stop. We're not going to go look for Gabi."

Sadie was stunned speechless.

"Look, I know you mean well, but Gabi didn't just leave, she abandoned me. She made a choice, and I didn't even factor into the equation."

The hurt was evident in the furious set of his shoulders, the downturn of his usually smiling mouth. Sadie could feel it radiating off him in waves, and she wondered what exactly happened to drive such a devastating wedge between brother and sister. What could sour blood so completely?

But beneath her husband's overt anger, Sadie could see the hurt. Whatever had happened between them, the wound Felix nursed was still open and oozing, the pain so close to the surface, it was impossible to contain.

"Okay," Sadie said. "We won't look for Gabi."

They rallied then, as much as they could, and took the Jeep down to Requiem for whiskey and street tacos from a truck that was painted the color of raspberry sorbet. Sadie held their half-finished conversation carefully, swaddling the sharp corners with the promise to herself that she'd try again.

They would work through it together, slowly, if necessary, but somehow, someway, Hemlock House would lose its power over Felix. And maybe she could convince him that they shouldn't close the door on the possibility of Gabi. Sometimes the thing you want most of all is the thing you don't dare to hope for.

Before they lost cell coverage on the way home, Sadie glanced at her phone and realized the date. "It's midsummer night!" she exclaimed, shocked that Felix had let the occasion pass without mention. He was forever alerting her to the most inconsequential celestial events, supermoons and meteor showers and eclipses that went largely unnoticed by the general population but became holidays in their tiny family of two. Sadie had grown accustomed to midnight stargazing and rising well before dawn, marking each astronomical phenomenon with gravity and celebration. How on earth could Felix have overlooked summer solstice?

"It is?" he said, turning onto the logging road. His voice was flat, expressionless.

Sadie's mouth went dry. "Come on," she coaxed. "Tell me all about it. Tell me about how the earth is at maximum tilt toward the sun and how there's continuous daylight at the North Pole."

Felix glanced at her out of the corner of his eye. "Sounds like you already know all about it."

"But . . . " Sadie trailed off. There was nothing left for her to say.

Felix didn't apologize, but he did reach for her, and when they pulled into the yard at Hemlock House, he stood with her in the twilight and pointed out some of the stars that she had come to know by heart. He tucked Sadie under his arm so that she could follow the line of his finger, but when she stepped away, she found that he wasn't watching the sky at all. Felix's gaze was trained on the edge of the forest, the trees shoulder-to-shoulder like good soldiers keeping safe the wild.

Felix stared north as if he knew there was something hiding just out of sight. As if he was looking for something. Or someone.

CHAPTER 16

THURSDAY

The path between the split in the rock and the place that Henry calls home is marked with deer antlers that have been nailed to the trees. After I first spot a fresh, bloodied skull topped with arching, jagged bone, my stomach twists so hard I stagger to a stop. Henry sees it, I know he does, but his pace never wavers, and I realize that these ghastly talismans are not a surprise to him. When we stumbled upon that deranged clearing on our doomed trip to Requiem, Henry knew exactly what he was looking at.

Ben did this, I realize. He did it here, on this shadowed north side of the mountain, and he did it near Hemlock House. His profanity spans decades. It's sick and twisted.

But I don't have time to consider it. The hike is cold and exhausting, the snow pummeling us in relentless waves, and when we finally crest a small rise and the cabin comes into view, it's nothing like I expected it to be. The picture in my head was of a rustic alpine chalet, maybe rough-hewn logs and a stone chimney set against the backdrop of the rugged north side of the mountain. But Henry and Finn's so-called home is a shack.

Between swirling gusts of snow, I can see that it's small and unwelcoming, held upright by mismatched lengths of untreated wood and plywood sheets that have been unceremoniously nailed over what I can only assume are holes in the original siding. The shingles are an odd assortment of shake, asphalt, and moldering two-by-fours, and an electric-blue tarp has been stretched across one corner of the roof. It's held in place by a few crumbling bricks that look as if they'd disintegrate if a bird ever deigned to land on them. Even the fresh covering of snow does little to soften the grim reality of this awful place. A residue of rot and neglect hangs in the air around us, accentuated by the oily smoke that belches from the single, crooked stove pipe in the roof.

Although everything inside of me recoils at the sight of the shack, a pinprick of hope punctures my sense of doom. If there is a fire roaring inside that miserable hovel, it means somebody is home.

"What are you going to do?" I whisper, even though we are a good fifty yards from the clearing where the shack decays into the earth.

Henry doesn't glance at me, his eyes resolutely fixed on the single window in the side of the cabin that faces us. There's a plaid blanket hung over it, a makeshift curtain that has not budged an inch since we've taken up residence beside a small outbuilding on the property. It's a ramshackle shed of sorts, and a rusting truck with a lift kit and roll bar is parked nearby beside an old UTV that's in terrible disrepair. Both are draped in snow. It appears no one has been in or out for quite some time.

"I'm going to see who's inside," Henry eventually says, and there's an air of hysteria in his tone.

I can't shake the feeling that this is a very bad idea. "How?" I ask.

"There's a window over the kitchen sink that we leave uncovered. I can see into most of the house from there."

It's generous to call the building before us a house. My guess is that it was once a single-room shanty that was added onto over the years. There's an annex off to one side that's leaning precariously. A bedroom? Maybe two if they're small. But I'm guessing the only warm room is the one with the stove, and I assume that's the main living space. The kitchen window must be on the back side—I won't be able to see Henry when he goes to investigate. A ripple of misgiving crawls over my already clammy skin.

"And then what?" I ask Henry, fishing. What I want him to say is: *I'll come straight back, report what I've seen, and we'll escape to Hemlock House.* But I already know who he *won't* see inside, and I'm worried about how he'll react.

"I'll come right back," Henry says dutifully, but I'm not sure that I believe him.

"You have to," I press. "Finn is counting on us." Maybe it's manipulative to bring up his brother, but I feel like I have no choice.

This seems to get through to Henry, even if only for a second. His face softens in the wintery half-light, and for just a moment I wonder if I can push him to come back with me right now. This excursion feels like a terrible mistake, and my hand twitches, desperate to grab Henry by the sleeve and drag him back the way we came. But then he gives his head a little shake and he takes one step away from the side of the shed. He's in the open, half of his body silhouetted against the pale snowscape of the forest, but there's no one around to bear witness but me. That first step is a big one, and once he's taken it and nothing immediately terrible happens, Henry is off.

"Be careful!" I call after him, maybe louder than I should, but my heart has begun to pound a drumbeat that can surely be heard for miles.

Henry is already gone. I watch as he weaves through the

trees in a zigzag pattern that makes him hard to track. He disappears and reappears so quickly I keep losing sight of him. Even in his dark coat—Felix's coat—he is just another shadow in the forest, a wraith among the relentless snowfall that continues to bury the world in white.

The half mile or so from the slot canyon to the shack was hard going—we made slow progress as our feet began to freeze in spite of our sturdy boots—but watching Henry now, I realize that he set such a sedate pace for my benefit. It's obvious that he knows these woods as well as he knows his own body. Every tree, every tract of stinging nettle, every boulder and waterway and blackberry patch are accounted for, and in no time, he has vanished from my sight altogether.

I send up a wordless prayer for Henry's safety, a groan that feels wrenched from the deepest part of my soul.

I'd give anything to have a do-over, for the chance to wind back the clock and start this week from scratch. A week ago today, Felix left for his nonexistent conference, and if I could have that morning back, I would wrap my arms around his neck and pull him into bed. I wouldn't let him leave without the love he promised me, and maybe if I would have pressed him—kissed the spot in the hollow of his neck that always makes him melt or questioned why his eyes were so sad—he would have given in.

Where would we be now if he had told me the truth? Would Gabi still be alive? Would Henry and Finn be safe? Perhaps in one of Felix's infinite universes we are all together at this very moment, warm and out of harm's way at Hemlock House, while Gabi proudly introduces me to her boys, and Finn gives me a shy wave from behind the sanctuary of his watchful big brother.

I want to be in that world so badly it aches. This moment in time is a shattered-glass, bloodied-mouth, record-scratch of a nightmare, and I would give anything for it all to be over and for the boys that I love—all three of them—to be safe.

Suddenly, the sound of a slamming door pierces the stillness, followed by: "Who's out there?" The man's voice is loud and distinct, commanding. The tone and tenor of someone who is well accustomed to being immediately obeyed.

Even though I'm tucked against the far side of the shed, I freeze. It's Benjamin Abbott, it has to be. What did he hear? What happened to draw him out of the cabin? My heart flaps weakly in my chest and my knees buckle beneath me. *Where's Henry?*

I don't recognize the sound of a shotgun loading until a blast splits the air. It shudders between the flakes of falling snow, a detonation that sends a strong, clear message: *run*. I could. I could slip back the way that I came, using the trees for cover the same way I saw Henry do just minutes ago. How long has he been gone? Time has lost all relevance out here, the interminable storm rendering minutes and hours meaningless. It's all the same gray nothingness, and I bite the damp fabric of my gloved hand to stop myself from screaming.

Of course, I'm not going anywhere. Not with Henry out there. There's simply no way I'm abandoning him. Or Felix, if he is indeed in the shack, injured or imprisoned or otherwise incapable of coming home to me.

Silence stretches for a second or two, and I force myself to exhale slowly, then inch forward just enough to peer around the corner of the shed. My blood is thumping so hard it momentarily blinds me, but then my vision clears, and I can see Benjamin Abbott standing in the snow several feet in front of the cabin. His eyes are trained on the opposite side of the shed, to the corner where Henry disappeared into the forest. Ben is so focused that he doesn't see the paper-thin sliver of my face in his peripheral vision, and I don't dare to so much as blink in case the movement draws his gaze.

He's leaner than I expected, and he looks so much older than he is. Wrinkled, sagging skin, wispy hair, black pools for eyes. His jeans are threadbare and his Carhartt jacket has seen better days. I would pity him if I didn't know who he is, what he's done. I could almost feel sorry for the shriveled hull of a man before me if it wasn't for the shotgun held taut across his body, trained at the place where Henry and I stepped out of the trees.

I don't know what to do.

"If I find you, I'll kill you," Ben calls, mean and mocking. "You're trespassing on my property."

I hear the distinctive metallic snitch of the shotgun loading, and then the resounding boom of another blast. A nanosecond later, there's a crack as a slug hits the far corner of the shed. An explosion of debris—dust and splinters and chunks of moldy wood—erupts twenty feet from where I'm hiding and rains down on my head and shoulders. My cheek stings, and when I raise my hand to it, my glove comes away red. A scratch, nothing but a scratch, but all at once I know that Ben means it: he will kill me.

For a few panicked seconds I consider my options. I can wait where I am, but barely concealed behind the shed, I'm a sitting duck. I could step out with my hands up—but I don't know if Ben will instantly make good on his promise and shoot. I consider and discard trying to go after Henry or calling out his name, but every scenario seems utterly hopeless, and I find myself pressed tight to the shed, with hot tears dripping from my chin. What have we done? Why did we come here?

Turning my face to the sky, I realize that the snow is letting up. The wind has died down and the snowflakes that still drift around me are brittle shards that seem to fall out of spite and nothing more. For the first time in days, it's almost quiet. I shift my weight and the packed snow beneath my boots groans. There will be no hiding now.

"Show yourself!" Ben screams.

My choices are gone. I take a shuddering breath and prepare myself to move out into the open. I manage a half step, just enough to peer around the corner and take terrified stock of the man with a gun trained on the place where he thinks I'll appear. Ben is still shifted slightly away from me, and I'm grateful for that one small mercy. But as I watch, my whole body tensed and waiting, there's sound and movement from the back side of the makeshift cabin. The forest goes still and silent as a crypt, as if somehow every particle, every atom of *everything* knows that this moment is singular.

"Benjamin, don't." Henry's voice is clear and powerful, ringing like a bell among the sanctuary of the trees. He steps into the clearing behind Ben, coming from the far side of the shack. Lifting his hands, he shows his father his open palms, proving that he's unarmed.

I watch, paralyzed, as Ben glances over his shoulder, taking stock of his eldest son, and then just as quickly turns back to the shed. He knows that I'm here. But he doesn't know who I am or what kind of threat I pose.

"Where's Mom?" Henry barks, fighting for Ben's attention. I don't know if he can see me half-hidden behind the rotting building and the vengeful slivers of snow. But I know he's trying to distract his father, to draw his attention away from me. A cruel smile cracks Ben's face, and he turns back to Henry, grinning.

Suddenly I'm moving. My mind barely has time to register what pure instinct has made me do before I find myself sprinting across the clearing. Eight long strides, nine, ten. I duck behind the tree nearest to the dilapidated shed, pinning my back against the rough bark. I'm breathless, my head spinning, but a quick glance around the wide trunk assures me that neither Ben nor Henry saw me move. The shotgun in Benjamin Abbott's hands commands the singular attention of his son, and Ben seems distracted by hate.

My whole life feels condensed into these fleeting, horrific minutes, and the clock that has ticked beneath my skin ever since I realized Felix wasn't coming home picks up its relentless beat. Nothing else in all the world matters right now but the double-edged sword of this terrible truth: I believe my husband is in that wretched excuse for a home, and his nephew is in grave danger. I can't let anything happen to either of them.

I carefully slide the rucksack from my shoulders, making sure to keep my silhouette well behind the refuge of the tree, and drop to my knees so I can dig through the contents. The stun gun and baton are both for close range, but the mace might be enough to disable Ben so that I can make use of them. For the first time in my life, I wish I could lay hands on something truly powerful. Fear and rage are a lethal combo, and I can feel them both frothing in my veins. I will tear into Ben with my bare hands if I must, an understanding that both startles and galvanizes me.

I tuck the stun gun in my pocket. Hold the mace in my left hand, the baton in my right. I give the cold rod a flick and the full length of it snaps into place, a sound so small and quick I don't worry about anyone hearing it. For just a second, I consider the so-called weapons at my disposal and feel a wave of panic. But before it can crest, I think of Felix, and without pausing to consider the consequences, I take off at a run.

Sticking to the very edge of the small yard, I race along the perimeter of the encroaching forest, deep enough in the veil of trees and brush that I can't see the clearing—and Henry and Ben can't see me. The snow muffles my progress, creaking softly with each furious stride, but I pray it's subtle enough that the men don't notice. I'm going in the opposite direction that Henry struck out in less than half an hour before. Vaguely, I realize that his footprints and mine likely loop around the shack, circling the hovel as if we have drawn a bullseye around the target of our search. *Here*, I think, and my heart echoes the cry: *right here*.

I'm nearly even with Henry and Ben when I realize I don't really know what to do. I can't rush the house without alerting Ben to my presence. I can't sneak up behind them without putting Henry in the crosshairs. I'm alight with a jealous sort of reckless love and longing, but I'm not a fool. Crouching behind the cover of thick underbrush almost directly behind Henry, I swallow a few ragged breaths and assess the situation.

Ben's gun is trained on his son, and neither he nor Henry has moved. We are a jagged line of potential disaster.

As my pounding heart slows, I realize that Ben is talking to Henry. His voice is too low for me to make out what he's saying, but he spills a steady stream of words that have a visible effect on Henry. First, the teenager's shoulders slump. Then his head hangs low. His hands go limp and drop to his sides, and I half expect him to go to his knees in the snow. I can't stop myself; I rise and take a single step toward him. And then a raw, angular wail is ripped from his throat. It's rough and excruciating, and Henry throws back his head and cries, the sound of an animal in pain. Dying.

Everything happens all at once. Henry's keening turns into a howl, a wicked, predatory sound that fills me with an ice-cold dread. He launches himself at his father, and Ben barely has time to load the shotgun before Henry is within arm's reach.

My fingers go limp, dropping the pathetic, ineffectual weapons I planned to use just moments ago. Charging out into the clearing, I scream: "Henry!"

He whips his head around, his eyes finding mine at the exact moment a third and final gunshot tears the day in half. The earth stutters and pauses in its rotation. I go rigid, my whole being focused on Henry as I wait, breathless, for the moment that he crumples to the ground. The last few days flash through my mind: my first glimpse of Henry on David Graham's Sasquatch cam, a lanky boy with a swollen black eye glaring at me in the greenhouse, his unexpected, tender care for his sick little brother. We've somehow lived a lifetime together in the span of these impossible, stolen hours, and my heart is a ghost town when I imagine this mountain without Henry on it.

But he doesn't fall. I blink, and fresh tears race down my icy cheeks as the freeze-frame judders to life before me. Henry takes a step back. The shotgun in Benjamin Abbott's hands slips from his fingers and disappears in a poof of snow at his feet. A second later his body follows.

Before Ben has fully settled, I'm moving again, sprinting to the place where Henry stands shaking, staring at his father prone on the ground. Dragging off my hat and my gloves, I drop them as I go. And when I can finally put my hands on Henry, I press my bare, cold fingers against every inch of him: his chest and stomach, his shoulders and neck. His arms, pale hands, blond head. I steel myself, ready for the ooze of warm blood that's pumping from some unseen wound.

There's nothing.

"This is Chief Colin Brandt with the Whatcom Sheriff's Department!" someone shouts from the direction of the shed. "Put your hands where we can see them!"

I can hear the thump of the stranger's words, but it's as if my ears are stuffed with cotton. My fingers are twisted up in Henry's coat, and I'm vaguely aware that we're holding each other up.

"Sadie!" he hisses, trying to pry me loose. "Put up your hands!"

But I can't comply until he grasps one of my wrists and raises it high overhead, spinning us both to face the forest. We're side by side, hands knotted together as we stand over Benjamin Abbott's body.

In a moment, two men emerge from the dark cover of the trees, running low to the ground with guns held out before them. They are both wearing green, fleece-lined uniforms with tall collars and thick, waterproof pants. On their chests I can see the gold, six-point star of the Whatcom County Sheriff's Department.

When they reach us, one drops to his knees, pressing a gloved hand to the place where blood gurgles out of Ben's back. His khaki coat is crimson with it, a stunning, winter bloom that my eyes simply refuse to focus on.

"Sadie Sheridan?" the other man asks, his tone commanding.

"Yes," I manage, too shocked by this sudden turn of events to say anything else.

He roughly pulls me away from Henry and pats me down, making sure I don't have a weapon. Yanking the stun gun from my pocket, he merely glances at it and then tucks it in one of the pockets of his jacket. When he's finished, he repeats the process with Henry. The officer steps back when he's satisfied that we're not armed, but his gun remains in hand.

"Chief Colin Brandt. We spoke on the phone a few days ago. Your friend Cleo Peters called in for a wellness check yesterday, and we've just managed to make it up to your residence."

"How did you find us?" I croak.

"The little boy told us. Your tracks were a dead giveaway, but he pointed us in the right direction."

"Finn talked?" I gape. "He *talked* to you?"

Chief Brandt ignores me, his eyes flicking to Henry. It's obvious that he's trying to make sense of the situation, but the man on his knees suddenly shouts: "We're losing him!"

And then they are both on the ground beside Ben, packing his wound with snow.

I should help. I should get a blanket or assist them as they attempt to roll Ben over. I know CPR. But Henry's eyes are unfocused, his legs unsteady, and I instinctively slip his arm over my shoulder and grab him around the waist so that I can help him to the warmth of the little, leaning shack. He's in shock, his lips turning blue and his jaw slack, and all I know to do is find a place to lay him down before he joins his father on the ground.

Officer Brandt yells after us, but I don't stop.

The cabin is dark and smells of cooking grease and unwashed bodies. It's too hot, too close, and I fumble frantically at the zipper of my coat, suddenly afraid that I'm going to pass out. I can't take care of Henry—of anyone—if I go to pieces. Sucking in the fetid air, I try to ground myself in the single room: along the back wall, a propane stove, a few crooked-door cabinets, a sink piled high with dirty dishes; beside me, an old couch, a wooden rocking chair, a round table. It's dark and depressing, but there are bits of beauty amid the squalor. A knit blanket in the colors of a sun-kissed sea. A mason jar with a handful of drooping wild sunflowers on the table, gathered before the storm. In the windowsill, a pretty cairn of smooth, blue stones.

I can breathe again, shallowly, and I lower Henry to the ratty couch, sloughing off my coat and tucking it around him as he starts to shiver. I can't bring myself to touch the lovely blanket (made by Gabi?) with my filthy hands. "You're safe," I tell

Henry, smoothing his hair from his damp forehead, but I'm not sure that he understands.

Henry is mumbling, his eyes blank and fixed in the middle distance, and from the open cabin door I can still hear Chief Brandt shouting outside. But only one sound pierces through my daze. A single word.

My name on his lips: "Sadie."

My hand is still on Henry's head when I finally spot him, tucked deep in the shadows where a black hallway leads to the little annex. One arm is chained to a copper pipe, and he's wearing the red sweater he left Hemlock House in, the same jeans. There's a week's worth of scruffy beard on his face, but I can tell that beneath all that hair, his cheeks are gaunt, his lips cracked and dry. Still, they pull into a faint smile for me.

"*Felix.*" His name is a whisper, an invocation. Then I'm across the small room in a few wobbling strides and sinking to my knees before my husband.

He's an apparition, a wish granted, and I'm not even sure that I dare to touch him for fear that he'll evaporate before I can prove to myself that he's real. But his eyes crease in that way that I love—just a hint of the sparkle that charmed me on a football field in Iowa glinting in his watery gaze—and I know my husband is not lost to me forever. I reach out to gently cup his face in both of my hands, and his unchained arm lifts to tangle grubby fingers into my hair. Snowflakes tumble free, cold droplets that bead on his hot skin and melt away, and then I'm kissing his face. His warm temple, his forehead, his closed eyes, the bridge of his nose. I taste salt and smoke and longing. When I pull his head into the crook of my neck, I don't know if the tears are mine or Felix's. Or Gabi's or Henry's or Finn's. Maybe the earth is crying with us, each snowflake a teardrop for every hidden hurt, bearing witness to all the pain we cannot see.

There are a hundred things I want to say to Felix, a thousand, but the words won't come. And maybe it's for the best, because in the silence of everything unsaid, in the dank and dingy cabin where nightmares once lived, a different sound fills the hollow space.

A baby begins to cry.

CHAPTER 17

FRIDAY

Felix holds a paper cup of peppermint tea in both hands and inhales the steam. His dark head bent over the rim, hair still damp from a long, hot shower, might just be the most beautiful thing I've ever seen. I can't stop myself: I reach one finger and trail it across his skin, tracing the ridges of his knuckles. He looks up.

"Hey, you."

"Hey, yourself." I sink to the hospital bed beside him and kiss his shoulder through the clean sweatshirt I grabbed from Hemlock House. It was a quick stop, a frantic grab and go that resulted in a hodgepodge of mismatched items with varying degrees of practicality. There are fresh clothes and a toothbrush, but for some reason I also snagged a book from his nightstand, a pair of plaid pajamas he's never once worn, and his favorite bottle of cologne. My mind lurched as I blindly threw stuff in an overnight bag, and then I went back for more because Henry and Finn would need things, too. Now, the overflowing duffel sits on a visitor's chair in Felix's hospital room, spilling all the trimmings of a second chance. It's an extravagance of riches.

It took hours for help to arrive at the cabin in the woods, but it felt like mere minutes. When Chief Brandt realized there was nothing more that could be done for Benjamin Abbott, he came inside the cabin to find Henry shaking on the couch and Felix still chained to the pipe. I had my hands full—literally—with a newborn baby girl who was single-handedly taking care of all the screaming the situation required. There was nothing for me to do but hold her and shush her, one hand methodically patting her back as I assured her over and over and over that everything was going to be okay. I couldn't decide if she was crying because she didn't believe me or because she did.

The snow stopped completely around the same time the stars came out, and I stepped into a velvet night beneath a sweep of infinity so clear and bright it was dazzling. Felix had one arm draped around my shoulders, and it took all my strength to hold him up. He was dehydrated and shivering and weak, but he tipped his head up anyway and traced the great square of Pegasus because he could.

"It's upside down, you know," he told me, not for the first time. But I didn't stop him. I would listen to his explanation again and again, a thousand times over if only he'd keep talking to me. "The constellation, I mean. A white-winged horse galloping to another galaxy."

"I thought there was no upside down or right side up in space."

"That's my girl," Felix murmured, and he kissed my crown with his chapped lips.

"In every world," I whispered.

And without missing a beat he whispered back: "You found me."

The clear night made it possible for the helicopters to fly. There were two emergency chopper flights from the St. Joseph Medical Center that lifted first Felix, Henry, and the baby, and then came back for Finn. My journey to Bellingham was a bit more complicated and included a couple of snowmobile rides and then an escort in one of the sheriff's department Ford F-

150s, sirens blaring whenever we reached an intersection that the officer who was driving didn't care to slow down for.

On the way, Chief Brandt explained that Cleo had assured them the situation at Hemlock House was life or death. Of course, there's no way that she could have known what we were going through on the homestead, but when she wasn't able to get through, she panicked and called in the cavalry. The officers knew something was very wrong when they found Finn alone. And then Gabi's body in the Jeep near the pass. They abandoned their snowmobiles long before they reached the cabin where Ben held his family hostage for nearly two decades, and arrived just in time to watch him fire his second shot into the side of the shed.

I imagine it was a lot of excitement for the entire department. Two bodies, a run-down shack in the woods, a handful of malnourished and clearly neglected kids—two of whom didn't even exist in the eyes of the state because they had been born on the mountain. It was a smorgasbord of transgressions, a sordid tale that would no doubt keep a team of investigators busy for weeks if not months to come.

It was also our story. Our lives snarled up in the sort of chaos I couldn't have even begun to imagine only a week ago.

"I don't know what to say," Felix whispers against my neck, his warm breath coaxing goose bumps along my arms.

"Say everything," I tell him. "Out of order, in a hot, jumbled mess, I don't care. Just start somewhere. Get it out."

He sighs and leans over to put his still-full cup on the rolling tray beside the bed. It's well after midnight, his hospital room finally dim and quiet. The ER doctor insisted on keeping him overnight for observation, and an IV drips fluid into his left wrist. I'm grateful for it, even though I know in my bones that Felix's body is fine. It's his heart I'm worried about.

"Start with her," I say, shifting so that I can peer into the bassinet one of the nurses rolled into the room. They weren't sure what to do with the baby, but Felix was insistent—he wouldn't let her out of his sight. So, after determining that despite being a bit underweight, she was perfectly whole and healthy, the pediatrician on call acquiesced.

Now she's swaddled in a blanket the color of fresh pistachios and sleeping soundly on her side. She's gorgeous. A sweep of soft black hair, pink cheeks, a tiny bow of a mouth making little sucking movements as she dreams.

"What's her name?" I ask.

Felix wraps a tentative arm around my waist and pulls me to him, but the movement is hesitant. It's as if he's afraid I'll pull away. I don't. I swing my legs up onto the bed and cuddle into his side, keeping my eyes on the baby.

"I've been calling her Juliet."

He can't see the hint of a smile that shadows my lips. "As in Romeo and?"

"As in one of the twenty-seven moons of Uranus."

I snort a quiet laugh. "Of course."

Felix squeezes me tighter. "Juliet Gabriella."

"It's perfect."

I've already guessed this part of the story, but I let Felix tell me anyway. About how Gabi wasn't due for a couple of weeks yet. How on the day that Felix allegedly left for the Planetary Sciences Symposium in San Diego, he really went to buy groceries and pay the first and last month's rent on the little apartment that he had found for his sister and nephews in Sumas. Gabi was supposed to be safely ensconced there long before Juliet was born.

There is wonder in Felix's voice as he tells me about their plan. About how easy and airtight it had all seemed. He got everything ready on Thursday and was supposed to transport them on Friday when Ben left to get supplies. In and out. A simple extraction and a brand-new life. Ben would never know. He could never know because he wouldn't let them go.

"He'll kill me," Gabi had whispered on the phone one of the few times she was able to call. "He'll kill all of us."

At first, Gabi refused to tell Felix where she was. He just listened while she told him little things about Henry and Finn, the men they were becoming. And then, mid-sentence, she'd be gone. But one night she called, and everything had changed. She wanted out. *Now*. She wanted Felix to help her.

They had to craft a plan in stolen moments, laying the ragged groundwork for an escape that allowed them to slip away unnoticed and disappear. Felix had wanted to call the police or hop in the Jeep to rescue his sister himself, but she had convinced him that it was too dangerous. Someone would get hurt. Most likely Finn or Henry. It was better—*safer*—to be sneaky about it. To wait until the second Friday of the month when Ben would leave the mountain for supplies. They couldn't go to Hemlock House because it was one of the first places Ben would look, so instead Felix created a haven.

He had three weeks to pull it off. But almost as if it had been divinely appointed, everything fell into place. The apartment he had found for Gabi was a basement suite on a cute acreage with a property line that skirted the Canadian border. The couple who lived upstairs were retired but eager to have kids around, and they had even strung a swing in a backyard tree for Finn. There was a small but wonderful hospital nearby, a good school system, a church with a robust ministry that helped women in unsafe or abusive situations find refuge. It was a fairy tale of sorts, and over the course of those stolen days—in furtive, randomly timed calls whenever Gabi could manage it—brother and sister crafted a getaway so filled with promise it was hard to believe anything could go wrong.

Until it all did.

"What are the chances?" Felix asks, more to himself than to me. "That when Gabi finally gathered the courage to reach out, the only phone number she remembered, rang in the kitchen at Hemlock House."

"And you were there," I finish. "I don't think that was an accident."

He gives a soft humph. "What's that supposed to mean?"

"That you were exactly where you were supposed to be, exactly when you were supposed to be there."

"Are you telling me you believe in God, Sadie?"

I nestle deeper into Felix's chest. "Are you telling me you don't?"

He sighs, long and low. "I don't know what I believe about anything anymore."

"Tell me what happened that day," I say, partly to distract him from the chasm of an existential crisis, but also because I need to know. Henry already told me his side of the story, about the crowbar and their attempted escape from the cellar. About Ben's early return. What happened after Henry took Finn by the hand and ran? "She went into labor, didn't she?"

I can feel Felix nod.

While the boys were escaping and Ben was hauling Gabi back to the cabin, Felix was on the road by the canyon, their meeting place. He waited impatiently for the sound of Ben's truck leaving the mountain farther down the logging road—on the rarely used back loop—but it never came. When he couldn't stand it a moment longer, Felix hiked through the ravine and found the cabin himself. Ben was there; the boys were long gone. Gabi was already near delivery. There was nothing for him to do but rely on everything television and movies had taught him about childbirth. Towels, hot water, scissors that had been dipped into a pot of boiling water.

"She gave birth on the floor of that shack," Felix says, the words flat and dull. "Apparently, it wasn't the first time."

He's still in shock, I realize. *Convinced that maybe he can rewrite the ending, if only.*

"If only Ben would have listened," Felix says, unknowingly echoing my thoughts. "After the baby was born, I knew something was wrong. If he would've let me take her in the Jeep sooner, I might have been able to get her to a hospital in time."

Of course, there's no way to know that for sure, but I don't question his conviction. Felix needs that anger right now to power through all that is to come. Without a bit of a blunt edge, I'm afraid he'll be tempted to curl up in a corner and sob.

Felix has only cried once since I found him in the cabin, and it was alone in the hospital shower while the rush of running water muffled his groans. I leaned against the bathroom door and listened to him weep, the grief surging out of him like a flood. It's the saddest thing I've ever heard, and I pressed my forehead to the metal door and cried right along with him. But when he came out, his eyes were dry.

"My sister died in the back seat of my car," Felix whispers.

His arm is still wrapped around me, and I weave my fingers through his, hanging on for dear life.

The rest of the story trickles out slow and steady, a fragment here, a memory there. When Gabi's breathing became irregular, and her blood had soaked through every towel they could find, Ben finally agreed it was time to get help. They swaddled the baby, tucked both mother and daughter into the UTV, and raced to where Felix's Jeep was parked and waiting on the logging road. But it was too late. Felix barely had time to settle his sister into the back seat before she took her last breath. There were no poignant final words, no tearful goodbye. One minute she was still clinging to life, the next, she was gone.

When it was over, Ben seemed to realize that he was culpable for her death, guilty of negligence at best, though second-degree manslaughter was certainly not out of the question. And once authorities started digging, what else would they uncover? What would Henry and Finn say when they eventually turned up? Ben couldn't let any of that happen, and before Felix had even begun to mourn his sister's death, he found a gun pointed at his head. Never mind that he was still clutching Gabi's newborn baby to his chest. Ben took little interest in her.

The weather was antithetically lovely when they trekked back to the cabin, and Felix was already improvising a plan. There was a tin of baby formula in the kitchen, along with a pack of newborn diapers and some of the boys' old baby clothes. Felix knew next to nothing about infants, but he knew enough to tie off the umbilical cord, offer her a bottle, and change her diaper when she was wet or dirty. She slept a lot and ate a little, and while Felix held her, he sketched their getaway in his mind.

Ben was smaller than him, shorter and slight from years of poor nutrition and back-breaking labor from their off-the-grid lifestyle. Felix could easily overpower him, take the UTV and run. But then it began to rain, and when the rain turned to snow, Ben took a bottle of homemade mash bourbon from beneath the pump sink in the kitchen. Before he began pouring out the eighty-proof liquor, he padlocked Felix to a pipe with a length of rusty chain, and that was that.

"Ben didn't kill you," I say, and there's wonder in my voice.

"I don't think he dared. I was his older brother for a season. Besides, he needed me for Juliet."

I run my fingertips gently over the white bandages around

Felix's wrist, my touch a benediction for healing and wholeness. The ugly bruising isn't quite covered by the snug wrap, but the cuts are cleaned and covered, no stitches required.

"Did she love him?" I ask.

Felix thinks about it. "In the beginning, I suppose. Because he was sad, and she thought she could change that. He wasn't evil or anything—not when we were kids anyway. He was just . . . really messed up."

I know more of Ben's story now. Of the abuse and addiction, the fractures in his psyche that were invisible but that permeated every part of his being. I can't help but think about how some people grow strong in all their broken places, and others never mend. Their wounds seem to fester and rot, poisoning their blood—and everyone who gets close enough to touch. I can't decide if it's grace or dumb luck that our hurts have healed over. We're scarred, but somehow still whole. I just hope that this doesn't break us.

"You're a good man, Felix. Good and kind and tenacious." I roll over to face him and press my body against his, my head tucked beneath his chin where I can feel his heart beat. "I just wish . . ."

"You wish what?" he prompts.

And suddenly I can't breathe. Here it is, a flood of emotion that blindsides me: all the pain and anger that I have shoved aside to embrace the joy and wonder of Felix's homecoming. I've spent most of my life feeling unworthy, unseen. Alone. Loving my husband—and believing that he loved me in return—is probably the greatest risk I've ever taken.

"I can't talk about this right now," I manage, my voice husky with hurt. I try to push away, but Felix's arms tighten around me.

"I hid this all from you," he whispers against my hair, automatically recognizing the reason for my sudden distress. "Sadie, I'm so sorry."

They're just words, but Felix's sincerity is gutting, especially in the face of what he did to me. To us. "Why?" I demand, forcefully tugging out of his embrace and sitting on the very edge of the bed. I'm over him, my body angled away, arms crossed tight against my chest in a defensive posture that makes me feel like a kid again. As if my arms can somehow protect my splintered heart. I wish that I could bury my questions and ignore my doubt, but Felix betrayed me in a way that just a week ago I would have bet my life he'd never even consider. "Why?" I demand again.

"I never told you about Ben because I was ashamed." Felix's head dips, and then he looks up, forces himself to hold my gaze. "He moved in my junior year of high school and ruined our family. He ruined my life."

There's heat in his words, and I listen as he tries to explain the upheaval that Ben brought into the Graham home. They were hanging on by a tendril before he arrived, but the traumatized boy inflicted his own brand of trouble that turned Hemlock House into a tinderbox.

"It split us apart. He was messed up. Dangerous. But Mom defended Ben, trying to love him back to health and wholeness, and I guess Gabi ended up doing the same. I didn't realize that she was falling for him until it was too late." Felix's voice cracks. "And then I just left. I abandoned them all the first chance I got."

There's real grief in his words, mingled with shame. I trace circles on his thigh, but I can't bring myself to look at him.

"I lost my family because of Benjamin Abbott," Felix says. "Twenty years ago, and then all over again."

I want to comfort him, but it's not that simple. "That doesn't explain why you kept it from me when we moved to Hemlock House."

"I wanted to keep you safe!" Felix grabs my hand, stilling the feather-like movement of my finger. "To keep you far away from all of this. You saw who Ben was, what he could do without a second thought. I didn't want you anywhere near him. And I didn't want him to know that you even *existed*."

"I'm not a child," I remind him. "I could have helped. I *did* help."

"I know."

"You lied to me." I make myself admit the truth, say those awful words out loud. But in the space between us, they lose a bit of their power. We're not perfect. We never claimed to be. And though I'll have to find a way to forgive my husband for what he did—and how we almost lost everything because of it—I can't help but wonder if I would do the same thing if the roles were reversed. What would I do to protect the man I love? Lie? Steal? Make impossible, life-changing choices that could never be undone?

Would I wish for a gun, my finger trembling on the trigger that would remake the world?

Yes.

"I'm sorry," Felix says again. "I'll keep saying it until—"

"Stop." I pick at a snag on the blanket covering Felix's legs, and study my husband. He's propped on the pillows, dark circles beneath his sad brown eyes. He seems thin to me, and he looks exhausted, his whole countenance heavy with anguish and regret. But there's a spark there. He stares back at me, ready to fight for us if it comes to that. My husband is still fierce and defiant. Hopeful. Our story isn't over yet.

"You did the best you could," I tell him, holding all my hurt and his reasons why in the same, splintered space. "You did everything you could to save Gabi and her kids. Henry and Finn and Juliet are okay because of you."

"But—"

"I think I can forgive you," I interrupt him, "if you can promise no more secrets. No more lies."

Felix has the audacity to snort. "Never again," he says, sliding his hand across the blanket and wrapping his pinky around mine. "I swear."

"You and me. Come what may."

Felix gives me a wry smile. "'Doubt thou the stars are fire; doubt that the sun doth move.'"

"Are you quoting *Hamlet* to me, Dr. Graham?"

"Shush," he says, squeezing his eyes shut, trying to remember. "Something, something about a liar."

"'But never doubt I love,'" I finish for him.

"Yeah," Felix's eyes go soft. "That's the one."

My husband takes my face in his hands and pulls me down, pressing his lips to mine so gently I moan. The whole world is a mess, but Felix is here. We're together.

I'm fading into him, letting love wipe every ledger clean, when there's a sound like a kitten mewing from somewhere beside us. It takes a moment for me to remember that there is a baby in the room, a little girl who has known no mother or father but my Felix. I push myself out of the way so that he can go to her, bending low over the bassinet and soothing her with murmured words that only Juliet can hear. When he lifts her into his arms, Felix is the perfect mix of tough and tender, mess and miracle, and I fall in love with him all over again.

◆

Our story has spread like wildfire through St. Joseph, and no one tries to stop us when we lift the receiver for admittance to the pediatric ward. It's the middle of the night, but the nurse on the video feed just waves us in.

"Well, aren't you a pretty one?" the night nurse coos, coming from behind the desk to smile down at Juliet bundled in Felix's arms. She's wearing a cheerful set of scrubs with cartoon dogs printed all over them, and her name tag says "Kayla." Stroking the shell of the baby's tiny, curled hand she asks: "How's she doing?"

"She's good," I say, answering for Felix. His eyes are already roving over Kayla's shoulder, looking for the room where his nephews have been settled into side-by-side beds. I was right from the beginning: Finn has a bad case of double pneumonia. It must have been brewing since before the boys spent a couple of nights on the mountain and in the greenhouse. And the doctors are holding Henry for observation. The brothers are in the same room because I assured everyone separation wasn't an option.

Now, I tell Kayla, "She's just had a bottle, and we wanted to see how the boys are doing. Any chance we could peek in on them?"

Kayla stares at the baby for a moment, her bottom lip between her teeth, considering. Juliet's eyes are wide and shining in the glow of the fluorescent lights. They're blue now, navy almost, but I have no doubt they'll fade into the same deep brown as Finn's. She looks just like him.

"If you're quick," Kayla finally concedes, sighing. "And quiet. They both need their rest. And frankly, so do you."

We know. Chief Brandt stopped in before lights out and assured us he'd be back in the morning for a series of formal interviews. We will all have to give statements, and I'm already worried about how that process will go with Finn. I saw him for a few brief moments upon my arrival at St. Joseph, but the next time I peeked in on him, he was settled in his room and sleeping soundly. Likely medically induced.

I still have no idea how Finn told Chief Brandt and Officer

Jameson where to find me and Henry. I still have no idea what his voice sounds like or if he'll ever use it again. Maybe his spoken words were a feat borne of fear and necessity that will never be repeated. Especially now, in this world remade without his mother or his father. My heart seizes just thinking about how awful that conversation will be.

Shaking off that bit of borrowed trouble, I thank nurse Kayla and take Felix's IV cart in hand. Leading him to Henry and Finn's shared room, I carefully push open the door.

Felix hasn't met his nephews. He doesn't know how hard Henry worked to keep Finn safe. Sheltering him on the mountain, lying about their ages so that if things didn't work out the way he was hoping, they wouldn't be separated. There was a stack of old Boxcar Children books in the shack, and I wonder how much of Henry's information about unaccompanied minors and precarious situations came from the dog-eared novels. These boys are living, breathing wonders, and Felix knows it the second he steps into the room. I can tell by the way his chest expands as he carefully passes Juliet into my waiting arms.

Finn is sound asleep in the bed nearest the door. A strip of recessed lighting on the wall behind him casts a halo on his chocolate-colored curls, and his eyelashes flutter against his cheeks as he dreams. I can tell the magic of modern medicine is already healing him from the inside out because his skin looks warm instead of sallow.

I'm not sure if I should quietly introduce Felix to Finn, but I don't have to wonder long because Felix pads silently to stand vigil beside Finn's bed. He stares at his nephew for several long moments, and then he lowers his head and covers his eyes with his good hand. His shoulders heave, and I can't tell if he's crying or taking deep, steadying breaths. Drawing Juliet tighter to my chest, I force myself to stay put and let Felix have this moment.

It's Henry who breaks the spell. "You look just like her," he says.

Startled, Felix's head snaps up.

Henry's bed is next to the window, and it appears neither of us realized that he was awake all along. His brow is a defiant, harsh line in the muted glow of the track lights, and he studies Felix with open suspicion. There's no question who he's talking about. Henry has never met Juliet—he thinks that Felix looks just like his mother.

"People used to mistake us for twins," Felix says, not missing a beat. He steps out from behind Finn's bed and slowly crosses the room, pulling his IV stand beside him. It's a visual reminder that they're in the same boat, and I'm suddenly grateful that for his first meeting with Henry, Felix is pale and wearing pajama pants. It levels the playing field somehow. "When we were kids," Felix continues. "Did you know that there's only eleven months between us?"

Henry gives a barely perceptible shake of his head.

"We were about the same size for a couple years in elementary school. You know, before I hit my growth spurt." Felix waves one hand at his six-two frame and lifts a shoulder as if to say: *That didn't last long.*

"I was taller than her, too," Henry says.

The use of the past tense guts me. Of course he knows that Gabi is gone, but the news must still be so fresh it burns like a raging fire. I want to comfort him, but I stay in the shadows, rocking Juliet side to side so that Felix can focus all his attention on his sister's firstborn son.

"I don't look like her though." There's raw sorrow in Henry's voice, as if he thinks that resembling Ben is a blight on his character.

Felix grunts his disagreement. "Yes, you do. You don't have

the same hair color or eyes, but you're a Graham through and through. It's in the cheekbones, the high forehead. I'd have known you in a sea of strangers."

Henry blinks hard, and then passes a hand over his face as if he can erase the raw emotion on display there. "So, what?" he says almost angrily. "Are you, like, my dad now?"

Felix is silent for a moment. "Is that what you want?"

"I'll be eighteen in the spring. I don't need a dad."

The rest is left unspoken, but it lingers in the room. Henry doesn't need—or want—another dad or a mom or a family. He's not ready for a guardian or father figure to try to erase the horror that was his biological dad. Ben was a train wreck of trauma and dysfunction and suffering. No thank you. Never again.

But I know Henry knew love. That there is no way he could be the man that he is without experiencing the love that Gabi so clearly poured out on her sons. Henry is in agony now, but it'll get better, bit by bit, day by day. And maybe someday I'll be able to share with him what I saw in the snow outside the rotting shack where he grew up. In the moment that Ben cocked the gun and raised it, he faltered. He saw Henry's face, and the barrel of the shotgun dipped toward the ground.

I know that Benjamin Abbott had a chance to kill his son, and he couldn't do it. He may have threatened it, and in a different time or place he might have followed through, but just hours ago, looking into Henry's eyes, Ben didn't even try to pull the trigger.

There's grace in that. A brutal, hard-won mercy that speaks of the man that Ben could have been if he had been born under different circumstances. To a mother who didn't send him to the NICU with meth in his veins. Who didn't routinely leave him in the insufficient care of a rotating collection of chemically dependent and perpetually indifferent family members.

Whether it was addiction or mental illness or something more sinister and spiritual doesn't matter. Ben was a monster, but he was also the broken boy who Gabi had once loved when no one else would.

"Maybe we could just be a safe place to land," I say, stepping out of the shadows. "The state will have to figure out custody, but Felix is your only blood relative, so I don't think it'll be an issue. You are welcome at Hemlock House in whatever capacity you choose, for as long or as short as you'd like."

Felix's eyes flash to mine. We haven't talked about this, not yet, but his expression is pure gratitude and disbelief. I almost roll my eyes at him. Of course we'll stay. Of course we'll fill in whatever gaps we can and provide the stable home that Finn and Juliet—and hopefully Henry—need. There was never any doubt.

I expect Henry to push back, to be disagreeable and angry and rude, but his gaze is fixed on the bundle in my arms. I smile a little. "You didn't tell me your mother was pregnant."

He shakes his head as if to clear it. "She wasn't due until November. It didn't seem important."

"Would you like to meet your baby sister?"

Henry only pretends to wrestle with himself for a moment. Then he puts out his hands for her and I close the space between us. Juliet has worked both arms free from the blanket and her little fists are opening and closing, reaching for something that's not there. When she's settled into the crook of Henry's arm, he holds one finger in front or her and Juliet grasps it as if she was waiting for her brother all along.

"What's her name?" Henry asks.

"I've been calling her Juliet," Felix says. "Juliet Gabriella. But if there's something else—"

"No," Henry interrupts. "I like it."

Later, there will be time to tell him what it means. How his sister is named after a different tragic love story and the winter-white moon of a far-flung planet. There will be talk of classic literature and astrophysics, stargazing and Bard on the Beach, strawberry ice cream and his first trip to the ocean. There will be time for everything we want to say, and for dreams that Henry doesn't even know how to hope for, to grow in the fertile soil of his imagination.

But for now, Felix just lays a careful hand on Henry's shoulder, and the young man doesn't shrug it off. It's a beginning.

EPILOGUE

SIX MONTHS LATER

The chime above the door jangles when Finn bursts into Trilogy, and Cleo automatically looks up from the till.

"Finny, my boy!" she calls, a smile crinkling her eyes at the corners. Passing change to an elderly woman in a duckling-yellow raincoat, Cleo comes out from behind the counter and puts out her right hand.

Finn shakes it, slaps it, pounds it, and then ends their special handshake with a forearm bump and a *too cool for school* sidestep around Cleo to study the display case of freshly baked goods. She laughs and lets him go, then envelops me in a hug.

"Good to see you," I tell her.

"You, too! Welcome back. How was Guemes?"

The little island across the channel from Anacortes was the perfect weeklong getaway, and I tell her so. We rented a house overlooking Padilla Bay and spent hours combing the windswept beaches hunting for agates. We were unsuccessful, but Finn has an ice cream bucket of ocean-smoothed stones to show for our efforts. He'll use them to build perfectly balanced cairns and rustic inukshuks on the windowsills all around Hemlock House. We're already running out of space for his increasingly complicated sculptures.

"Any progress?" Cleo asks, glancing over her shoulder to make sure that Finn can't hear her.

I shake my head. Beyond the words that Finn uttered for Chief Brandt, he's yet to speak again. His counselor has encouraged us to be patient, but there's a part of me that wonders if this silence is just a part of who Finn is. I've been taking sign language classes with him online, and it's been a good thing for both of us. A step forward into a future that is every bit as bright as one filled with words formed on his tongue instead of with his beautiful, expressive hands.

The trio of doorbells jingles a second time, and Cleo and I turn to watch Felix step into Trilogy with Juliet in his arms. She's a chubby six-month-old with thigh rolls that cause complete strangers to stop and admire. Her black newborn hair has lightened to tawny brown, and her eyes remain an almost haunting twilight blue that is like nothing I've ever seen before. In short, she's gorgeous—the spitting image of Henry. And funny and sweet and a complete-and-utter joy.

"She had a blowout," Felix informs me, passing Juliet over and obliterating any delusions I harbored about her pure perfection. The baby grins at me and then reaches up as if just remembering and yanks a purple Velcro bow out of her tangled curls. It sticks to her fingers, and I pry it away, stuffing the accessory in my pocket and smacking her cheek with a loud kiss. Juliet's eyes light up at the initiation of her favorite game and she kisses me back, slobbering on my chin with her wide-open mouth.

"Give her to me," Cleo demands, snagging Juliet under the arms and swinging her up and away. The baby giggles as Cleo bops back to the counter where she grabs a chocolate croissant for Finn and hands it to him with a few of her warm, candied hazelnuts sprinkled on the plate.

Trilogy is half-full, but Finn's favorite table by the floor-to-ceiling windows is open, and he settles himself in with a view of the river without waiting to see if we'll follow.

Routine is important in the aftermath of trauma, a schedule and clear boundaries as comforting and safe as a favorite lovey. That's why when Finn's counselor suggested he'd thrive with a focused, stay-at-home parent, Felix applied for an extension on his grant.

"I want to do this," he said, then asked uncertainly: "What if I do this?"

"Become a stay-at-home dad?" I quirked an eyebrow.

"Just for a season. What do you think? We have just over a year left on our sabbatical. We're not due back in Newcastle until a year from August."

"But—"

"The kids need some stability," Felix interrupted, wrapped up in a daydream that was unfurling behind his eyes. "Besides, you're teaching all those online classes, *and* you have a novel to finish. Then edits and a book launch . . . My brown dwarfs aren't going anywhere."

I had laughed, trying to imagine Felix handling midnight feedings and wiggly diaper changes and homeschool. "Okay," I said, because I was curious to see what would happen, but also because I could no longer imagine our life without Henry, Finn, and Juliet in it.

Neither of us knew the first thing about being parents, but Felix accepted the challenge with gravity and resolve. He watched YouTube videos and joined an online dads group. He interrogated his coworkers and friends, writing down bits of advice on Post-it notes, and then sticking them all over the house so he wouldn't forget the wisdom they imparted.

> Consistency
> is
> key.

> Sleep when the
> baby sleeps.

> 8 hugs a day
> for maintenance.
> 12 for growth.

But for all his seriousness, for all the books he reads and parenting best practices he tries to follow, Felix is a natural. He's Juliet's person, period. The one she reaches for, her forever first choice. Maybe it's because he cared for her in those awful days after Gabi died, but I think it has more to do with the fact that she knows down to her DNA that he loves her unconditionally. And Finn is Felix's shadow. The little boy can't get enough of stars and space, planets and supernovas, black holes and gas giants.

For Christmas, I bought Finn a book for kids about relativity, and we all learned about how mass drags space and space drags mass and mass warps space. I know the center of a black hole is called a singularity, and I think Finn kind of grasps how gravitational waves work, but I know the only one of us who really gets it is Henry.

He's the last of our little entourage to darken the door of Trilogy, and when I see the bouquet of wild daffodils he's clutching, my eyes mist. We passed a field of the cheerful flowers on our way into town, but when he said, "Back in a sec," I hadn't realized what he intended to do.

"Large black?" Cleo calls, and Henry nods, bypassing Felix and me to join Finn overlooking the water.

Henry had only lived with us for a few weeks when Felix realized just what we were dealing with. "You think I'm smart," he'd whispered as we were lying side by side in bed one night. "You should've met my sister."

There were gaps, of course, in Henry's limited, homeschool education, but after three months of working with Felix, he took a placement exam, and it was decided he could get his high school diploma by backfilling several required classes: a foreign language, US government, and art among others. He's doing it mostly online—with Felix's help—and hopes to apply to the University of Washington in a year.

"He'll be okay," Felix whispers, reading my mind as I watch Henry show Finn the flowers and begin to explain what they're for.

"Will he?" I lean against Felix and his arms go around me. I want an ironclad guarantee. A blood covenant. I want someone to assure me that the pain these kids have endured was more than anyone should face in a lifetime and that from here on out their lives will be smooth sailing. I'd open my own veins to make it so. But that's impossible. In the fall, Henry will take physical education and oil painting at the same high school that Felix and his parents once attended. And Finn will go to fifth grade. Felix and I have been thrown into the deep end of parenting three, after concluding that we would never have kids.

"Hey! A little help here?" Cleo calls, motioning us over and handing the baby back across the counter.

Juliet squeals and grabs a handful of my hair, stuffing it into her mouth before gagging and spitting it back out. I can't help but laugh.

Henry and Finn slip out of Trilogy before Felix and I have our coffees, but we don't mind. Through the wide front window we can see them cross the street and slip beneath the wrought-iron arch of the Lutheran church. The little graveyard is a slightly unkempt garden beside the white-washed building, and near the back is a new gray stone.

We've been gone for a week, and the tulips Henry and Finn put in the stake vase are no doubt wilted and brown. The daffodils are a good choice. Bright as sunshine and wild across the mountain. Maybe last spring, Gabi picked her own bouquet and displayed it in a mason jar on the little round table.

And maybe in another world she's picking them now, gathering flowers for a table where we will all gather round.

ACKNOWLEDGMENTS

ONE DOZEN BOOKS IN and I still find myself staring at a blank screen wondering where on earth to begin with the acknowledgements. As with every single book that came before this one, I owe a debt of gratitude to so many people. Family and friends, of course, but also an entire community of professionals, new acquaintances, and even total strangers who have put their stamp on *Where He Left Me*. I'm grateful down to my bones for each and every one of you, and I hope that I remember to mention you all! Of course, I won't, and I pray that you'll forgive any oversights and know that you are forever appreciated. This book exists because of you.

Huge thanks to the team at Browne & Miller, Danielle Egan-Miller and Mariana Fisher, for spending so much time helping me get the story just right. Mariana came up with the line "in every world I'd love you" and not only did it just *fit*, it captured the overarching theme of inevitability and permanence and wonder in love and life.

I'm so grateful for my writing sisters in the Story Society of Iowa: Heather Gudenkauf, Kali VanBaale, Tracey Garvis-Graves, Kimberly Stuart, and Julie Stone. Banding together was a brilliant move that has led to so much laughter and so many memories. The wisdom, advice, and camaraderie of this group is unparalleled.

When I accepted an invitation to speak at the Okoboji Writers' Retreat, I never imagined how much it would impact my professional life. The indomitable Julie Gammack has created something truly special in OWR and the Iowa Writers' Collaborative, and I still can't quite believe that I get to be a part of such an incredible collection of world class journalists, writers, and creatives. I wish I could name all 70+ of you, but suffice it to say I think you are all amazing. Thanks for letting me sit at the table.

Writing friends Tosca Lee, Kimi Cunningham Grant, William Kent Krueger, Ellen Won Steil, Beth Hoffman, Caleb Rainey, and Kelsey Bigelow—among so many others—provided everything from advice and encouragement to much needed hugs and gifts of snacks all along the way. Sometimes the littlest things mean the very most. And to friends Dean and Gail Douma, thank you so much for allowing Aaron and me to spend a couple of days at your place on Guemes Island. It was just the research getaway I needed.

My entire publishing team, including all three of my editors (Kaitlin Olsen, Jade Hui, and Sarah Grill) leveled up *Where He Left Me* at every turn. So many people had a hand in the process: Ifeoma Anyoku, Stacey Sakal, Megan Rudloff, Maudee Genao, Libby McGuire, Abel Berriz, Yvonne Taylor, Tania Bissel, and Min Choi, who designed the gorgeous cover. I'm forever thankful for you all. Working with the Atria team is a dream come true.

Bookstore owners are the real MVPs of the publishing world, and I'm blessed to know the best. Terri LeBlanc and company at Swamp Fox Bookstore in Marion, Iowa, Hunter Gillum and Alice Meyer (and the whole team!) at Beaverdale Books in Des Moines, Leslie Huerta and her amazing staff at Francie & Finch in Lincoln, Nebraska, and Mollie Loughlin and the girls at the Book Vine in Cherokee, Iowa are just a few of my favorites—but there are so many more! If you haven't been to Valley Bookseller in Stillwater, Minnesota, Book People in Sioux City, Iowa, Dog-Eared Books in Ames, Iowa, The Bookworm in Omaha, Nebraska, Dragonfly Books in Decorah, Iowa, and/or River Lights Bookstore in Dubuque, Iowa, my friends, you are missing out. Local gems exist in the most unexpected corners, and they deserve our time, attention, and book budgets. Shop small and shop local!

I'd be remiss not to mention one of my favorite places on earth: libraries. My local libraries in Sioux Center, Orange City, Hull, and Rock Valley—as well as innumerable libraries all across the Midwest—have invited me into their communities and been havens of fellowship for years. It doesn't matter where the library is: the second I step inside, I feel like I'm home. I write in libraries, browse for books, have great conversations, and, of course, read. If you haven't been to your local library lately, I encourage you to stop in to find a book and thank a librarian. The service they perform in our communities is often underappreciated but indispensable.

Of course, none of this would be possible without the support and encouragement of my family. Isaac, Judah, Eve, Matthias, and Anneka: *mwah*! I love you. Dad and Mom, I can't believe that you are still my biggest fans. And Aaron, thanks for always knowing what I need long before I know it myself. Writing trips will always be my love language.

Last, but never least, if you've made it this far: thank you for picking up my book. Whether you are a new reader, or you've been with me all along, I am so insanely grateful to you. Because of my readers I get to do this thing that I love so much. I hope I'm writing when I'm eighty—and I hope you'll stick around for the ride.

xoxo – Nicole

ABOUT THE AUTHOR

NICOLE BAART is the author of several novels, including *Where He Left Me* and *Everything We Didn't Say*. The cofounder of a nonprofit and mother of five, she lives in Iowa with her family. Learn more at NicoleBaart.com.